LIFE SENTENCES

TEKLA DENNISON MILLER

Gold Imprint
Medallion Press, Inc.
Florida, USA

Published 2005 by Medallion Press, Inc.
225 Seabreeze Ave.
Palm Beach, FL 33480

Printed in the United States of America

Library of Congress Cataloging-in-Publication Data

Miller, Tekla Dennison.
  Life sentence / Tekla Dennison Miller.
    p. cm.
  ISBN 1-932815-25-2
  1. Prisons--Officials and employees--Fiction.
  2. Mothers and daughters--Fiction. 3. Serial murderers--Fiction.
  4. Abused wives--Fiction. 5. Prisoners--Fiction.
  6. Prisons--Fiction. I. Title.
  PS3613.I558L54 2005
  813'.54--dc22

                              2005009435

ACKNOWLEDGEMENTS:

A novel is created in an author's mind long before the first word is put on paper. Such is the case with this one. Often fiction is derived from true events. In my case, the episodes that inspired this novel occurred over the twenty years I was employed by the Michigan Department of Corrections. I learned during those challenging years that truth is mysterious, bizarre and often difficult.

So many thoughtful people supported me throughout the writing of Life Sentences. Thank you to all of you: Perry Johnson, Elizabeth Testa, Joan Green, Joyce Alexander, Shannon Richardson, Leslie Doran, Linda Thompson, and Candice Carson.

A special thanks to the wonderful staff at Medallion Press — Helen, Pam, Leslie and Jamie — and my husband, Chet Peterson, who has always encouraged me and supported all my endeavors.

TABLE OF CONTENTS

chapter one

GRADUATING

THE SERIAL KILLER WAS sentenced to life without parole on the same morning Pilar Brookstone graduated from medical school. Her mother shared that news as Pilar queued for the processional. Now, stepping away from the provost's handshake, the new Dr. Brookstone was still thinking about her mother's announcement. "Chad Wilbanks is permanently off the streets," Celeste had said as though presenting Pilar with an extra-special gift. "You'll feel safe enough to come home, at last."

On this of all days, Pilar didn't want to think about the murders or the man responsible. This was the moment to concentrate on the diploma she clutched to her chest, the sweet triumph of a hard-won degree. But instead, memories of her friend Susan Mitchell rose up to block Pilar's view of her classmates. Chad Wilbanks had first charmed Susan, then brutally murdered her. Susan was a statistic now, one of eight young women Wilbanks victimized during a vicious two-year spree near the University of Michigan.

Would Pilar feel safe in either Ann Arbor or in her Gross Pointe Shores home now? True, she had left medical school there because of the murders, transferring to Wisconsin after the first year. But Celeste's words brought no real comfort, because in the intervening years Pilar had come to realize fear of Chad Wilbanks was not the real reason she dreaded going home.

As Pilar searched the audience seated under the vast striped tent, her mother's aqua silk suit stood out like a large flower among a field of weeds. Seeing her always impeccably dressed mother gave Pilar a brief elated moment — how often people thought they looked alike, how often people said they could easily pass for sisters. At forty-eight, Celeste still resembled a youthful model, slender, graceful, and no gray hair. Pilar remembered how her friends envied her good fortune to have inherited Celeste's naturally curly auburn locks and high cheek bones. Pilar believed she was even luckier to have inherited her mother's intelligence. Unlike her mother, however, Pilar put her smarts to good use.

Like a victorious athlete Pilar hoisted her diploma into the air. In response, Celeste made large circles with her arms, nodded her head, which was covered in a wide-brim aqua hat. Then she checked the others near her. Surely, her look said, everyone watching knew her daughter graduated fifth in the class.

Pilar descended the stairs with her diploma still triumphantly raised and caught a glimpse of her father's steel-wool-gray hair. Marcus Nathaniel Brookstone, III, forever tan and fit, sat to the right of Celeste. To Celeste's excited nudges, his body stiffened, and he crossed his arms over the chest of his navy double-breasted jacket. Despite her mother's proud gaze, Pilar felt her enthusiasm fade as she returned to her place in the front row. Her father remained rigid, eyes focused on the podium.

After the ceremony, Pilar lingered in the shade of a huge oak tree, giving brief hugs and short, bittersweet farewells to several women students. As they promised each other to keep in touch, Pilar's roommate and closest friend, Julie, threaded her arm through Pilar's. She steered Pilar through the crowd and said, "I truly wish you'd reconsider OB/GYN. You're a natural. Your compassion alone would be such an asset."

Pilar stopped and pulled away from Julie. "I haven't totally decided what I'm going to do. Perhaps I'll have a better idea after my residency."

"But," Julie scrunched her face, "we'll be so far apart. You in Detroit and me in Oregon."

Pilar hugged the short, perky woman. "Don't fret. There's always the phone. Besides, that separation may not be forever. Who knows where I'll end up?" Her own eyes tear-blurred, Pilar took in Julie's pouting lips and wished for a moment that she was going west with her friend.

Julie's parents whisked her away. As she bounced along

beside them, Julie looked over her shoulder and called out, "Don't forget me."

Her remark seemed strange to Pilar, since they'd been so close all through med school. "Julie," Pilar teased in response, "you won't let me forget you." She tried to ignore the lump that formed like a huge fist in her throat.

Pilar watched the crowd fill in around Julie. Then, when Pilar could no longer see Julie, she scanned the well-wishers and excited parents. Finally, she spotted her mother, tall like Pilar, struggling through the sweltering crush. When Celeste saw her daughter, she waved one gloved hand, while the other held her hat fast against the breeze from Lake Mendota, a graceful motion practiced all her married life lived on a lake shore. Odd though, were the gloves in an age when most women had freed themselves of such restraint. Perhaps she and her mother weren't really so alike — beneath the black commencement robe, Pilar wore Birkenstock sandals and a sun dress.

"Where's Daddy?" Pilar asked as they embraced. She immediately regretted the endearing, childish title.

"He's getting the car," Celeste answered. She held Pilar at an arm's length.

Although her mother's eyes were shaded behind large, Jackie Kennedy-style sunglasses, Pilar knew her mother watched her face register disappointment. In fact, Pilar knew her mother wouldn't have to look at her at all. Celeste had been confronted with that expression so many times before.

"You know how he is, dear," Celeste added in a resigned tone.

"Just this once, Mother, he could have been here for me. Just this once." Pilar silently cursed her VW for dying a week earlier. She had no choice but to be a prisoner in her father's car for the long ride home.

Pilar wanted to shred her diploma and toss it into the wind. Better yet, she wanted to throw it in her father's face. Instead, she yielded as her mother wrapped a comforting arm around her shoulder and guided Pilar through the throng. Like Julie's unfailing friendship, Celeste's loyalty had been one of few morsels of happiness in Pilar's life. Most times, Pilar was delighted that her mother had never given up on her, especially when Pilar knew how stubborn she herself could be.

"Mother, I'm only doing this for you," Pilar told her. "I could have gotten a ride with friends."

"I know, dear," Celeste squeezed Pilar closer. "I know."

Did her mother realize she couldn't acquiesce forever? Pilar's clenched hands hid in her robe. Did Celeste know how she needed to get out?

THE HEAT FROM THE soft asphalt lot reminded Pilar of walking barefoot on hot sand, but the small sense of vacation lasted only until Pilar caught sight of her father. Marcus was already seated behind the steering wheel of the idling car, cooling off in the air conditioning. Though he glanced at

Celeste and Pilar, he made no attempt to get their attention. He hadn't taken off his jacket or loosened his tie, a brief, hopeful sign. Perhaps his immediate departure from the ceremony was really a gallant move. Perhaps he just wanted to make the car more comfortable for them. "Perhaps I'm kidding myself again," Pilar mumbled to herself.

As Pilar gathered the robe around her and hoisted it up so she could get into the back seat, Marcus turned to her and said, completely without warmth, "Congratulations, Pilar. Your mother and I are very proud of you." Then, with a total change in tone, he scolded, "But if you had stayed at the University of Michigan, we could be at the club for dinner rather than some restaurant where they don't know how to make a proper martini." He followed that with a forced chuckle.

Pilar found no humor in his remark. More than any thing, more than any one, Marcus loved the Grosse Pointe Yacht Club which nestled the shores of Lake St. Clair, a short drive from the Brookstone family estate.

"I thought we could have champagne," Celeste soothed as she patted his arm. "You know, to celebrate."

Marcus shook her hand away and drove out of the lot, almost laying a patch of rubber like a kid with his first car. Disheartened, Pilar rested her head against the window to catch glimpses of the university buildings as the car sped past. When the familiar, comfortable brick buildings of the University of Wisconsin Hospital and Clinics slipped from sight, she clenched the folds of the robe. What made her more tense — the looming residency at Detroit Receiving Hospital, or the prospect of spending three years at home?

Determined to salvage her special day, Pilar announced with too much cheer, "You'll enjoy the restaurant I picked, Father." Her voice gained strength when she added, "Everyone will be there." Then her bubble of self-assurance popped. She pressed her nose against the window like a child looking through the glass display case in a candy store. As she watched the hospital merge into the sun low in the spring sky, she mumbled, "I promise you'll get a perfect martini."

"We're not stopping." Marcus' voice broke the silence like a sudden thunder clap.

Pilar raised her head far enough to see him peer in the rear view mirror. Did he want to see how unhappy he was making her? It was a game they'd played too often. As Pilar was drawn to the mean creases surrounding her father's eyes, she wondered who had coined the phrase "laugh lines." Feeling her own face tighten like a mask, Pilar looked away from her father's spiteful challenge and immersed herself in the fleeting sights of Madison and Lake Mendota.

She could almost smell Marcus' discomfort when she didn't respond, but she also knew he wouldn't let the issue go, so his next statement held little surprise. "I want to get as far today as we can. I have to prepare for an important meeting."

He baited Pilar one more time, "You understand?"

"Sure." Pilar's tone could have etched glass. Of course, Marcus always put his needs before everything else. As usual, she was in the way but didn't know why.

When she remained silent, Marcus continued, "Besides, I don't want to meet any more of your radical do-gooder, liberal friends. I had enough of them when you went to Michigan."

Pilar slumped into the corner. If she squeezed her eyes shut, would her father disappear? She tucked her nose into the seat. "New car?" she asked as she breathed in the scent of fresh leather.

"It's your graduation gift," Marcus announced, like a fulsome CEO buying loyalty from a subordinate. "It's more reliable than that VW."

Pilar bolted straight up. "Mine?" She slapped the leather and added with some sarcasm, "Your generosity is over-whelming. Besides, I don't want some bourgeois Mercedes." She'd been proud to earn the money to buy the VW.

"Bourgeois went out of style in the seventies, Pilar," Marcus chided. His face creased with disapproving furrows as he again sought out Pilar's reaction in the rear view mirror.

"Not among my peers, Father." Pilar glared back.

"Oh, Pilar, get a grip on your life." He made the turn onto eastbound I-94, heading to Michigan, dismissing her opinion, as usual. "If you plan to be a doctor, you'll need to think more clearly."

Celeste, straightening her suit where it tangled in the seat belt, turned to Marcus and Pilar. "Need I remind you two that today is a celebration?" She removed her sunglasses. "Besides, Pilar, when you join Daddy's practice, you'll want a car that . . ."

Her mother's pleas had too often trapped her in the past. "I have to return this robe before we skip town." Pilar fanned the material up and down. "Do you think you have time for that, Father?" She no longer could accept her mother's pretense of maintaining a happy family. Didn't she get it? Their happy family had never existed.

"We'll mail it back," Marcus clipped as he tapped his fingers on the steering wheel. Then he sighed deeply and stretched one arm over the back of Celeste's seat.

Celeste smiled, though Pilar knew her mother didn't understand. Marcus' newly relaxed state wasn't due to getting out of Wisconsin, but was because Pilar ignored her mother's statement about working in his practice as a neurosurgeon.

Pilar studied the backs of her parents' heads. It was a good thing all her personal belongings had already been shipped home. Her father probably would have left them in her apartment for the next renter. And the Mercedes — it was just like him. Appearances were what counted. Her father never missed an opportunity for him and his family to look good.

They might look good, but they'd never win an award

for family of the year.

The car's claustrophobic interior made it hard to breathe. Pilar sniffed deeply several times to bring oxygen back into her brain. She only smelled leather and made herself dizzy.

PILAR CLAWED AT HER neck. Who was strangling her? Her body shuddered awake as she struggled to pull the robe away from where it had crept above her shoulders and tightened like a noose. She interlocked her fingers, pushed her arms forward and stretched. As the fuzziness cleared from her head, Pilar recognized her surroundings. "Can we stop? I have to pee."

"Didn't they teach you anything at that med school?" Marcus asked as he engaged the turn signal and exited I-94 East of Kalamazoo.

"Yes. We all must pee sometime." Pilar's acerbic response was wasted on deaf ears.

"I had just decided to take a break anyway," her father remarked. Celeste's sigh was deliberate and loud.

The illuminated arches of McDonald's created eerie shadows over the entry to an otherwise dark parking lot. "Are you sure you can afford to eat here?" Pilar asked. "I've heard the martinis aren't very good." Why could she not resist baiting her father?

Pilar hopped out of the car almost before it came to a complete stop. She pulled the robe over her head, tossed it on the seat, and after slammed the car door. No matter her rush to reach the bathroom, Pilar couldn't help but shout out one last comment over her shoulder, well aware that she often provoked a confrontation with her father.

"I thought as a graduate of Michigan med school, you'd earn more money."

Before Pilar slipped inside the restaurant, she heard her mother say, "You know, Marcus, you could be just a tad more happy for your only daughter." Pilar's shoulders slouched at the challenge in her mother's exhausted voice. "You should be thrilled that she wants to follow in your footsteps."

Berating herself for making her mother's life more difficult, Pilar stopped long enough to hear her father answer, "I didn't ask Pilar to do that." Leaving Celeste behind he headed to the restaurant, and yelled to her as he looked at Pilar, "She'll just get married and waste my investment."

At that moment, Pilar prayed her mother would get back in the car and drive off. Pilar knew she couldn't. Where would she have gone?

AFTER SPLASHING COLD WATER on her face, Pilar stared at the person looking back at her in the restroom mirror. Even without makeup and with a head of thick, sometimes unruly hair, she was pretty. Over the years, she hadn't always felt that way. She thought her full, naturally red lips overpowered her face. Who would have guessed full lips would come into vogue? Who would have guessed women would pump their lips with silicone to have a mouth like hers? She snickered at that image. "Little does my father know there's not much chance that his investment in my medical career will be wasted. No man at the moment wants my full lips."

Pilar lifted her hair to the top of her ahead and then let it drop. "You know as well as I do," she said to the vision in the mirror like a friend, "marriage is out of the question. The one-night stands I've known don't want a doctor for a wife." She leaned into the mirror to more closely examine her features. "Besides, only Barbara Streisand could love that nose."

Pilar thumped the mirror and headed out the door. By the time she got to the counter, her parents were in a booth eating Quarter Pounders and drinking coffee. When Pilar started to order her father yelled, "I have your hamburger here."

The clerk raised his eyebrows as though he knew what it was like to have a father like that. Pilar shrugged in response.

"Marcus," Celeste said with a hint of ire in her voice, "maybe Pilar would like to order for herself. She is capable."

Though shocked by her mother's uncommon, forceful tone, Pilar didn't turn away from the young man taking orders and asked for a grilled chicken sandwich and a diet Coke. She paid him with a ten-dollar bill she had tucked into her pocket. When the clerk finished the order, Pilar grabbed the tray and slid into the booth beside her mother, while the other customers, clad in shorts and T-shirts, eyed the more formal trio with suspicion.

On their way back to the car, Marcus announced, "We'll drive straight home."

"What? We're not stopping overnight?" Pilar shouted loud enough to draw the attention of the group parking nearby. How many hours would she be stuck with him? "How could you make that decision without asking Mother or me?" Pilar plopped into the car and again slammed the door.

Marcus slid behind the wheel. "In case you haven't noticed, this isn't a democracy."

Celeste gingerly eased herself into the passenger's seat as Marcus started the engine. "I thought I made it clear earlier," he stated, and checked the lot for traffic. "I must get home."

Pilar curled up on the back seat. A familiar fatigue, induced by anger and depression, set in, as it had each time she'd gone home to Grosse Pointe Shores. Using her graduation robe as a pillow, she let the repetitive sound of the clicking tires along the highway lull her into a fitful sleep.

MUTILATED WOMEN'S BODIES. PILES of them in a field. Murky light. A stench. Screams. Pilar woke with a start.

Marcus tapped the brake. Everyone lunged forward. "What the hell," he shouted.

The screams were from Pilar.

"Nightmare, Father," she whispered, feeling as though she had had an out-of-body experience. "I had a nightmare."

Pilar looked out the window at the green-and -white road sign that read, "University of Michigan next right."   They must have passed the Ann Arbor exit.

Why had she really left?   Was it to defy her father's insistence that she attend his alma mater?   Susan's smile appeared to Pilar as clearly as though her friend were in the car.   Or had she really been afraid and fled because of the student murders?   Had she been frightened that she would be Chad Wilbanks next victim?   It was odd though, his face was plastered everywhere in the media, Pilar hardly remembered what he looked like.

MARCUS HAD MET CELESTE at the University of Michigan. She had thought he was quite a catch – handsome, rich, and well-established in Michigan society.   Somehow, Celeste managed to ignore his need to control others.   Unlike Celeste, Pilar held the opinion that her father's arrogance overshadowed any positive attributes.   She often wondered why she saw that and her mother didn't.

As the new Mercedes sped on, Pilar stared at the back of her father's head.   Repulsed by his carefully tended hair, his manicured life, she wished that the burning in her eyes would become a laser beam and sear his locks.   The wish was as dreamy and hopeless as a child's on the evening's first star.

True, Marcus had never been violent to Celeste or Pilar.   And true, he'd always made sure his smart, talented daughter had attended the best schools, had the best piano and ballet teachers, gone to the best arts camp. Yet childhood memories plagued Pilar, countless times of being ignored or worse, of being ridiculed for not "having what it takes like a boy does."

In imitation of her mother's futile attempts with Marcus, Pilar spent the better part of her childhood trying, and failing, to please her father. Though he never said it outright, Pilar was convinced Marcus kept his distance from both of them because he harbored a deep resentment that Celeste had never given him a son, a boy he would have considered a rightful heir. That rancor spilled over into his feelings about Pilar. No matter how bright, gifted, or successful she was, she could never be the son he wanted.

She got an inkling of how hopeless her efforts were the day she won the third grade spelling bee. Victorious, she flashed her parents a radiant smile. "Exclusionary" was a tough word.

"You'll have to do more than that if you want to make it in this world," he said. Then he turned his attention to other fathers gathered in the auditorium, while Pilar savored what little comfort her mother's ever-ready embrace gave her. Except for Pilar's high school and college graduations, Marcus never attended another activity, feigning a burdensome work schedule. The same all-powerful timetable that had them speeding to Grosse Pointe Shores.

Yet, she never gave up trying.

PILAR RESTED HER HEAD against the car seat. As she listened to the click, click, click of the tires, she reviewed a scene that had played over and over in her mind during the past years. Shortly after she decided to change medical schools, Pilar, at home packing, heard angry words between her parents. It was the cocktail hour, normally a time when they made small talk and sipped their evening martinis in the library, a floor below. Her mother's hurt tone drew Pilar to the edge of the stairs to eavesdrop. Without knowing how she got there, a few minutes later Pilar stood outside the library door listening to Celeste's accusation, "You never cared about Pilar or me."

"Care!" Marcus' enraged voice boomed. "Care! I'm a good provider for you and Pilar. I've spent my life providing for you. Look at this house, look at your clothes, your car, the servants. Look at Pilar's education."

As Pilar listened, an image emerged in her mind's eye of her father flailing his arms around while his face reddened with each thundering word.

"That's not love. And now," Celeste stopped to take in air like an oxygen-deprived mountain climber, "now you confirm the dirty rumor spreading at the club."

Pilar hugged her chest to stop the shaking as the word "rumor" assaulted her. She couldn't imagine her conservative, boring father would do anything to raise an eyebrow let alone become a rumor.

Just as Pilar decided to knock and enter the library, Celeste amazed Pilar by screaming, "If you wanted a son of your own so badly why didn't we adopt one?"

"It wouldn't be the same — from my making. I've tried to explain it to you before, but you don't want to know."

Suddenly, Marcus opened the door. His face came within inches of Pilar's as Celeste yelled after him, "It's better to have a bastard born to some white trash?"

Marcus pushed by Pilar. She didn't exist.

Pilar stood frozen, the confusing words whirling around in her head, *a bastard son, a bastard son*. All those days her father wasn't with the family, her birthdays, her school honors and piano recitals, he must have been with his illegitimate son. Had he been with that son, too, when he didn't take her to the father-daughter dance?

Bracing a hand against the paneled wall, Pilar steadied herself. Her chest heaved with the slamming of the front door. She was positive her father's cowardly departure was bitter proof that there could be more to the rumor than her mother knew.

Celeste crossed the room and placed her hand on Pilar's shoulder. "I'm so sorry you had to hear that," she said in the same calm voice she used to console a young Pilar after she scraped her knee. "It means nothing. We're still his real family."

Pilar glared and said, "He's never hugged me, Mother. How real is that?"

At that moment, Pilar vowed she would never drop another tear for her father. She finally understood that she no longer had to feel guilty about choosing a lifestyle different from her parents. In fact, Pilar began to find enjoyment goading her father into a frantic tirade about the responsibility to which a woman of her background should be committed. "Look at your mother," he often shouted when Pilar pushed him over the brink. "She knows her place."

Over the years Pilar had looked at her mother, who was often cowering in some corner of their house. Tonight, as they sped homeward from graduation, it was no different. Her mother did know her place. There she sat, as far as she could from Marcus, using the window rather than his shoulder as a pillow. Marcus was totally clueless about Pilar's need for independence and personal success. As to the idea of status, Pilar's definition was the polar opposite of her father's.

So why was she still crying? Pilar covered her face in the robe.

LIGHTS FROM A FREIGHTER defined the dark, placid waters of Lake Saint Clare. The Mercedes turned up the driveway marked by an electric gate with *The Brookstones* etched in brass. Pilar opened a window. The familiar damp air had been one of few comforts during her bleak childhood, and brought back memories of a little girl awakened by the sun shimmering off the water and across her bedroom wall.

Back then, she raced down the manicured front lawn to play with Bud, her yellow lab, in the waves lapping the beach.

Pilar raised her still sore body to an upright position and rubbed her eyes with her fists the way that child would have done. Marcus rounded the circle of the drive and parked in front of the nine-foot mahogany entrance doors. The gray stone building, Marcus' inheritance, loomed in the darkness, as cold and brooding as a Gothic mansion from a Daphne du Maurier novel. Pilar remembered no casual visits from friends dropping by, ever.

There had been little honest cheerfulness here. Yet Pilar couldn't help smile at the one thing that once had brightened each homecoming – Bud jumping up to lick her face. He was the only dog her father allowed in the echoing house. Bud died when Pilar was 12.

THE NEXT MORNING, PILAR awakened to the mauve curtains fluttering in the open window opposite her bed. She stretched and inhaled. The breeze from the lake came sweetened with spring fragrances, and when she threw the bed covers off, the lemon scent of fresh laundry filled the air. Pilar grinned, thinking how her mother wanted everything perfect and sometimes that wasn't a bad trait. Her smile faded when she scanned the day-lit room. Her mother tried too hard to ensconce Pilar in their old ways.

Nothing had changed except for a fresh coat of soft pink paint on the walls. The antique white canopy bed in the center was anchored by identical tables on either side. As a child, when Pilar lay in bed, the canopy of mauve and plum flowers spread above and sheltered her like a secret garden. A large chest snugged its foot. Pilar knew her childhood toys would be neatly stored inside. An American Girl doll collection sat like rows of ladies-in-waiting on shelves that lined the walls. Pilar long ago had stuffed the Barbie Dolls in boxes and packed them away in her closet.

On the dresser sat a silver-framed photo of a ten-year-old Pilar and her parents. She and her mother were smiling and squinting into the sun. They had their arms around each other's waist, while Marcus, thin lipped, stood stiffly off to the side. He didn't touch either Pilar or Celeste. "Like the old saying goes," Pilar commented as she glowered at the photograph, "a picture says a thousand words."

Reluctant to get out of her garden bed, Pilar finally sat up, back propped against a pillow, and gazed out the window at the sun-rays streaking like glass ribbons across the lake. She doubted her mother would ever come to grips with the reality that Pilar wouldn't stay longer than the three years she contracted with Detroit Receiving.

It was a compromise, because Pilar had been accepted and wanted to attend the Cleveland Clinic. But, that four-hour drive wasn't close enough for her mother. Though disappointed, Pilar again gave into her mother's appeal. "You'll be gone from me soon enough," Celeste said. "Just stay with me a few more years."   Pilar felt her mother sounded as though once Pilar was finished with her residency, they would soon be forever separated. Had Celeste feared facing an empty nest with her distant husband? Or had she seen something in Pilar's future?

Pilar shivered about her mother's unusual premonitions. For instance, Celeste often knew the grades Pilar got on important tests before she could tell her. Like the time Pilar raced home to show Celeste her grade on her biology test. "You got a 98 on that test. Good for you," Celeste blurted out. She tried to cover up her insight by adding, "Let me see it."

"How did you know my exact grade?" Pilar asked, stunned by her mother's uncanny ability to always know things before she could tell or show her. "Did you call the school?"

"No, dear. A lucky guess."

"You have a lot of those, Mom." Pilar handed her the test.

Pilar shuffled to the window and breathed another gulp of lake air. For that moment she only wanted to enjoy the short two weeks before she embarked on her residency. She planned to fill the hours reading good books and making up for sleep lost during exams.

A large crystal vase, an anniversary gift from Pilar's father to her mother, (no doubt purchased by his secretary) today filled with vibrant pink roses, adorned the desk beneath the window. So many nights her teen self had sat there talking on the telephone, rather than doing homework. In that at least she'd felt normal. Now, she swept her hand across the polished wood top and thought about her best childhood friend, Trish. Pilar never kept in touch. They had drifted in such different directions. Trish, with her stuffy stockbroker husband, was more like their mothers than Pilar would ever be. Julie on the other hand — well. Pilar already missed her.

The sight of her father maneuvering his Lexus past the silver Mercedes onto Lake Shore Road was as familiar as the view of the lake: Pilar had often stood in the same window and watched him drive away, even after her mother begged him to stay. The result was always the same; he'd rather go to the club or wherever — maybe with his son.

Today, when his car vanished into the trees along the road, she imagined her father and the Lexus had been swallowed by the leaves as if by a giant man-eating plant. Most likely he was listening to his cherished tapes of Rush Limbaugh. "Perhaps Father and Rush will never come back," she chirped like a bird after a summer rain, then shrugged. "Too bad. He'll only be gone a week to a conference."

His absence would allow just enough time for Pilar and her mother to share quiet times without interruptions from his confrontations. Pilar daydreamed of renewing the friendship she once had with her mother, one where they confided their deepest secrets to each other. Pilar scrunched her face. All she really foresaw was her mother repeating her father's party line: "You think you can get anywhere without a man. Just try it."

"Well, guess what?" Pilar said to her father's departing car, "I will."

Pilar turned from the window to clench Emma, a fuzzy white rabbit, tightly to her chest. Emma had come as an Easter gift from her father, or so Celeste said, when Pilar was six. Pilar's father, who was out of town that Easter, would never have selected the rabbit. Marcus would have found Emma frivolous. He would also have admonished Celeste for acknowledging a Christian occasion, though the Brookstones only participated in their faith on special Jewish occasions like Rosh Hashanah and Yom Kippur. Pilar suspected her father worked hard at not attracting attention to his ethnicity. He wanted to blend in at the club.

Though Pilar was well aware her mother had bought Emma, she reacted with the proper amount of joy about her father remembering her, while she hid her hurt over his absence. Emma became Pilar's favorite toy. She believed the rabbit had the power to chase away all her pre-teen-age pimples, help capture the heart of her latest crush, stop her from covering her head in lightning storms, and scare off any sadness. Emma and Pilar spent hours dancing and singing in the bedroom to Bruce Springsteen. One night Pilar must have gotten carried away to "Born in the USA", because her loud renditions brought her father to the place he so rarely ventured.

"Turn that damn thing off and practice your Mozart," he shouted.

Pilar was more stupefied by his knowledge of her piano skills than his vocal intrusion.

Emma also accompanied Pilar on walks along the shores of Lake Michigan where she and her mother spent their annual two weeks at the summer home of Celeste's brother in Harbor Springs. Pilar left Emma on the cottage bed when she turned thirteen, though, and traded in her make-believe affection for the real thing, holding hands with Joey, Pilar's first boyfriend. He summered with his parents in the cottage next door. Even at gawky thirteen, Joey squeezed Pilar's hand in his as they haunted the beach front. Emma couldn't match that.

Other teenagers also shared Harbor Springs cottages with their families, while Marcus rarely joined Pilar and Celeste on any vacation. In fact, for Pilar's high school graduation, he sent Celeste and her on a two-month tour of Europe.

Pilar confided to Emma, "It probably gave him more time for the Tiger baseball games with his son, whoever he is."

Though Pilar left Emma behind when she headed off to the University of Michigan as an undergraduate, there were many times Pilar thought she needed the funny rabbit. Now, Pilar hugged Emma and, petting her velvet fur, swayed as she hummed Madonna's song "Boy Toy." Emma's lanky legs and pink satin lined ears and feet bounced to Pilar's body's motion. "Remember this song, Emma?" Pilar asked the mute stuffed toy.

Pilar held her at arm's length, and confided, "Life on my own is going to be tough, Emma, but I know I can make it without leaning on a man." She squeezed the rabbit and laughed. "And, hey! I've still got you!"

chapter two

DOCTOR BROOKSTONE

ON HER FIRST DAY at Detroit Receiving Hospital, Pilar decided to take East Jefferson rather than westbound I-94 into Detroit. Faced with a resident's grueling schedule, especially ER's twenty-four-hour shifts, it would be the last chance Pilar would have for a year to enjoy a leisurely drive along the waterfront.

Within ten miles from her parents' house, the posh Lake Shore Road, lined with a diverse collection of somber mansions, became East Jefferson Avenue. Jefferson meandered through middle class neighborhoods and into eastside Detroit near Belle Isle where Lake St. Clair squeezed into the Detroit River. Pilar had sailed those waters often. From that point the waterway rushed at seven knots past the city. Did it want to put the glass and concrete towers far behind?

As Pilar listened to Bob Edwards on NPR's "Morning Edition" report about another ethnic cleansing in a country whose name she could hardly spell, she looked out at the boarded-up buildings, empty lots, drug dealers, and thugs of East Jefferson Avenue. Bob probably didn't know about eastside Detroit.

Pilar dreamily watched the sun spread across the river. The rays peeked through a mantle of tree leaves, forming a lace arbor over side streets crowded with ramshackle homes, trash-strewn lots and cars on blocks waiting to be repaired once the owner got a job. The green canopy seemed to mask the hopeless lives secreted behind doors and curtained windows. Every so often, Pilar glimpsed pots of red and pink geraniums lining a porch, a momentary brightening for what could only be the residents' despair. She saw few people out so early. From what Pilar had heard, there was little to get up for. "That's why people like us take the freeway," she told herself. Her own sarcasm made her cringe. How well she had learned to stay out of the wrong part of the county.

After lowering the visor against the sun's glare, Pilar slid her hand to the *Detroit Free Press* that lay on the passenger seat. The paper was folded open to the third page where she had circled the four-inch story on Chad Wilbanks. His name had been in the news off and on since she returned home. This article assured the reader that the murderer at that very moment boarded a bus, leaving the Reception and Guidance Center in Jackson to transfer to his permanent home at Hawk Haven Prison in the Upper Peninsula.

Permanent home. Forever imprisoned. Pilar wondered

what it would feel like to be trapped behind bars for the rest of one's life. Chad was what? Twenty-something, she thought she remembered reading. No matter how awful the crime, forever was a long time. At least her incarceration in Grosse Pointe Shores was temporary. She could leave after the three years she'd promised Celeste. To Pilar, those years would be enough of a prison because of her father.

Over breakfast, her usual English muffin and two cups of black coffee, Pilar read and reread the section of the article that said, "As part of his sentence, Wilbanks will never return to Washtenaw County where he was found guilty of first degree murder." Instead of the relief she expected to feel, something in her felt regret. What made her want to confront this man, the killer of her good friend?

Susan's smile came to Pilar's mind, a sweet smile that belied Susan's quick and unexpected temper. It was probably that same smile, a little tentative, a little timid, that attracted Chad's attention.

As Pilar maneuvered her car into the right lane, she wondered about Chad's smile. The murders and subsequent trial had been front page news even in Wisconsin. She recalled a picture of him, not a mugshot. Like most handsome male students, he sported good clothes, styled hair, an athletic physique. But he gazed intensely, almost Pilar, would swear, passionately into the camera. She wondered who had taken the photograph, who had earned that heated stare.

What was this obsession she was developing? Once, after a brief local radio report about Wilbanks' pending transfer, Pilar found herself in front of the bathroom mirror with toothpaste dripping down her chin. She clutched the brush so tightly it cracked. What she saw was her own auburn, shoulder length hair, her own large, cinnamon-colored eyes. So like Susan's. So like the other victims'.

Yet, she thought she knew Chad's smile already, almost as though she had felt it directed at her before. In fact, as bizarre as it seemed even to her, she felt she had encountered this man somewhere, had felt the intensity of his gaze upon her.

Pilar shivered. Enough. Out on the river a lone sailboat struggled against the swift current. She would drive these thoughts away. She would concentrate instead on her residency. What a privilege it was to work at Receiving, a leader in emergency medicine. And what an experience she was likely to be signing up for; the hospital was located in the heart of Detroit.

Emergencies there were more likely than car accidents. Pilar would also see her share of domestic violence victims, and gun and knife wounds, mostly the result of neighborhood street battles, and drug turf wars. Though ER at Receiving would be only one of Pilar's rotations at the hospital during her first year, she had already chosen trauma medicine as her specialty. She hadn't shared that with anyone, even Julie, because she didn't want to spend hours defending her choice.   ER at Receiving wouldn't be anything like Father's serene Mission-style office, nor would it be patronized by elite members of his club. She hoped she was a match for the challenges of this volatile environment. And anything would be better that a position in her father's sterile milieu.

The stark gray stone and glass towers of the Renaissance Center, the Ren Cen, emerged from the shores of the Detroit River. She had only a few miles before she'd be in the parking lot at the hospital complex. She hoped the Center's name was an omen for her own future. After all, the Ren Cen had its share of ups and downs and was on an upswing. She also heard about attempts to revive other city neighborhoods close to the hospital, so maybe Receiving's ER wouldn't be as bad as Pilar envisioned. Still, the queasiness she felt made her regret that second cup of coffee.

Pilar squeezed her shoulders to her ears and sighed. That exercise didn't ease the tension. So, she massaged her neck. The pressure remained.

As she turned right onto Beaubien and away from the tidy line of condominiums edging the river, Pilar agreed with her father about one thing: she was a liberal do-gooder. "And I'm glad," she said, and slapped the steering wheel. She smiled into the rearview mirror like the Cheshire cat in "Alice in Wonderland", then had to slam on the brakes to avoid a collision with a sheriff's car, red and blue lights circling and sirens blaring, that shot onto the street from the bowels of the Wayne County Jail. Once Pilar regained her composure, she resumed her journey with a more cautious concentration.

Soon the hospital complex came into view. As she circled the parking lot to find the employee area, humid air rose up from the asphalt like steam from a boiling pot. Pilar parked, exhaled loudly and got out of the car.

"Check out the new nurse," one male doctor said to another when they passed by Pilar outside the employee entrance. She looked forward to their reactions when they discovered she was a peer. Perhaps not exactly a peer. Not until Pilar at least completed her first year of residency.

With fluttering stomach, Pilar practiced her new title to herself, Doctor Brookstone. She chuckled over the two doctors who undoubtedly only saw a good-looking one-night-stand. When the two Don Juans turned to check Pilar out one more time, an unappealing memory from med school surfaced: The dean telling her he doubted any woman could handle the burden of medical career and family. "So, it really is a waste of time, isn't it?" he asked.

Often, the dreadful truth about careers and relationships were delivered to Pilar and similar women like a scalpel which cut into the brain. The comment made by the dean gave Pilar a sound shove into the feminist fight, where she was determined to come out a winner.

Pilar waited until the two doctors were out of sight before she approached the entrance. She stopped for a moment to

gloat over the sign that read, "Hospital Employees Only."
Then she drew in a long sustaining breath, pulled the door
open, and crossed the threshold.

ON MONDAYS, ER WAS considered quiet, especially after
the carnage brought in on Friday and Saturday nights. So
after Pilar's initial orientation, meeting the patients assigned
to her and making rounds was easy. As she left her supervising doctor after a scheduled lecture and headed to the lounge
for lunch, Pilar met one of the doctors from the parking lot.
His eyebrows shot up into surprised peaks. "Look who's
here", his witching smile seemed to say. When he noticed
Pilar's lab coat and checked her name tag, a dropped jaw
replaced his momentary seduction. Any pleasure Pilar had
from that encounter with the thunderstruck doctor became
history when he quickly gathered his poise, leaned his body
toward her, and said, "You're too pretty to be a doctor."

Pilar glanced at his name tag — Jeremy Peters. "You
sound like my father, Doctor Peters," she told the brash
young man. "And I don't like him either."

He backed away and grunted, "No need to get testy."

"No need to be disrespectful," Pilar retorted and held out
her hand. "I'm Doctor Pilar Brookstone and you're going to
have to get used to me around here for a few years."

Doctor Peters' unenthusiastic hand shake reminded
Pilar of those she detested, like a limp offering of dead
fish. "You know what I discovered in med school?" Pilar

asked as she dropped his hand and wiped hers against her lab coat.

He shrugged and looked uninterested.

"You don't need a high testosterone level to be a doctor."

"Yeah, well tell me that after a Saturday night of removing bullets and sewing up ten-inch gashes when you've been up twenty-four hours." The two doctors walked through the doors to the physicians' lounge and straight to a large, stainless steel coffee pot.

"I will, Doctor Peters," Pilar stated, and handed him a steaming cup. "Coffee?" Pilar winked and noted she'd caught him off guard while she scoped his body as he had hers in the parking lot. Though he seemed ill at ease under Pilar's scrutiny, he showed no other signs of timidness. Pilar noted that his rugged good looks were more like Indiana Jones than a doctor, who in her mind should fit the likeness of the white-haired, bespeckled pediatrician of her childhood. Now, Pilar sounded like the male colleagues she accused of stereotyping. Still, no one would question that Doctor Peters' self-assured good looks would interfere with his ability to suture the wounded.

As he took the cup from Pilar, Doctor Peters reminded her, "Remember you're only a resident. You have a lot to learn."

Pilar grabbed her sandwich and coffee. Eating alone at the outdoor picnic table seemed more congenial than any further confrontation. Had her heated face revealed her true reaction to his admonishment? Pilar regained her composure and headed out the door, waving, "See you Saturday then?"

As Jeremy Peters stood motionless, mouth hinged open like a ventriloquist's dummy, Pilar whispered to herself, "Round one is mine." But was that a good way to start her first year?

The rest of the week didn't go smoothly, but not because of the job. In fact, Pilar seemed to have impressed her supervising doctor by her no-nonsense manner and desire to help anyone in need of care. Everyone else, however, especially Doctor Peters, seemed put-off, Pilar guessed, by her looks. Any skills Pilar displayed intimidated, rather than engaged her co-workers. The two qualities, beauty and talent, seemed like oil and water. They just didn't seem to mix. Disappointed, Pilar found that the work world was no different from her college experiences. Though there were women doctors on staff at Receiving, most female employees were nurses who clearly had learned their place in hospital hierarchy. Pilar believed she was treated more like the nurses. For instance, one time an orderly quickly retrieved the pen she dropped and returned it, commenting, "You're too pretty to do the heavy work." Had she noted sarcasm, or just disrespect in his tone?

Another time a male nurse asked Pilar out for "a friendly cup of coffee." She declined, of course, only to be assaulted by unkind words. "Do you think you're too good for me, Doc?" She told him no, that she was his supervisor and dating was against the hospital rules even though she had been well aware that male doctors broke that regulation regularly.

When Pilar and other doctors crowded around the coffee pot one morning she wanted to ask, "You can't seem to make up your minds. Am I too bright or too pretty?" Instead, she held back her question and took her coffee to a corner table where she sat alone. The group seated at the table next to her laughed and chatted comfortably. Would she ever loosen up enough to join them? What held her back?

If Julie had been in the Detroit area, Pilar would have made arrangements to meet her for a drink after their shifts that day, just as they had done at the University of Wisconsin. While they sipped wine, they'd lean their heads together and recount the daily events, punctuated by poking fun at their colleagues whom they either felt superior to or feared. Often, they'd share an especially humorous moment in uproarious laughter and attract unwanted attention from the other patrons in the dimly lit cocktail lounge. Julie and Pilar also would listen to each other for as long as it took to air an annoyance or concern. Then they'd get down to more serious medical issues, family problems and relationships. The two friends would part from the session refreshed and ready to do battle again. "I miss Julie." Pilar sighed.

SATURDAY NIGHT CAME WITH the vengeance Peters promised. Pilar sat in the lounge after she had worked almost nineteen hours straight. She could hardly remember the first victim — a thirteen-year-old shot in the arm in a gang turf quarrel. Thinking back to him, Pilar fell asleep in a chair. She woke up after an hour's nap, threw water on her face, and did a final check of the ER. When satisfied everything was in order, she drove home in a stupor and fell fully clothed into bed.

On the following afternoon, Pilar dragged her exhausted body back to the hospital expecting a worse evening than the one before. Halfway through her shift, an EMT found a teenage girl at the emergency entrance slouched on the ground and leaning against the wall. She was unresponsive and appeared to have been beaten. Once the girl had been placed on a gurney and wheeled into a vacant space in triage, Pilar saw that the bruises weren't fresh, but the track marks on her arms were.

"Get an IV of Naloxone in her, one milligram to start," Pilar barked to the nurse at her side. "And I'll begin CPR. She's fading fast. It looks like a heroin overdose."

"Are you sure?" Peters asked as he hovered near Pilar's right shoulder.

"Check her arms," Pilar directed. "And since you seem not to know the signs," she added, ignoring his seniority, "she's hardly conscious. In fact, she's in acute narcosis.

She gurgles with each labored breath. Her pupils are constricted. There's indication of depressed respiration. The bruises are not new. And she smells of alcohol." When Pilar completed her diatribe, she wondered if Peters had been testing her. Surely, with his experience he would know an overdose.

The nurse inserted the IV and delivered the first milligram of Naloxone with little response. Pilar ordered another milligram.

"What does alcohol have to do with it?" Peters shouted over the loud, controlled confusion in the crowded area. "Oh, never mind. Dumb question. I know polydrug use like alcohol is common with heroin overdoses."

"Did anyone see who brought her in?" Pilar asked without realizing how naive the question sounded. "We could use more information on what exactly she ingested." The second milligram of Naloxone worked. The patient came out of unconsciousness.

"No one is going to stick around to be questioned by the police." Peters rolled his eyes. "And if she dies, yadda, yadda, yadda."

"Oh, right," Pilar mumbled. "Her breathing and pulse are stable. I think she'll make it."

"This time," one of the nurses snickered.

When Pilar chided her for that remark, the nurse snapped, "If she doesn't kill herself, her boyfriend will." She pointed to the fading black and blue mark over her eye.

"Yeah, well," Pilar fumbled over her words and examined the bruise. "Maybe the police can talk some sense into her. Or better yet, find her parents."

"You may know diagnostic systems and treatment, but you have a lot to learn about girls like her." Peters shook his head as he answered. He tipped a finger to his forehead. "See you. Car accident victim."

Exhausted and shaken by the pragmatic way everyone dismissed that poor girl, Pilar turned to the same nurse she reproached earlier and asked, "Do you think the police will get her counseling, maybe on Methadone?"

"Ha!" the nurse sneered. "She'll be lucky if the police will keep her overnight. To them she's just another Cass Corridor hooker with a drug problem. She'll probably die of AIDS anyway." The nurse shrugged. "Many of them do."

"I need help in here," Peters shouted.

Reluctantly leaving the teenager to be picked up by the police, Pilar raced to help Peters with a patient whose puncture wound spurted blood in rhythm, like one of those fountains that squirted water to music. Pilar secretly admired Peters' unflustered composure and precise movements. It was obvious he'd been in that situation many times. As Pilar pressed a sterile cloth over the wound to slow the bleeding, she peered back over her shoulder to watch a policeman wheel the young girl away.

chapter three

CHOICES

HALFWAY THROUGH HER SECOND year of residency, Pilar decided what direction she wanted to go in medicine. One night during a rare dinner with her parents, Pilar mapped out her plans. "I'm applying to the Department of Corrections so I can work in a prison," she announced.

Marcus carefully placed his knife and fork down and gestured the maid out of the dining room. He might have been waving a fly away. His eyes never veered from Pilar. When the door closed behind the servant, he exploded. "I have had enough of you and your arrogant confidence," he said. "What makes you so sure you can save the world?" His mouth tensed into a thin line and hardly moved as the veins in his forehead pulsated with each angry word.

Pilar lowered her fork and smiled, pleased with the way the assured, controlled words flowed from her mouth. "First of all, Father, my future is not your decision." His chin jutted out and he raised an eyebrow. Her calm response appeared to surprise him. "If you're worried about your investment, I'll pay every dime back."

"Pilar," Celeste interrupted as she dabbed a white linen napkin at the corners of her mouth. Pilar had forgotten Celeste was in the room. She held up her hand to stop further comment. Her composure changed into contempt. "You have no idea about the real world, Mother, the one filled with the less fortunate who have no way to care for themselves. Well, Father dear, and Mother," she nodded at them both, "I now know that world all too well."

"I volunteer at Saint Johns, Pilar, remember?" Celeste fidgeted with her pearl necklace.

"Saint Johns is a hospital where the rich go, not the people I see every day." Pilar scraped the chair across the hardwood floor, secretly hoping to leave a gouge. She stood to face her father, seated opposite at the end of the twelve-foot table. As he adjusted his silk, handmade tie, Pilar made clear her feelings. "You could never understand the difference, or maybe, Father, you don't want to understand."

Marcus tried to regain his control when he answered, "Just because you've joined N.O.W. doesn't mean you've learned anything, Pilar."

Did he always think he could have the last word? Pilar's jaw stiffened, "You've been reading my mail." Her crooked smile showed as much scorn for him as she'd ever felt. "Can't handle the fact that one of your GIRLS has found her own way in life? That I can be a damn good doctor despite the fact I won't follow in your footsteps as you think a son would? Too bad. This is the twenty-first century."

She studied her father. The deep lines from his nostrils to the corners of his mouth had turned into a permanent frown. She recognized a lifelong signal in the slight nervous twitch of his nose. He was truly uneasy. Maybe even he realized he'd crossed an unforgivable line.

Head bent, Celeste twisted her napkin in silent frustration.

Pilar felt for her mother's distress. Yet she was also angry. How had Celeste stayed so long with that hateful, controlling man?

As Marcus lifted his wine glass, Pilar strutted to his side, curbing her urge to laugh at the time it took her to reach him in that obscenely long room. She stood as close to him as possible. Though he didn't flinch or change the position of his erect back against the mahogany chair, Pilar towered over him and defiantly spit out, "And stay out of my mail."

Celeste slapped the napkin on the table. "I've had enough of both of you," she shouted.

Startled by her mother's unnatural outburst, Pilar was tongue-tied, while Marcus nearly dropped his glass. For a moment neither seemed to know the woman at the other end of the table.

Celeste looked at Pilar, then Marcus, and stated clearly, "Neither of you can see beyond your own little world. You treat me like I don't exist. Well, for your information, others think I'm worth something."

"What are you talking about?" Marcus shouted.

"For the past year I've done more than volunteer at the hospital. I've put my college degree to work. I counsel battered women and rape victims." Celeste stood and faced Pilar squarely. "The poor aren't the only ones who are assaulted."

Marcus' face turned red. "No wife of mine . . ."

"I didn't know, Mother," Pilar interrupted. "Why didn't you tell me?" Pilar never thought of Celeste as anyone but just her mother. And her father's puppet.

"Would you have cared? Either of you? Look at your father, Pilar. He's mad, not happy for me. But I'm more alive now than I've been in ages."

"That's ridiculous." Marcus punched the table with his fist. The silverware bounced.

"Get over it, Father," Pilar smirked. "It looks like you're losing authority over both your girls." Suddenly anxious to be out of the tension, she moved toward the door, cool, determined. Would there never be an end to this conflict?

"Pilar," Celeste begged.

Pilar waved her hand in front of her face to let her mother know not to say anything else. Pilar wondered how she could have been so self-centered and blind about Celeste. "I need time to think. I don't seem to know either of you."

As soon as Pilar entered the hallway, she leaned her forehead against the wall. Guilt filled her, crown to toe, for faulting her mother. Hadn't Pilar always thought of her as a quiet, pliable person? Trained to be compliant at all costs?

"Mother's right," Pilar whispered. "I've not paid much attention to her. And here she is, taking steps to be in control of her own life."

Still, she remained angry with her mother for putting up with Marcus for so long. Pilar vowed never to give into another for so many years. She banged through the door down the front steps, kicked the Mercedes' front tire, threw herself behind the steering wheel and drove off.

MOTORING ALONG LAKE SHORE Road, Pilar let the natural world eclipse any thoughts she had about that evening. The sun reflected that brief pink moment in the east just before it disappeared for another day behind the western sky. As usual, that sensual union with the horizon raised Pilar's spirits, but short-lived euphoria was replaced with the image of her father's lips coupled with his wine glass.

Her father couldn't behave any other way than he did that night at dinner. Yet at the very least he could have listened to her reasons for wanting to work with prisoners. He would have learned about the two incidents that were key to Pilar's decision. First, she would have told him about Maria, a fifteen-year-old, barely four months pregnant.

In Pilar's third month in ER, someone dumped Maria at the emergency entrance, like a bag of trash, with two bullets lodged in her abdomen. Maria clutched Pilar's hand to her chest, familiar eyes pleading to save her. This time, she looked more like a fifty-year-old rather than a child. Maria was the same girl who had overdosed Pilar's first weekend in ER.

Maria was a runaway and a prostitute in Cass Corridor. Her infamous pimp was known on the streets as Johnny Good Time. From the buzz in the emergency room, Maria hadn't been his only victim. Johnny Good Time was un-happy with his women if they didn't bring in enough money, pregnant or not. Watching the life fade from Maria, Pilar believed Johnny wanted to abort the baby and not kill off his income. But he used too many bullets.

Maria and her baby died before reaching the operating table. Maria's death certificate read *Jane Doe A.K.A. Maria*.

That night Pilar decided to take a tour of the Corridor.

CASS CORRIDOR, THE SEEDIER part of the avenue that drew Pilar's interest, was sandwiched between Wayne State University on the north end, and Cass Tech High School on the south end. The unlikely setting for both prestigious schools was about a mile west of Detroit Receiving. Drunks and addicts lurked in the alleys, slumped against buildings, and slept on doorsteps. Even though she could outrun the healthiest of them, Pilar didn't feel safe. So, she chose to cruise the streets rather than walk. She needed to absorb as much as possible without the fear of being accosted, with-out anyone recognizing that, though ashamed about it, she harbored some unpleasant, inherited prejudices. She didn't think about the attention a new Mercedes would get in such an environment.

Brown-toothed teenage girls, some with children perched on hips, lingered in doorways of boarded up buildings. They took no precautions to hide the needle tracks in their bare arms, or the yellowed baby diapers that drooped from the unchanged load. Dressed in shorts that only covered half their behinds, halters or Spandex cropped shirts and four inch heels from Wal-Mart, they teetered toward possible Johns who exited the many decaying bars which lined the avenue.

It was hard to tell if any of the prostitutes had ever been pretty. Most looked like photographs of Appalachian women from the Depression – blanched, emaciated faces, vacant, weathered eyes, toothless mouths gumming cigarettes, and wisps of hair escaping from plastic clasps fastened at the back of their necks. Few Corridor women took the time to wear makeup. That's not what a trick was looking for. The nurses in ER told Pilar that many hookers had all their teeth removed to enhance a trick's oral sex pleasures. Pilar couldn't believe it.

After several visits to the Cass Corridor, Pilar gained the courage to question Jodie, a teen prostitute, who was soliciting from the shadows of a condemned apartment building. Jodie had known Maria. "We all knows each other here," she said as she swept one arm in front of her like a magician at the end of his sleight.

Her welcoming expression quickly changed to suspicion. She crinkled her face into an extraordinary mass of lines. "You a parole agent?" she asked.

Pilar chuckled, "No. I'm a doctor." But, she thought maybe she should have become a social worker.

Jodie tilted her head to the side, her brow furrowed into a huge valley above her nose. "What's a doctor doin' here? Ya with the health department? Because if ya are, this whole street should be quarantined." Then she pursed her lips. "I take that back. If it was, whadda I do?" She glanced at the needle tracks on her arm.

On Pilar's third visit, Jodie invited her to her room in a condemned structure next door to one of the bars. "Is it safe to go in here?" Pilar asked as Jodie slid a board to one side and crawled through the opening.

Once on the other side Jodie motioned Pilar through. "Sure. I live here, don't I?" she answered as if that should be explanation enough for trespassing. "Besides, it's a helluva lot safer in here than your wheels parked on the street. You be lucky the car's there when ya get back." She laughed, showing off the dark cavern that once held teeth. The nurse's tale must be true.

Jodie's apartment was on street level at the rear, so they avoided the ancient stairwell where steps were either rotted or gone. Pilar gagged when Jodie shoved the warped door open. The smells overwhelmed her — dirty diapers, unwashed dishes, and human waste. Pilar covered her nose. Flies swarmed unrecognizable chunks of food on plates left out on the table.

Gray, threadbare sheets covered a mattress in the corner. Spent syringes lay in complete view on the floor next to the bed. The table, one chair, and the mattress were the only furnishings. Jodie let her baby spill to the gummy floor as if he were a bag of laundry. A fleeting vision of Maria slumped against the hospital wall filled Pilar's head, to be quickly erased by the horror of the baby crawling through the cockroaches and dried feces. Jodie was too high to care. Did Jodie bring her Johns here?

Jodie recounted that she, like Maria, had run away from an alcoholic mother who let her boyfriend teach Jodie about sex. She had just got back on the streets after six months in the county jail. "I can do six months easy, but them girls that go to Scott, that's another thing all together. That's hard time."

As Pilar surveyed Jodie's hostile environment, she was convinced that six months in any prison or jail had to be better than the Corridor. Or it should have been. The women's prison had made the headlines and onto national news programs when inmates filed a class action suit against the state over the sexual abuse and harassment they endured at the hands of male guards. Even Geraldo Rivera did a special about abuse of women prisoners that featured Michigan. He reported that those women had few choices but to accommodate their keepers. Any harassment Pilar thought she faced paled in comparison.

"What happened to your baby while you were in jail?" Pilar asked.

Jodie's head jolted up. Though she spoke with a drug-induced slur, she made it clear that Pilar had better not tell social services about her baby. "They'll take Clifford away from me as sure as not." Her face filled with intense distrust. "My social worker already took Cassandra, my three-year-old."

Meeting Jodie inspired Pilar to read the special report by Amnesty International that Geraldo Rivera had referred to on his broadcast. Pilar was especially interested in the lengthy section on women in Michigan prisons. When she finished the report, Pilar was positive she could help those women.

The report also opened the guilt she felt about her friend Susan's murder. Why had Chad Wilbanks picked Susan as his mark, and not her? More troubling, why hadn't Susan told her about Chad? She and Susan had been inseparable at the University of Michigan, yet she had somehow failed her friend. She couldn't help Susan now, but perhaps she could help others, including women prisoners. Pilar saw them as victims just like Susan. So, Pilar prevailed upon her medical supervisor to let her volunteer at the Scott Correctional Facility for Women once a week, when she got to her third year of residency and wasn't on duty in the

ER. Though a long way off, Pilar would use the time until then to gather as much experience as she could to aid those needy prisoners.

The other event that made Pilar decide to work in corrections was the night an ambulance brought in a walkaway from Northeast Corrections Center, a halfway house for men about to be paroled. He had jumped from a fourth-floor window, crushed his legs, and broke his arm. When Pilar met him, he was in traction and confined to a hospital bed in a private room. Both his legs were in casts attached to wires and a pulley that raised them about six-inches off the bed. His right arm, the only limb not in a cast, was handcuffed to the metal bed frame behind his head. The position of his shackled arm seemed uncomfortable for the prisoner. Each time he tried to reposition himself, he winced as his arm twisted in the chain.

Pilar asked the sheriff's deputy who guarded the escapee why the patient needed to be cuffed when there was no way he was capable of leaving the hospital in his condition. The deputy simply shrugged and said, "It's regulation." His large lips flapped as moisture slipped from the corners. He shifted his body, which hadn't seen exercise in years, so he could rest his feet on the bed rail. The lumbering motion strained the seams of his brown uniform pants. The prisoner's face paled when the deputy's heavy booted foot forced his body to bounce. The unconcerned guard never noticed.

Regulations, Pilar discovered, often appeared to get in

the way of humane and healthful treatment when it came to criminals and the poor. And in the case of the walkaway, he wanted to go back to prison rather than be paroled into the hell of eastside Detroit. The inmate's eyes widened with terror when he told Pilar that. He wanted her to swear to him that he would not be put back on the streets. So, the handcuffing was a superfluous, bureaucratic mandate. That escapee was only going where he and the corrections department wanted him anyway — back inside the walls.

When Pilar's residency ended, she joined the Michigan Department of Corrections. She was disheartened when she was denied a position to work with women prisoners at Scott Correctional Facility, a decision made despite the self-education programs she had developed on venereal disease, birth control, and breast exams. Maybe Warden Cooper at Scott was uneasy when she discovered Pilar, while volunteering at the prison, also counseled the inmates on their right of choice when it came to their bodies and partners. Cooper was a no-nonsense policy administrator and Pilar knew that kind of counseling wasn't among any outlined by the MDOC. Yet Pilar had hoped that during the third year in her impeccable residency, her credibility would outweigh any uneasiness about her motives.

While Pilar had her heart set on helping young women like Maria, Jodie, and Susan, the correctional administrators had other ideas. So, instead of the Scott Women's Prison, Pilar was assigned to work in the Upper Peninsula at Hawk

Haven Men's Prison. Though there was a greater need for physicians at that prison because of its remote location, it did little to appease Pilar's disappointment. The good news, Pilar decided, was that the prison was near Marquette on the southern shore of Lake Superior which put it about as far as she could get from Grosse Pointe Shores and still be in Michigan.

chapter four
MICHIGAN MURDERS

THE MICHIGAN DEPARTMENT OF Corrections' Training Academy was on the west side of Lansing, almost a two-hour drive from the Grosse Pointe Shores house. Though Pilar thought the school didn't have the best accommodations, more like a boot camp than a campus, staying there was easier than a daily drive for the six-week program.

Pilar's days were filled with classes on correctional policies and procedures. Other sessions concentrated on how to interact with prisoners. The evenings were usually spent reading department manuals and doing homework before lights out. The dormitory reminded Pilar of her freshman year in college.

Pilar met Lorrie during lunch on the second day of training. Lorrie sat in a chair next to Pilar at an otherwise vacant table. She was a petite, rather frail woman, two years younger than Pilar, in training to be a probation officer. Her large eyes peered from under the bangs of her short auburn hair.

"You can't go to Hawk Haven," Lorrie insisted after she swallowed a mouthful of mashed potatoes. Her eyes were wide, filled with panic

"What's the difference?" Pilar asked, puzzled by the anxious look on Lorrie's face.

Lorrie pushed her tray of food to the side. "Chad Wilbanks is there," she said as she leaned closer to Pilar. "He charmed his way into the lives of at least eight women, and they're all dead. "

Pilar shrugged to let Lorrie know that he and his where-abouts had nothing to do with her, despite the chill that flowed through her veins. For a second Pilar wondered how she could have forgotten Chad Wilbanks was sent to Hawk Haven. Or, did she deliberately not want to remember?

Then Lorrie whispered in Pilar's ear, "I was engaged to Chad Wilbanks."

Pilar put down her fork and tried to absorb what she heard. Her hands trembled at the thought she knew two women who were involved with the same murderer.

Without coaxing, Lorrie blurted out the details. "I was lucky," she acknowledged as her eyes darted around the room. "I broke the engagement, because Chad had changed. I lived across the street from him most my life, but . . ." Lorrie paused for a moment and gazed at the wall behind Pilar. "He wasn't the same person after he graduated from high school."

When Lorrie resumed her narrative, her voice filled

with odd displeasure. "My therapist has tried to convince me that breaking my engagement to Chad had nothing to do with his murderous rampage two months later."

She lowered her head and again engaged Pilar. "I knew he could be violent and the coincidence was too obvious." Lorrie reached across the table and clutched Pilar's wrist. Her grip tightened when she admitted, "Chad broke my arm. That ended it for us." She raised her right arm as though showing Pilar a cast. "We were both at Eastern Michigan University then." Her voice was wispy, almost other-world-like. "We had been sweethearts since middle school."

Pilar was mesmerized by Lorrie's appearance because she resembled every dead woman pictured in the newspapers, except she had short hair. Her enormous, cinnamon-colored, puppy-like eyes, now calm, framed in lush raven black lashes, projected provocative purity.

As though she had read Pilar's mind, Lorrie told her she'd cut her hair after she saw photos of Chad's victims in the newspapers. "I didn't want to look like them," Lorrie added. Then she pulled an album filled with the victims' pictures from her backpack.

Stunned at such a macabre keepsake, Pilar couldn't comprehend why anyone would want a constant reminder of poor, helpless women, especially if she knew the murderer. Lorrie handed the album to Pilar. "You look similar to them, too," she said as she reached out to flip Pilar's hair. Pilar recoiled.

When Lorrie first mentioned photos, Pilar suddenly re-called a yellow rain slicker. It reminded her of Gerri Hearn's picture and description in the newspaper. Gerri, a twenty-three-year-old, five foot-six woman with dark auburn, shoulder-length hair, was a law student at the University of Michigan hitching a ride home to the other side of the state for the Christmas holidays. Gerri Hearn never made it. A young mother and her son found Gerri's naked body in the park across from their house. Gerri Hearn had been raped, strangled, and stabbed 25 times. A yellow slicker covered her body. Pilar stared at Gerri's picture in Lorrie's album.

Pilar, too lost in her own morbid reverie, only realized Lorrie was still talking when she saw her mouth open and close. When Pilar tuned back in, Lorrie was saying that shortly before she applied to be a probation officer, she married her therapist.

Pilar shook her head. How could such a partnership allow Lorrie recovery? More curious, why was Lorrie freely telling her story to Pilar, a stranger?

As Lorrie chattered away like a wind up, talking doll whose mechanics had gone awry, speedier and speedier, Pilar saw Lorrie's mangled body on top of a chaotic pile of corpses left behind by her former beau. The entire mound was covered by a giant yellow slicker.

"What?" Pilar asked when Lorrie whispered in Pilar's ear.

"We never had sex. He wanted to marry a virgin."

The words *Virgin Mary, marry a virgin* whirled around

in Pilar's head. All the newspaper articles said Chad Wilbanks had raped his victims.

"I've got to get back to my class," Pilar told Lorrie, though they had another twenty minutes. She left the table, went to the bathroom, and threw-up. Lorrie followed Pilar and posted herself outside the door.

After Pilar determined a reasonable time had passed for Lorrie to become bored and give up her station, Pilar walked back into the hallway. Lorrie startled her when she grabbed her arm and said, "Please don't tell anyone about my past." Lorrie didn't let go. She glanced around the area and added, "I'm sure they won't let me be a probation officer if they know about Chad."

"No problem," Pilar answered and unclenched Lorrie's hand, finger by finger, exposing red prints. "But why do you want that job anyway?"

Lorrie's eyes became seething slits, angry at Pilar's doubting tone. She didn't answer for a moment. "You don't understand. I have to help others like Chad. Even he could have been turned around if . . . " Lorrie stopped in mid-sentence, and left Pilar pressing her purse against her chest as though fearful it would be snatched.

DURING TRAINING LORRIE AND Pilar became casual friends, or at least casual for Pilar. Lorrie seemed to need a more intimate link. One day, Lorrie revealed that desire when out of the blue she rambled, "Perhaps if I stayed with

Chad, he wouldn't have sought revenge. He wouldn't have taken our split-up out on those young women."

Pilar reminded her that Chad was suspected of two murders in California a year before the Michigan murders started. "If you stayed with him, you'd probably be dead," Pilar consoled. "Not in training to be a probation officer."

Lorrie was silent. Apparently, she needed to feel guilty.

With each ensuing encounter with Lorrie, Pilar was learning more about Chad Wilbanks and his family than she had ever wanted to know.   Yet she could never stop listening. It was like the time she found herself in front of the mirror with toothpaste running down her chin. She had a deep seated, strange, and unexplainable desire to know all she could about Chad.

Lorrie had lived in Center Line across the street from the Wilbanks family since she was in the fifth grade. Though she and Chad had become quick friends, they hadn't started to date until high school. They had planned to marry when both graduated from college.

Pilar laid her text aside whenever Lorrie appeared in her dorm room. There was no escape once Lorrie set her mind to talking. In their short relationship, Pilar felt she was becoming Lorrie's therapist though she hadn't sought that connection. Was she a better listener and more objective than Lorrie's husband?

Lorrie usually showed up in Pilar's room just before lights out to talk. One night early in their training, she recounted the saga about Chad as though she thought Pilar asked to hear the tale. Lorrie pointed out that Chad's mother never married his father because he was married to someone else. He kept Maryann like a mistress.

Lorrie wore a long-sleeve, white cotton nightgown. She sat cross-legged at the end of Pilar's cot sipping Diet Coke.

"Why do you drink diet pop?" Pilar asked. "You're too thin as it is." Pilar suspected Lorrie was anorexic. Wouldn't that be one more way to punish herself for the murders Chad committed? As a doctor, Pilar was becoming concerned about Lorrie's emotional state.

"When Chad was little, he didn't know his parents weren't married, of course. He thought his father had to be gone for long periods of time on business." Her eyes glazed over. Her tone was slight and flat, and she never attempted to engage Pilar. Rather, she no longer seemed to know Pilar was present.

"One night, Chad overheard an argument between his parents. That's when he learned the truth about his birth — that he was a bastard." Lorrie picked at something on her nightgown. She flicked it and went on. "And that his father was married to someone he had no intention of leaving. It would ruin his reputation, you see." Lorrie got up and stood at the window and watched the full moon rise beyond the trees, sending shafts of light through the leaves.

Pilar's text slid from her hands and thumped on the floor. Amazed by how closely Chad's life paralleled hers,

Pilar experienced again that disquieting moment of sympathy. There were many men in the world like Chad's father, Pilar's for one. She was so tired, but allowed Lorrie to go on. The story was surprisingly compelling.

As Lorrie folded and unfolded the curtain, she continued her trance-like soliloquy. She explained that one night Chad barged into his mother's bedroom. He grabbed his father by the throat. His father pushed him off and fled from the house. It was the last time Chad ever saw that man. Chad was a senior in high school.

When Pilar shifted in the bed, the sheets rustled and distracted Lorrie. She walked to Pilar and sat at her side. "He didn't mean to call you a whore. But what did you expect when you slept around like you did after that?"

Shaken, Pilar finally spoke. "I'm Pilar, Lorrie, not Maryann." Pilar leaned over, picked up the fallen text, and clutched it to her chest. It was time to send Lorrie away. She knew they both should be studying.

Lorrie snapped her head up and smiled. "Of course you are. What makes you think you're Maryann?"

Goose-bumps shot up Pilar's arms and into the base of her neck as she tried to ease away from the whole scene without seeming uncharitable. "Is Chad the only child?"

"No." Lorrie sounded exhausted. Yet she told an even more bizarre tale than the one Pilar had already heard. Lorrie told Pilar about Chad's younger sister, Amy. Chad beat her, almost killed her, because he said that Amy was a tramp like his mother. Apparently it was a well-known fact in the neighborhood that Maryann entertained many men after his father left. Everyone suspected that was how she made a living. At least she didn't have any other visible income, except the child support Chad's father gave her.

Pilar lowered her head and smoothed the sheet. She didn't want to engage Lorrie's gaze. Instead, she envisioned a long line of men outside the Wilbanks' front door. Each looked like her own father. Each held a pair of tickets to a ball game.

For some reason, Pilar simply had to know more. Was this relentless need to hear Lorrie out really a form of therapy for herself? "Didn't Chad have anyone else to turn to?" Pilar asked as she fluffed a pillow and rested her head against it.

"Christy, his mother's sister. Chad adored her. She married Joey, a state cop. After his father disappeared, Chad and Joey were really close." Lorrie finished her Coke and tossed the empty can into the trash. She faced Pilar, her face streaked with mascara tears. "It was hard on Joey when he found evidence in his own home that connected Chad to Susan Mitchell's murder."

Pilar bolted upright. "What do you mean?"

"Chad was house-sitting for his aunt and uncle when he killed Susan Mitchell in their basement."

Pilar wanted to cover her ears, and yet she still couldn't stop listening. Lorrie told Pilar that after Joey faced the unthinkable truth, he arrested Chad. Joey had to tell Chad's mother, who at first wouldn't believe her loving son could be that evil. Maryann had shared all the details with Lorrie. That she begged Chad to tell the truth. Lorrie felt Maryann at first believed he was covering for someone else — but she got what she asked for. Chad confessed. When their hour-long conversation ended, they both came out of the interrogation room. Joey told Lorrie that from the way their eyes were so red and puffy, they both had to have been crying.

Pilar visualized deformed faces, swollen until they were shiny, like grotesquely pleading wax museum figures. She imagined Maryann groping her way from the small chamber after she heard Chad's confession. Maryann must never have suspected her son's wickedness. No mother like her would believe the light of her life had committed such horrendous crimes. He was no monster. How could he have turned out this way?

When she finished, Lorrie swiped away drips from her nose as though incensed they had formed. "In the end," Lorrie's voice trailed off, "we all deserted Chad."

Did Lorrie still love him?

Though the July evening held the day's heat, Pilar shivered uncontrollably. She saw Susan having dinner with Chad, sharing a bottle of wine. Then here was Susan alone in a basement with Chad, struggling while Chad repeatedly stabbed her. Susan, falling limp to the concrete floor.

Chad, covering Susan's body with a yellow slicker. She saw Maryann twisting her hands in despair at a courtroom exit.

How much blame, Pilar wondered, could be placed upon Maryann for Chad's behavior? How much are any of us independent of our parents' influence? She remembered the newspaper photograph, that handsome face, the searing gaze, those intelligent eyes. That was the question, wasn't it — how did that man become a murderer?

Pilar pulled the blanket up to her chin.

"But," she jumped when Lorrie shouted, "how can we blame Chad for feeling betrayed and hurt by his own family?" She raised her fist into the air and slammed it against the bed as though Pilar caused the betrayal to happen.

Pilar pulled the blanket away from Lorrie's fist. "I know how Chad feels," Pilar confided. "My father abandoned me, too. I hate him, but I'm not going to kill every man that reminds me of him." She tried to laugh. "Even if I'm tempted."

Suddenly Lorrie changed her tone. "Just be sure you're not taken in by Chad's charms like the rest of us." Her voice was cold, secretive. "And don't forget, you said I was lucky."

ON THE LAST TRAINING DAY, Pilar clutched Lorrie hard to her chest. If she let go, Pilar was afraid Lorrie would spin out of control, then crash to earth in flames like a meteor. Yet, despite Pilar's urgent desire to help Lorrie, she also felt an intense pressure to get as far away from her as possible. One thing Pilar knew for sure, though, was that somehow she herself embraced Lorrie's history — and Chad's.

chapter five

THE MEETING

"NICE ASS, LADY," AN inmate called out.

Pilar winced at the catcall as she bent forward to grab her briefcase from the Mercedes' front seat. When she straightened and self-consciously brushed her slim linen skirt in place, Pilar noticed Warden Max Whitefeather watching her from the lobby window. Whitefeather licked his lower lip and stepped back into the shadows. It was stupid to have worn a hip-hugging skirt.

When she wrapped a matching jacket over her shoulders, another inmate yelled out, "Show us your tits." Several other men chuckled as they lock-stepped to a prisoner transportation bus idling near the sallyport.

Though the air was unusually cool for early August, Pilar's hands were moist when she gripped her briefcase. She knew that if she acknowledged the men, even with a slight tilt of her head, she'd only encourage more insults. She kept her head held high and chin forward. Yet her eyes shifted slowly toward the voices. With a trembling hand

Pilar reached for the door handle just below the words Hawk Haven Prison, etched in the glass. She hesitated. Then, Pilar turned and faced the taunting men.

Pilar focused on an officer standing at the front of the bus. He leveled a shotgun at a line of men chained together wearing orange jump suits with Michigan Department of Corrections printed across their backs in large black letters. Ankles clad in iron, the prisoners shuffled by the officer and awkwardly climbed the stairs. Pilar knew from training videos that once they boarded the bus, another officer would guide each prisoner to a seat, unhook him from the tether, and handcuff him in place to a steel eye bolt welded to the chair.

As Pilar laughed at her concern over what that group said to her, she noticed the armed guard never flinched when prisoners insulted him. Even the unarmed officers appeared menacing in their black slacks and gray shirts, colors Pilar associated with the likes of Darth Vader. When one unintimidated prisoner spit on the guard's uniform shoulder, the officer lodged a shotgun butt in the offender's groin. The injured prisoner tumbled to the ground. The others linked to him crumbled as well. They cursed as they pulled the first man from the top bus stair.

A flash of light drew Pilar's attention away from the cascading inmates to the gun tower perched on the rooftop just above the sallyport. The ever-vigilant tower officer lifted his M15 automatic rifle and aimed it at the confused pile of orange bodies. Then, he pointed the rifle into the air just above the human mass and fired a warning shot. The report sliced the air.

Pilar flinched and sought refuge inside the lobby. She leaned against the door, hyperventilating, and damned her faintheartedness. The smirking front desk officer raised the forefinger of his right hand to the side of his head like a salute and asked, "Dr. Brookstone, I presume?"

Pilar regained her composure and faced the officer. She stretched to her full 5'8" height, back-board straight and snapped, "Yes." She tossed her hair away from her face and chastised herself for the second time that morning. She should have secured her hair in a clip at the nape of her neck so she'd look professional.

The officer started at the unexpectedly loud response and stated, "You're expected. The warden is waiting in the auditorium with the other 'fish'." His eyes roamed over Pilar's body.

Pilar recognized the insulting term "fish," a derogatory expression for someone new. She arched her right eyebrow and checked the officer's name tag. "You were correct the first time. Call me Doctor Brookstone," she instructed in a harsh, sarcastic tone, "Officer Leonard."

The unflustered officer smiled and motioned her through a steel security gate into a small enclosure. "After you, DOCTOR Brookstone."

Why was it, she wondered, the jerks were always good

looking? She jumped when the gate struggled to close behind her, and noted the mocking grin on Leonard's face.

"Put your briefcase down," he ordered.

Pilar looked in the direction of his nod. She placed her newly purchased calfskin case on a stainless steel table bolted to the wall. A sour liquid stung her throat. She swallowed hard and forced it back down while Officer Leonard rifled through the briefcase like a cop looking for drugs.

"Routine search," he said. "You'll get used to it." His face brightened. He commanded Pilar to spread her legs apart and lift her arms out to her side level with her shoulders. He lowered his eyes to the slit in Pilar's skirt that exposed the section of her left thigh two inches above the knee.

Pilar glanced at him, wrinkling her face into a disdainful question. Ignoring her, Officer Leonard circled behind Pilar. A heavy scent of Stetson cologne filled the cage. As he completed the shakedown his fingers combed through Pilar's hair down to the collar of her silk shirt. He pressed the seams and massaged his way across her outstretched arms and then back to her breasts.

Paralyzed, Pilar faced the bars of the gate that shut her away from the outside world as Officer Leonard caressed her breasts and slid his hands along her thighs into her crotch. Pilar's eyes burned as she strained to keep the tears away. She was too new to know if that was a normal search or one given to all "fish" to put them in their place.

When he finished his exploration of her body, Leonard

yelled, "Gate Two."

An officer, beads of sweat formed on his upper lip, pushed a button. He was seated inside the bubble, a small room to the right of the gates, and screened behind bullet proof glass. He had watched the shakedown and winked at Leonard to show his approval. Gate Two slid open with the same uneasy effort as gate one. Leonard motioned Pilar to follow another officer who waited nearby. Pilar felt Leonard's scorching stare as he watched her walk the corridor that took her behind the walls.

AS PILAR ENTERED THE auditorium, Warden Whitefeather was being introduced. He stood in front of two rows of newly hired "fish" officers. He was shorter and stockier than Pilar remembered from their interview. His crooked smile greeted Pilar. "Doctor Brookstone," he nodded. "Take a seat here." He pointed to the one right in front of him.

The new male and female officers of varying ages and racial and ethnic backgrounds studied Pilar as she moved to the first row, the one they avoided. She took deliberate steps to control her nervousness while twelve pairs of eyes followed her. Pilar's heels, the only noise in the auditorium, sounded like hail hitting a metal roof. Painfully aware of her unsteadiness, it seemed like hours before she finally sat alone in the center of an empty line of chairs.

Whitefeather tossed his charcoal-tweed sports coat into the chair next to Pilar. Its sleeve brushed against her arm.

Pilar blanched when the warden clapped his hands and shouted, "Let's get this orientation over." He loosened his tie, unfastened the top button of his white, synthetic shirt and rolled up his sleeves.

The officers fidgeted with their own ties, shirt cuffs, and buttons. Pilar tugged her skirt over her knees. Warden Whitefeather eyed the motion when she tucked her legs under the seat. As he regarded her, the warden barked like a drill sergeant, "Some of you won't make it." His eyes moved to Pilar's face. His voice echoed in the nearly empty assembly hall.

Though certain that the remark was directed at her, Pilar couldn't let on that she was humiliated. Instead, she elevated her chin and stared the warden down.

He grinned, then looked at the others. "I don't know which of you, maybe a third, won't be here this time next year."

While Whitefeather waited for a few to clear their throats and change positions, he examined Pilar. He pushed his thick salt and pepper hair away from his forehead. One stubborn tuft returned to its place above his right eye.

"Prisoners have all day to watch you, to find your vulnerabilities." Pilar felt she was the only person in the room. Whitefeather finally looked away and checked each face in the audience. He appeared to note who would be a prisoner's target. "Be aware of the set-up." His eyes settled back on Pilar.

Heat filled Pilar's face. Why did he single her out? She

needed to determine what indicators she had displayed in that short time to make people think she was vulnerable. In training she had heard the warden's wife had died. Killed by a drunk female driver. Was he upset with all women at that moment?

"Some of you," the warden waved his right hand in an arch across the front of his slight middle-aged paunch, his intense eyes moving from one face to another, "will leave of your own free will. Others will be fired for a variety of reasons from drug abuse to," he hesitated and glanced at Pilar again, "improper relationships with prisoners."

It took every bit of Pilar's energy to stay still and not react with a nervous twitch or movement. Though desperate to challenge his obvious accusation, Pilar also knew that the orientation wasn't the time or place. Pilar looked from the warden's round stomach to his face. Despite the obvious physical differences, she saw only her father. The rest of the orientation was a blur.

ONCE IN THE INFIRMARY, Pilar collapsed into a chair, glad that her office was part of the prison's administration building rather than inside, beyond the security gates. Yet, she was curious about the security risk. So many inpatient rooms faced the parking lot with nothing more than locked windows to prevent an escape. Pilar shrugged. How silly! No one had gotten out of Hawk Haven in its one hundred-year history. Besides, there was no place an escapee could go.   The prison was in the middle of the Hiawatha National Forest in the UP, the Upper Peninsula.

Built in the late 1800's, Hawk Haven looked like a state hospital from a Dickens' novel.   The still-occupied warden's house, a reminder of past days when most prison administrators lived on grounds, sat to the left of the Gothic administration building.   Both buildings were incorporated into the thirty-foot concrete wall, an ominous perimeter protected by razor ribbon, electronic detection system, and eight gun towers.   It was almost too hard for employees to get out of there let alone a prisoner, unless, of course, an inmate exited through an infirmary window.

Pilar had more pressing concerns than a possible escape.   She laughed at the absurdity of her position: Could a debutante from Grosse Pointe Shores work in one of the toughest prisons in Michigan caring for rapists, murderers and child abusers?   She was going to give it one helluva try. And the first thing she'd do was figure out how she came across as susceptible to Whitefeather.

As Pilar removed a department manual from her briefcase, she thought back to her six weeks in training. Remembering Lorrie's cautions, it seemed an uncanny co-incidence that Pilar would have trained with someone who knew Chad Wilbanks, a serial killer.

Pilar retrieved her stethoscope, the last item in her at-tache.   Then, she lifted a white lab coat from a wall hook, caressing it as though the coat were a symbol of honor.

Maybe the coat would erase any misconceptions about her. Pilar had one arm in the sleeve when someone knocked. The door opened before she could acknowledge the caller. An African-American woman poked her head through the opening and announced, "I'm Jane Carson, day shift nurse. Your first patient is here."

Pilar nodded. "I'll see him in the exam room." She walked through the door, but stopped as she searched the long, impeccably clean corridor, lined with closed doors and smelling of disinfectant and old gym shoes. Pilar turned to the nurse. "Where's the exam room?"

Nurse Carson chuckled in a good-natured way. "We have several, but he's in number three." She pointed down the narrow hallway. "By the end of today, you'll be well acquainted with each room."

"Why's that?" Pilar asked.

"The word's out about the new good-looking female doctor, so our clinic call is higher than normal. They knew about you a week ago." Nurse Carson giggled like a girl. "Boys will be boys, locked up or not. Besides, sick call gets them out of their cells." Her eyes shone like two small suns and lit up her dark face. "You'll get used to the attention. We all do."

Pilar watched Jane Carson return to the nurses' station. She had to be one of few African-Americans who worked in the UP. She was short, maybe 5'2", a little on the plump side, in her late twenties, with classic good features rather than prettiness. Her black hair was cut close to her almost perfect skull. Her noticeably buoyant personality captivated Pilar.

AFTER A MORNING OF checking pulses, heart beats, and sore throats, Pilar had just enough time to eat an apple from an infirmary tray before Nurse Carson appeared at the door. "No rest for the weary, I'm afraid, doctor. Your first patient for this afternoon is here. And he's a doozy." She handed Pilar a file. "In here for natural life."

Pilar took the folder and asked, "Aren't most of the prisoners in here for life?"

"Yes, but he's special. Murdered seven, maybe eight women, but still thinks he's a lady's man."

Pilar checked the file. Chad Wilbanks' name stared back at her. A hundred icicles might be massaging her spine. "First day jitters," she muttered to herself, and headed for the consultation.

"We all have them," Carson said as Pilar passed her.

Upset at being heard, Pilar acted like she didn't understand. "What do we have?" she asked.

"First day jitters." She frowned at Pilar as though she shared a deep secret.

CHAD WILBANKS SAT IN a chair, his right wrist handcuffed to the arm. Pilar noted that he didn't raise his head when she entered, but she was sure he appraised her from the corner of his eyes.

"Good morning Mr. Wilbanks. What . . .?"

"Call me Chad." Now he looked directly at her. Here was that newspaper photo, come to life. His smile was as engaging as she'd suspected.

She quickly looked away and thumbed through his medical record. The typewritten words made no sense. Pilar faced Chad. "What brings you to the infirmary, Mr. Wilbanks?" She willed herself not to think of women's mutilated bodies.

"You look pale, Doctor Brookstone. Maybe someone should see you and not me." His tone was pleasant, not condescending. He had a slight lisp, something she hadn't expected.

Two sentences, and Pilar was disarmed.

This was not the monster she had read about in the newspaper. Pilar could see why Lorrie and the others were drawn to him. In fact, he seemed almost shy, vulnerable. He reminded Pilar of the many boys with whom she'd gone to Grosse Pointe Country Day School; dark, nicely cut short hair, a creamy complexion, and healthy, flushed cheeks. She pictured him in white tennis shorts and shirt. Chad was the very image of the man Pilar's father had hoped she'd marry.

Lorrie's warnings echoed in Pilar's ears, and put steel in her spine. "Mr. Wilbanks," she commanded as she tossed his file onto a table, "if you don't have a medical problem, then I need to send you back to your cell and tend to the other prisoners. My schedule is full."

"Sorry, ma'am. I didn't mean to speak out of place." He waited for a few moments before he looked away from Pilar's face to her trembling hands.

Pilar stuffed them into her lab coat pockets. Chad raised his head and studied her face again. "I have a sore throat," he finally reported. "Strep has been going around the joint, so the block sergeant thought I should get in here before I got too bad."

"I see," Pilar answered. She pointed to the exam table. "Sit there."

Chad chuckled as he jangled his cuffed wrist. "I can't move from this chair."

"Oh, sorry." Pilar's faced heated, again. "Is that the policy for everyone?" She recalled the walk-away at Detroit Receiving Hospital chained to his bed.

"Only if a guy tried to escape." Chad shifted in the chair. His mouth formed a half- deriding smile. "But, a doctor can order them taken off if she wants." Pilar was fully aware he noticed the tension in her shoulders.

Here were those victims' bodies again, cluttering her thoughts. She also remembered something she'd heard at the academy about a prisoner caught trying to tunnel his way to freedom. Hard for her to imagine someone as calm, engaging, and handsome as Chad could be a brutal murderer and an escapee. "I have a lot to learn," Pilar mumbled. Once again, she regretted revealing her thoughts out loud.

"Ma'am?"

"Nothing. I'll examine you where you are." Pilar leaned over Chad. He made no attempt to hide his interest in her breasts. And, instead of being insulted, Pilar felt her increased heartbeat stimulate an adrenaline rush. The sensation was probably from her nervousness over treating a notorious killer. She was sure she'd soon get over it.

Pilar manipulated a tongue depressor inside Chad's mouth and softly said, "I'll take a culture and send it to the lab."

She reached for a Q-tip and swabbed his throat, then wiped the specimen onto a glass slide. When she straightened, their eyes locked. "Meanwhile, I'll give you a prescription," she said. "Your throat does look red and swollen." Suddenly dizzy, she stepped away to lean against a table, hoping he hadn't noticed her unprofessional demeanor.

"Aren't you going to check out my heart and lungs?" Chad asked. How did he manage to make such a simple sentence sound so seductive?

"No need." Pilar turned away from his probing gaze and fussed with papers. "I'll get the officer to take you back. Your prescription will be ready for the afternoon med call."

"Thank you," he responded in stilted sincerity. "You're more efficient than the last doctor we had here. He was just waiting on his retirement."

"That's a high appraisal for a routine exam," Pilar

answered as she turned to him. "But, I appreciate the compliment." At the moment, everything she'd learned in training was fuzzy. Maybe she shouldn't have been so quick to acknowledge his praise. No, first day jitters, that was all.

When Chad left, Pilar wanted to lock the door and sit alone for a while to go over what had just happened. She had treated a handsome, articulate man about her age who happened to be a serial murderer. Was she attracted to him? Or, did he frighten her? For a moment, she brushed the ideas away and attributed her ease with Chad Wilbanks to knowing so much about him. He had become too familiar.

Images of Lorrie's agonized face and Susan Mitchell's smile complicated her thoughts.

MID AFTERNOON, PILAR WAS coming down the hall when she saw a prisoner hand Nurse Carson a stack of forms. Pilar noticed Jane's body stiffen when the man ran his forefinger along her wrist. Hearing Pilar's footsteps, they moved apart and Jane called out, "Doctor Brookstone. Wilbanks' tests are back from the lab." Her face glowed. She never looked away from the sullen man whose institutional pallor made his skin look like ash. Pilar couldn't help compare his color to Chad's healthy flesh tone.

"Since when do we allow prisoners to work in the lab?" Pilar asked the nurse, and motioned to the man as he left the area.

"Since we can't get enough help," Jane answered.

"Besides, he's smart, a low security risk; it's good training. And, in Johnson's case, I keep a close watch on him." She handed Pilar the lab results. She noticed Jane didn't wear any rings, despite having told Pilar about her husband and two children. "Tommy's real job is the main porter for the infirmary," Jane explained further. "When we're short handed, he's our runner."

Jane sounded too enthusiastic. But, Pilar was exhausted from the day's call-outs. She didn't want to discuss the issue further. She probably over-reacted anyway. "Call Wilbanks up for his meds then, Mrs. Carson."

"Done. And, please call me Jane or Carson. We're going to be together too long to be so formal."

The nurse appeared to wait for Pilar to offer the same privilege, but Pilar didn't. Not yet. Not until she knew what was going on. Anyway, Pilar didn't know how long she'd be at Hawk Haven and she didn't want to risk a whole career on a moment of poor judgment.

Pilar glanced at prisoner Johnson's stringy, shoulder-length, dishwater blond hair as he walked through the gate toward the cell blocks. Jane, face flushed, also watched Tommy's exit, though unconcerned that Pilar may have detected her dreamy state.

"Why is Johnson in prison?" Pilar asked.

Jane jerked around so fast she dropped a bottle of aspirin. She ignored the scattered pills and asked "Why do you want to know?"

"Just curious how prisoners get to work in an area I consider high security."

"They earn it, just like Tommy did. He kept his nose clean and stayed out of trouble." Clearly, there was more to their relationship than nurse and prisoner.

"Will you elaborate, please?" Pilar asked.

"Tommy has been a good prisoner. He's had no bad behavior reports, so he has reduced his security level from close to medium custody. If he continues on that path, his level will go to minimum."

"At which time I assume he will be paroled."

"Yes." Jane picked up the clipboard and went to the nurses' station across from Pilar's office. Another patient waited. Her curt answer let Pilar know that the conversation was finished for her. But not for Pilar. She decided that she might have a few more questions about him. She planned to keep her eye on both of them, and would definitely check into Johnson's file. Meanwhile, Pilar picked up the spilled aspirins Jane left on the floor.

CHAD RETURNED LATE THAT afternoon for his meds. Jane had finished distributing prescriptions to a line of prisoners from a small opening in the shield surrounding the nurses' station. Pilar was writing up a chart behind the counter. One other prisoner was in the waiting room near the entry gate. He was the afternoon porter who, like Tommy, was assigned to keep the infirmary hospital sterile.

Pilar looked up from the chart briefly. Chad's eyes were focused on her while Jane, her hands in surgical gloves, explored his mouth to make sure he'd swallowed the dose. Holding his tongue, Jane fingered Chad's gums.

Trying unsuccessfully to concentrate on the notes in front of her, Pilar was positive that Chad had been admiring the way her body curved over the chart rack. She sneaked a look.

The nurse tugged hard on Chad's tongue. He winced and shifted his attention to the ceiling above Jane. "Get a good look," the nurse said. "That's as close as you're going to get to that doctor." She yanked off the gloves, tossed them into the trash, and reached for another pair.

"A man can dream, can't he?"

An arresting smile lighted Chad's face. Pilar slowed her writing and tilted her head to eavesdrop. Suddenly, she felt as though a cold wind blew through her body. Pilar inspected the air-conditioning vent above. It was motionless.

Jane wasn't charmed. Instead, she placed her hands on her hips like a mother about to scold her son. "That's about all you can do in here, Wilbanks, is dream. Now, get on your way."

"See you tomorrow then," Chad told the nurse, but still he gazed at Pilar.

A shaft of afternoon sun sliced through the narrow window, warming the top of Pilar's head. No doubt it also highlighted the red in her hair. Pilar shivered.

Chad nodded in a way that indicated he fully enjoyed Pilar's awareness of his flirtations.

chapter six

MAKING ROUNDS

PILAR HAD TO MAKE rounds in the segregation units. There was no way to get out of it. Rounds were required. So, she finally faced the inevitable. Wearing a lab coat and carrying a clipboard with note paper, she left the administration building, "The Building" as the prisoners called it, for the cellblock. It was the first time she had been inside since the warden's orientation the day she arrived nearly a month earlier. The idea of meeting prisoners on their turf was unsettling.

The security gate shuddered until it finally slammed closed with an earsplitting bang. Pilar was locked outside of her protected environment and deposited alone into the bowels of the institution. Pilar patted her pocket to make sure she hadn't forgotten her personal body alarm. If she needed help, she could push the alarm and alert central control who would send officers to her aid. It was often the only thing that saved a victim from her assailant in a prison.

As Pilar walked past the recreation yard, she marveled

at how the prisoners' uniforms created a wall of blue. The men huddled near the yard fence in small groups. She searched for Chad in each gathering, though he wouldn't hang out with just any crowd. She guessed his congregation would be of a higher quality than the usual yard gangs.

Most prisoners moved like robots near the yard's perimeter, while others jogged or jumped in place to keep warm. They all kept their distance from the fence so as not to set off the alarm or attract the gun tower officers. While they talked and smoked, their eyes followed three other officers circulating among them; their heavy breathing became mist that spiraled into the cold air which hinted at an early autumn. The ever-vigilant tower sentry peered through high-power binoculars at the yard below. Every now and then, Pilar caught him lifting the weapon to site an inmate in the rifle's scope. She thought she saw the officer mouth, "Bang, bang."

None of the prisoners seemed to notice the refreshing wind that kept the sky an uncommonly cloudless and deep blue for the time of year. No doubt they only saw the razor ribbon lining the tops of the twelve-foot high double row of fences. Pilar glimpsed the perimeter security vehicle circling on the road outside that barricade, but the inmates paid little attention. Both the fence and the vehicle patrol segregated them from the woods and the outside world. The unpredictable cold waters of Lake Superior were on the other side of the northern stand of trees. That environment was a formidable deterrent to any escape plan. Sadness filled Pilar when she thought about the many inmates, particularly Chad, stuck in these unforgiving surroundings.

A few special prisoners meandered through the mass of blue uniforms. When they walked near a group, the other inmates acknowledged them with hesitant nods and quickly moved out of their way. Even a "fish" like Pilar knew they were the leaders, the ones in control. The ones to fear.

Pilar recognized two prisoners from past infirmary call outs. One was Tiger. He headed toward the weight pit. Breeze, the other familiar inmate, puffed at a cigarette that dangled from the left side of his mouth. Pilar had already learned that both were well-known, young Detroit drug dealers. Pilar stopped on the walk beside the yard fence to watch the two for a moment.

Breeze stuffed his hands into his jacket pockets as he ambled over to Tiger. The others he passed stayed their distance. Breeze stood to Tiger's left, away from the gun tower officer's prying vigil. Breeze took the cigarette from his mouth and flicked it at the fence. He leaned into Tiger. His mouth moved as though he was talking to Tiger, but he stared straight ahead at the officers traveling through the yard.

The scene seemed more like a movie set than an actual prison. Everything appeared as Hollywood might have portrayed, every motion contrived, though at that moment less sinister.

Without responding, Tiger suddenly moved away from Breeze and walked toward the yard gate. Breeze bit his lower lip, his eyes raised to the gun tower. He spit on the ground and followed Tiger. They waited at the gate in silence while the officer tucked his hand-held radio into a black leather pouch hanging from his belt. After he signed the prisoners' yard passes, he unlocked the gate to let the two inmates return to their house, the place where they bunked. House was another prisoner slang term like "The Building" that Pilar learned in the short time she'd been at Hawk Haven. The prisoners' jargon was like a foreign language.

Pilar remained in place and watched the two inmates head to their cell block. Though curious about their uneasy encounter she really didn't want the details. By the looks of the track marks she had seen on their arms, Pilar was sure whatever they were into had to do with drugs. How naive she had once been to think there were no drugs in prison.

"Let's get this over," Pilar mumbled, and turned toward Block One. By sounding the bell outside the unit's door she alerted a housing officer of her arrival. No doubt the tower guard had already given him a heads up. There was no way anyone could sneak around the grounds without one of those sentries spotting them.

A buzzer sounded and Pilar pushed the door open. Immediately she held her hands over her ears to stop the unbelievably loud and unintelligible din of male voices. When the door closed, all her senses jumped into gear. The smell of disinfectant overpowered her, while at the same time she was blinded by the glare from the freshly polished linoleum floor. Keeping a segregation unit as clean as possible supposedly helped employees feel less oppressed by the environment. Yet Pilar, despite what she had learned in training, doubted whether the prisoners gave a damn. They only left their cells one hour a day, alone, in cuffs and leg irons and escorted by two to three officers.

After signing in at the officers' station tucked in the apex of the L-shaped multi-tier building, Pilar spoke with the first prisoner. His only comment was, "You sure smell good, Doc. Better than the last guy."

The man in the next cell confirmed that and added, "Sexier, too."

"Is there any prisoner here who has a medical problem?" Pilar asked a passing officer.

"Other than mental, ma'am?" he snickered.

Before Pilar had a chance to answer, prisoners shouted as though singing a round. "The new Doc is here."

"Quiet, you idiots. The Doc is here."

"Look at those legs."

"How 'bout that hair?"

Pilar walked to the cell of the inmate who yelled last. "How 'bout a health problem? Got any, hot shot?" she asked.

He backed away from the door as another man called out, "I have ta see you, Doctor."

Pilar looked around to see from where the voice had

come. "Over here," the prisoner yelled louder. "Cell 103."

She leaned her head against the scratched, Plexiglas window of the cell to hear the prisoner's medical complaint without it being broadcasted to the entire gallery. Instead of getting the anticipated litany of medical problems, Pilar was greeted with a masturbating inmate. He chuckled at Pilar; her mouth dropped to her chin. Semen poured over his shorts. Though horrified, Pilar couldn't show any embarrassment. "Got any other skills?" she asked.

The prisoner's smile faded. Other inmates nearby laughed and shouted, "Got any other skills? That's a good one, Doc."

"He doesn't even got a brain."

"All's he knows is how to jack off."

"That's enough," Pilar ordered. "If this is all you have to say to me today, I'm out of here and won't be back for while. Meanwhile, mister," she turned to the offender's cell door tag, "I'm writing you up on a sexual misconduct."

The officer who passed by earlier walked by again and said, "It won't be his first. Besides, what else can happen to him? He's already serving life."

"He'll have to do his time then without some of his personal property like that TV, I guess." Pilar was about to say more when she heard a loud commotion at the end of gallery B. Officers, including the one at her side, ran toward the sound. Pilar followed. When she made it to the officers' station, three guards from other posts came through the outside door.

"Suit up," the unit sergeant commanded. "Baker's at it again. He's bleeding badly."

Sergeant Turner faced Pilar. "Stand by, Doctor Brookstone. We may need your help." Turner then talked into his radio. "The team is ready, Captain. We're going in."

Awed by the precise movements of the officers dressing out for the emergency cell extraction team, Pilar was happy to oblige the sergeant's orders. She'd stand by, but out of the way. Until now, Pilar had only seen the special team perform on video. In silence, the five-man team donned their battle attire, helmets with Plexiglas face shields, and gloves and vests that prevented sharp objects from penetrating. The lead person also carried a large Plexiglas shield like those that safeguard riot police.

Once the team was in their fighting gear, Sergeant Turner stood to the side of the offending prisoner's cell. Blood trickled in a long wormlike stream under the door. From behind the closure, ear piercing crashes were heard as the prisoner continued to bust up his room. Every so often Pilar heard the prisoner shout, "aaaahhhhh". Pilar pictured him lifting something he had torn apart. Maybe the radiator. Whenever he smashed it into the wall, door, or window, he let out that eerie sound.

As the team marched down the hall toward Baker's cell, other inmates taunted, "Baker, the goon squad's here."

"Better get it over with, Baker. Just finish yourself off."

"Yeah, or the goons will."

"Baker, listen up," the sergeant ordered loud enough to be heard over the noise and the egging-on of the inmates in nearby cells.

Baker slammed something against the door. Turner jumped back. The blood streaming from under the door thickened. How could Baker have that much energy left?

"Baker," the sergeant shouted again, "I'm going to gas you if you don't come out of the cell calmly."

Whack. Baker's response resounded down the gallery.

"Okay, Baker, here it goes." Sergeant Turner opened the door slot and delivered a spray of pepper. The prisoner rushed the door; "Aaaaaaaaaaaahhhhhhhhhhh." Then *thump*. The steel door shook from Baker's body being hurled against it.

"Get ready," the sergeant directed the suited team standing by. They lined up, the shielded man in front of the other four, and queued in a single line, each placing his hands on the one in front to strengthen the massed impact. Sergeant Turner then ordered an officer to tape the entry on the video camera he had already retrieved from the storage locker. Pilar sneaked closer to watch the action.

The prisoners' taunts were silenced as though reacting to a choir director. Pilar supposed they had been through those attacks so often, they knew the good part was about to begin. They didn't want to miss a single moment.

Turner unlocked Baker's cell. As soon as the door

opened the team rushed through. Crashing and thrashing resonated from the interior as Baker was pushed to the floor. Pilar moved closer. The other prisoners cheered.

The floor was covered by a carpet of fresh blood and spattered the entire team. It was hard to tell from where on Baker the blood came.

Each of the four team members held a limb as the leader shackled Baker. Once restrained, they carried Baker from the cell and placed him onto a waiting gurney. Pilar chastised herself for being so unprepared when she discovered someone else called for that transport. Once they'd secured Baker, the officers rolled him into the day room. Pilar ran alongside the moving table and examined him. He was spurting blood from punctures to his right arm and chest.

"Call for an ambulance," she ordered without halting her inspection of Baker's wounds. "He'll need to get to ER."

HAVING HAD THE SENSE to grab the medical kit from the block locker, Pilar used whatever available to slow his bleeding. That confident response to the situation lessened any doubts she had about who was in control when it came to medical care. "Give me the gauze from the kit, Sergeant Turner." Pilar gave the directive, but never diverted her attention from the patient.

The sergeant handed Pilar an opened package from which she retrieved a large bandage. She folded it several times to give it thickness, making it highly absorbent. She laid it across one wound in his upper arm. "Put your hand on top of the bandage and apply pressure. Don't let up until I tell you," she instructed Turner.

Next she gave an order to an officer standing nearby. "Get some baking soda and water and wipe the pepper spray remains from Baker's face."

The officer scurried away and returned in a flash. He was surprisingly gentle with his touch. The officer obviously understood that Baker was no longer a threat.

Pilar methodically tended to Baker's chest. Using a second bandage, she applied pressure to that wound. Once the bleeding subsided, she cleaned the wound and searched for chips of porcelain from the sink that should have been replaced long ago with stainless steel. Thank goodness the chest puncture was not as deep as the arm wound, though Pilar believed internal bleeding could also be a problem.

Another bandage was prepared for the arm which had not stopped bleeding. Pilar relieved the sergeant and pressed it on top of the gauze already in place. She kept a steady pressure on the wound. Baker fell into unconsciousness.

"The ambulance is here," an officer announced. The EMT truck backed up to the building's entrance. It was one of the few times a non-institution vehicle was allowed inside. As officers rolled the gurney to the waiting EMT, Pilar maintained pressure on Baker's arm until the newly arrived crew took over.

Once Baker was off to the hospital, Pilar noticed Officer

Cleaver, the lead team member, collapsed on the floor. He was bleeding just below his knee.

"I'm fine," he said when Pilar attempted to examine him. Though he waved her away, his hand was limp. "It's a minor cut. These things happen all the time. I only fell on a piece of glass."

"No need to be ashamed." Pilar consoled the officer. Showing pain wasn't acceptable behavior for a trained emergency team member. "That puncture is deep and needs immediate attention, maybe stitches."

Pilar faced the officers' station. "Sergeant Turner, send someone to the infirmary for the wheelchair and get this man there pronto."

"I can walk, Doctor," Cleaver's face paled when he tried to stand. He slid back to the floor. The blood from his soaked uniform streaked the wall.

"I am the doctor and you'll do as I say. Meanwhile, I've got to get back to the infirmary and get the medical transfer completed for Baker." Pilar started to walk away, but stopped. "I'll see you shortly, right?"

"Right," Sergeant Turner answered for Officer Cleaver.

Pilar passed Warden Whitefeather near the officers' station. He apparently had been called to the scene earlier. "Impressive work, Doctor Brookstone," he said as his eyes followed the line of blood leading to Baker's cell.

"This wasn't as bad as what I saw in Detroit. But, thanks anyway." Pilar was pleased he had seen her in a different light from that of orientation when he ogled her legs. Maybe now he would accept her as a colleague.

JANE GREETED PILAR WITH Baker's transfer orders as she rushed through the infirmary gates. Pilar signed it and gave it to a waiting officer. He immediately headed for the gate as Cleaver was wheeled by. "Get him into an exam room and prepped." Pilar was impressed by the quick response and preparedness of all the employees. It brought home how routine those emergencies were to everyone. Would they ever seem that way to her?

After Officer Cleaver's wound was cleaned and sutured, he was sent home to recuperate. Pilar sequestered herself in her office. Her knees gave way and she fell into the chair. Jane burst through the door unannounced. "So, how was your first day on rounds?"

Was she being sarcastic? Pilar wanted to slap her rather than answer her. In fact, she didn't want her there at all. "Well, to tell the truth," she said instead, forcing herself to be calm, "a little hectic and quite different from sick call."

They looked at each other for a few seconds. Then, the absurdity of the whole morning hit and they laughed. Pilar regained her composure. "It's not exactly what I thought making rounds meant. I hope this doesn't happen every time I go inside."

"Me, too." Jane chuckled. "It makes us work too hard. And yet, there may be days that are even tougher if things get out of hand."

"It gets worse?"

"Could," Jane affirmed. "We've had hostage situations, officers assaulted, yard stabbings, and a couple of small riots. Never can tell what will set the masses off."

"It doesn't happen often though, right?" Pilar asked.

"Right," Jane nodded and left.

"Right." How could all of that chaos happen in less than an hour? It was as though Pilar was back in Detroit Receiving's ER. Though she saved Baker's life and gained the warden's approval, she hoped it would be awhile before she had to make rounds again.

chapter seven

VISITING

"YOU MADE IT THROUGH your first month," Jane said as she walked with Pilar to the parking lot. "Better than most "fish", I might add."

Judging by the nervous undercurrent in Jane's voice, Pilar believed the nurse was testing her. She chose not to get caught up in the game, instead responding in good cheer, "And, I didn't make a complete fool of myself."

While they talked, Pilar rummaged through her real thoughts — that she was glad those weeks were over; that she was upset for being more uncomfortable with the prisoners than she would be with other new patients. Pilar felt certain that in time her uneasiness with most of them would pass. Yet, her concern about her schoolgirl's reaction to a murderer like Chad still confused her. How could she explain why she looked forward to his weekly clinic appointments? Perhaps Chad's magnetism was more due to his notoriety rather an attraction? Hadn't she been intrigued with him since Susan's murder? Wasn't it natural to be curious?

Jane eased alongside Pilar like a best friend and asked, "What are you doing this weekend up here in the wilderness?"

"I'm going home to Grosse Point Shores." As soon as those words came out of her mouth, Pilar regretted them. When would she learn not to speak without thinking? Jane's expression conveyed what Pilar dreaded. Jane no doubt thought Pilar was a rich wimp who would run back to her wealthy parents every chance she got. She didn't particularly want to be Jane's friend, just accepted as a good doctor and without any hassle. She'd have to learn to govern her tongue.

At least she had already decided to ditch the Mercedes. A less ostentatious and more practical car for that northern climate would change the prison employees' first impressions, and make her more like them.

"Don't blame you for going down. Not much to do up here on this side of the bridge but drink. I'd tag along with you, but . . ." Jane swept her hand from her head down her body as though she was showing off a new outfit. She didn't have to finish her statement. Her narrowed and suddenly mean eyes revealed what she thought. Someone of her race wasn't usually welcomed in the Pointes.

"After you met my father, you'd change your mind about the best place to spend your time," Pilar said.

Jane pursed lips and remained silent. Was she waiting

for Pilar to feed her more information about her private life? Jane finally laughed. "We all have our crosses to bear."

Jane was right about the drinking habits in the north country. From what Pilar had heard, when the men weren't at work, they hunted and fished. If they weren't doing any of those, they were in the bars drinking and fighting. It didn't matter who you were, either: lawyer, doctor, prison guard, or police officer. Those guys were on equal turf when in the woods, on a stream, or downing a couple of beers.

Jane lingered nearby. She appeared to wait for more details about Pilar's weekend. Pilar was not about to share that with anyone. "What are your plans?" Pilar asked in an attempt to change the direction of the conversation.

"Me? Same ol', same 'ol." Jane laughed. "Pizza Hut with my husband and the kids. Maybe pick up a movie at Blockbuster."

"Sounds cozy," Pilar remarked with a wee bit too much sarcasm. "But, I've got to get going if I intend to make those two-hundred miles tonight." Pilar hoped to avoid the Labor Day weekend traffic.

Jane grimaced at the brush off. "Have fun," she said, but not with any sincerity.

"See you Monday."

Pilar smiled. Monday couldn't come soon enough. She dreaded the family reunion. Though she had promised herself to stay away, once again Pilar had let Celeste talk her into going home to celebrate her first month on the job.

It was one more silly idea among many Celeste had over the years, one more time when against her own wishes, Pilar gave into her mother's lonely appeals. Now that Celeste was a rape and victim counselor, shouldn't her mother be too busy to worry about her? Celeste's weekly calls ought to have been a clue.

Pilar glanced at the menacing prison towers fading into the dusk and backed out of the parking spot. She was sure her mother had hoped that after a month on the job, she'd be ready to work with her father, or at the very least find a place in a more suitable practice. Pilar still heard her father's final words when she left for the UP. "You know being a doctor is tough work, more suited for a man." Too bad he hadn't seen Pilar's performance in the ER. As for his parting shot, what did she care? "Besides," he sneered, "you won't find a suitable husband at Hawk Haven."

Marcus' words repeated over and over like a mantra. Pilar tapped her fingers against the steering wheel in rhythm. While she waited for the light to change, Pilar tried to forget his comment and examined her nails; the ragged tips flicked up and down. She analyzed the cuticle on one nail. Where would she get a manicure in the Upper Peninsula? Who cared anyway?

As soon as Pilar glimpsed the moonlit waves lapping the shore of Lake St. Clair, the tension lessened in her shoulders. But, despite that brief sweet moment, loneliness crept back when she opened the front door to her parents' house. How that prodigious mansion had been wasted on an only child. Pilar's illegitimate half-brother might have enjoyed romping through the rooms. At least the noise would have been a welcomed change.

From out of nowhere, the maid rushed to Pilar's side and took her jacket and attache. "Ah, home, sweet home," Pilar snipped as she practically grabbed them back.

The maid smiled, ignored the irony, and greeted Pilar cheerfully, "It's good to have you here, Miss Brookstone." Then she fled to her appropriate place in the back of the house like the servants on "Upstairs, Downstairs."

A light from the library radiated a warm glow across the foyer floor. Pilar peeked into the book-lined chamber and found her mother asleep in the Queen Anne chair beside the fireplace. A magazine lay open in her lap. When Pilar kissed her forehead Celeste jerked awake. "You're home." She yawned. Celeste closed the magazine and set it aside.

Pilar took hold of both her hands and tugged her to a standing position. "It's well past midnight. Let's go to bed and talk in the morning."

"Good idea." Celeste stretched. "I doubt I'd make much sense in this drowsy state."

After they embraced outside Pilar's bedroom, Celeste reached for the door knob. Pilar grabbed her hand. "I know what you're thinking," she giggled. "But you're not tucking me in." Pilar nudged her mother toward her own quarters across the hall from her father's room. How long had it been since they've shared the same bed? When Pilar switched on the light and closed the door to her own bedroom, she realized she hadn't asked about her father.

At breakfast, Celeste told Pilar that Marcus wouldn't be home that weekend. "Urgent business," she explained. She averted her apologetic eyes from Pilar.

"Same ol', same ol'."

Celeste lifted her head and stared at Pilar. "What did you say, dear?" she asked.

"Oh, nothing. Just repeating something a nurse said to me recently."

"Umm," Celeste said, and turned toward the lake. She still held a forkful of eggs as she slid the lace curtains to one side and gazed dreamily out the window, staying in that position for several moments, like a mannequin.

Posing there was the resplendent woman of Pilar's childhood. Her fine chin proudly raised, exposing a long neck like Audrey Hepburn's. Beautiful, high cheekbones, full lips, and a Greek profile.   As a child Pilar's friends envied her for having such an enchanting, devoted mother, who would give up tennis, bridge, and lunch at the club to be a part of her daughter's life. Over the years Pilar learned the real truth. Beneath Celeste's handsomeness lay a lonely person who, like the women prisoners Pilar had once worked with, had no way out of a life-style known from birth. Celeste Brookstone had played the role of a high society mom and perfect wife well. Now, though, Pilar hoped she was finding her way to more rewarding pursuits.

Pilar half-wished her mother would turn to her, find a teenager, and say, "Hurry up or we'll be late for your sailing lessons," or wherever they would go on such a flawless day. Instead, Celeste remained immobilized by deep thoughts which seemed to distance her from that time and place. She looked proud yet wounded, like an abandoned fawn alone in the woods, lost and incredibly tired.

"Mother, is there something wrong?" Pilar finally asked.

Celeste snapped out of her dreaminess as though a loud sound startled her. She blinked while she examined Pilar at the other end of the table. "I don't know. I guess I'm uneasy about you working in that prison. I have this vision . . ." She didn't complete her thought.

For a moment, Pilar wished she hadn't come home. Her mother's darkened eyes gave Pilar an eerie sensation. Celeste was troubled by more than Pilar's job. But, what?

Celeste's eyes drifted upward, above Pilar as though something else caught her attention. She put her fork down, eggs untouched. She dabbed her mouth with a napkin and asked, "What should we do today?" The question seemed to drift across the placemats and silver.

"It's your call." Pilar finished her coffee. She pushed away from the table and waited for her to answer. When none came, Pilar asked, "Mother, do you have any plans?"

"No, not really," she said in a wispy, unfamiliar,

Marilyn Monroe voice.

"My new apartment needs everything and there are few decent stores up north." Pilar waited for a response. "How about we shop for some of the basics I need?   Then, we could have lunch."

"That would be fun, like old times." Celeste raised her fingers to her cheek as an unexpected tear released. "Where should we go?" she asked, yet appeared to slip again into another world.

Pilar wanted to press Celeste about her mood, but relented and answered, "I think to Eastland Mall. It's close and everything's there." Pilar waited for Celeste's endorsement.

Celeste scrunched up her nose as though she were smelling spoiled milk. "That mall? But if you want . . ."

"I do want," Pilar whined as though begging for a candy bar. "I'm not buying expensive items. I'd be more of an outsider than I already am driving a Mercedes when all the other Yupers drive 4x4 pickups. And," she added more forcefully than she intended, "we are not eating lunch at the club!"

Celeste placed a hand over her lips and appeared to process the day Pilar planned. Then she bolted up from the table and retrieved her purse from the hall stand. Pilar followed.

Celeste yelled over her shoulder, "Let's go. I'll powder my nose in that Mercedes." She was out the front door before Pilar found her keys. Her sudden devil-may-care attitude surprised Pilar. After all, her mother still dressed for dinner, and never, ever went anywhere without her makeup applied. Celeste's abrupt mood change promised a pleasant day, yet her overall demeanor that morning concerned Pilar. What was really going on in her mother's head?

T.G.I.FRIDAY'S WAS NOISY, INCONSPICUOUS, and delightful for their lunch. The two women feasted on hamburgers and french fries, forgetting about their usual constant calorie counting. They tattled about everyone they knew from the club. Celeste glowed like a teenager sharing a morning at the mall and secrets with her best friend. "You remember that Muffy girl you went to high school with?" she asked.

"Yes."

"She had her nose done. Weren't you thinking about that, too?"

"How dare you bring up changing a part of me I've grown to love?" Both women laughed. It was an old joke. Pilar had fretted about her nose all through high school. Gradually, it became less of an issue. "If Ms. Streisand can live with her distinctive breather, so can I."

"Good for you," Celeste cheered. "You were the only one troubled by it anyway." She paused, then added, "This is so much fun. I wish we could do this more often."

As they sipped their ice teas, it seemed like the old days when Pilar and her mother shopped for school clothes. "This has been a great day," Pilar finally agreed. "I miss being with you." With few friends and Julie so far away,

Pilar was happy to have her mother to talk to.

"We must do this more often, no matter how far apart from each other we live," Celeste affirmed. They clinked their tea glasses in agreement.

They devoured their food. They giggled like girls, heads bent close together as Celeste revealed the latest Pointe gossip. Once freed from her Gothic prison, she was self-assured, even flamboyant, outspoken, and young again. At that moment the two beauties passed for sisters, rather than mother and daughter. Marcus wasn't there to tell them, "Don't be so silly", or "Act your age."

Pilar sighed. Her father would have made a fine Puritan. Like the Puritans, a few righteous men wandered from the fold as Marcus had. He spent his life rationalizing his sinful behavior and projecting his guilt onto Celeste and Pilar. That anger, deception, and rigidity aged him while it destroyed Celeste's confidence and Pilar's trust — their real selves forever lost to him. His loss. Pilar grinned at her mother.

Celeste's face became serious as she dabbed her napkin around her mouth, a familiar and perpetual habit. "Are you happy at the prison, dear?" she asked.

Pilar sensed an ulterior motive to her question. "Yes, I suppose," she answered. "But, it's hard to tell. I haven't been there that long."

Celeste leaned forward. "Give me your word that you won't let your pride get in the way if you decide that prison work isn't for you." Celeste paused and bit her lower lip, a more recent habit than the napkin routine. "You are always welcome in my home."

"Thanks." Pilar made a mental note about how she emphasized "my home." "But if I decide to change jobs, I will live in my own place. I think I'm old enough for that."

Celeste laughed. "I guess you are, but I don't want to believe it." She surveyed the restaurant and focused on the young couple snuggled together at the bar. "Have you made any friends yet, Pilar? It can be very lonely without friends."

Believing Celeste spoke about her own life as well as her daughter's, Pilar answered, "That will take a little time." She followed her mother's gaze to the couple. "There is one person. Jane. A nurse. She's about my age, married with two children. She seems to be bright and fun. She doesn't take the job personally." Surprised that she didn't hesitate to tell her mother about Jane, Pilar was nevertheless careful not to let on that she was suspicious of Jane's overly friendly relationship with Tommy Johnson. If Jane wasn't careful about her flirtation, she'd get fired. And as her supervisor, would Pilar also be accused of being an accomplice?

"She's married?" Celeste stirred a spoon in her tea and appeared caught in a dream.

"Yes, why?"

"It would be nice to have grandchildren, that's all." She shrugged.

"You sound like Father, except he only wants grandsons."

Pilar frowned at the direction the conversation had taken. "The best thing I could give him, no doubt."

"No. Not I." Celeste tilted her head and peered at Pilar as though she looked over the top of reading glasses. "You have always given me your best. Grandchildren would just be the frosting. Besides, I'd be a wonderful grandmother."

Pilar pushed her hair from her face and smiled. "Don't hold your breath. Husband prospects are slim, at the moment. Besides, you're too young to be a grandmother."

"There's still hope, and a lot of time for even some-one as ugly and incompetent as you to find the right man," Celeste teased. "And, there's always that nose. You could get it fixed."

They laughed momentarily, but finished their tea in silence. After Celeste paid the restaurant bill, they walked arm in arm to the Mercedes.

SUNDAY MORNING PILAR PILED her purchases into the car's trunk. One of the first things she would do back in Marquette was to trade in the car. She closed the trunk lid.

Celeste handed Pilar a plastic bag filled with homemade scones. "Thanks. Did you bake these?"

Celeste nodded. "It's a newly acquired skill to fill my free time — what little I have these days with my counsel-ing work."

Pilar hugged Celeste. "Maybe you should visit me the next time. A change of scenery would do you good."

Celeste pecked Pilar on the cheek. "Yes, perhaps." She took a quick breath. "Yes, I'd like that. I have this odd feeling . . .

"What? What kind of feeling?" Pilar asked as she remembered so many similar moments when her mother had had a premonition. Usually her insights turned out to come true, which made Pilar uneasy.

"Oh, it's just a silly, motherly thought. It's foolish, really. I feel like I'm going to lose you."

"How could that be?" Pilar smiled and shook her head. "No matter where I live I'm still your daughter. And, we can always visit."

"Yes. Well, I said it was foolish." Celeste started to stand away from the car door, but stopped and asked, "Whatever happened to your yellow slicker?"

"I never had one. Mine was red, remember?

"Umm. That's odd," Celeste said, more to herself than Pilar.

"Odd? How?" Pilar's voice became tense.

"I seem to recall a yellow slicker, that's all." Celeste leaned away from the car. "Oh, well. Its' just one of those silly, aging memory things." She bent forward and kissed Pilar's cheek. Have a safe trip, dear." Celeste turned and walked to the house.

As Pilar drove away, she watched Celeste who remained at the front door. Celeste waved once and then rested the tips of her fingers on her lips.

PILAR PULLED THE CAR into her designated spot, thankful to have any place to park. The prison lot was crowded even that early on a Monday morning. The line of visitors, mostly women and a few children, wound its way through the waiting area and out the front door of the administration building. As Pilar passed the lobby desk, the officer announced over the telephone to central control, "There are five separate women here already to visit Chad Wilbanks and it's only eight. How'd ya wanna handle it?"

Pilar analyzed the line of women. Which of them would visit a man like Wilbanks? She experienced an odd twinge, almost like the time her best friend stole the boy she had a crush on. She sighed and went to the front of the line, a privilege held for employees.

A new officer searched her. He was young, a recent hire like Pilar. The fish officer was a lot less thorough than Leonard.

"What's up with all the visitors?" Pilar asked, trying not to sound too nosy.

"It's like this once a week, on Mondays. Chad Wilbanks' visiting day." The officer shook his head. "It sure baffles me."

"How's that?" He had piqued Pilar's curiosity. She was surprised she hadn't noticed the large group on other Mondays. She probably got to work on those days before the visitors had arrived.

The officer contemplated the crowd in the lobby. "Those women don't even know Chad Wilbanks. They've only read about him in the news, or got information on him from the Internet. Some of them travel more than two hundred miles to visit."

"The Internet?" She was so astounded, her voice squeaked.

"Yes, ma'am. There are web sites that post pictures and information about prisoners interested in pen pals, but often the relationship goes further." The officer thumbed toward the growing line of visitors.

"Web sites?" she asked, sounding like an echo. "I didn't think prisoners had access."

"They don't directly. They send the information via snail mail to the web site host organization." He chuckled. "It sure pays off."

"That is odd." Pilar glanced at the group. "I guess Wilbanks,"she said, then quickly added, "and several other prisoners, won't have time for sick call today." What could be on the Internet that would bring those women up here?

"No ma'am. Wilbanks is one of the most popular. Those women also deposit money in his account. He's not likely to give that up for a few meds." He called out to have Gate Two opened. "Have a good one, Doctor Brookstone."

"You, too." Pilar was delighted that the officer seemed so nice after Leonard's treatment. As the gate closed, she peeked one more time at the lobby. Such ordinary looking women. She heard Lorrie's singsong voice; "Virgin Mary, marry a virgin." Pilar headed for her office.

Officer Leonard escorted Chad Wilbanks past Pilar to check him in for his day of visits. Chad smiled. Leonard nodded. "Ma'am." She'd been so engrossed with Lorrie and the female visitors. Had Chad's elbow deliberately brushed against her arm?

Then she heard Chad whistle. "There's more than usual, today." He sounded amazed. Pilar touched the place where Chad's elbow nudged her and caught his eyes following the motion. Pilar was intrigued by his obvious lusting, and felt relieved that he was interested in her even with a bevy of cash-carrying women at the prison to visit him.

Today, Chad wore the street clothes permitted for visits rather than the usual prison blues that resembled hospital scrubs. The red crewneck sweater and white shirt brought out his large, sensual, mink eyes. His alluring smile invited an encounter.

Pilar squeezed her attache to her chest and lowered her head to hide her burning cheeks as she fled to the solitude of her office. Had Leonard noticed her foolish behavior?

While Pilar waited for the first patient, she started a list of reasons she might be acting like a teenager with a crush. The only thing she wrote was *Father*. What was she searching for? How could she harbor even the slightest belief she'd find whatever she sought in a murderer she hardly knew, no matter how charming he was?

Jane knocked on the door and teased, "No more napping, Doctor Brookstone. Your first client is here."

"I'm on my way," she yelled with too much exuberance. The inmate's arrival was perfect. Pilar had no desire to waste any more time on her father or Chad Wilbanks.

LATE IN THE AFTERNOON, Jane knocked again. "Sorry to tell you this, but you have one more patient." Her face formed an exaggerated grimace, turning the corners of her mouth so hard her bottom teeth were exposed.

Pilar checked her watch. "So late?" She had hoped to finish the ever-growing pile of paperwork before she left for the day. She closed the folder she was writing in and placed it on top of Tommy Johnson's institutional file. Jane focused on Johnson's name.

"What room?" Pilar asked quickly without hiding her exasperation, and to allay Jane's obvious curiosity.

"One." An unexpected smile filled Jane's face as the two left the office.

Pilar grabbed the medical record Jane handed her and pushed the exam room door open. The folder slipped to the floor at Chad Wilbanks' feet.

"Hey, Doctor Brookstone! How's it going?" He leaned from his chair, one hand cuffed as usual, and picked up the file. When he handed it to Pilar, their hands touched. They lingered in that space. Then, Pilar yanked the folder away.

Chad relaxed into the chair. His confidence suffocated

Pilar.

"I'm surprised you have time for sick call with all those visitors," Pilar said, then hastily chided herself for the friendliness. And, even she recognized a jealous undertone — had Chad? She was like an open book when she acknowledged her awareness of the other women.

"No big deal. They come every week. Amazing, huh?"

"Yeah," she answered, "amazing."

"But," Chad rapidly added, "those women aren't real friends. They don't understand me."

"Umm," Pilar waited for him to tell her why he was there. "Well?" she asked.

"Well, what? Oh. Why am I here?"

Pilar tapped her foot.

"My throat's gotten sore again." Chad opened his mouth wide and showed off nearly perfect teeth free of fillings.

Pilar leaned against the exam table and folded her arms over her chest. "Not good enough, Mr. Wilbanks." Her hand was still warm where he had touched it. "Are you trying to get out of a work assignment? Because your throat is fine."

"You haven't checked it." He pointed to the jar which held tongue depressors. "So, how do you know? Besides, it's not time for me to work yet. I'm the night block porter." He pointed at the container again. "I used to be the librarian before I tried to escape."

Pilar snatched a depressor and a small flashlight. As she approached him, she said, "Open wide." She jammed the wooden stick on his tongue and to the edge of his throat. His eyes narrowed as he choked. Pilar retracted the wooden stick. "Like I said, you're fine." She walked around to the other side of the exam table to keep her distance.

"Thanks, Doctor Brookstone."

She nodded.

"Do you like to read?" Chad asked, and went on before Pilar answered. "I sure do."

"Yes, I do like to read," she responded, taken off-guard by his question. "When I have time."

"What kind of books?" Chad sat tall and appeared hungry for the exchange.

"If I'm not reading a professional journal, I guess I like true adventures like *Into Thin Air* and biographies or memoirs. *Angela's Ashes,* that kind of book." Pilar thoughtfully gave into his appeal.

"Me, too," Chad said. "But, since I lost my librarian job, I can't seem to get the stuff I like. Our library is really short on good books."

"Get me a list of books you might want and I'll ask the program director for his help," Pilar offered, before she realized she was in a conversation with an inmate that should be reserved for a friend or colleague. She had been warned in training not to get involved in such a personal chat. Embarrassed by how easily Chad lured her into that dialogue, Pilar started for the door.

"Thanks. Do what you can, but the program director will take forever." Chad's tone became sad.

"Well, maybe I can bring some of my books in, as a loan." After all, Pilar was willing to help anyone eager to better themselves. How could fudging the rules for a good cause do any harm?

"Why are you here?" Chad asked in an amiable tone, as if he sensed Pilar's ease of conversation.

"What?" She faced him.

"You're pretty, and intelligent, and you care about us. Why would someone like you work in corrections, especially in the UP?" His voice could soothe anyone into a dreamy state.

"No choice about where I'm assigned. As for corrections, it's like my father says. I'm just a do-gooder hunting for a man." Immediately, she regretted the words. How could she confide in a prisoner?

Chad smiled.

Pilar pressed the button that alerted the officer to take Chad back to his cell. He followed her every move. "I'll be back real soon." Chad hesitated. "With that list of books."

Pilar, unable to move, watched Chad's cocky retreat. What on earth are you doing? Pilar slammed the door shut, condemning her immature reaction.

AFTER SHE PACED HER living room floor for an hour, Pilar

finally gave in to her overwhelming curiosity. She slumped into the chair at her computer and searched for the prisoner pen pal web site. Shock overcame her when she discovered there were several. She surfed through each until she found Chad's name on prisonpenpals.com.

An unsmiling Chad was pictured in full color. His expression offered the viewer a childlike plea which made him appear shy. At first, Pilar was suspicious and angry. The ad seemed so manipulative.

"Hello, ladies," it read. "My name is Chad Wilbanks. I'm twenty-eight years old and a college graduate. Though I have been accused of first degree murder, I'm pursuing legal alternatives to the life sentence I'm serving. I have a good sense of humor and I'm sensitive, intelligent, a good listener, a little shy, and I love reading and all kinds of music. Because I have been incarcerated for more than two years, my friends have abandoned me. I've learned what it's like to be lonely."

That last phrase pulled Pilar into Chad's eyes. Did she see hurt in them? She shook her head. How could she, an intelligent doctor, be caught by his self-serving advertisement?

Once freed from his eyes' magnetism, she read on: "Though I've made a mistake that put me behind bars, I'm not a bad person. So, please don't judge me by my crime. Give me a chance to tell you my side of the story. I'm not interested in money or what anyone can do for me. I would just love to hear from you. I hope to find a woman who is easy-going, kind, caring, and emotionally and financially stable who also wants to develop a friendship, or perhaps more? So, please write. Let's meet and build a friendship."

PILAR READ THE TEXT through twice, and finally felt the real loneliness behind the man's words. She could almost hear that endearing lisp.

Judging by the number of women who visited Chad, his plea for friendship seemed to be working. If those women wanted to go against his claim not to want money, was that his fault? So what if he appeared too eager for a relationship? The guy was lonely and being forthright about it. Why not use the Internet?

She searched next for Tommy Johnson's name. He wasn't listed on any site Pilar found. He wasn't lonely, though, like Chad. He had Jane in his corner.

chapter eight

CALL OUT

EACH MORNING PILAR SEARCHED the appointment list for Chad's name. When she didn't find it, she was both relieved and hurt. "What is going on with me?" Pilar threw the clipboard against the wall. "Why do I care if he comes here or not? He's probably too busy with all his women visitors anyway." Pilar leaned against the wall. "No money in my office for him."

Jane opened the door. "Who you talking to?" she asked as she inspected the room. "I heard a crash. I thought some inmate slipped by me and you were in trouble."

"No. No trouble here. I dropped the clipboard, that's all." Jane studied her as Pilar picked up the board. Her interest made Pilar uncomfortable.

"Let's get this day started," Pilar stated with as much cheerfulness as she could come up with at that moment.

"Right," Jane agreed. "Follow me." Her rapid steps were accentuated by rubber soled shoes that squeaked against the linoleum. She was difficult to keep pace with.

"We have an emergency in room two," Jane reported as she pushed the door open. "Stab wound."

"A fight so early?" Pilar asked. "Incredible."

"These guys only got time, Doc, and fights aren't usually scheduled."

Tiger slouched over his stomach on the end of the exam table, feet dangling like a rag doll. His bloody hand held together the edges of a jagged tear that almost covered his entire abdomen.

"Who'd you piss off so early in the day, Tiger?" Pilar asked as she peeled his hand away from the wound. He didn't respond. He didn't have to. Pilar knew the answer. Tiger probably didn't deliver the goods as guaranteed, or maybe he took some drugs for a private stash rather than turn the cache over to his buyer.

"At any rate," Pilar consoled as she cleansed the ragged slice and looked for any unwanted particles left behind, "you'll live." Tiger squeezed his eyes into slits and flinched. "The wound isn't too bad this time. A few stitches and a tetanus shot and you'll be on your way. By the way, you must have had some previous practice in first aid."

"What d'ya mean, Doc?" Tiger mumbled his first words.

"You did a nice job stopping the bleeding." Pilar pointed to the finger prints still visible where he had applied pressure to form a makeshift tourniquet.

Tiger examined his wound and grunted, "Practice. Right."

"It's a good idea to stay inactive for a couple of days," Pilar instructed. "I'll let the unit sergeant know you're excused from any work detail until after I see you in ten days."

When Pilar finished bandaging his wound, she asked, "By the way, do you have any Tylenol?"

"What for?" Tiger mustered his tough-guy voice.

"Pain." Pilar again pointed to his wrapped stomach.

"Won't need any." He used his macho street tone.

"Right, okay. I almost forgot. A nurse will change your dressing when she makes block rounds."

"Hmm," Tiger replied, "I'll probably be in the hole for this." He jutted his stomach at Pilar.

"She'll still change your dressing and I must see you in ten days wherever you are." Pilar pressed the buzzer and waited for the officer to take Tiger back to his cell.

"Don't forget the Tylenol," she reminded as Tiger was ushered away.

Two weeks to the day Pilar last examined Chad his name was on the infirmary call out list. When Pilar saw his name in print her spine tickled as if someone stroked it with a feather. She threw off the sensation and admonished herself for her silly behavior. Again, she reminded herself that her interest in Chad had been fueled by his notoriety, and Lorrie's rendition of her relationship with him. "Normal curiosity," she assured herself.

Marcus' warnings also sounded in her head. He had

often brought to Pilar's attention her "unhealthy" need to help the underdog. He lectured Pilar on many occasions about her reactions to people Pilar perceived as mistreated or helpless. "Your emotions will get you in trouble one day," he had told Pilar more times than either cared to recall. Regardless, Pilar didn't really believe her own social work mentality was a bad thing.

Though Pilar rushed through each patient's problem and dispensed prescriptions as fast as possible, it wouldn't bring Chad any sooner. He would be delivered when scheduled and only after Pilar completed the examinations on all those who came before him.

Tommy Johnson entered Pilar's office halfway through the morning. She'd missed his name, or perhaps ignored it once she zeroed in on Chad's. His sudden appearance at Pilar's office door made her uneasy. "What are you doing here?" she asked, her tone more defensive than professional.

"I'm on call out." He pointed to the clipboard in Pilar's hand.

After Pilar confirmed his appointment, she walked to the door. "That's not what I mean. Even if you are on the call out, you're supposed to wait for the nurse to secure you in an exam room. I rarely see patients here." Pilar motioned him to the nurses' station.

"She told me to come here." Tommy shrugged as he tilted his head at Jane. He seemed unruffled.

Jane, on the other hand, appeared flustered in his

presence and apologized for her error. She directed Tommy to a room. "The doctor will see you in there."

Tommy ambled away as Jane passed his file to Pilar. She didn't release her grip right away. For several seconds they searched each other's expressions. For what? Understanding? Forgiveness?

"Sorry," Jane said. "I'm so used to letting him in your office to clean; I forgot."

"An easy mistake," Pilar responded.

Pilar seized the file and slipped into the room where Tommy waited. She had forgotten that he was the infirmary porter. He had almost free access to her office. Pilar needed to be more careful about what she left out for him to see — if it wasn't too late.

Unlike Chad, Tommy emoted danger. His dark, mean eyes were topped by full brows as black as a Halloween cat's. Those dark brows were a remarkable, almost contrived-looking contrast to his dishwater blonde hair. They knitted together in a V over his nose and appeared like a bat flying. Pilar shivered at the thought and rubbed her upper arms.

"Cold?" Tommy asked. His voice startled Pilar. Had she thought he couldn't talk? Or perhaps she didn't think he was capable of considerate words. Pilar didn't answer. Instead, she studied his file and then scrutinized him. Johnson unsettled her, but she hadn't a clue why she felt more that way about him than other prisoners. "Why are you here, Mr. Johnson?"

"I wanna quit smoking." He sounded like a wise guy from that organized crime TV series, "The Sopranos".

"That's commendable. How can I help?" Pilar sat in a chair next to him.

His brows fluttered like wings when he answered. "I wanna get inta counseling so I can wear one of them patches. But, you need to order it."

"I see. I can only recommend that you go to group. The therapist determines whether a prescription is warranted for the patch. Once he notifies me, I'll write it up."

"What's the use of seeing you then if you can't do nothing for me?" he asked, visibly agitated.

Pilar remained calm on the outside, but edgy on the inside when she answered, "Without my initial recommendation, nothing will happen for you." She gained control for the moment. Then, she recalled information in his file. Tommy was quick to anger. He even murdered his rap partner. It was that murder that got him sentenced to prison, if only for a short time. Pilar didn't have any intention of being Tommy's next victim.

He stood up unexpectedly. Pilar leaned away.

"Did I scare ya, Doc?"

"No. Only surprised me."

He smiled with half his mouth. That did scare her.

"Don't worry. I won't never hurt you. We need ya round here." He paused and seemed to consider his next step.

"You're a good doctor and ya care 'bout us." At that moment he didn't appear to be the volatile murderer described in his prison file. Tommy seemed almost considerate.

"Thank you. I just do my job as I see fit." Feeling more relaxed, Pilar sat at the chart table to make notes. Tommy turned to leave without permission. "I haven't said you could leave yet," she scolded. She continued with more softness, "We haven't settled your smoking issue." She pointed to his arm as though he already wore the patch he'd asked for.

"Forget about it. I'll take my chances with cancer. Gonna die somehow." He placed his hand on the door knob.

"Mr. Johnson, I think what you want to do, quit smoking, is worthy and difficult for someone locked up." Pilar was willing to help a patient like Tommy who asked for assistance.

"Thanks, but I don't wanna get ya in no trouble or do something not in policy, Doc." Tommy sat down again. "You already do more than any other doctor in this joint."

"I appreciate your compliment." Pilar smiled. His sudden kindness was unexpected. Maybe there was more to him than met the eye, as the cliche went. "I do what I have to for the sake of good health. So, let me write a script for the patch and get you started in a support group. Agreed?" Without waiting for an answer, she wrote the prescription and made a notation in his medical record.

"That's great, Doc." Tommy got up. Once through the

door, he said over his shoulder, "I'll pay ya back soon. I'll clean your office with extra special care."

"God knows," Pilar chuckled, "it could use it." She didn't want to do anything to provoke his angry side. Moreover, Pilar enjoyed that new, kinder facet of Tommy. She started to follow him out into the hall.

Jane was obviously waiting outside the exam room. Not wanting to intrude, Pilar stepped back into the room just out of sight, but within hearing range.

"How did it go?" she heard Jane ask.

"Piece of cake. A soft touch. She's eager to help, and that makes her mellow. The perfect "Duck". She'll give in when the time's right."

"How do you know all that?" Jane pressed.

"I listen and observe," Tommy whispered. "The clues are out there." He sounded like a detective from a film noir style movie. "And she wrote the script."

Pilar peeked out just in time to catch him stroking Jane's cheek.

"I'll tell you more later," Tommy said in almost a loving tone. He glanced toward Pilar and withdrew his hand. Lightning quick, he exited the waiting area on his own. His medium security level gave him a lot more freedom of movement than Chad. A lot more than most prisoners at Hawk Haven. When the gate closed behind him, Pilar watched Jane's reaction. She lowered her head and shuffled papers on her desk as if to avoid Pilar's scrutiny.

Pilar gave Jane the script for the patch and counseling. "Process this today," she ordered more harshly than needed.

Jane picked up the paper and file. "I didn't know he wanted to quit smoking. Good for Tommy."

"Yeah, good for Tommy," Pilar repeated as she looked back at the gate. What had she gotten in to? Helping Tommy quit a harmful health habit couldn't be all bad even if Pilar went outside policy a little. But, what did Tommy think she'd give in to? When would the time be right? She decided to find out what "Duck" meant.

A half hour before the noon inmate count, Jane tapped on Pilar's open door. "Chad Wilbanks is in exam room one."

Pilar's heart stopped for a brief moment. She occupied herself by straightening a row of pens. She hoped Jane didn't notice the color blazing in her face and down into her chest like a pink river. "I'll be right along." Did she sound too solicitous?

As soon as Jane left, Pilar inhaled ten times, a technique learned in a relaxation class. She checked her face and hair in the mirror near the door. Jane looked up from her station and noted the care Pilar took. Pilar smiled and hustled to see Chad, sure the flush had deepened the red in her cheeks. She stuffed back the familiar question: Why was she acting like this?

When Pilar walked through the door and let her eyes connect with Chad's, she knew the answer. It was carnal.

"I haven't seen you in a while, Chad," she said. "What

brings you today?" She pretended to review his history in his medical record.

Casually, Chad leaned back in his chair, letting his knees part. "You," he smiled. "And your scent. What is the perfume you always wear?"

"Lauren." Pilar rubbed her hand lightly across her neck where she had applied perfume earlier. "I know you're here to see me, but for what medical reason?" She brushed her hair off her forehead, pulled the exam stool forward and dropped gracefully onto it.

Chad considered her for several moments. Pilar heard footsteps in the corridor as the employees made their way out the gate for lunch. She crossed her legs, shifted on the stool. Clearly, they were taking each other's measures.

Chad leaned forward and almost whispered, "I waited for as long as I could before coming back. I may be taking a chance today, but . . ." He reached his free hand toward Pilar.

Pilar wrapped it in both of her hands and lowered her face into his palm.

chapter nine

FETISH

MIDWAY THROUGH A BRUTALLY cold November morning in her fourth month at Hawk Haven, Pilar wasn't surprised to find Chad waiting in an exam room. He sat in the same chair as he did on the first day they met.

"So, what brings you here today, Mr. Wilbanks?" Pilar asked. As she took the medical folder from the door pocket, Pilar caught Jane observing her. Pilar's glare challenged Jane's inquisitive stare. Jane turned away.

Pilar walked close to Chad's chair. Her lab coat brushed against his hand. His now twice-weekly visits had become a normal part of her schedule at Hawk Haven, were so routine in fact, no one, except Jane, seemed to question them. Even the officers stopped cuffing him in the second month after Pilar reported to Jane that Chad had an inoperable brain tumor. She had to make up some chronic medical problem. Otherwise, he couldn't see her so often without arousing suspicion.

As Pilar passed Chad, he reached behind her and

closed the door. Pilar's hair prickled at the base of her neck. Without turning she ordered him to get on the exam table.

He obeyed.

Pilar stationed herself behind him so she could watch the door. She circled her arms around his chest and reached her hand inside his pressed uniform shirt. His sinewy muscles tightened in response. Pilar kissed his neck and the top of his head. A thin flame ran under her skin.

Chad caressed Pilar's hand. "We've got to be careful," he cautioned. His hand was warm, assuring. "You know I'm working on something." His grip tightened and then he let go. Pilar's hand hurt.

"I know." Pilar massaged his shoulders. "But, it's getting tougher to wait. My nerves are raw." She imagined his fine-toned, naked body entwined in hers. She massaged her hand.

Chad turned to Pilar and brushed his lips lightly against hers like a child's butterfly kiss. Heat flowed into her groin.

"All you need to worry about are the babies we'll make once I'm out of here," he said as he rubbed her stomach.

Pilar combed her fingers through his silky hair. He pulled away. "Remember that day I asked why you work here?"

"Yes, why?"

"I want to know the real answer. I may be the reason you stay . . ."

"You are." She dropped a kiss on his nose. He waved

her back.

"Okay, but why did you start?"

"Is that today's topic?" she teased. Pilar relished his questions. He wanted to know everything about her. What she did every day, what her life was like growing up, everything. His appetite to know was insatiable, and she was the center of his attention in a way she'd never been for any man before.

"Yes, and I want you here beside me when you answer it." Chad patted the examination table.

Pilar hitched herself up onto it, letting her long legs dangle beside his. She began to relate the story of an incident that instigated her desire to help others, long before she ever met the prostitutes of Cass Corridor.

"My grandfather, my mother's father," she began, "told me that when he was a child in a small Polish village all the stores in the Jewish neighborhood where he lived remained closed on Christmas Day. The Jewish owners feared that if they opened they would be called Jesus killers." Pilar noted Chad's forehead crinkle in surprise. "You didn't know I was Jewish?"

"No. I didn't," he whispered.

"Does it matter?"

Chad inspected her face. After a few seconds he answered, "No. Why should it?"

"Good." Pilar continued with the story. "My grandfather said that no Jew would dare show his face on the streets in old Poland on Christmas day. They feared some reprisal would take place, like being physically abused or having their property destroyed."

Chad shifted. "What does this have to do with you today?" he asked.

"One Christmas day when I was about seven, my grand-father and I ate in the only open Jewish deli in the Detroit area. To entertain me and help me forget about all my friends celebrating a holiday I didn't understand, my grand-father told me stories." She chuckled quietly. "One was about the doctors in his village who used leeches to draw out the evil spirits. Imagine." She looked deep into Chad's eyes, hoping to find understanding there. "My grandfather looked so lonely, so lost. And, though we wouldn't be in-jured or called Jesus killers, that Christmas day I knew I never wanted anyone else to suffer as he had."

Chad cocked his head to the side. "So, you want to help the underdog, is that it?"

"Yes, I suppose, simply put, that's it."

"Am I one of your underdogs?" he asked. His lisp was obvious.

"Of course not. You're my Chad."

From the first time Pilar blurted out family secrets to Chad, there was no turning back. How could she not surrender to him? Pilar was so caught up by him, by the way he listened closely to her every word, by his track-ing her every motion, by his physical beauty — so like a

Michelangelo sculpture – she could hardly think of anything else. His attention held her spellbound. She loved everything about him: his touch, his voice, especially his seductive, hypnotic eyes.

Chad broke her train of thought when suddenly he took her face in his gentle hands and said, "You are the most exciting person I have ever known."

Pilar blushed like a school girl.

He chuckled. "And I want you to be the mother of my children. But," he winked, "I don't want you to quit working. We don't want to waste your brain on housework, do we?"

When Pilar was slow to respond, Chad kissed her nose and said, "I could be Mr. Mom."

They laughed so loud Pilar feared others in the infirmary would hear them. Yet, that easy laughter gave Pilar the courage to dig deeper into Chad's secretive past. Except for the few crumbs he offered about his college psychology major, his father, Maryann, and fraternity life, Pilar knew little else. She accepted that as part of his shyness, or even an institutionalized caution. In fact, when she prodded him for details about his childhood, his lisp became more pronounced. So Pilar had yielded to his need for privacy, therefore, confident that as their relationship grew, so would his trust in her.

But, Pilar had excused Chad's clever avoidance of his personal history for long enough. The time had come to hear about Chad Wilbanks from other sources than Lorrie and the news. The time had come to test that new trust.

"Tell me more about your father." Pilar slipped down to stand facing him between his legs.

Chad's eyes narrowed. "What can I tell you that I already haven't?" he asked.

"I don't know." Pilar offered a comforting smile. "Anything."

"You know he was a duplicate of your father. Dominating, rich, and an angry perfectionist. He believed that showering a person with money was equal to affection and a way to make up for his absence, which was most of my life." Chad paused and stared at a spot above Pilar's head. "He abandoned me." Chad spoke those last words with such a chill, Pilar shivered.

"Yes," Pilar agreed. "My father was a duplicate." It consoled her to know she hadn't been the only one to suffer a relationship with an unloving father.

"Except," Chad said, and stopped.

"Except what?"

"They didn't look alike."

Though neither Chad nor Pilar shared pictures of their fathers, Pilar had often described Marcus in great sarcastic detail. Chad had never described his father. "What do you mean? You never have told me how your father looked. In fact, I don't even know his name."

"I fortunately take after my mother," Chad said. "I wouldn't want to remind her of him." Chad still didn't say his name.

Pilar believed Chad and she were joined together by their comparable relationships with their fathers. Though unconcerned about either father interfering in her future with Chad, Pilar wasn't so sure about the role Maryann Wilbanks would play.

Standing face to face in that sensual moment of faith, Pilar's confidence about her closeness to Chad was clear. Pilar decided to take a chance and ask Chad to give up more information about his own past that he held so dear, so secret. "I've shared a lot of my family history with you, Chad. And, today I told you the special story about my grandfather." She stroked his cheek. "Do you trust me enough now to tell me about your family?"

Chad's body stiffened. He pushed her away and turned his back. Hurt, she placed her hand on his shoulder to let him know it was okay. Chad lifted his hand to hers. They remained in that silent space for several moments.

Chad released Pilar's hand and faced her. "My mother, Maryann, is the most beautiful and caring woman I have ever known," he said as his eyes filled. He quickly added, "Next to you of course, Pilar."

Pilar didn't want to hear about his mother in those terms. Often in the past, Chad had slipped out endearing remarks about Maryann. Remarks that had intruded on their limited sessions. In those moments Pilar reeled with jealousy and, yes, even hatred of a woman she had never met.

Chad reached into his pocket. "Here," he said, and offered Pilar a letter. "It's from today's mail."

The letter from Maryann read like a love note. As she read, Pilar's sight froze for a long moment on the words, "I long to hold you in my arms." The vision of son and mother romantically entwined nauseated her. Serves me right for probing, Pilar thought. And surely, she'd misunderstood. His family history really didn't matter after all, because no matter how secretive he chose to be, she would do anything to be with Chad. Anything.

"I know you'll do anything for me," he said, refolding the letter and returning it to his pocket. How had he gotten inside Pilar's head?

"But," he added, "I don't want you to do something foolish or before it's the right time."

Pilar's mouth dropped into an exaggerated pout. Chad stood and tilted his head to one side. "Gotta go," he said "before someone gets a crazy idea that we have more than a doctor-patient relationship."

Pilar laughed. "Now, how would they get that idea?" She reached for Chad's hand, glad that the tense moment had passed. She decided to risk one more inquiry into Chad's background before he left. "Since we're being so honest with each other, did you know I met Lorrie in training?"

Chad stepped back. "Yes," he admitted. "She wrote to me." Though his lisp was conspicuous, his calm, matter-of-fact answer cooled Pilar's momentary conviction that they were ready for such a baring of their souls. Her jealousy suddenly transferred from Maryann to Lorrie. Chad must have recognized her anxiety because he rested his hand on Pilar's arm to reassure her.

Pilar pulled away, but Chad's grip tightened around her arm. "She's an old friend," he consoled. "A youthful sweetheart. College changed us, so we went our different ways."

"She's still in love with you," Pilar blurted.

Chad smiled sympathetically. "Lorrie is not a stable person."

"I know." Then clasping his hand into hers, Pilar walked him into the corridor. Her heart skipped when Jane glanced at their interlocked fingers.

"Jane won't say anything. I know Tommy and she have been going at it for more than a year." He touched Pilar's cheek. His eyes connected with hers. "Tommy's a good friend." Chad winked at Pilar and nodded at Jane.

Pilar scanned the area to make sure no one else had seen that exchange, especially Officer Leonard. He had shown up at unusual places and times. It was almost as though he followed Pilar to catch her in a mistake. Sometimes, Pilar thought she heard him breathing outside her office door. Often when she flung the door open to surprise the spy, she'd spot him dashing out the infirmary gate.

After Chad left, Pilar went back to her office in a daze. She leaned against the closed door, her heart pumping in a feverish rush. She sat at the desk, fingering Chad's institutional file. Did Lorrie write to Chad before she got to Hawk Haven? So what? If she did, Lorrie's plan to get him back hadn't worked. And, Maryann wouldn't get him either.

Instead of spending any more time on Lorrie and Maryann, Pilar dreamily reviewed the past glorious months she shared with Chad and focused on her second month at the prison. She remembered Chad's name was listed on the afternoon sick call. When the consultation began, Chad boldly spoke first. "Let's cut to the chase. We both know how we feel about each other." He sat very still, resting his unshackled hand in his lap.

Pilar stepped away from him. She steadied herself against the exam table, an unsubtle, bad habit in his presence. Words didn't come. Instead, she simply stood there and placed her hand over her open mouth. There was no defense. Any astute observer would notice how she had been taken with Chad's flirting from the start. Marcus' words mocked Pilar. "You're nothing without a man."

Pilar finally forced a response to Chad's confession. "What do you mean?"

Before Chad could answer, they heard footsteps and a knock at the door. Jane opened the door and said, "There's an emergency." She glanced at Chad and shrugged. "You're needed, Doctor Brookstone, in room two."

Pilar was relieved for the moment that her question went unanswered. She feared what Chad would tell her if he had the chance. She feared her own reaction as well.

It wasn't long before Chad had the opportunity to get his answer. It came much quicker than Pilar anticipated. Two weeks later Chad returned to the infirmary. "I'm here to answer that question you asked the last time we were together."

He remembered. And of course, Pilar had no doubt what he had to say. Since they met she had given him nothing but positive, encouraging signals. Pilar stood before him, ready.

"You know as well as I do that from the very first time we met," Chad whispered, "we were drawn to each other like magnets." His voice became louder, more confident. "I feel as though I've always known you. And . . ."

Pilar lifted her hand to stop him. She fell to her knees and kissed his lips. "And that we have always been in love," she whispered into his neck.

"Whew," Chad sighed. "This is better than I had expected. I had hoped I wasn't misreading you, us."

How could he have thought that? Pilar's immediate and strange fascination for him was as odd as something in a Steven King novel. Pilar hadn't been good at hiding those feelings from Chad right from the first day. It was as though they had been lovers, unwillingly separated, and finally reunited. It was the most intense, and perhaps irrational sensation Pilar had ever had. She would never be able to explain. Hadn't she read as much as she could about him in newspapers before she stepped inside the prison? Perhaps she was just like those women who made the weekly trek to visit Chad. Did she feel sorry for Chad? Had she thought she would be his savior? Or, did she love him? Silly questions. Of course she loved him — every inch. Besides, Chad didn't want pity and didn't need to be saved. He wanted her.

PILAR BROUGHT HERSELF BACK to the present and gazed out her office window at a winter sky that held a late-day pink glow. Now, after four months at the prison, she realized that nothing seemed to matter to her but Chad. Consumed with that insane love, she was determined to get Chad out of prison despite his life sentence. Nothing could stop her. She would find one technicality in his case, like a cop slip-up, some bit of evidence that would set Chad free. Maybe even DNA. She'd read about all those others who had been wrongly accused and then set free because of DNA.

Pilar believed with all her heart that there was more to Chad's story than what she had heard from Lorrie or read in the newspapers. He may have murdered one woman, but there had to have been a good reason. One thing was for sure — Chad was the most engaging person Pilar had ever known, both physically and emotionally. In him she found the uncertainty of good and evil. The evil of a known killer. And, odd as it seemed, evil had become attractive, glamorous in a way.

Then, there was Lorrie. Did she have a hidden motive

for warning Pilar about Chad? She must still love him. Pilar had become a threat. "Lorrie," Pilar sighed, "are you a nut or a clever seductress?"

But, the other women visitors had dwindled down to just the curious. After a heated discussion Chad took his name off prisonpenpals.com. At first he was hurt that Pilar checked up on him, and so uptight he slammed his fist into the wall when they talked about the web site. Why no one checked on the commotion in her office was amazing. When Chad discovered Pilar's investigation was done before he and Pilar became intimate, he calmed down. He even seemed flattered by how early she'd shown an interest. Yet, it still took some persuading to get him to remove his vitae from the Internet. "It's fun to get mail and visitors," he said. "Besides, I can't see you all the time when you're working and gone on the weekends. And, my mother can only come to see me once a month."

Though erasing his information from the list of pen pals didn't stop the already established friends from communicating, no new women showed up at the prison. Pilar faithfully checked the visitors' names each Monday. That was a monumental task. She had to conceal her search and sneak a look at the list of names by pretending it was a way to gauge her likely call outs. Was she jealous or suspicious? Jealous, she decided.

Pilar made notes in Chad's medical record and set it aside. Rather than see another patient, she wanted the day to be over. Pilar could hardly wait to take her next planned step toward liberation from the Pointes: After work she was trading in the Mercedes for a four-wheel drive Subaru station wagon. Though not quite a pick-up truck, the wagon was more appropriate in the north where residents liked to say, "We have two seasons — winter and July 4th."

Before the next prisoner, Pilar retrieved Chad's institutional file, hidden from the curious under a pile of papers. She made a copy and placed it in her attache. It was part of her research on Chad Wilbanks. She was convinced the information she gathered would prove Chad's innocence.

AT THE CAR DEALERSHIP the salesman seemed in a hurry to take the Mercedes in trade for the Subaru. Pilar suspected he'd keep the luxury sedan for himself. She had given into his rather low trade-in value. What did it matter? Pilar wanted to get rid of the car that made her stand out in the land of trucks and SUVs. The luxury car was also a daily reminder of Marcus.   She had already decided the profit made on the deal would go in the bank for a rainy day and Chad's legal fund. What would Marcus say to that?

As the salesman handed Pilar the keys, he regarded her body from her head to her ankles. Clearly, his intentions were lascivious. His lack of subtleness brought back memories of Doctor Peters at Detroit Receiving Hospital. Chad never approached Pilar in such a lustful manner. Rather, he was always gentle, admiring, but never lecherous.

Pilar snatched the keys from the salesman before he could make a verbal pass. She dashed to her forest green wagon and slid behind the wheel, then spun out of the lot like a teenager in a drag race.

On the way home, Pilar made one other planned stop at the public library on Presque Isle Avenue. She searched for a book about women becoming involved with prisoners. The search took longer than expected, but she didn't want to ask for help from a small town librarian eager for some juicy gossip. Finally, Pilar found *Women Who Love Men Who Kill,* by a reporter named Sheila Isenberg.

When Pilar checked out the book, the librarian asked, "Are you doing research for a class?"

"No. I work at the prison. I'm curious about why all the women visit."

"You're a counselor, then?" The librarian's abundant gray eyebrows knotted together to form a magnificent line across her brow. She looked like a sinister old maid from a Grimm's fairytale.

"No. I'm a concerned physician." Pilar's acid response didn't change the librarian's expression. She made it obvious she didn't believe Pilar. Would Pilar be the topic of local gossip shared over a cup of evening tea?

Pilar was on a mission and had no time to worry about that. She raced to her car, humming, anxious to get home and see what Ms. Isenberg had to say.

SINCE THE TREES HAD shed their leaves, Pilar caught glimpses of Lake Superior from her living room window. When she arrived in Marquette, the trees were in full green dress. Within two months, flawless northern autumn weather accompanied the vibrant reds and oranges of the maple trees, the perfect complements to the golds of the birch and the greens of the spruce and fir. Fall skies were clear azure during the day. Pilar missed that time and the kaleidoscopic sunsets ending most days. November had ushered in nothing but bleak, overcast winter horizons. The churning, dreary lake waters that reminded her of day-old oatmeal greeted Pilar each winter morning, warning her to bundle up. Superior took on a meanness in the winter which was hardly welcoming. Yet, like her days on Lake St. Clair, water, even at its ugliest or most challenging, had always calmed Pilar.

It was evident winter came early in the Upper Peninsula when Pilar discovered most new apartments had fireplaces. Though she had little time or desire to decorate, except for the shopping spree with her mother, she was glad she made arrangements for a regular wood delivery. That evening Pilar built a fire to ward off the dampness.

Pilar grabbed the book and studied her sterile sur-roundings. Maybe she should do something about the white walls and sparse furnishings. Everything in her life seemed washed in a non-color, starting with the beige walls and floors of the prison. Adding some periwinkle and green to her world could transport her from this dreamlike stillness of aging gauze and into the warmth and new growth of a sunny spring day. She needed a real home.

A glass of merlot, an apple, and a ham and cheese Hot Pocket were the perfect accompaniments to the fire. Surely they would nourish Pilar for a night of research. Curling up on the couch, she began to read, and experienced a rush like an archeologist about to unearth an ancient artifact. She felt like a female Indiana Jones on the threshold of discovering primordial love and sex secrets.

At midnight Pilar finished reading about women in love with murderers. Undressing for bed, she thought about what she'd read. Women like her. Or, were they? On one hand, she was relieved to know she wasn't alone or crazy. She wasn't the only woman who had an unconsummated affair with a man behind bars. Yet, she wasn't like some of those women Isenberg reported about. Those poor souls, most coming from abusive partnerships, sought out relationships with prisoners, especially lifers, to keep them from performing intimate acts. That was not Pilar. Yet, what could she want from a murderer?

Pilar posed in front of the mirror. She knew what she wanted. She brushed her hand across her bare breasts. Pilar longed to make love with Chad. She dropped her hand and examined the woman before her. Ms. Isenberg was right about one thing. The fathers of women like Pilar raised their daughters on a diet of emotional neglect, while discounting them and their achievements. She was also right about two other things. In many of the cases Ms. Isenberg recounted, the man looked like the woman's father. Chad did have some physical similarities to Marcus: dark hair, creamy complexion, same height, but that was where the likeness stopped. Chad, unlike Marcus, was caring, understanding, and appreciated Pilar.

There was a second resemblance to those in the study. For instance, Pilar knew without a doubt Chad accidently killed Susan. Pilar believed her lover was as much a scapegoat for other murders as the women in Isenberg's study believed about their men. Pilar, like them, felt she was the only person left on her lover's side. She tried not to think about Maryann.

"I'm no groupie, either," she announced to the woman staring from the mirror. "I didn't follow Chad to prison and stand in an endless visiting line. Our meeting was serendipitous. Our love for each other is real."

Pilar slid the book onto the night stand and crawled into bed. Once she turned off the light, she fantasized about making love to Chad. His naked body was as vivid as though she had seen it every day of her life. Pilar's hand roamed over her body. She imagined Chad lying next to her. Pilar dreamed of his tender caress. As she touched her pubic hair intending to bring pleasure, Chad's face was displaced by her father's. Pilar leaped from bed clawing at the air. "Leave me alone."

Crumbling to the floor, Pilar held her knees to her breasts. She remained huddled there until she heard the clock strike two.

chapter ten

DISCOVERY

"I READ YOUR INSTITUTIONAL file," Pilar announced to Chad on his next call out. "And, I've ordered the transcripts from your trial." She didn't mention Sheila Isenberg's study.

Chad's face wrinkled in surprise. His expression quickly changed. "I thought you trusted me."

"Oh, I do." Why would he question that? "But," Pilar explained, "if we're going to find a way to get you out of here, legally," she brushed the back of her hand down his cheek, "I need to know every detail of your case, even something you may have forgotten or don't think is important."

"You sound like an attorney, not a doctor." He teased. "I told you I'm working on something. But, we'll need money to pay off the attorney. And, he'll need money to convince the governor to commute my sentence."

"YOU DIDN'T TELL ME you had an attorney."

Chad shrugged. "I don't, but we'll need a lawyer, and they aren't cheap." He studied Pilar. His eyes seemed to become smaller, a shade darker. Was he waiting for her to reject his idea?

"Of course we'll need an attorney," Pilar agreed. "But, I guess I didn't understand the whole plan that included the governor."

Chad didn't answer.

"No matter," Pilar added when Chad remained silent. "I have already started liquidating my assets, so to speak." Pilar placed a hand on his arm. "I'll do anything we think will work so we can be together."

Chad wrapped a hand around Pilar's and squeezed it so tightly it hurt. He had done that before. Perhaps out of fear. "Good," he said. "Just so we understand what we're getting into. We don't want to strap you financially or jeopardize your job right now."

"I've sold some stock my father gave me, and I plan to sell most of my jewelry," Pilar assured him.

Chad removed his hand and stroked Pilar's hair away from her cheek. Her groin moistened in response. "I have a comfortable income that will keep me," she whispered.

Chad's hand slipped to Pilar's breasts. Her nipples hardened with intense sensation. She wanted to rip his clothes away.

"I have contacts to help us, but we must be careful." Chad's mouth brushed against Pilar's ear. Then, he held her head in both his hands. "All in due time, though."

She pressed into his hardness. What contacts? No, she

wouldn't ask that. She didn't want to interrupt the moment with that question. Certainly, she didn't want to make him think she had no faith in him or his plan. Not when he considered her participation with such hope. But, why couldn't he be as open with her as she was with him?

Instead of pushing the issue further, Pilar forced a smile and kissed his soft cheek. Chad patted her back like a consoling father.

"By the way," Chad said as he backed away, his voice raising a little, "What did you find out about me that I haven't already told you?"

Teasing, Pilar bent her head to one side, fluttered her lashes, and rubbed her hand along her shirt collar to where it ended at a hint of cleavage. She licked her lower lip to bait him further. "I learned that you murdered Susan."

Chad's body tensed. "You knew that."

"But, I believe it was an accident. She provoked it." Pilar fluffed his hair as she would do to a child. "Remember, I know about her quick temper."

"Oh, Pilar." Chad lowered his head to nuzzle into her breasts. Did she feel him crying? Confused by this unexpected and uncharacteristic outburst, Pilar circled her arms around him.

"I didn't rape Susan." Chad's muffled sobs were barely audible. "We had already been sleeping together." He sniffled. "That night she got mad when she found a letter from Lorrie. She started hitting me and came after me with a knife." He turned his head to the side. "We were both high. I just tried to stop her, not strangle her."

Pilar pulled his head closer to her breasts again and rubbed his back. "Ssshh. I know." Lorrie again. That demon. She hadn't told Pilar the truth. Apparently, neither had Susan. Pilar didn't know she had been sleeping with Chad when she died.

"The cops needed to pin all those other murders on someone so they'd stop looking bad." Chad sounded like a little boy, a voice he often used. "I was as good a candidate as any for them."

"I know," Pilar repeated. She didn't question why he never mentioned he also stabbed Susan, or why he never called the police that night.

"Why do you care about me, Pilar?" Chad asked. "You could have anyone."

"But, I only want you." She lifted his head away, leaving tear-dampened circles near her breasts.

When they heard a rustle outside the door, Pilar pushed Chad away. Straightening her clothes, Pilar leaned toward the door. Nothing. Perhaps it was Jane passing by.

Pilar and Chad never talked about the murders again.

SOON AFTER THAT, JANE Carson asked to meet Pilar at Flanigan's Bar on Washington. Though unsure about having a drink with someone Pilar suspected knew of her involvement with Chad, she agreed to go. The decision was fueled by what Chad said about Tommy Johnson and Jane. At first, Pilar thought perhaps Tommy was being a typical prisoner, bragging about an imaginary affair with an employee to boost both his ego and stature among his block mates. After all, Jane was married with two kids. "But, so is my father married," Pilar snickered.

Throughout the many weeks at the prison, Pilar saw enough evidence of Tommy and Jane's affair to not question the reality. Every time Tommy was in the infirmary, Jane was flustered and silly. Pilar caught them touching more than once. Their body language gave away their yearning for each other. Hawk Haven was a regular "Peyton Place".

Pilar parked her Subaru among the 4x4 pickups, most with gun racks, and rushed inside the bar. She half expected to bump into a couple of prison employees in the midst of a parking lot peeing contest. It wouldn't be the first time for such a competition. One contest had taken place at the prison between a male and a female sergeant. The other custody staff found great joy in the rivalry, but not Warden Whitefeather, especially when he found out the woman won.

JANE WAS ALREADY AT a table in a dimly lit corner. It was like meeting a spy. The clandestine spell was broken when she waved enthusiastically, not fearing any attention she attracted. Her brazen greeting gave the impression Jane hung out at Flanigan's a lot. As Pilar sat across the table from her, Jane said, "I'm glad you came."

Her casual, cheerful attire — a rose and purple print sweater, rose knit above-the-knee skirt, purple tights and black boots — gave her a more youthful look than the starched nurse's uniform she wore at the prison. Her maple brown eyes shone like a child's spotting a pile of gifts under the family Christmas tree. Jane had definitely donned an off-work persona.

Jane sipped her margarita as the waitress took Pilar's order, a glass of merlot as usual. Pilar sensed Jane's intense scrutiny. Yet, Pilar realized she did need a friend. Someone she could confide in. Still, Pilar must be careful. Though it seemed a long time since they first met, Pilar knew baby steps were in order with Jane. See what game she played. Pilar sounded like a prisoner herself. But, why shouldn't she? None of the employees had gone out of the way to befriend her until Jane.

Pilar wanted to share her current situation with someone. It had been difficult for her to keep the affair with Chad hidden. She desperately wanted to celebrate her love in the open. Yet, she hadn't even had the courage to tell her best friend Julie about Chad. So, how could she tell the nurse who worked for her?

Jane waited for the waitress to serve the wine before she said anything. When she finally talked, she stunned Pilar.

"I know you are fully aware of my relationship with Tommy. We're deeply in love and I need you on my side.

I can't afford to have anyone squeal on us, not after we've kept it quiet for almost two years." Jane looked at the people seated at the bar. She smiled at an officer, a man Pilar had seen escorting prisoners to the infirmary.

"There's no sense beating around the bush," Jane said. She took a long swig of her margarita as though she needed the alcohol's help. "You and Chad have been having a thing, too."

Heat ran through Pilar's veins. How could she and Chad have been so careless, so stupid? Pilar sipped her wine. How could she respond to Jane without either revealing too much or appearing defensive? Pilar couldn't win.

"What I'm saying," Jane pressed. She was tearing the shells from one peanut after another, assembling a pile of nuts on her napkin. "We're in the same boat. We can use each other's support."

"Support?" Pilar asked cautiously. "What kind of support?"

Jane pursed her lips. "Like tonight. Someone to talk to so we don't feel like such sneaks, or outsiders, or dirty."

"I don't feel dirty," Pilar answered too quickly. "I have nothing to be ashamed of."

"Me either. And that's what I mean. Maybe we can help each other." She almost begged.

What is Jane up to? Pilar decided not to tell her anything just yet. Not until she was damn sure about Jane's motives.

"Look," Jane confided. "I'm going to be honest with

you." She popped a handful of peanuts into her mouth.

"I may not be ready for your honesty." Pilar rested her back against the chair. She admired Jane's classic features. Even chewing a wad of nuts, she looked like the bust of Nefertiti pictured in "National Geographic".

"Too late." Jane licked the salt from her lips. "I want you to know so you don't think you're alone." Jane lowered her eyes to Pilar's tapping foot. Jane knew what was going on in Pilar's head, all right. Maybe she wanted more than to be Pilar's confidante. Maybe even blackmail her.

Was Pilar reacting again like a paranoid inmate?

"Whether you want to admit it or not, except for the drastic differences in our backgrounds, you're a lot like me." A self-satisfied smile crossed Jane's face. "I've been studying you since you got to Hawk Haven."

A golf ball size lump formed in Pilar's throat at the thought Jane had learned more than she wished anyone to know, except Chad. She and Chad had been too obvious. They knew better. Training taught Pilar that prisoners and staff are experts at finding that weak link to set up for their own purposes. Pilar had been visible to Jane, and who else? She had no one to turn to. She was like Maria, the fifteen-year-old prostitute.

Jane examined Pilar like an artist about to paint a portrait. "You don't have to worry. I'm not telling anyone else. We need each other, now and in the future. As I said, you're more like me than you think."

Jane snagged her. Pilar finally bit. "How do you mean?"

"This is the first time either of us have found a man who listens to us and makes us feel important." Jane smiled and nodded several times. "Right?"

Pilar was drawn to the loud laughter coming from the crowd at the bar, as though they had overheard the absurd conversation. She wanted to be with friends, drinking, laughing, and sharing small talk. She wanted to be with Julie. She didn't want to be in this intense, prying conversation. Pilar quietly answered, "Yes."

Jane's self-assured and accurate accounting of their likeness was uncanny. She might have eavesdropped on Pilar's thoughts since Chad came into her life. More likely, Pilar had revealed all to Jane through her own body language.

"We've been the perfect daughters," Jane continued. "And now we've each become the center of one man's attention."

Jane hesitated, anticipating a response. Pilar felt the dampness in her armpits and on her forehead. She didn't want to wipe the sweat away and give Jane a heads-up about how nervous she made her. Jane had pegged Pilar.

Jane eased back and signaled the waitress. "You might as well face it, Pilar." It's the only time she had used her given name since Pilar's first day on the job. "We're just two good girls finding bad boys who need us."

Jane played with the straw in her empty margarita glass. When the waitress pushed through the growing throng of Friday night patrons to their table Jane asked,

"Want another drink?" She pointed the straw at Pilar's half-empty glass.

"No. I'll finish this wine and then I have to be on my way." Pilar swallowed the remainder almost choking.

"Too bad. I'm not ready to do Mommy duty yet." Jane ordered another margarita. "Besides, this place is better than our double-wide in the trailer park, and my husband slugging down beers and bitchin' about his dinner."

In the bar's atmosphere, Jane wasn't the efficient Nurse Carson. It was almost like she was three different persons. She was a nurse, a wife and mother, and a woman, like Pilar, in a forbidden affair.

Jane walked Pilar to the door with the freshened drink in her hand. "One more thing," Jane said as she nudged Pilar's arm. "Do you think Chad can get approved for all those infirmary appointments if I'm not making sure they're processed?"

Pilar was too confused to utter a word.

"I HOPE WE CAN do this another time," Jane offered. "When you can stay longer. When you're ready to combine forces." She turned away and joined a group at the bar.

Pilar marveled at the easy way Jane maneuvered between two prison officers. Pilar envied their acceptance of her. She had never felt that comfortable around people.

Was Jane really like Pilar? Was she seeking a woman friend with whom she could confide, compare aggravations, bitch about her husband, kids, and fathers?   Someone with whom to share the darkest secrets and dreams?   Someone like Julie? Pilar wasn't sure. Jane's obvious hunger for such a relationship made Pilar uneasy. What were Jane's real reasons for the rendezvous at Flanigan's? Why did Jane think they had a future together?

Driving home, Pilar tried to picture a young Jane at her house for a sleep-over. It would never have happened. Was it because of the color of her skin, or because of her distinct neediness?

Pilar let go of those worries for the moment and concentrated on Chad, a much happier and sure prospect. Despite Jane's awareness, Pilar wouldn't trade in the past months for anything. She was enthralled with every conversation with Chad, and every common taste they discovered. As with books, their tastes in music were similar. Though neither was fond of opera, they loved Mozart and Verdi mixed in with a little Earl Klug and Madonna.

That wasn't all of it. Pilar admired Chad's interaction with the other inmates, every instance confirming her belief that he shouldn't be in prison. One day when twenty-year-old Murphy was supposed to see the psychiatrist, Chad happened to be in the hall at the same time. Murphy had slid to the floor, rocking on his heels. He held his head in his hands and cried. Chad squatted at his side and circled his arm around Murphy.

Though the officer approached them intending to break

them apart, Pilar stopped him. Murphy and Chad stayed in that position, Chad talking softly. After fifteen minutes both stood and Murphy went to see the psychiatrist. He had kept that appointment every day since.

As Pilar watched that interaction, she had wiped away her own tears. No transcript or trial could reveal the real Chad Wilbanks she saw that day.

chapter eleven

LETTERS

MONDAY BEFORE THANKSGIVING PILAR was reading the normal pile of prisoner communications, called "kites", when her phone rang. The prisoner operator clipped, "You have an outside call, Doctor Brookstone."

Surprised by an early morning caller, Pilar was hesitant to answer. She feared bad news from her mother. When she finally lifted the receiver, Pilar heard a male voice on the other end and it was not Celeste's. "This is Larry Corbett's brother," he said in a muffled tone as though he was holding his hand over the phone's mouthpiece. "I'm only telling you this once."

"Who is this?" Pilar asked when the name didn't register.

"Listen up, lady. I don't have all day."

The caller paused. He seemed to adjust something. Pilar heard rustling, like paper being shuffled; or perhaps the caller rearranged a cloth over the mouthpiece. "You better take care of my brother, Larry," he insisted in a controlled and loud voice. "Do as he asks or . . . "

"I only treat prisoners who have a real problem." Pilar was annoyed by the intrusion. "If you are Larry Corbett's brother, you should caution him about having someone intercede from outside. I . . . "

"Doctor Brookstone, if you don't do as I say, I'll see to it you don't work again. You know about the information Larry has on you."

Pilar didn't comment. No need to let the caller, whoever he was, think he knew anything.

"Remember," he warned, "I'm on the outside and I've got a lot of friends who don't mind messing up a pretty face. Especially one that belongs to an uppity bitch. I know your address, so just take care of Larry or else."

The line went dead. "Or else what?" Pilar whimpered.

Staring at the telephone for several minutes Pilar recalled the many encounters she'd had with Larry Corbett. Like Tommy Johnson, he worked in the infirmary as a porter so it wasn't easy to avoid him. Each time Pilar bumped into him in the hall he pestered her. "When are you going to call me out to look at my back, Doc?"

"You know the procedure." Pilar's answer was always the same. "Sign up for sick call in the block like everyone else." Why would Corbett think he deserved special treatment?

After Corbett first approached Pilar, she reviewed his medical file. He had an old back injury and some osteo-arthritis. He took Vioxx. Nothing else could be done. He was prescribed physical therapy which he refused. In fact

Corbett could loose a good thirty pounds, which would be the best help for him and his weary joints.

That phone call was something else all together. Larry Corbett had obviously told someone about his last conversation with Pilar when she made rounds in his block. Corbett was a medium custody prisoner brought to Hawk Haven as part of the labor force to maintain the prison. The day Pilar circulated in his housing unit, he burst out of his cell when she passed. He had grabbed Pilar's arm. She yanked it away. "Watch who you're touching," she admonished.

Corbett raised both his hands, took a few steps back, and asked, "You selective about who touches you, Doc?"

"What are you talking about?"

A slow smile crossed Larry Corbett's face. He leaned toward Pilar. "I know about you. I've got pictures of you, and ya don't want no one else lookin' at 'em. I found 'em taped under one of the desk's in an office I clean."

What pictures could he be talking about? She'd given a couple to Chad. But, he wouldn't be that careless. "You're trying to create a story you think will persuade me to treat you," Pilar stated. "Well, Mr. Corbett, you have nothing on me and you know it."

"Look, Doc, I've overheard conversations about you and a prisoner here. I don't think ya want that kind of information out, understand what I'm sayin'?" He waited for an answer.

"I'm not going to do anything for you unless you follow

procedure," Pilar said as she turned and walked away.

"I know where you live." Corbett followed her. He handed her a piece of paper with her address written on it. Pilar's body flared up like someone torched it. She took the note from Corbett and left the cell block.

"Later," Corbett called out as he pointed at Pilar.

AT FIRST, PILAR ACCEPTED the conversation as just another angry inmate trying to persuade her to do something that didn't need to be done. It wasn't difficult to get an address from the desk of a careless employee, especially if he placed too much trust in a prisoner porter. Even Pilar found herself in that position. Since Corbett didn't show her any pictures, they could be ID photos taken from someone in the personnel office. He was the porter there, too.

Though Pilar let that incident go, she did make an appointment to see Corbett a few days after their conversation. But, the telephone call came first. Until then there was no reason to report Corbett.

Given the threats made by both Larry Corbett and the man who claimed to be his brother Pilar decided there could be a legitimate concern. So she made an appointment to see Warden Whitefeather. It was a tough decision in light of the warden's apparent assessment of her at orientation. On that day Pilar would have denied she'd ever be the rule-breaker she had become. She decided to prepare a written report to give the warden to help keep her factual and calm — if that was possible.

PILAR TOOK A DEEP breath and pushed open the door to the warden's office. His secretary greeted her with an efficient, cold nod, and directed Pilar through to the inner chamber. In seconds Pilar stood in front of Whitefeather.

The warden put down a file. "What brings you here today, Doctor?"

Pilar mentally composed herself before she answered. She had to use the right words so Whitefeather wouldn't think his orientation prediction had been on target. "My life has been threatened by an inmate and his brother," she said as collectedly as possible.

"We all get threats. It's part of the job." His lips pursed as he appeared to think about what she said. "Perhaps you should transfer to another prison." That was quick. Was he hoping that was why she was there?

"Transfer! I don't want a transfer." Pilar held up her report. "I want this investigated."

Whitefeather raised his hand like a patrolman stopping traffic. "There have been other rumors that you don't know about, which leads me to believe you have become a security risk."

Pilar leaned across his desk and asked, "Me, a security risk?" Now angry, she was trying not to get out of control. "What about the guy who threatened to kill me?" She threw her written account on the desk. "Read it. Read it now." She needed that time to quiet her nerves.

Whitefeather backed away; his chair squeaked from years of use. He read the report. Every now and then he peered over his glasses at Pilar. When he finished, the warden laid the narrative down. He said nothing.

Breathing hard, as if she had run a couple of miles, Pilar collapsed into a chair. Visibly shaken, she asked, "What about the guy that called me yesterday from outside who said he was Corbett's brother?" She was unable to hold back her tears any longer. She blubbered on, more afraid than angry or ashamed. "His brother said he was going to kill me. And, he's on the outside."

The warden shifted and cleared his throat. "What kind of signal are you giving these guys? I tried to warn you . . ."

Pilar jumped out of her chair. Whitefeather moved back again. Was he afraid Pilar would come at him over the desk? That was exactly what she wanted to do. "Warn me?" She over-pronounced the words. "What about the pervert who telephoned me? What signal have I given him? And, why haven't you mentioned these rumors before now?"

"Calm down. I'm trying to help." Warden Whitefeather raised both his hands. Palms faced out. "Do you know what a "Duck" is in prison?"

"No," Pilar answered as Tommy's conversation with Jane came back to her. "But, I've heard the term."

"It's when prisoners set up a vulnerable employee. Are you sure you haven't put yourself in that kind of position, consciously or unconsciously?"

"What? How can you say that after what I just told you?" Pilar pointed to the paper on his desk.

"Think about it, Doctor Brookstone. Your intentions are noble, but they could mislead prisoners into believing you care more personally about them than you might a patient. Meanwhile, I'll turn your report over to the state police."

"That's not enough." Pilar pounded her fist on his desk. "We're talking about my life."

"There's little else we can do right now, but investigate this just as you asked." He brushed his hand through his hair. "Until we get to the bottom of these threats, be careful."

"CAREFUL. What does that mean?" Without waiting for an answer Pilar marched out, slamming the door. Did the warden know about Chad? She was in trouble, and there was no one to help.

THE SUNDAY OF THANKSGIVING weekend, Pilar drove to Thunder Bay Inn. Despite Celeste's unrelenting pleas for Pilar to come home for the holiday, a turkey sandwich and NPR were more appetizing than a seven-course meal with her parents. After her conversation with Whitefeather the week before, and the disturbing telephone call she received earlier that morning from Chad, Pilar needed to unwind. Chad had accused her of having a boyfriend on the outside. He wasn't about to be convinced that Pilar was alone at a movie at the Delft Theater Saturday night when he called.

How could she explain her own desperation? Without Chad, especially on a holiday, she too was lonely, but chose to stay close to the prison. As close as she could be to Chad.

Pilar decided that a drive along Lake Superior for a late lunch at Thunder Bay Inn was the right treatment for her blues. But then, a black Ford pickup truck followed her from Marquette to Big Bay on the remote two-lane road going to the inn. Pilar noticed it right away, when she turned out of the apartment complex.

Normally she wouldn't be concerned, but she drove slowly because of the rain. Most cars passed her and the truck. When she slowed, the truck slowed, too. Whoever was behind her had to be as cautious or as unfamiliar with the roads as Pilar, though she was surprised that anyone driving such a big truck had anything to fear.

Rain turned to snow as Pilar stopped outside the white clapboard inn made famous by the movie, *Anatomy of a Murder*. The truck parked down the street alongside Lake Independence, opposite the inn. The truck's windows were tinted. This was no coincidence. The driver was heading anywhere Pilar was. But, why?

Pilar waited for the driver to get out. When he didn't, she decided not to go inside. Why take a chance the driver would tail Pilar in the dark the twenty-five wilderness miles back to Marquette? She certainly would be vulnerable if he decided to play games. The highway bordered the isolated, rocky cliffs of Lake Superior along an unpopulated and heavily wooded area. It was a perfect place for someone to get away with a murder. No witnesses.

She locked the car doors, then reluctantly turned her car around and headed back to town. She'd be in for a night of TV, a frozen dinner, and dreaming about seeing Chad the next day. The truck followed. Again if she speeded up, so did the truck. If she slowed, it did, too. Whoever was driving, possibly Corbett's brother, made no attempt at concealing his mission. Pilar's eyes darted rapidly back and forth from the road in front to the rear view mirror. Snow came down as hard as hail. Though it was only mid-afternoon, it looked like dusk. The windshield wipers slapped loudly in rapid, constant motion. Pilar's heart kept pace.

Once Pilar pulled into her carport in her apartment complex the truck sped past and out of sight, taillights blurred into the falling snow. Pilar's hands froze to the steering wheel as though the tight grip protected her. In that position, she waited in the idling Subaru for what seemed like hours. Not until her neighbors came home did Pilar have the courage to leave. When they parked nearby, she turned off the engine, got out, and followed them inside.

After Pilar double-locked the front door, she checked the windows, thankful her rooms faced the lake and not the street. She didn't want to know if the truck was still out there, like someone on surveillance. If it was, who could she call for help?

Feeling consoled for the first time by the barren,

cheerless rooms, Pilar built a fire and put the kettle on for tea.   The blinking light on the answering machine was probably her mother calling for the tenth time. Who really needed the comforting? At least she wasn't sharing another meal with her and Marcus.

Prepared to choke back the guilt she felt when she heard her mother's sad voice, Pilar punched the button on the machine and waited for her words. Instead, Chad's voice came on the line. "I'm sorry for what I said earlier," he said with sadness that rivaled Celeste's. "I miss you. Sweet dreams."

Pilar listened again to Chad's message. She was intrigued by how he was able to telephone without going through an operator to place a collect call. Chad's call must have been placed by a third party. Perhaps it was some kind of a scam the prisoners dreamed up.   In any case, she and Chad still had to be careful. Suspicious calls were traced and monitored from the prison.

The second message was from Julie. "Where have you been, old girl? I haven't heard from you since you went to that prison in the wilderness. Don't they have phones in that place? It's been too long. I think I can get a way for a long weekend to visit. Give me a call, pronto."

Julie's perky voice made Pilar laugh out loud. She dialed Julie's number. After the second ring, she hung up. Pilar wanted to confide in her about what she'd been up to. She wanted to believe Julie could accept her relationship with Chad. Most desperately, she wanted to see Julie's cheery face. But, could she trust her?

Pilar picked up the receiver again. She held it to her ear and stared at the key pad. She slammed the phone down and cleared all the messages. Pilar grabbed her cup of Good Earth Tea and plopped down in front of the fire. "I'm in this alone," she told the flames.

ON MONDAY PILAR'S INBOX was overflowing. In her lab coat and settled at the desk, she tackled the pile before her first patient reported. Her hands shook when she finished the threatening kite from a prisoner.

> Dear Dr. Brookstone, M.D.
> We know you for what you are — a whore. The AMA is about to investigate you. You've had your big dick, but you had to be a one-man whore. So there's a contract out on you and you won't live long no matter where you are going. Watch your step, bitch.
> Jameson #200801

Her picture was attached to the paper. The photo wasn't from any ID. It was the one she gave to Chad. She was sitting on the bed in her apartment. It was innocent enough, but Chad had other photos that are far more incriminating.

There was no way Jameson could get a picture like that unless Chad had been careless. How could she have been so stupid to believe they could hide such evidence from those who wanted to find it?

Pilar turned the piece of paper over and over. The truck driver came to mind. Was he connected to Jameson?

A computer search of both medical and institutional files revealed no prisoner by his name or number existed in the entire system. Despite having to face Warden Whitefeather a second time, Pilar had to show him that letter, too.

Rocking her head in her hands, Pilar laughed. Whitefeather was right. She may have to leave because of her involvement with a prisoner. How did she get into this? Never mind. Who was the snitch? Someone who had seen Chad and her together. Jane? Tommy Johnson? Officer Leonard? Who?

LEONARD STOPPED PILAR IN the hallway on the way to the warden's office. "You look mighty upset, Doctor Brookstone," he said, apparently enjoying her agitation. He focused on the "kite" she clenched. Perhaps he knew about the warnings and the death threats. Perhaps he helped send them.

"Nothing I can't handle." She had to squeeze by him since he didn't relinquish enough space for her to pass. Their bodies touched and Leonard sighed. He nauseated Pilar.

The warden's secretary signaled Pilar into his office. He looked up from a stack of files, removed his out-of-style

wire rim glasses, and said, "I've been expecting this meeting." He motioned her to sit.

"Why?" Pilar was feeling more and more like she was
the object of a conspiracy. She sat, careful not to expose too
much leg. "Do you have some other information I should
know about?"

"No." He replaced his glasses and leaned back. The
familiar chair squeak was almost soothing. Whitefeather
rested his hands, fingertips pressed together, at his chest.
"But, I did warn you there could be trouble for a young,
attractive woman working in this prison, and after our last
talk . . . " He shrugged.

Pilar straightened, ready to do battle, and handed him
the letter. "Why would I want to be the recipient of anything like this? I'm not a masochist."

Warden Whitefeather took the letter and read it. He
fluttered the picture and asked, "How do you suppose he
got this?"

"My ID picture was recently stolen from an employee's
office and sent to me with a "kite"." Pilar moved forward
and stared so hard it was as though she could see inside the
warden's mind. "Now, how do you suppose that happened?
A careless employee? Or, perhaps an employee bent on getting me in trouble? Maybe Officer Leonard?"

Whitefeather furrowed his forehead. Though he ignored that question, Pilar was sure he tucked it away in his
memory bank to use in the future if he needed.

"Perhaps," he slid the photograph into a desk drawer, "you should transfer to another prison, as I have already suggested. There's an opening for a medical director at Scott Correctional Facility. You should think about applying."

Relieved he wouldn't pursue the picture at that moment, Pilar stood. "That's how you'll deal with the fact that someone wants to kill me? Send me away? How thoughtful."

Whitefeather thrust the letter at her. Pilar raised her hand. "That's your copy. I have plenty more. Who knows, maybe I'll put together a scrapbook about my happy days at Hawk Haven Prison." She didn't ask for the photograph. She didn't want the warden to think it was important.

WHEN CHAD APPEARED FOR the afternoon infirmary call out, Pilar ushered him into her office instead of going to an exam room. A thoughtless move perhaps, especially after she admonished Tommy Johnson for being in there. But, why should she care how she behaved? Pilar was desperate. Jane was the only other person in the area, and she wouldn't tell anyone anything, if only to protect herself.

As soon as Chad stepped inside, Pilar disclosed everything about the two letters and let him read them. She paced and listened to the pages turn. Chad slumped into a chair. The papers he held quaked like leaves in the wind. He raised his eyes to the ceiling.

The silence in the room hurt Pilar's ears more than banging gates. Tired of waiting for a response, she spoke. "That's not all. Whitefeather wants me to transfer to Scott."

Chad bolted upright, eyes wild. "I'm not ready."

"What?" Pilar stood in front of him.

His face flushed as he explained. "We haven't made our plans. We need more time."

"I may have no time. Doesn't that matter to you?" She pointed at the "kites" in his hand, and told him about the black truck.

Chad lifted her hand to his cheek and slowly lowered it to his mouth. They both calmed.

"I'm as frightened as you are about these." Chad threw the "'kites'" on the desk. "But, if you transfer, how will we be able to get me out of here?"

Pilar rubbed her forehead. "I don't think I have a choice. Someone here knows about us and is out to get me. Maybe even blackmail me for money and my job."

"Blackmail?"

"It's no secret that I have money. And, I want to keep all the funds I have so we can get a good lawyer." Pilar circled her arms around him.

He left his arms at his sides and whispered, "What if an attorney, if we get one, can't get me out? Or, doesn't have the contacts or enough money to get the governor to commute my sentence."

Pilar pushed away. "Then, we'll just find a way for you to escape. After that, we'll head for Canada."

"Are you crazy?" Chad yelled. "I tried that before."

Pilar placed a finger to his mouth to quiet him. "Not with my help, you haven't. I may have a plan. I'll tell you about it when I've thought it through. We won't use plan B unless the attorney doesn't work out." She drew him close, and they kissed. "Better go," she said, and released him. Yet, she never wanted to let him go, fearing it would be a long time before she'd embrace Chad again.

"Yeah. I've got some planning to do myself." Chad scrambled out the door.

THAT EVENING, BEFORE A fire, Pilar wrote several entries in her almost-filled journal. If her words were ever read by someone other than Chad, their eyes would burn. Pilar's deepest desires, fantasies, and plans were vividly penned along with her observations and descriptions of prison employees. Both Whitefeather and Leonard would love to get their hands on that kind of information. It would condemn her at last.

As she jotted down notes about plan B, Pilar decided to collect her jewelry. Once assembled, she would look for a place to sell it without revealing her identity. She needed a trusted buyer who wouldn't expose her. Anyone dumping large quantities of expensive jewelry in that small community would not go unnoticed. Chad had bragged about his connections on the streets. He'd know the right contact.

When Pilar piled the gathered diamonds, pearls, and what looked like a ton of gold on the bed, her heart raced.

chapter twelve

OUT OF CONTROL

LEONARD MARCHED INTO PILAR'S office. He kicked the door closed. As he swaggered toward her desk, he dangled a piece of paper in the air and taunted, "Guess what I have?"

"I can hardly imagine. Maybe a Christmas gift?" His boldness concerned Pilar. She followed his every move like a cat hunting mice. What would he do next?

Officer Leonard's gray shirt, taut against his muscular chest, was pressed military style and tucked firmly into his black slacks which were creased as though just ironed. Pilar fancied him staying that neat even in a fight.

"It's a "kite"." He passed the paper in front of her face.

"So?" Pilar backed away from him.

Leonard let out a low, sadistic laugh and displayed straight teeth, their perfection spoiled by too many cigarettes. "It's a special "kite"," he teased. He tossed the paper into the air. It floated in slow motion and landed in front of Pilar. Standing tall, back straight as a board, Leonard's stomach flattened. He must spend hours working out.

Happy her desk separated them, Pilar placed her tell-tale, shaking hands in her lap out of sight. Chad was upset when he left her office the other day. Had he been that foolish to send a note saying more than he was requesting an appointment?

"Read it." Leonard placed both hands on Pilar's desk and leaned across. Pilar felt his breath. "You may enjoy it as much as I do."

Pilar lifted the paper. The handwriting was as familiar to her as her own. Ice ran through her veins. She read the words without showing any reaction. How much did Leonard know?

> Pilar, love
> I am so sorry I was distant when we last met. I hate wasting any precious time we have together. I blame my selfishness. But I am concerned if you leave our plans will be destroyed.
> I love you
> C

Pilar laid the "kite" down and folded her hands together on top of the desk. Her eyes engaged Leonard's. She said nothing. Every muscle in her body ached. Yet, Pilar would not give in. She must think clearly.

Leonard massaged his hands for a few moments and then

sat. "Well?" he asked, no doubt waiting for the frightened reaction Pilar was experiencing, but straining not to reveal.

"Well, what, Officer Leonard?"

He tilted his head to the side. He pushed his fingers through hair as blond and thin as Chad's was black and thick. Leonard's frigid stare remained fixed on Pilar's. "Don't play stupid with me." He leaned back in the chair. "You know exactly what that "kite" says."

"Exactly what does it say?" Pilar took a chance Leonard was only guessing about an affair she was having with an inmate.

Leonard blasted from the chair as though he'd been fired from a cannon. The chair screeched against the floor and slammed into the shelves behind. "You're involved with a prisoner, and I think I know who it is." His Kentucky accent became more pronounced with his increased frustration.

Pilar bit her lower lip and smiled at the same time. "Officer Leonard, do you know how many love letters I get in a week?" She tore the "kite" into tiny pieces.

His smirk showed he was ready to make his next move. It was like a chess game, and one of the players would soon yell out "gotcha" instead of "check mate." "I have copies of that 'kite'." He pointed to the pieces of paper in the trash, but continued to stare at Pilar.

Though hoping he hadn't been that smart, Pilar answered, "I'm sure you do."

"Where are those other "kites" you've gotten? Are

they in the trash, too?" Leonard seemed comfortable in the interrogator's role.

"I don't keep them. There's no need." When his face brightened like a cartoon character who had just been given a clue, Pilar wished she had kept the other "kites". She quickly added, "There'll be plenty more to replace them."

Pilar stood. She walked around the desk to face Leonard head to head. They were about the same height, so their eyes were level. "What do you want, Officer Leonard?"

He flipped Pilar's hair. "I want you."

Pilar's heart felt as though it had jumped into her throat. She hadn't expected a sexual proposition. Blackmail seemed more Leonard's style. Blood pulsated through the veins in her jaw. "I'm not sure what you mean." She clenched her teeth so hard pain shot into her temples. "But, if that was a pass, you've embarked on dangerous ground."

Leonard tossed his head back and released a self-assured laugh. His mouth opened wide enough to show the dark cave where his tonsils were once embedded. In a sudden jerk of his head, Leonard stopped. "You think you're too good for me, but you'll bang a prisoner."

Pilar's jaw tightened even more. She must not be defensive. Leonard needed to let off steam. And, she needed to remain level-headed. Several moments passed as the two stared each other down. Suddenly, Leonard grabbed Pilar's arm. She wrenched it loose. His hand dropped to his side. "You'll be sorry, Doctor." His fingers twitched like a gun fighter's. "I have enough evidence in that "kite" to get you canned."

Gaining confidence by the minute, Pilar jumped at the clue he slipped. Leonard only had one "kite". "All you have, Officer Leonard, is one among many love letters from fantasizing inmates." She walked to the door. She placed her hand on the handle and threatened, "What I have is enough to file sexual harassment charges on you." She opened the door. "However, I won't tell anyone what happened here today if you stay away from me." Pilar directed him into the hallway with a sweep of her hand. As Leonard walked by, she leaned toward him so her mouth was close to his ear. "And I had better not hear any rumors, either."

Crimson flowed from Leonard's cheeks to the tip of his ears. "This is not over, Doctor."

Pilar whispered, "Oh, yes, it is." Then, in a voice loud enough for anyone in the waiting area to hear, she stated, "Thank you for sharing that "kite" with me, Officer Leonard. I'm sure it means nothing. So, don't worry."

Leonard's back muscles tensed when he answered, "Ma'am." He tipped his finger to his forehead as he did on the first day they met, and headed for the gate.

Jane glanced up and then quickly turned away.

Pilar closed the door. She braced herself against the desk, brushing her fingers through her hair several times. After such a close call with Leonard, what choice did she have? She had to transfer to Scott Correctional Facility.

Two months had already passed since the encounter with Officer Leonard. No one said anything, and to Pilar's delight she didn't receive any "kites" other than those related to medical needs. Leonard had been silenced for now. She had gained the necessary time to take the promotion to medical director at the women's prison.

Tommy Johnson's transfer to the trustee camp came up suddenly. Pilar rushed to complete his medical file and forward it. Happy that he was one less person for her to worry about until she was out of Hawk Haven, she sighed, sounding like a hot air balloon. Leaving couldn't happen soon enough, though it wouldn't be any too fast if she didn't let Warden Whitefeather know her decision.

Jane, tears moistening her cheeks, crashed through Pilar's office door. "I won't see Tommy anymore," she wailed.

"Ssshh," Pilar scolded, cringing at her unabashed confession.

Jane swung her arms as though she was batting cobwebs away. "I don't care who knows."

"But I do." Pilar yanked her further inside and shut the door. "If they think I know about you and Tommy, I'm as guilty as you."

Jane flopped into a chair. She hit the seat so hard she sounded like a sack of potatoes being dropped. Jane blew her red nose. "I'm quitting."

"What? Are you insane?" Pilar sat in the chair next to

hers. "If you do, they'll know something's up."

"I can't go on if I don't see him," Jane cried, and blew her nose again.

"They aren't going to let a former employee visit Tommy." Pilar handed her another tissue. "So quitting isn't the answer." Suddenly, Pilar was sucked into the friendship that Jane foresaw would happen the night they had met for drinks.

Jane lowered her head into her hands. "They won't let an employee visit him either," she sobbed. "I thought you understood." She lifted her puffed face. "I never thought I was anything until I met Tommy."

Pilar understood all too well what Jane meant. But, she also knew that if Jane left, she'd accomplish nothing. "He's a trustee," Pilar commented as though that would change everything. "He'll be paroled soon."

"How will that help?" Jane slumped further into the chair. She looked small and vulnerable. "This is a small town," she sniffled. "If we're caught seeing each other, it'll be no different. I'll still lose my job."

Jane was right. Not only would she lose her job, but her husband and maybe her children, too. Worse yet, she and Tommy were an interracial couple. If they stayed in the Upper Peninsula, they'd stick out like palms at the North Pole. That wouldn't be the only obstacle to overcome. Tommy, himself, was troublesome. The few times Pilar had contact with him made one thing clear: he wasn't someone to mess with. His unsmiling demeanor pierced her own confidence. He was colder than dry ice. He spoke few words, making each one count, each calculated. What did such an unemotional man, a murderer, really want from Jane? Why had he selected her?

For that fact, what did Jane want with Tommy? His records described Tommy as showing no remorse for any of his actions, even the murder of his rap partner. He wasn't attractive either, especially with that creepy hair, long, and most often unwashed. He had neither money nor the legal means to get any. He reminded Pilar of a 1960's hippy throwback, a mean and dangerous one.

"Jane," Pilar finally said, "remember Tommy is a killer."

Jane snickered. "And Chad's not?" She moved to the office door. "I'll be in touch." Like a flash of light, Jane was gone.

WHEN PILAR THREW THE last towel into a box, she was glad she hadn't decorated her apartment after all. It was as though that collection of rooms had been rented by an anonymous person. The impersonal aspects of these surroundings did make it easier to move. Even the furniture didn't seem to matter, although it would eventually be trucked to her new place in the Lower Peninsula. As she made one last sweep of the rooms, the telephone rang. Pilar dove for it, expecting it was Chad. She hadn't seen or talked with him for several days. She was disappointed when she heard Jane's voice.

"I need to see you," Jane said, more like an order than a plea.

Pilar hadn't seen or heard from Jane since she left her office almost a month before. Jane had quit her job, and when she tried to visit Tommy, was denied entry as predicted. Pilar's situation would soon parallel Jane's. She wouldn't be able to see Chad, either.

"Why? I can't help you." Pilar reached for a glass of wine. She was becoming more dependent on her daily sipping.

"But, I can help you," Jane said.

Pilar noticed the lake waters had taken on their spring blue-green softness. "I don't understand what you're talking about." Pilar twisted the curtain cord. "I don't need any help."

"I can help you get Chad out of prison," she announced.

Pilar kept her attention on the lake that had become so familiar over the past nine months. She needed to think about what she said next to Jane. She didn't want to do something stupid. So, for several long moments Pilar only heard Jane's breathing. "Look, Jane," Pilar finally said, "I appreciate your concern about my well-being, but believe me, I can handle my own life."

"I'll be in touch," Jane said as she had the last time they were together. Then the line went dead.

Were Jane's parting words a threat?

ON PILAR'S LAST DAY at Hawk Haven, Chad appeared for one final time. She took a chance and broke another rule. She locked the exam room door.

Chad looked from the latch to Pilar. "What's up?"

Pilar unbuttoned her blouse to expose her breasts. As she walked toward him, she dropped the shirt to the floor. She placed his hands on her breasts. "No matter what happens, these will always be yours."

He caressed the nipples. "You sound like you're going to have an affair."

Without answering, Pilar backed away still holding one hand. She lifted her skirt to her waist. "Take this," she whispered, and lowered his hand to her vagina. She felt as though she would explode. The throbbing in Chad's pants was certain to push her over the edge.

"As much as I want to," Chad said out of breath, "we just can't take the chance."

Pilar knew he was right. Yet, her whole body shuddered with desire. When Chad backed away, Pilar lowered her skirt and put her blouse on. "Virgin Mary, marry a virgin," reeled in her head.

Like a woman possessed, Pilar knelt on the floor in front of Chad. She unzipped his pants and took his pulsating penis into her mouth. Within seconds it erupted, thick as cream. Chad grunted. Pilar replaced his penis and zipped his pants. She stood, cleaned the evidence from her mouth, and promised, "There'll be more of that soon."

Jane's offer echoed in Pilar's head. What was she thinking? She had already made up her mind.

Footsteps rushed by the door. Neither she nor Chad moved. Little else could scare Pilar once her life had been threatened. She washed her hands and splashed cold water on her face. The unusual silence signaled their shared uncertainty about the future.   And, of course, sadness. It would be their last meeting for a while.

Chad spoke first. "Tommy escaped yesterday."

Pilar straightened, but kept her back to Chad.

When she didn't respond, Chad continued. "I heard the officers talking. They think Jane helped him."

How could he not even acknowledge her uninhibited display? Though wounded, Pilar decided he was so taken off-guard by the chance she took, he was unsure of what to do or say. He probably took the easiest way out by diverting his sexual tension to another pressure point in their relationship.

Pilar turned to him. "Tommy's escape shouldn't stop us from our plans." She searched his expression for reassurance.

"He was going to help me. But now . . ."

"I didn't know you had talked with Tommy about getting out." Pilar didn't mention her conversations with Jane.

Chad looked like a child caught stealing candy from a store counter. "I thought since he would be out soon and had a lot of contacts, Tommy could help you find an attorney." He almost whined.

"We don't need Tommy's help." Pilar didn't hide her anger over that new development. "Why did he escape so close to being paroled?"

Chad laughed. "The man can't stand being controlled when he's on the streets. He likes his freedom to roam the country. That can't happen when he has to report to an agent every week and that guy's breathing down his neck."

Clearing the sleazy image of Tommy from her mind, Pilar massaged Chad's neck. "Don't worry about Tommy. He doesn't sound reliable anyway." She placed a key into his open palm. "Plan B." Searching his face for a sign, her confidence waned a bit. She was sure Chad knew about Jane and her.

"What's this?" Chad rotated the piece of metal. "The key to your heart?"

"In a way."

"Pilar, quit playing games."

"It's the key to the infirmary windows. If I can't get you out legally, you'll go the same way Tommy did."

"I don't know," he said, still examining the key.

"We'll keep in touch using my code name, Carol Jones, just like we've been doing. But be mindful who you talk to. And watch where you keep my letters, and that key. Better yet, burn the letters." Her own criminal mind amused Pilar. "You never know who can get a hold of them," she warned as though Chad didn't know it. For the moment Leonard would remain her secret.

"Don't take too long to get that attorney." Chad slipped the key into his pocket. "I don't think I can stand it in here without you."

"Well, I'm hopeful my exit will give whoever is after me fewer reasons to set me up, or . . ."

"Or what?"

"Nothing, I don't know." Could Chad tell how scared Pilar really was about someone trying to kill her? Maybe even Tommy. He was in prison for manslaughter, after all. But then, what would he gain by getting rid of her now?

"Go, but remember what's waiting for you," Pilar forced a smile and winked. "We'll be together soon."

Chad traced her cheek with his finger. "Be careful."

"You, too," Pilar whispered.

When Chad left, Pilar looked out the window for the last time. It had taken more than two months to finalize her transfer to Scott. Though it meant a temporary separation from Chad, she was happy she would never see the Hawk Haven parking lot again. As Pilar tossed the thoughts about, her eyes focused on Officer Leonard driving away in a black Ford pickup truck.

chapter thirteen
GOING HOME

MARCUS OBJECTED RIGHT FROM the start to Pilar renting an apartment in Ann Arbor. "It's just your defiance showing through again," he said as he toured the rooms and swirled a martini, a drink he enjoyed earlier in each day. He brought the ingredients. Pilar never touched the vile stuff.

Celeste and Pilar chatted over champagne and Brie spread on sourdough slices. "You seem on edge, Mother." Pilar refilled their glasses, crystal house-warming gifts from Celeste.

"Umm." She raised her champagne. "I'm making plans, but we'll have to talk later," she whispered, and nodded at Marcus as he joined them.

Though puzzled by Celeste's comment, Pilar realized she had made other hints over the past year. Something was up. For instance, Celeste's surprise visit to Marquette a couple of months ago to "just hang out" as she called it, sounding less like a Grosse Pointe mother and more like a college friend passing through.

Then there was their conversation a couple of weeks ago when Pilar told her about the transfer. "Great, Pilar," she sang. "Your timing is perfect."

"What do you mean?"

"I'll tell you everything when you've relocated. But, why are you moving to Ann Arbor? Scott Facility is so close to that lovely town, Plymouth. And," Celeste quietly added, "Ann Arbor holds such bad memories."

"I'm not afraid any longer, Mother." She didn't want to tell Celeste she now felt she had left the University of Michigan because of Marcus and not because of the murders. To justify her decision further meant she would also have to tell Celeste about Chad. Pilar wasn't ready for that. Neither was Celeste. "We'll talk when I get home," Pilar said, almost mimicking Celeste. Both were harboring secrets. Whose would be the juiciest?

As EVERYONE SIPPED THEIR drinks, their momentary silence was interrupted by a beeping sound. Celeste, rather than Marcus, retrieved a pager and checked the message screen.

"May I use your phone, Pilar?" Celeste asked. "It seems there's an emergency with one of the women I counsel."

"S-sure." Pilar stumbled over her answer. Celeste was about to unmask yet another facet of her personality. One hidden, or perhaps ignored by Pilar. What else didn't Pilar know about her own mother?

Celeste turned her back to Marcus. She held a quiet,

steady telephone dialogue. After a few minutes, she returned the portable receiver to its proper place, unlike Pilar, who was always searching for where she'd left it last. "Well," Celeste announced, "that emergency is taken care of for the moment, at least." She touched her eye and wiped her nose. Her face twisted in pain.

Marcus appeared put off by the interruption. "I hope we don't have to hear that damn thing go off all night."

Celeste seemed to take a few moments to focus her eyes, as if she were just awakening. She breathed deeply. "Marcus, I'm only on call every third week," Celeste answered with confidence. "I've listened to your pager and phone ring for what seems a hundred years, and usually just when I've fallen to sleep."

"Mother?" Pilar touched Celeste's arm. "Are you okay?"

Before Celeste could answer, Marcus said, "She'll tell you she had one of her visions. Your mother thinks she has ESP, or some damn thing." Marcus snickered. "She claims she is an eyewitness to events her clients have experienced, but she's not even there." Marcus quickly ushered Celeste to the door. He turned to Pilar. "Can you believe this nonsense?"

Pilar didn't answer. Though she had only become more aware of that peculiar trait of her mother's, how had her father missed it? Despite Marcus' mockery of Celeste, Pilar was amazed at the positive, if perhaps odd, changes in her mother taking place right before her. But then, Pilar remembered, her mother had always seemed to know what was going to happen. "You go, girl," she whispered into Celeste's ear when they hugged good-by.

As soon as her parents left, Pilar poured the remainder of the champagne. She lifted the glass to the door and toasted, "To you, Mother." When she finished the drink, she updated her journal, beginning with her mother's question about why she chose Ann Arbor. Pilar felt different about living in the town from which she ran away so many years earlier. There was nothing there to frighten her, and Marcus' opinions truly no longer mattered.

On a more frivolous note, Pilar wrote that she rented this particular apartment despite the cost. It had a fireplace. She had grown used to one while up north. If everything went the way she'd hoped, she and Chad would need the two bedrooms. And it was in the perfect location — near M-14, US23, and I-94. Getting to the prison was a piece of cake.

"I'm no longer afraid of the so-called serial killer or my Father," Pilar stated as she wrote. She penned the realization: *No one is stalking me. Those evil intentions, whatever they were, went away when I left Hawk Haven.* Her sigh of relief was long and hard.

Pilar pushed open the sliding glass door leading to the deck. She inhaled the humid air, filled with the sweetness of lilacs and daffodils. The scents tickled her nose. "It's good to be back." Here Pilar would be able to enjoy a real summer, unlike the iffy ones in Marquette.

She jumped when the phone rang. Only a few people knew her unlisted number. On the third ring, Pilar determined it was either Chad or her mother calling to let her know she got home.

The voice was neither. It was that of Jane's estranged husband. "Where's Jane?" he demanded in a sinister tone. A figure hiding in the shadows crept into Pilar's imagination.

"I don't know." Pilar had no intention of prolonging the unwanted contact.

"You're her friend. You must know."

"I only saw her at work, not personally." Pilar's wet hands clutched the receiver. The caller's breathing became louder and faster.

"Liar," he screamed. Pilar held the receiver away from her ear, but she still heard him. "You had drinks together."

Had he been following Jane?

Pilar couldn't hang up. It might upset him more. So much for her journal entries. "The last time I saw her, Mr. Carson, was the day she quit her job." Pilar took a deep breath. "She came to my office to say good-by. I haven't seen or heard from her since."

"Don't do anything foolish," he warned. "I know where you live." The telephone went dead.

Did everyone know where she lived? Pilar collapsed into a chair. She repeated those same words she'd heard too many times before; "I know where you live."

How did Emmet Carson uncover her unlisted phone

number and address?   She had only met him once. It was months ago when he picked Jane up at the prison. She didn't pay much attention, so his looks were a blur. If Pilar couldn't picture him mentally, she wouldn't see him coming.

Pilar made a quick decision. She snatched a piece of paper and wrote her will. She left everything to Chad. If she was going to die . . . What was she thinking? Was she setting up a self fulfilling prophecy? "Damn!"

She read the will out loud for clarity:

I, Pilar Brookstone, M.D., being of sound mind and body and being under no duress, proclaim on this day, May 8, 2003, the following to be my last will and testament:

I wish all of my money, including the contents of my checking and savings accounts at Citizens Bank in Ypsilanti, any salary owed me, the cash value of the sale of my car (2003 Subaru Outback) and a $15,000 stock share in Fidelity be given to Mr. Chad Wilbanks, Hawk Haven Men's Facility, Marquette, Michigan.

The rest of my worldly goods are to be given to my mother, Celeste Brookstone.

"Being under no duress. What a joke." Did that include the fear someone was going to murder her?

Pilar stuffed the will into her attache. She'd go to the

bank in the morning. She made one more entry in her journal, listing the names of people who might have even the slightest intention to kill her — Officer Leonard, Emmet Carson, Jane Carson, Father. She drew a line through Father. That was a silly notion. She added Tommy Johnson.

A MANAGER AT CITIZENS Bank struggled to remain aloof when he read the will. His furrowed brow gave away his obvious concern. He straightened his already perfect tie. He glanced at Pilar several times as he checked the document. He placed the will in front of him and removed his glasses. "Are you sure you want to do this?"

"You're not my attorney or a friend. So, why are you reading it? Just sign the damn paper." Pilar made no attempt to conceal her irritation.

The manager hesitated, then reached for a pen. He signed and notarized the will. "No need to get upset," he said. "I was just . . ."

"Thanks," Pilar grabbed the papers.

She felt his gaze follow her to the door. It *schwooshed* closed. Pilar descended the stairs to the secured area of the bank.

Sickened by her persistent thoughts of death, she leaned her forehead against the wall stacked with locked boxes. Her chest heaved with each deep breath. A clerk peeked in. "Are you okay, Doctor Brookstone?"

"Fine." Pilar placed a copy of the will and a letter she

wrote to her mother on top of those she had received from Chad. She would file the original copy of the will with the county clerk the next day. She slammed the box into its hole and turned to the clerk. "Yes. I'm quite fine. Thank you." She handed the clerk the duplicate key and left for Scott, about a half hour drive on US14.

Halfway to the prison, Pilar pulled her car onto the shoulder. She clutched the steering wheel to stop her uncontrollable shaking. "Maybe I should go to the police. But what would I say to them? Would I tell them I'm helping a known killer to get out of prison? Some unidentified person wants me dead? What?" She released her hands, one finger at a time.

Pilar started the car and drove on.

"GOOD MORNING, DOCTOR BROOKSTONE." Officer Leah Whalen's cheerfulness belied the unexplainable contempt that most employees, including her, displayed toward Pilar. After all, she'd only been at Scott a little over five weeks. Pilar attributed the general attitude toward her to rumors and envy. At least the shakedowns at the women's prison were less offensive and done by a female.

Though rushed, Pilar smiled and made small talk with Whalen. She didn't want to offend the officer. Yet, Pilar also didn't want to be late for her appointment with Jodie who was about to deliver her third baby, this time while a prisoner at Scott, the very place she feared. Pilar had always held the memory of her first meeting with Jodie in Cass Corridor close to her heart. Jodie had a tough time coping with correctional policy which mandated she give up her baby to foster care the day after the birth. She had already lost custody of her other two children. She threatened to kill herself if that policy was implemented and she lost yet another child. Pilar had doubts she'd follow through on that threat. Even so, she wanted to be around to give Jodie support.

Pilar hastened through the corridors and endless gates. She hardly noticed others she passed. She was preoccupied with Jodie and her plight. Pilar was also immersed in her dislike of Warden Cooper. She never had listened to Pilar's proposal for a nursery so the prisoner mothers could live and bond with their babies for one year. Pilar offered a plan for a nursery shortly after she transferred to Scott. It was one she had originally started planning when she volunteered at the prison while still an intern at Detroit Receiving. The day Pilar offered her idea, Sharon Cooper nearly vaulted over her desk. "So, the rumors are true," she shouted.

"What rumors?" Pilar was taken back. How could there be rumors so soon? The prison grapevine was daunting.

"That you want to change how we do things at Scott." Cooper came around the desk and stood over Pilar who held the arms of her chair like someone afloat clinging to a life ring. "And you're too close to the prisoners," she said in a quieter, but forceful tone.

"I only want what's best for these women." The warden hovered so close Pilar strained her head backwards to see Cooper. "How can that be wrong?" Pilar asked, her grip tightening around the chair's arms.

Warden Cooper scowled. "Is that what you also had in mind for the prisoners at Hawk Haven?"

"I'm not sure what you're asking. But, I repeat," Pilar sounded more in control and loosened her grip. "I just want prisoners to be treated humanely. I want them to have hope."

"We have enough trouble keeping up with the programs the courts and state policies mandate," Cooper said, "without some do-gooder like you adding more grief." As she said that Warden Cooper walked to the door. Pilar noted her shoes. They were sensible loafers, but they teamed well with the conservative suits she always wore.

When she reached for the handle, Pilar blurted, "You sound like my father." Perhaps her shoes brought out the similarities.

"What?"

"Sorry. Just thinking out loud."

"Well, Doctor Brookstone, stick to the plan and stop trying to make so many waves." Warden Cooper opened the door indicating their discussion, if it was one, was over.

What did the warden really know? Had anything leaked out about Chad and her? She hadn't hinted at an affair, so maybe Pilar was still in the clear. Pilar wasn't sure how much longer she could exist like that — always looking over her shoulder, always questioning.

As PILAR NEARED THE infirmary, she let those distasteful memories go and concentrated on Jodie. The waiting room was empty. Jodie wasn't in Pilar's office either. "Where's Jodie?" she asked Cleo, the duty nurse, in a voice too loud and squeaky.

"She's at the university hospital," she answered "She went into labor about an hour ago. I thought you knew."

"Damn." Pilar grabbed her attache. "Cancel the rest of my appointments. I'm going to the hospital."

"You shouldn't just leave . . ."

"Cancel my appointments, I said. I don't need you to tell me how to handle my job."

Cleo's face turned red as Pilar sped past. The nurse didn't deserve to be snapped at. Cleo was Pilar's only friend at Scott, but she didn't have the time to apologize for her insensitive outburst.

"YOU'RE JUST IN TIME," the female officer greeted Pilar. She stood guard outside the hospital room. "Jodie's about to deliver."

The first thing that caught Pilar's eye when she entered the hospital room was Jodie hadn't been handcuffed to the bed. That change had taken a lawsuit and a lengthy trial. It was an improvement, although the new procedure only applied to pregnant prisoners no matter how ill other inmates were. Fortunately, the medical director before Pilar successfully argued that leg irons and body chains could cause a pregnant woman to fall, or if secured too tightly, could traumatize the fetus.

"Hi, Jodie." Pilar picked up her hand. "How are you doing?"

"You made it," she murmured.

"I said I'd be here when you delivered. Or, did you wait for me?"

Jodie's cracked lips formed a weak smile. It lasted only a second and was erased by her response to a contraction. "Shit, these hurt." She squeezed the words out through her swollen gums.

Pilar had arrived in the nick of time. Only a few minutes into the visit, she watched a nurse wheel Jodie to the delivery room. The officer followed. Despite Warden Cooper's attitude, Pilar vowed to continue the fight for a prison nursery. "Things have got to change for these poor women, inside and outside the walls," she murmured.

The officer turned around. "Did you say something, Doctor Brookstone?"

Sure the officer actually heard her, Pilar waved her off.

THE NEXT AFTERNOON LUCINDA, Jodie's cell mate, handed Pilar a large, colorful bundle. "It's an afghan. Me and Jodie made it for you."

"How thoughtful." Pilar unfolded the blue, purple, and green zigzag knitted pattern. "It's beautiful. But why?" She laid it across her desk chair.

Lucinda scuffed her toe against the carpet. "We made it in crafts. We want ya to have it 'cause of all the things ya do for us." Lucinda shoved her hands into her pants' pockets and lowered her head the way a shy child would. "No one else cares 'round here but you."

Pilar hugged Lucinda. "Plenty care about you. It just doesn't seem that way sometimes." Pilar stepped back and retrieved the afghan. She held it in front of her to appraise it. "Thank you. The afghan will come in handy on cold nights. I'll be sure to thank Jodie personally."

Lucinda erupted into tears.

"What's the matter?" Pilar returned the afghan to the chair.

"She's not coming back. She died."

Had Pilar been so engrossed in her own world that she hadn't noticed Jodie didn't come back as scheduled? And no one bothered to tell her. Pilar reached for her pager. "Damn." She hadn't answered the prison's call last night. That alone would be enough fodder to feed the warden's negative impressions of Pilar, and even possible disciplinary charges.

If Lucinda heard the curse, she didn't acknowledge it. "Lucinda, I didn't know," Pilar consoled in a feeble attempt to hide her own guilt. "Is there anything I can do for you?"

Though Pilar empathized with Lucinda, she really wanted her to go. She needed to find out what happened to Jodie. But, Lucinda required her attention; Pilar's needs would have to wait.

Lucinda shook her head and wiped away her tears. "I've gotta get back for count." She shuffled out the door.

"I'll talk with you soon," Pilar called after her.

"Yeah," she said.

Pilar rifled through the files piled on the desk. She opened Jodie's, only to find the death certificate in plain view. Jodie committed suicide as she vowed. Though Pilar had promised to help women, she let both Maria and Jodie down. She was unable to save them. Who would be next?

Pilar thought back to the day before at the hospital. Pilar let Jodie and her baby have those last moments to themselves before they were separated. Who knew how long it would take before someone brought the child to see Jodie at the prison? When Jodie turned her baby over to a social worker, Pilar returned to comfort her. Once Pilar felt Jodie was okay and had fallen asleep, she left the hospital. She needed to get back to the prison to tend to her other patients. The officer later reported she had taken a break to use the restroom thinking Pilar would remain to supervise Jodie. Apparently, as soon as Jodie was alone it only took a few minutes for her to gather sheets from the bed and hang herself. "She fooled us all," Pilar murmured.

THE SUN WAS LOW in the sky when Pilar realized she hadn't moved for over an hour. She rubbed her temples to ease the raging headache. She needed the upcoming weekend to clear her head. "Oh, God. It's Mother's Day." She remembered the occasion as she collected a week's worth of material to read during the next two days. "I promised Mother I'd take her to brunch."

Pilar looked around to see if anyone heard her talk to herself. Fortunately, nearly all the infirmary employees had left for the night. She lifted the afghan and folded it over her arm.

The gate officer searched Pilar with unusual intent. She went over every inch with the agonizing speed of a snail. "Is this a new procedure?" Pilar asked. Shakedowns were meant to stop contraband from coming into prison, not going out. Though inmates sometimes asked staff to carry letters for them, it wasn't allowed and generally meant the prisoner wrote something they didn't want a chance reading to catch.

"We're told to do random checks, ma'am," the officer said like a cartoon detective. More obvious was her attempt to lower her voice so she sounded masculine. Perhaps that made her feel competent.

"Umm." Pilar was suspicious, but repacked her belongings that the officer had strewn all over the table between the gates. The officers seemed to be searching her more often of late. What on earth was going on? Why was she singled out again?

"Nice afghan, Doctor."

"Thanks." Pilar heard Warden Whitefeather's warning about the prisoners accusing her of playing favorites. That she accepted gifts from the inmates in return for sexual favors. The only gift she ever took before now was from Chad. But other envious inmates, the ones who probably found out about their affair, had obviously spread rumors.

"A PRISONER DIDN'T GIVE this to you, did she?" The officer was almost drooling for some disparaging evidence as she lifted the afghan. "You know it's against the rules to take gifts from the inmates."

"I know the rules. I've been through training just like you." Pilar deflected the question not only to protect herself, but Lucinda as well. "In the winter I keep it around for warmth." Pilar yanked the afghan from the officer. "Good night."

"Have a good weekend, Doctor Brookstone."

"Thanks." Facing Celeste, dealing with Jodie's death, and now the officer's suspicions would make the weekend difficult, at best.

chapter foureen
MOTHER'S DAY

AT FIRST PILAR DIDN'T see the paper stuck into the wind-shield wiper. The note crossed in front of her when the blade swiped over the glass as she squirted washer fluid. She turned off the wipers and got out of the car to retrieve the paper, thinking it was some kind of advertisement. Instead, the typed note stated those same damnable words; "Be careful."

Pilar's heartbeat drummed in her ears. She frantically searched the lot for any sign of a voyeur. Seeing no one, she jammed the damp missive into her pocket and climbed back into the car. Before she pulled out of the carport, she checked the lot again. There was no movement. Ever vigilant as she drove to Grosse Pointe Shores, Pilar didn't look away from the rear view mirror for long. No one followed. No black Ford truck. But, someone wanted her to be aware that they really did know where she lived. Emmet Carson?

Things were getting out of hand. Pilar couldn't screw

up now. Not when she was so close to getting Chad out.

She dropped the letter she wrote to Chad the night before into a post box. Had she said what she wanted to?

> Dearest C
>
> I was so frustrated a minute ago when I got home and found that I had missed your call. I got a late start on my bike ride. I know I'm unpredictable and undependable but never uncaring for you. I thought I would be back in time but rode to the botanical gardens and sat by the stream dreaming about us and wishing you could have been there with me. Before I knew it, I had been there for over an hour. Weekends are the hardest without you. It would be so different if you were here to share them with me. I am always amazed how in tune we are even though we are separated. I love the way you understand me even when the truth may be uncomfortable.

That sounded like a confession. For what? What would Chad read into those words? That she desired companionship, someone to touch her? Chad wouldn't understand that from where he sat. No need to make him any more anxious than he already was. Though she'd been tempted a time or two, she hadn't given into her sexual needs. What else did she say in the letter?

> I'm feeling settled in my apartment and in this town – certainly more happy about my general lifestyle than back in September when I was under the burden of indecision and fear. Oh, but the waiting for you is hell.   When will it be over?   I've learned to live with delayed gratification, though not well. Few could understand how we have managed to sustain a strong relationship.   All they understand is lust, drugs, and wallowing in the fantasies of eroticism.   Certainly, there is no evidence we have done anything wrong or criminal unless caring for and loving and respecting each other could be construed as antisocial behavior.

Pilar crinkled the paper in her pocket. Perhaps the idiot who left it thought she was a criminal or . . . or what?

The rest of her letter to Chad was typical. And it wasn't criminal or weird.

> I haven't learned to live with this whole rotten, sadistic prison system though.   The latest is that Jodie killed herself. If that witch, Warden Cooper, and the department would do something for the pregnant prisoners

and their newborn, at least they'd have a small thread of hope. You know you'd think by now I would have some understanding of what prisons are all about, but when it comes to times like this, especially for the women prisoners on Mother's Day. Well, I don't. They're so lonely and despondent, and there's no relief. I can't understand anything beyond the fact that prisons are painful.

But, I swear having you here right now would make my life complete. If I could only convince you what a disappointment all other men have been you wouldn't feel jealous of my life. There is no one now or ever that has been as gorgeous to look at, sensuous, gentle, and warm as you, my love. I miss you. I know if you were here things would be so different.

Pilar pulled into her parent's drive murmuring, *I'll love you always, Chad*.

CELESTE WAITED AT THE door. Lately each time Pilar saw her, she had changed a little. Her hair was cut in a shorter, more youthful style rather than the rigid Gross Pointe page boy. She had even taken to wearing chic casual slack outfits, shedding years of skirts, panty hose, and heels.

Pilar barely got out of the car before Celeste circled her arms around her. "It's so good to have you living close by." She held Pilar at arm's length. "And you look so much better than when you were up north. That red dress is perfect for you."

"You look great, too." They walked arm in arm to the entrance. "If I didn't know better," Pilar giggled, "I'd think you've found a boyfriend. You're acting like a girl in love."

Celeste laughed. "You'd be surprised what's going on inside this old girl." She swept her right hand down her body and twirled.

Pilar would like to know what was going on. She acted peculiar, and it wasn't because Pilar moved nearby. "Is Father away?" Pilar looked inside the library.

"Yes," she answered quickly and with obvious satisfaction. "We have so much to talk about." Celeste changed the subject with ease. "Where are we going for brunch?"

Something was definitely up. "I made reservations at the Dearborn Inn."

"That's such a long drive."

"No matter. It's a gorgeous day. And you deserve the best." Pilar handed Celeste her purse and green silk jacket and nudged her through the door. "Let's go."

"I had forgotten you traded in your Mercedes for this wagon thing," Celeste commented as she glided into the front seat.

"It's a Subaru, not a wagon thing," Pilar chuckled.

"Whatever," she said in a valley girl accent. " It does suit you better."

"Where'd you pick up that slang and accent?"

"From you, of course." Celeste gave Pilar "the whatever" hand movement – both hands held at the side of her face, forefingers pointed forward.

Pilar guided the car onto I-94. The world was alive with the aromatic spring newness. The scent was both dizzying and inspiring. "Mother?"

"Umm," she answered as though in a dream.

"You seem different."

Celeste lowered her sunglasses to the tip of her nose and peered at Pilar. "How do you mean? I hope younger." She laughed.

"I don't know. You are so . . . happy. And I guess, glowing."

"I've decided to divorce your father."

Her answer came out so fast and without concern, Pilar almost pulled to the shoulder. "What!" she screeched. "What brought this on? Not that . . ."

"Not that you blame me? Is that what you were going to say?" Her smile filled her face.

Pilar slapped her hand over her mouth in mock horror. "You have always deserved better."

Pilar mentally rehearsed how to interrogate Celeste later about her amazing decision.

AFTER THE VALET TOOK the car, the two women were ushered to a window table bathed in sunlight. The waiter poured champagne. Pilar raised her glass. "Happy Mother's Day." They clicked their glasses.

"Pilar?" Celeste asked before Pilar was able to start her gentle inquiry about her mother's major life change. "I'm worried about you."

Pilar spilled some champagne. "You needn't be, Mother." She dabbed the liquid with her napkin. "There's nothing to worry about." She noticed the napkin was pink, a traditional and stereotypical Mother's Day color.

Celeste laid her hand on Pilar's to stop the cleanup. "You seem so on edge. Since you went to Hawk Haven you haven't been the same girl I've always known. Did something happen there?"

"No. Everything's fine. In fact, I'm thinking about going to work in Africa. I'm not fulfilled working in corrections. There are too many policies which prevent any lasting reforms. I'm sure I can do more good working in a third world country. Though, I sometimes think a prison is the third world. Maybe I'll work with Doctors Without Borders." Until Celeste's surprise registered, Pilar hadn't realized how fast she babbled on about those ill-thought-out plans.

"What? You just got settled here." Celeste's mouth dropped open, her eyes lost their glow. "What are you running from?"

"Mother, I'm not running away from anything. It's just that the administration won't listen to me about what the women need. Here I am the medical director, yet any requests I make go on deaf ears. I can't stand how the pregnant inmates are treated, like mules tethered together and led down narrow paths." She slowed her pace and added in a deliberate, less manic state, "Pregnant women need to have rest, more food and nourishing snacks. And why are prostitutes in prison, for God's sake?"

Celeste listened to her rambling, her mouth slowly turning down into a half moon. Pilar waited for her to respond to what must have appeared to be a stream of irrational prattle. Her mother only said, "Oh, Pilar, are you sure you know what you're doing?"

Pilar abruptly stood. "Let's get some food. I'm starved." She pulled her mother's chair out, almost toppling Celeste. How much did Celeste know about her plans, Chad, or at least someone like him? She couldn't know much unless Celeste talked with someone when she visited Marquette. But, Pilar had made sure they didn't speak to anyone from the prison. Who would tell her? Perhaps the same person putting messages on Pilar's windshield.

"Good. I'm starved, too." Celeste steadied herself and the chair as she stood. "But, I still need some answers."

"I want to feel I'm actually making a difference, that's all. In Africa I will."

They ate in silence for what seemed like hours. The break gave Pilar the time to formulate an explanation about her planned departure. Though she had been thinking about it for a while, Chad and she had only recently agreed Africa would be a perfect place for them to hide, if it came to that. Better than Canada. It was too close.

"Pilar?" Celeste put her fork down. She leaned into the table as though she was about to reveal a dark family secret. "Do you date?"

"Of course." Pilar laughed, but fidgeted with her napkin. "I was planning to tell you today about Chad."

Celeste sipped her champagne. "Chad?" She set the glass down in slow motion.

"Yes. He's someone I met in Marquette." Pilar's arms were damp.

"You never mentioned him before. Are you hiding him?"

Pilar wanted to tell her the truth. She wasn't hiding him. The state of Michigan was. Pilar wanted to share everything with her. She needed to share it with someone, but . . . "No, Mother," she answered instead. "Chad and I didn't understand how we felt about each other until I made the decision to transfer back here."

"What does he do?" Celeste's uncertainty was clear in her tone.

Pilar bit into the quiche. She should have rehearsed the conversation better. "He's finishing his term. After that he's joining me," she answered, with not quite a lie.

Celeste stared at her for several moments. "So, he's a student?"

"Yes."

"In what, Pilar? Do I have to pull every word from your mouth?"

Pilar sighed loudly enough to attract the attention of the couple at the next table. "He's studying criminal justice. He wants to go to Africa with me."

The other patrons' cheerful chatter and the clink of flatware striking against plates were all that was heard for several minutes. "Mother," Pilar pressed, "I think I deserve an explanation about you and Father."

"You're right, dear." She gulped her drink. "I've consulted an attorney, but I haven't made any final plans. I want to do this whole thing right so you and I aren't cheated by that self-centered miser."

"Those are strong words."

Celeste nodded.

"But," Pilar pried further, "when did you make the decision to leave?"

"Easy. The night you overheard your Father and me talking about his son. I knew then I could no longer live with that man."

"Why didn't you leave him after that?" For the first time in her life, Pilar wished she smoked.

"I stayed because of you."

Her mouth opened to speak. Celeste raised her hand

to stop her. "You can think what you want. I believed you needed an intact family until you got on your own. Now that you are, I'm free to follow my dream."

"I never wanted to stop you from being your own woman." Pilar's voice quavered.

Celeste reached across the table and patted Pilar's hand. "It has nothing to do with you. It was entirely my decision as a mother who thought she knew what was best for her daughter. I may have been wrong about both of us. But, like George Elliot once said, 'It's never too late to be what you could have been.'"

Would Celeste understand and accept what Pilar had become? A prisoner's girlfriend? Perhaps in due time. Right now, Pilar only wanted to celebrate her mother's new-found fearless self. Or, was that strength always there and Pilar hadn't seen it? "Cheers, Mother." They both finished their drinks.

Over coffee and dessert, Celeste described her plans to move from the Grosse Pointe house into a chic condo on the water at Nine Mile Road. "I don't want anything to take care of and I want plenty of freedom to travel. Maybe I'll visit you in Africa."

Pilar's heart skipped. If Chad and she were on the run, knowing their whereabouts would make Celeste a conspirator. She hadn't thought about losing her mother if she fled the country.

"I certainly don't want to live in that mausoleum

anymore," Celeste continued. "Besides, it's your father's family home." She paused to look at the happy groups gathered at other tables. "I should have visited you more often in Marquette," she said with quiet resignation.

Celeste chattered on as though she were merely planning a vacation. She sounded sure and positive about her decision. "I can't wait to get started on my new life. I have a few more details to attend to, then I'll let your father in on my decision."

"He won't be happy," Pilar tittered. "I'd love to be there when you tell him. He'd never guess you'd have the spunk to do it."

"Spunk, schmunck. I want to live the rest of my life my way." She actually sang the last part like Frank Sinatra. Her determination made her so youthful.

When Pilar dropped her mother off at the "mausoleum", Celeste leaned into the driver's window. "Pilar, I'm still worried about you. If there is anything you need to talk about, please, please, come to me. You couldn't do or say anything that could stop me from loving you with all my heart."

Pilar kissed her on the cheek. "Don't fret. It's just the new job, the move, and all the recent changes. I'll be okay."

"You need friends, like that Jane up in Marquette."

Hearing her name sent electricity up Pilar's back. "I have friends, and I have Chad." She smiled.

"Yes, Chad," Celeste answered as though she questioned

his existence.

To ward off any more skepticism on her part, Pilar fed her a little more information. "Rest assured, he's the best thing that ever happened to me."

"How's that, dear?"

"Chad not only thinks I'm beautiful, even my nose, he respects my brains and doesn't ridicule me for my career choice. That's never happened to me before. His total acceptance of me is worth more then just about anything."

"Anything?" Celeste squeezed Pilar's hand and quickly added, "I understand. But I still worry."

"You'll meet him soon."

"Promise?"

"I promise."

"Good," Celeste nodded. "I look forward to it." Though Celeste sounded reassured, her face was gnarled in worry and question. She stepped away from the driver's window.

Pilar put the car in gear. As she drove away, Celeste called out, "Don't be a stranger."

Pilar waved out the window. "Love you, Mother."

AN HOUR LATER, PILAR parked in front of Maryann Wilbanks' house in Center Line. She called Chad's mother from her cell phone as soon as she was out of Celeste's sight. She was determined to meet Maryann. She also wanted to explain her relationship with Chad. Pilar had to make it quite clear how much they meant to each other. It was the only way Pilar could fight the jealousy that stabbed her each time Chad talked about Maryann. Chad and his mother were too close.

Pilar collected the pink baby roses she had purchased from a corner vendor and slid out of the car. While gathering her confidence, she studied the house for a few minutes. She was interrupted by a familiar voice calling her name. Pilar's heart dropped into her stomach. She turned to the greeter.

Lorrie walked across the street. She hugged Pilar as though she, and not Maryann had been waiting for her. Lorrie pushed Pilar away. "You didn't heed my warning, did you?"

"Lorrie, how grand to see you," Pilar screeched like a Grosse Pointe debutante. "What's it been? A year?" How could she have forgotten that Lorrie's parents still lived across from Chad's childhood home?

"Yes." Lorrie eyed the flowers and then the Wilbanks' house. "Why are you here?"

Pilar was caught and decided not to lie to Lorrie who sounded as if she already realized what was going on. Before she knew it, Pilar blurted out the entire tale. As Pilar related almost every detail, her narrative sounded more like a soap opera than her own life over the past year.

Lorrie listened without interrupting. One moment her face expressed joy, the next pain. She raised her hand to Pilar's cheek and wiped away a tear. "You should've listened to me. It's not too late. Just get in the car and drive out of all their lives. Chad's included."

Lorrie could be right. She sounded more calm than Pilar had remembered during those many nights at the training academy. But, Pilar was in too deep now. She couldn't let go of the only man she truly ever cared about. "Let's get together soon, Lorrie," Pilar said.

"Sure. Great."

Pilar turned away from Lorrie and walked to her meeting with Maryann Wilbanks. She would never attempt to see Lorrie again.

The Wilbanks' house was similar to every house on the street. Most were three-bedroom, beige or light pink brick ranches with two-car attached garages and well-kept yards. Fresh budding maple trees planted when the subdivision was first developed were now mature and edged the curbs. The serenity of this all-American thoroughfare apparently had hidden many family truths.

Pilar ambled up the sidewalk to the Wilbanks' front door. The concrete path was like all the others, lined with newly blooming tulips and daffodils. Maryann Wilbanks pushed the screen door wide, banging it against the porch railing. "Come on in." She held the door to allow Pilar through. Had she been waiting in that spot since Pilar called earlier? Had she seen her run-in with Lorrie?

"Thank you." Pilar handed her the bouquet. "I bought them for you from Chad. He asked me to since he can't do it himself."

"What a doll he is." Maryann nuzzled her nose in the flowers. "It's just like him. I'll get a vase." She headed to the kitchen. "Make yourself at home," she called from the kitchen.

Maryann seemed younger than Pilar had expected and though she had had a hard life as a single mother, there were few telltale aging signs. She reminded Pilar of the ads with the Ivory soap girl. Both had dark, curly hair surrounding a creamy, flawless complexion accented by rosy cheeks. Maryann's athletic physique gave her the appearance of spending her life on the tennis courts rather than as a lady of the night.

Family pictures lined the pale yellow walls of the small living room. Chad and a girl Pilar assumed was his sister, Amy, smiled out from most of them. They looked exactly like each other and Maryann. None of the photographs showed a man, except his Uncle Joe in a state trooper's uniform. There was no hint of Chad's father. And apparently, Joe had been forgiven for Chad's arrest.

"Well, now." Maryann entered the room carrying a tray of iced tea and coconut cake. She nodded at the cake and said, "My daughter, Amy, baked it for Mother's Day."

"Is Amy here?" Pilar smiled politely. "I'd love to meet her."

"No. Y'all just missed her. Her and her boyfriend went to his mother's." Maryann must have noted the skepticism in Pilar's expression about Amy's sudden disappearance. She was quick to explain. "Amy's expecting a baby and plans to marry the guy real soon. They went shoppin' for baby things just yesterday."

"Oh. You'll be the youngest grandmother I've ever seen." Pilar was taken aback by the news.

Maryann giggled. "I try to stay fit." She poured the tea and handed Pilar a piece of cake.

Pilar almost dropped the dish. Taking a deep breath, she admitted, "I'm quite nervous being here."

"No need." Maryann's smile filled her face just like Chad's. It eased the moment. "We're just simple folk, hon." She waved an arm around.

They both surveyed the surroundings.

"I've wanted to meet you for so long," Pilar spoke faster than normal. "Chad talks about you a lot. I feel as though I already know you."

Maryann's face brightened. "We're very close. In fact," she pointed to a Victorian-style card on the mantle, "he sent that beautiful card." Then, she quickly changed the subject. "I'm surprised I never met you when I visited Chad."

Pilar detected a slight southern accent. That was another mystery to solve. Hadn't Chad said his family was from Michigan?

Pilar set the plate down. "That would have been difficult. Marquette is a small city. Our meeting could have made others more suspicious of my personal life than they already are."

"Hope this won't be the last I see you now that we've met." She hesitated. " 'Specially since you're workin' on gettin' Chad out."

"I didn't know Chad told you." Pilar bit her lower lip.

"Oh, honey, he tells me everythin'. Even about that little good-bye present you gave him." She giggled again.

Pilar perspired like a woman having a hot flash. Which present was she talking about, the key or the blow-job? "Oh yes," Pilar sounded agitated. "I keep forgetting how close you two are."

Pilar picked up the fork and took a small bite of the cake. She had no appetite.

Maryann studied her. "You're quite good lookin', ya know. Even more so than Chad said."

Did Pilar sense a slight note of jealousy in her compliment? "Thank you. " Pilar was uncomfortable with Maryann's unabashed ease.

"Ya know, hon," Maryann continued, "you look like . . ." She didn't finish the statement.

"Like?" Pilar let out a nervous laugh as she remembered pictures of the murdered students. Was Maryann recalling them as well?

Maryann was silent. Yet, she didn't hide her examination of Pilar, which made the moment even more awkward. "It's unreal" she whispered as though forgetting Pilar was still there.

"What?" Pilar asked.

"Nothin'. Just, oh nothin'." She waved her hand back and forth in front of her face like a fan.

"Maybe you miss Chad so much you want me to look like him?" As unrealistic as it was, Pilar fished for a reason her appearance had temporarily overwhelmed Maryann. Or, did she also recognize the resemblance between her and Chad's alleged victims? Even Pilar's friend Susan was always mistaken for her sister.

"Could be," she said without certainty.

The two women seemed to run out of things to say. The clinking of the fork against the plate when Pilar took another bite of cake was exaggerated by the silence. While her hair tightened into humidity-induced curls, Maryann appeared collected. She waited patiently for Pilar to talk.

"Wanna see Chad's childhood pictures?" Maryann broke the quiet. "I've kept an album, including some of his grade school drawings."

Maryann fetched the scrapbook before Pilar responded. As they browsed through the pages, Pilar discovered the normal little boy she had imagined. Chad's smiling face and bright, eager eyes peered out from each frame. That shared experience with Maryann temporarily lessened the tension of the meeting for Pilar.

When Chad reached his teen years, Pilar sensed both a moodiness and a smugness. The two women chuckled as Maryann interpreted each photo in detail. Especially endearing were those of Chad pouting – so typical of a teenager. Not so engaging were the many pictures of Chad hanging onto Maryann, no matter his age.

The final pages shocked Pilar. Before her lay the entire history of the student murders. Beside every victim's photograph or newspaper account was a handwritten notation explaining away any evidence pointing to Chad's guilt. Next to Susan's picture inked in red were the words, "Chad admits."

Maryann sat very still. She observed Pilar as though waiting for her to refute what was written there. Or, was Maryann confirming the resemblance between Pilar and the victims? Pilar flashed backed to Lorrie and her collection of victim's pictures.

Pilar wanted to run from the room. She wanted to hide from that likeness. She didn't want to admit that their similar physical aspects were one reason Chad had been attracted to her.

Maryann disrupted the momentary spell. "Y'all know Chad's innocent."

"Yes," Pilar whispered. "Yes, I do."

Maryann took the album from Pilar. "Some day y'all might like to have this, or a copy for you and Chad to keep as a memento."

Pilar looked at her watch as a way of ignoring the strange offer. She had visited with Maryann for more than two hours. "I must go. It's a long drive and I have early appointments at the prison tomorrow." Pilar stood and headed for the door. "Thanks for seeing me. And for the cake, too." She pointed to a half-eaten portion.

"It's nothin'." Maryann opened the door. "Don't be a stranger." She sounded like Celeste. "First meetings are always tough." She hugged Pilar and pecked her cheek. "Plan to stay longer next time."

"Thank you."

"After all," Maryann affirmed, "you're goin' to be my daughter-in-law. But, be careful who y'all deal with."

Dripping in sweat now, Pilar wanted to get out of there. Maryann knew too much already.

"I know about Tommy's offer to help Chad," she exclaimed, almost like an afterthought.

Pilar's shoulders stiffened. "I've had no contact with Tommy, except at Hawk Haven." Her voice revealed her anxiety. "I only know he's one of the few people Chad trusts."

"Just be careful," she warned again. Her voice blended with Lorrie's.

"I will." And then added, "Happy Mother's Day."

When Pilar was seated inside her car, she looked back at the Wilbanks' home. Maryann had already disappeared inside and closed the door. Pilar quickly checked for Lorrie, half expecting her to be hidden behind a bush like an animal ready to attack. There was no sign of her. The street was engulfed in eerie silence.

When Pilar pulled into her parking spot, she was

startled she had driven all the way home and didn't remember one mile. That whole day had been filled with astounding revelations. Celeste's delightful change, for one, and her courageous decision to divorce Marcus after all those years. Yet, Celeste's prodding troubled Pilar. What did she really know?

Maryann Wilbanks was also a concern. Pilar was unhappy that she knew so much about Chad and her. Could Maryann jeopardize her future with Chad? A fresh idea occurred to him — could Maryann be the stalker?

chapter fifteen

THE PROMISE

Dearest C

I was frustrated once again when I got home and found that I missed your calls. My timing sure is off lately. I took my mother out for brunch. After that I went to Center Line to meet your mother as I told you I would. She reminds me so much of you.

I didn't meet Amy. By the time I got there, she had left with her boyfriend.

Chad probably didn't know about Amy's pregnancy and marriage plans. She doubted he'd take the news well.

Your mother is just as you said. She's beautiful and younger looking than her actual age and totally at ease with strangers, if I qualify as a real stranger.

What had Chad really told Maryann? How much did she know?

> I told her the flowers I brought were from you since you couldn't send any from prison.
>
> She showed me the card you sent. You are so thoughtful and a good son. She misses you terribly. I miss you, too.
>
> After seeing my mother today, I'm not so worried about her any more. Remember how I was concerned about her loneliness and need to be with me to fill her time? Well, she's turning a new leaf. She's divorcing my father and getting on with her life. Can you believe that? My mother? She mentioned travel. She even wants to visit us in Africa if we end up there. She did try to pry out of me anything about my friends and dates. It's difficult not to blurt out everything. I must be patient though. I need to be sure she can handle our relationship and the chances we are taking. In time I believe she will understand.

If Pilar told Chad about seeing Lorrie he'd freak out, particularly if he knew that she had confided in Lorrie. Celeste was right that Pilar needed a close friend to share with. All women needed someone to talk to.

I've been reading several articles about criminal justice reform. I'll send you copies. They are very interesting and speak to how I feel about the void that faces the convicted.

I hope to talk to you soon. You are still my one and only. Please never feel as though I want to be with someone else. I do have a choice in partners, and I chose you. You have touched my soul and heart. I long for the day when you are here to touch my body. It is already spring. Soon it will be summer, and I am sure you will be free.

Yours always

CJ

PS   I've enclosed a $3000 money order for your account. This should keep you for a while.

The handwritten letter rather than the usual typed one was more intimate. That, coupled with the money, should guarantee Chad's trust in Pilar. He couldn't doubt her love after that.

Pilar fetched the *Sunday Free Press* from the table and settled into her favorite arm chair, ready for a quiet evening of reading. She immediately focused on pictures of Jane and Tommy. They stared from the front page as though accusing Pilar for their plight.

The article stated that the police had traced them to Florida where Tommy's father lived. And then perhaps to Colorado, where a male backpacker was killed in the Weminuche Wilderness. The article revealed that after the story ran with the murdered man's picture in the *Denver Post* and the *Durango Herald*, a witness came forward. He reported he saw the victim at a gas station. The witness said he had overheard him asking for a ride from a white man traveling with an African-American woman in an out-of-state car. The witness further reported that the victim was carrying hiking gear while the other two were not. The police believe an abandoned car found near the trail head in the area where the body was discovered had been rented by Tommy Johnson. No other details were given as to why the police linked Tommy to the murder.

Pilar placed the newspaper in her lap. "Now what?" None of her research or the contacts that Chad gave her had produced an attorney willing to take his case on. Instead, she had been left with no alternative but to give into Jane's offer to help Chad get out of prison she had made the week Pilar left Marquette. Pilar looked out the window into the dark. "Will this ever be over?"

There was still Plan B. She had been smart to have the infirmary window key duplicated for Chad. Pilar's devious behavior surprised even her. She and Chad had to plan a strategy without the authorities discovering what they were up to. That was tricky, but possible. They would need an escape route into the Canadian wilderness, new identifications, passports, and tickets to somewhere in Africa.

Pilar rummaged through the notes she had about people Chad met in prison who could get all the phony ID needed, for a handsome price no doubt. Never mind. Money didn't matter. She started a "to-do" list.

THE TELEPHONE'S RING AWAKENED Pilar. She snatched her clock. It was three in the morning. Who could be calling at that hour? Maybe it was an emergency at the prison. It wouldn't be the first time she had to go into work at a strange hour.

"Hello, Doctor Brookstone here." Pilar yawned.

"You need to be more watchful, Pilar," the male caller warned. "I know where you were today."

Pilar bolted upright and shouted, "Who is this?"

"You know what they're saying about you at Scott? You're bringing in drugs to those women."

"What's the matter with you? Who is this?" She was shrieking now.

The line went dead.

MONDAY MORNING AT THE prison was quiet. The gate officer hardly patted Pilar down. But she was more than thorough with Pilar's attache. Was she looking for drugs? Perhaps she was part of the scheme to make Pilar appear shady. Pilar watched the less-than-precise rifling through her belongings. What kind of negative signals had she given at Scott? The drug rumor was someone's way to force her out. It had to be the same person who was after her at Hawk Haven. But, how would they know Pilar's daily routine? Damn. She wanted this whole thing over. Chad must get prepared, pronto.

The officer handed the attache to Pilar. It was in total disarray. "Have a nice day." She sounded sarcastic.

"Thanks," Pilar snatched the case. The quick motion forced the officer to stand back. "I'm glad we can't take purses inside. After how this looks," Pilar lifted the attache near the officer's face, "I couldn't imagine how my bag would be returned."

The officer smirked. "Gate two," she shouted. She clearly enjoyed her brief moment of power.

Pilar gladly left the gated confines without another word, though she searched every face she passed looking for a clue that might identify the caller.

ONLY A FEW MINUTES after she settled in her office, an infirmary guard interrupted her. "Doctor Brookstone?"

"Yes."

"The warden wants to see you."

"What? Why didn't she call me?" Pilar sounded irritated. Why hadn't the warden requested an appointment directly?

"Don't know. She just called, and . . ."

"Okay, okay." Pilar motioned the officer out. "I'm on my way."

Sharon Cooper's secretary told Pilar to go right into the warden's office. Pilar knocked before she entered.

The warden looked up from a file. "Close the door," she ordered, "and sit down."

Cooper stayed seated behind her desk. Pilar noticed that the suit she wore was similar to the warden's others. They showed little imagination, like a uniform. Silly observation at a time like that, but one that could be useful for Pilar. The warden was unwilling to change.

Pilar recalled the many meetings she had with Whitefeather. Would this one be the same? "What can I do for you, Warden Cooper?" If the warden's lips were squeezed more tightly together there would be nothing but a thin red line marking her mouth.

"I won't beat around the bush. Remember our recent conversation about rumors I've heard about you?"

"Yes." Pilar couldn't keep from frowning.

"Well, they're getting worse. I'm not only getting letters," the warden fluttered sheets of paper she retrieved from a pile on her desk, "but phone calls saying you are bringing in drugs."

"I know." Pilar was resigned to the accusations.

"You know?"

"Yes. I've been getting the same letters and phone

calls," Pilar related in the same matter-of-fact way she handled Officer Leonard. "Makes you wonder how truthful they are, doesn't it?" Pilar crossed her legs and folded her hands in her lap, surprised they weren't shaking.

The warden tapped a pencil against her desk. "I just want you to know that I have no choice but to keep you under surveillance in order to prove you are not doing anything against policy."

Pilar's back tensed as though a steel rod had been wedged down her spine. "Surveillance?" she asked. "Are you going to have me tailed?" Pilar stood. "How about a stakeout team at my apartment? This is absurd."

"It's for your protection as well as my satisfaction." The warden stood, too, and headed for the exit. She opened the door in her usual way, signaling that their conversation was over. "I just want to give you a fair warning."

Pilar moved within inches of her; their nose almost touched. "You could have trusted me instead."

Warden Cooper closed the door so quickly it brushed Pilar's back. Her secretary smirked. Pilar wanted to give her the finger and yell, "Fuck you, bitch." Instead, she smiled sweetly. The secretary looked away.

AFTER WORK PILAR ENTERED her dark apartment. She immediately focused on the phone's blinking message indicator. Could she have missed yet another call from Chad? She pushed the button before taking off her jacket. "Pilar, it's Jane," the harried voice announced. "I'll call tonight around eight. Be there." Pilar's throat tensed as though something was wrapped too tightly around it.

The next message was from Celeste. "Things are moving faster than I had thought. The divorce papers should be served on your father in a couple of weeks." She sounded cheerful. "I've put a down payment on a two-bedroom penthouse unit at Nine-Mile Condominiums," she chattered on. "Can't wait for you to see it. Quite posh and liveable. Oh, by the way, did you see that article in the paper about the escapee and that nurse? That isn't the same Nurse Jane, is it? The friend you told me about? Talk to you later."

If Pilar hadn't known better, she would have believed her mother heard Jane's call. Pilar erased Celeste's message. How much did she know? Could Whitefeather have called her? Pilar was getting more unraveled by the minute. How much longer could she go on living like that?

Pilar punched the key to retrieve the last message. "Remember I'm watching you so don't do anything foolish," the voice from the night before cautioned. She rushed to the window as though he was outside observing her with binoculars. All she saw was an empty yard and the moon rising.

Everything was closing in. Pilar could hardly breathe, as if she were at the top of Mt. Everest without an oxygen tank. She poured a glass of wine and sat on the deck wrapped in Lucinda and Jodie's afghan and waited for the eight o'clock call.

Though she expected the ring, she jumped when the phone sounded. When Pilar answered on the second ring, she heard Tommy's voice rather than Jane's. "We need to talk. You're fully aware Jane and I know all about you and Chad. If we're caught and you won't cooperate, we'll squeal."

"What are you saying?" She was unhappy about where the conversation was headed. "I thought you told Chad you wanted to help me get an attorney."

"I do, but it will take a lot of money."

"Money's no problem." *Shit.* Pilar slapped the table. She shouldn't have been so eager.

"Money isn't the only problem. You probably know from the paper the cops are on our tails. So we need to be extra careful."

Pilar didn't know what to say.

"We need money for our efforts in this, too." Tommy's demand sounded threatening.

"I'm prepared to compensate you, Tommy, but we have to act fast. Someone is trying to get me in trouble — if not kill me."

Tommy laughed, "Aren't you being a little dramatic?"

"Maybe so." Pilar paced in front of the deck door and searched the area for the person watching her. Was it Tommy? He had her unlisted telephone number. Had Chad given it to him? "I still want to get this over so Chad

and I can get on with our lives. And so can you and Jane."
There was no movement outside.

"Don't you worry about us. You just do as you're told
and your lover will be out of prison." Tommy's tone was
sarcastic rather than sympathetic. Pilar imagined he curled
his lip back like a snarling dog.

Tommy explained that part of the money the attorney
got went to pay off a judge who would get Chad released.
"It happens all the time," he assured Pilar.

Tommy ended the conversation by telling Pilar, "I'll call
tomorrow night at the same time to give you instructions.
I gotta go now." Then he let out a sigh that was so loud
Pilar held the phone away from her ear for a moment until
he resumed talking. "I can't stay in one place for too long,
even a phone booth. My picture's been splashed across the
front page." He chuckled, almost proud of his star status.
"I don't want some do-gooder to see me and turn me in."

After she hung-up Pilar poured another glass of wine
and closed the sliding door to the deck. She caught a hint
of a cigarette's light. She pulled the curtains and peeked
through a crack between the panels. The light was gone.
She was letting her distrust control her. After all, people
were allowed to smoke and walk outside the building.

THE WAIT WAS EXCRUCIATING. Since Tommy's second call
and their planning a meeting, Pilar had been a bundle of

nerves. "Where the hell are you, Tommy?" she asked the rearview mirror. "Come on, come on," she chanted.

To get a better view of the lot Pilar decided to change parking spots. She backed out too fast and sideswiped the car next to her. She quickly wrote a note letting the owner know what happened and how to contact her, remembering as she snapped the wiper blade down on the paper, the threat she'd found on her own windshield. She got back into her car and parked in a space on the other side of the lot.

Every two minutes Pilar checked her watch. She grabbed the makeup pouch tucked inside her purse. Though she knew exactly how much there was, she counted the bills again. "Twenty-five thousand dollars for an attorney is a lot of money. And I'm sure it won't be all Tommy will want, but if it works . . ." She stuffed the money back into the pouch.

Pilar tapped her fingers against the steering wheel and chanted in rhythm, "This will be over soon, this will be over soon." She stopped when she saw a movement in the rearview mirror. Her hands tightened around the wheel. Her heart pumped frantically. There was no way to get enough blood through her veins.

Tommy's lurid face peered through the driver's window. "You got the money?"

Pilar showed him the pouch. How smart of her to have left a note by her telephone about their meeting. Just in case.

"Good." He opened the door and sat in the passenger's seat. He took the pouch and counted the bills

"Don't you trust me?" Pilar resumed the finger tapping and searched the parking lot.

"I don't trust no one." Tommy sounded so matter of fact. It made Pilar's hair stand on end.

"Twenty-five thousand, exactly." His smile was smug when he handed Pilar the lawyer's address and directions.

She read the information on the piece of paper.

"I'll ride with you. Jane will follow us in her car," Tommy directed, jerking his head toward the back window.

Pilar turned around and saw Jane's car parked several spaces away. Details of its occupant were obscured by the building's shadow. Only the dark shape of a head was apparent.

"When we get to the lawyer's parking lot, stay in the car," Tommy ordered. "I'll take the cash to him. He'll see you once I make the delivery. Got it?"

"Yes." This must be some lawyer. Well, Pilar would go along with the plan, though she was unhappy about how it was being played out. Tommy wasn't the only person who had little faith in other humans.

"You don't sound so sure." Tommy squeezed Pilar's arm. There would be a bruise.

Pilar inhaled deeply and practically barked, "I'm sure."

"Good, 'cause it's too late for you to back out now. Let's get outta here." Tommy let her go, smacked the console and waved out the window, motioning to Jane.

Pilar waited until the bronze Ford pulled close behind. This scheme might be crazy, but it sure beat escape as a way to get Chad out. They could move to Toronto and start over. They wouldn't have to be looking over their shoulders for the rest of their lives. She could also stay in contact with her mother.

Pilar took a few deep breaths as she pulled into traffic and headed to the lawyer's office in Southfield. Jane's car followed.

Half an hour later, Pilar turned onto I-696 from I-275. Almost there. Soon the ordeal would end. Soon she and Chad would be together. Together, what a wonderful word. She stole a glance at Tommy. His eyes were closed. Could he be dozing? See, how silly she was to have worried. Everything was going to work out fine. With every mile she became happier and more relieved. More certain.

Suddenly, red and blue flashing lights flickered in the mirror, maybe a mile back. A police car, and it was gaining on them. They'd been discovered. But how? Pilar's heart beat faster and faster, keeping pace with the twirling flashes. Panic replaced euphoria.

The flashing lights sped closer, half a mile, then a quarter. Pilar couldn't breathe. She choked back vomit.

What in hell were they doing? Had she gone crazy? Abruptly she twisted the wheel. The car veered off the road onto the shoulder. She would wait here for their pursuers.

But what would she say?

Tommy awoke with a start. "What are you doing?" he screamed

"I can't go through with this," she shouted back. "When the police get here I'll tell them you kidnapped me and forced me to withdraw the money."

"What police? Are you crazy?"

"I don't want to go to prison. I don't want to lose Chad." Pilar turned off the engine.

"You're a whore. Nothing more," Tommy hissed.

The police car rushed by. The uniformed occupants didn't even glance at them. Before she felt any relief, a motion in the rearview mirror drew her attention. The sun's glare distorted the figure's movement. Jane, advancing toward the car.

Like a flash of lightning, Tommy threw open his door, stood up and yelled to Jane, "Go back to your car and stay there."

Pilar was paralyzed. How could she get away? She fumbled with the seat belt and pushed her door open.

As suddenly as he'd left, Tommy was back. He reached across his seat, grabbed Pilar's hair and yanked her head back like a whiplash. "You stupid bitch," he shouted.

A spray of spit covered her face. She tried to turn away.

"You stupid bitch," he said again, more softly. He shook his head in wonder. "How could you be so dumb?" Then his rage seemed to surge up and again he yelled, "STUPID

BITCH." He wrapped her hair around his wrist for leverage, and dragged her to the passenger side. "Stupid," *yank*. "Bitch," *yank*. "Stupid." *Yank harder*.

Sobbing, Pilar crawled to lessen the pain. "Please, Tommy, no!"

"You blow this, Doc," he said, "you won't have a job anyway." He shook her head. "In fact, you won't even be a doctor no more."

No time to scream. No one would hear. She had to struggle for herself.

"Cut it out," he shouted. Still gripping her hair, Tommy twisted her body to the floor. "Stay still." He shoved her face into the floor mat. "I gotta think."

Pain charged across her scalp. A sharp piece of gravel pierced her cheek.

"Listen," he hissed, pressing on the back of her head. "We made a deal. You can't back out now. I've got too much to lose." He pulled her face up. "Get it?" This time with his hand around her neck, he pulled her into a kneeling position, mashing her face into the gray velour seat, her body contorted and her back jammed against the dash.

She wondered if her ankles would break. She wondered if she would suffocate. She wondered if it would matter. She heard cars passing on the freeway. She felt him reach into his jacket, hear the whisper of metal against cloth.

The driver's door was still open. She could feel the air, sense the motion of the passing cars. Didn't anyone see what was happening?

No one stopped.

The steel barrel pressed to her temple felt oddly cool against the humid July heat. She tried to talk. She tried to ask why he was so angry, to tell him that only she and Chad would be the losers. She tried to remind him that he and Jane were free. She tried to tell him he could have the money. But could this be her voice? All she heard were guttural sounds, gibberish into the upholstery.

She flailed.

Tommy tightened his grip. Now Tommy was talking. Words, words. What was he saying?

Pilar couldn't turn to see his face, read his lips. Where was Jane? Why wouldn't she help?

Tommy was so strong. He held her with one hand.

"Mother, please help me, please." A wild technicolor nightmare flooded Pilar's mind – scenes from the last year, scenes from childhood — lake water, Bud, intense eyes, cell doors.

She heard a loud crack.

Her nightmare exploded in fireworks of pain.

chapter sixteen

CHECKMATE

"Mrs. Brookstone?" A blonde, thirty-ish man dressed in a conservative dark blue suit stood in the door. He was more beautiful than handsome, perhaps Scandinavian.

Celeste hesitated before giving a cautious, "Yes." It wasn't usual to have strangers come to the front door late on Saturday afternoon. Most people she knew were getting ready for an evening at the club after a day of boating on Lake St. Clair.

As Celeste searched the young man's eyes, the image of Pilar's car flashed into her mind. It was parked at the side of the freeway. How odd. Celeste lifted her hand to her head to stop the sudden onset of pain. Fear rushed through her body. She pushed both the vision and the fear away.

"I'm Detective Patterson from the Southfield Police Department." The man showed her an official identification and badge.

Despite the lingering head pain, Celeste's reaction changed to a more hopeful interpretation. Had something happened to her husband, or rather her soon to be ex-husband, Marcus? He was often in Southfield for meetings. Had Marcus done her a favor and she wouldn't have to file for divorce after all? Insensitive of her, maybe, but honest.

"May I come in, Mrs. Brookstone?" he asked.

His question halted Celeste's ambivalent thoughts. "Of course." She led him into the library, motioned the detective to a chair and sat across from him. The image of Pilar's car flashed before her again.

"Mrs. Brookstone, is there anyone else in the house with you?" Patterson sat on the edge of Marcus' chair. He leaned his long, slender frame forward. His smoothly shaven face immediately turned into a series of concerned lines.

"No. I'm alone. That is, my husband is due home shortly." Still hopeful, Celeste checked his reaction.

The detective folded his hands in his lap. He studied Celeste for several moments and finally said, "What I'm about to tell you is difficult. So, after I explain why I'm here, I'll wait with you until your husband gets home."

Suddenly every nerve in Celeste's body was alive. "What are you saying?" She didn't have to ask. "Something has happened to my daughter, Pilar. Right? Where is she? What's happened? Let's go!"

Celeste was out of the chair heading for the door before the detective could speak. He chased after her and circled his arm around her shoulders. Patterson escorted her to the couch and waited until she was seated. He sat beside her.

"Mrs. Brookstone, I am so sorry, but there is no easy way to say this. Your daughter is dead."

Celeste's body stiffened, fists clenched. For several seconds she searched the detective's face. Had she heard him correctly? His eyes said, "yes."

"NOOOOOOOOO!" Celeste screamed and pounded the detective's chest. Patterson remained composed. He accepted the pummeling as though it was part of his job.

Celeste's stomach cramped, and vomit rose into her throat. She swallowed hard and sobbed, "How? When? Where?" She wiped her nose with the back of her hand, not caring for once about proper etiquette.

"A police officer on routine patrol found Pilar in her car on eastbound I-696," he responded in a practiced, controlled voice.

Celeste slumped into the cushion, her vision blurred by tears. The earlier image of Pilar's car sent a cold rush along the length of her spine.

"She'd been shot." He rose without looking away. "The officer found her about 11:50 A.M. The medical examiner says your daughter died about thirty minutes earlier."

Celeste doubled over into a fetal position. "No, no, no." Her moans sounded like a wild beast. "If only that officer . . ." She rocked back and forth asking, "How can this be? Who would do this?"

"We hope to have those answers shortly." He paused. "I'll need to ask you several questions. It won't be easy."

"I don't," Celeste took a long sniffling breath, "care. Nothing can be as hard as finding out your only child is dead." Saying it out loud renewed the pain. She sat up, bounced her back against the cushion and hugged a pillow to her stomach. "Whatever happened to parents dying before their children?"

Patterson stood in front of Celeste as though to hold her there. "Her wallet was found with money in it," he said. "So we don't believe the motive was robbery."

What was that detective saying? It was all too much. If it wasn't robbery, then what was it?

"We'll need your help, Mrs. Brookstone. When you're ready, that is."

Didn't Pilar need her help? Hadn't Celeste known that from their last meeting? She recognized that need too late. "When can I see her?" Celeste asked, and blew her nose.

"As soon as you're up to it. We do need an official identification." Patterson returned to Marcus' chair. "I thought we should wait for Doctor Brookstone," Patterson said as his face reddened slightly. "Your husband, that is."

"Have you been to Pilar's apartment?" Celeste ignored the offer to wait for Marcus.

"There's a crime scene team going over it now."

Sinking further into the couch, Celeste studied his face. "I'm not sure why I asked that question. What would searching her apartment have to do with a random freeway murder?" She quizzed. "You do think it was random, don't you?" But she already knew the answer. Pilar hadn't been herself for several months. Something was terribly wrong. Celeste believed she failed her daughter. She hadn't helped Pilar. Something happened at Hawk Haven, but what? That yellow slicker came to mind again.

"Mrs. Brookstone."

Celeste raised her head. The room seemed hazy. Perhaps it was a bad dream.

"We have reason to believe whoever killed Pilar was following her," Detective Patterson said, his tone hesitant. "We found another set of fresh tire tracks and foot prints behind your daughter's car. Plus, there was no sign of car trouble which might have caused a passerby to stop."

A hand of ice wrapped around Celeste's heart and squeezed it. "Pleeease. I'll do anything to help you find her killer."

"I do have one question. Did you know where she was going this morning? Maybe to meet a friend?"

"No, I don't know." Celeste's voice was barely audible. "She didn't have many friends that I knew of."

"You need to rest while we wait for your husband."

The kindness in the detective's voice gave Celeste strength. Why hadn't Pilar found a young man like him? "No. I want to deal with this now," she answered with as much force as she could muster. "I don't want to lose one second of valuable time." Her own strong voice amazed her. "Give me a moment to wash my face."

"Are you sure?" The detective stood.

"I'm very sure."

DETECTIVE PATTERSON STEADIED CELESTE when her legs gave way. She hadn't expected most of Pilar's face to be missing. "It's Pilar," she whispered, a remnant of her earlier, piercing headache returning. "She's wearing the blouse I gave her."

As Celeste balanced against the table, she began to sob. She touched the blood-spattered blouse and remembered the day she gave Pilar the silk top. It had been Pilar's twenty-seventh birthday. "We were so happy then," she whimpered.

Celeste raised her hand to touch Pilar's wounded, dead face. Rage boiled in her stomach like a witch's brew. She vomited what seemed to be everything she'd eaten in the past few days. The convulsive retching propelled her forward.

Patterson caught Celeste with little concern. Once he stabilized her, Patterson ushered Celeste away from the stainless steel morgue table and the unrelenting overhead lights and led her to a frayed chair in the corridor outside the medical examiner's office.

"I'll get you a glass of water," the detective said as he handed Celeste a wet towel he took from the exam room.

Silent, Celeste only had enough energy to stare at the white cinder block wall. Her hand floated into the air as though unattached. It was heavy. Then she felt the coolness of the damp cloth as the seemingly detached appendage wiped her face.

While Celeste waited for Patterson's return, a police officer escorted Marcus into the waiting area. He rushed to Celeste. "Why didn't you call me?" he asked. "You look terrible," he added.

His voice echoed. His lips kept moving, but Celeste was unable to understand what he was saying.

"Celeste, answer me," Marcus demanded; his body formed a shadow over her.

She closed her eyes and shook her head. The movement made her dizzy. "You'll never change." Celeste forced the words out as his greeting finally made sense. "Your daughter has been murdered and all you care about is yourself and how I look." Her dry mouth smacked as she spoke.

Celeste opened her eyes. They stung when she focused on Marcus' murky glare. "Don't you want to know that Pilar's face was blown off? Don't you want to know someone may have been following her?" She rubbed her aching head. "Why weren't you home? Why weren't you ever home, Marcus?"

"This is not the time to bring that up again." His jaw tightened with each word. He smoothed his tie and buttoned his sports jacket. "We need . . ."

"When is the right time?"

Celeste stood. Her legs trembled when she walked to Detective Patterson. He handed her the glass of water. Her parched mouth felt like she had been trekking across a desert for days. "Thank you," she said. She gulped the entire contents of the glass and turned back to Marcus. "And WE don't need to do anything. I must to do this on my own. You haven't been here for us for a long time. I don't need you now."

"She's my daughter, too," he screamed.

Others in the area glanced at them. Marcus' entire face turned as pink as the walls of Pilar's bedroom. The workers quickly went back to their tasks. They probably had been through such outbursts before.

A brief moment of pleasure relieved Celeste's numbness when she saw how uncomfortable Marcus seemed. "Pilar has never been your child," she boldly announced. "Just as I have never really been your wife, only a proper escort when your business engagements dictated." As she talked, her blood returned to an even flow. Standing up to Marcus at that moment was cathartic. Pilar would have approved.

Patterson stepped between them and introduced himself. The two men shook hands. Patterson looked from Marcus to Celeste. "I'll need both of you to help," he said. "Any information, even the absurd, could lead to Pilar's killer. Clues often come to us in unexpected ways."

"I'm sorry if I sound difficult, but . . ." Tears stung Celeste's face as they streaked uncontrolled to her chin. "It's so hard to believe. If only I was more insistent about knowing her friends and what she was doing."

Marcus grabbed her arm and spun her around to face

him. "Did you know something was wrong?"

She yanked free. "Not really. She just seemed so edgy. She said it was due to her move and job change. And . . ."

"And what, Celeste?" Marcus belted. "This is no time to protect her."

"What's wrong with you? What are you afraid of?" By the way his mouth formed a crooked, thin seam, Celeste was certain there was more to his past than he ever shared. "Is there something you don't want found out about you?" she asked, surprised by her own calmness. "Are you afraid Pilar had too much dirt on you? Perhaps you're the one who needs to be protected."

"That's absurd," he hissed. "You're crazy." Marcus engaged the detective's attention. "I've nothing to hide."

"What about that son of yours? Is he the only one?" Look at us, Celeste thought, arguing rather than comforting each other. How had she stayed with this man all these years?

Marcus stiffened. Small bubbles of perspiration formed above his upper lip. The veins in his neck grew and pulsed with angry blood. He wiped his mouth with a linen hanky Celeste had never seen before. "Don't bring him up," Marcus ordered in a quiet, forceful voice.

"He was always more important to you than," Celeste shuddered, "Pilar." A picture of a teenage boy flashed before her. Pain raged across her forehead like lightning bolts. She rubbed her brow and cried. Detective Patterson patted her shoulder. Marcus didn't move.

chapter seventeen

TRUTHS

CELESTE HOVERED IN THE middle of Pilar's apartment and inhaled the agonizingly familiar scent of Lauren perfume. It filled the stagnant air. A half-eaten English muffin sat on a plate next to an empty coffee cup. Celeste forced a meager smile when she spotted other dirty dishes filling the sink, a habit Pilar had never broken.

Seeing Pilar's usual disarray reminded Celeste of her first visit to the Ann Arbor apartment. She could still taste the Brie they had bought together at Zingermans, feel how the creamy, ripe cheese had slid across her tongue. The store was no bigger than a large bedroom, but every narrow aisle was crammed with heavy-laden shelves beckoning with one scrumptious treat after another – English Lemon shortbread cookies, imported Chinese teas, orange-infused olive oil. In the cooler, they found half-baked sourdough bread flown in from San Francisco each morning, patés, fresh baked scones, and creme fraische. The cozy aromas from the Jewish deli squeezed into the rear of the building floated them into a distant world. All together, it was a wonderful place to share. Celeste craved to be there with Pilar again.

The memory engulfed Celeste with such a heaviness she felt as though she was being buried in an avalanche. She crumpled onto a chair near the dining table.

"Mrs. Brookstone?"

Celeste looked toward the kind voice. For the first time she was aware of Detective Patterson's intense blue eyes. Until he called her name she had forgotten he brought her to the apartment. What a relief to be there without Marcus, as she had requested.

"Yes?" Celeste finally acknowledged Patterson in dreamy hoarseness.

He sat in another chair at the table. He wore the same navy suit, white shirt, and striped tie. It seemed like a uniform for the detectives; unassuming, yet authoritative. Patterson placed a stack of items in front of Celeste. "We haven't found Pilar's car keys and her purse held nothing unusual. From the search of the apartment we found these." He placed his hand on the pile of papers. "I thought you might find something in them to help us."

On top was a picture of a young man. Celeste dropped the framed photo.

"Do you recognize him?" Patterson asked as he picked up the picture and handed it back.

"Yes, no." Celeste shook her head. "What I mean is,

he reminds me of Marcus when he was a young man. So handsome, so young and healthy."

"Other than pictures of you and a dog, this is the only photograph we found so far. Could he be a boyfriend?"

Celeste took the picture from him and studied the smiling, rosy-cheeked face. "I guess. Pilar mentioned a young man she met in Marquette. Chad, I think she called him. She had promised I'd meet him soon."

"She never talked about him to you?" he asked without accusing. Celeste admired his tactfulness, and was grateful.

"Not really." She recalled her conversation with Pilar over Mother's Day brunch. Celeste rested her head in her hands and sobbed. Would she ever forgive herself for thinking only about her unhappy life with Marcus? If she hadn't been so self-absorbed she might have prevented Pilar's death. She should have paid attention to her premonition.

Detective Patterson waited a few minutes. Then he handed Celeste a tissue. "Do you recognize this key?" He lifted it from an envelope. Sunlight streaked across his close-cropped platinum hair.

Celeste blew her nose. "No. But it looks like a safe deposit box key."

"Do you know where Pilar did her banking?" He handed her the key.

As she stared at the small metal piece, Celeste realized how little she knew about Pilar's day-to-day life. She turned the key over in her hand as though it might reveal a clue. "I'm not sure," she whispered.

Celeste set the key on the table and perused the rest of the items Patterson gave her: dry-cleaning slips, address book, pictures of Pilar with her dog Bud, more bank statements. "What's this?" she asked herself rather than Patterson.

He leaned over her shoulder to examine the paper she held. "Citizens Bank in Ypsilanti. Do you know if that's Pilar's only bank?"

Celeste shrugged and asked, "A $3,000 withdrawal?"

Patterson paused for a moment to let Celeste absorb the receipt's meaning. "Is it unusual for Pilar to withdraw that much money?" he asked.

"Yes. She charges — charged — everything to get credit for frequent flyer miles." She studied the receipt. "Why would she need that much money? And where did it go?"

"There was only $49 in her wallet. But the $3,000 was withdrawn weeks ago. About the time she moved here."

"Just before Mother's Day," Celeste acknowledged. The memory of their brunch together on that sun-filled morning punctured Celeste's chest with stabbing pain.

Patterson picked up the bank receipt Celeste let fall from her hand. "Maybe she was buying things for this apartment." His arm flowed in front of him as though showing the rooms to a potential renter.

"No. Like I said, she charged everything, even groceries." Celeste paused. "For the miles." Her nose smarted as though she were peeling onions. "Even though she could afford a full price air fare, for Pilar," her voice quivered, "it was the principle." Celeste looked around the unadorned room. "Besides, there's nothing new here that I can tell."

Patterson was silent, as though allowing Celeste time to process the mounting facts. Then he said, "There could be some pertinent information in the safe deposit box, something that might help us." He took the key from the table. "Are you up to going to the bank to see what's in that box?"

"Yes." Though exhaustion tried to overpower every muscle, Celeste had to go on. "Of course." As she stood to leave, Celeste noticed the newspaper on the corner of the table. It was folded to reveal the pictures of the escapee and that woman Jane. "There is one thing." Celeste retrieved the paper. "Pilar told me she had a friend from Hawk Haven. A nurse named Jane." She handed the *Free Press* to Patterson. "Pilar never mentioned this man, though."

Detective Patterson stashed the newspaper into his attache. "That could be helpful information." Then he passed a piece of paper to her. "I found this by the telephone."

The note in Pilar's hand writing said, *10AM — Tommy, bank lot*. Celeste gave it back to him. "So, there is a connection."

"Could be," Patterson placed the note next to the newspaper. "But we need more evidence."

When they reached the door, another item caught

Celeste's eye. It was an overdo library book on top of an unpacked box. The title stopped her: *Women Who Love Men Who Kill.* An odd choice of reading material for Pilar. Maybe she was doing some research on the women prisoners. "May I take this?" she asked.

Patterson nodded. Celeste tucked the book into her purse to look over later.

THE BANK MANAGER GAVE Celeste copies of Pilar's records. Listed on the statement was a withdrawal of $25,000 from her savings account on July 17, the day she was murdered. Hands shaking, Celeste showed the statement to Patterson.

"It certainly wasn't found in her car or purse," he said, as though making the comment out loud to himself rather than to Celeste. "But that clarifies the note a bank patron gave to us."

"What note?" Celeste asked.

A man who had read about the police asking for any leads about Pilar's murder had contacted the detective. He reported finding a note on his car parked in the bank lot. It was from Pilar telling him she dented his car. She left her telephone number. The accident happened on the day she was murdered. The day she also withdrew the $25,000.

Celeste gazed at the people forming a snakelike line waiting to complete transactions with the tellers. Pilar stood in a line just like that only two days earlier. Her image emerged almost life-like into Celeste's mind. Pilar seemed anxious, perhaps scared. "Pilar must have sold everything to get that kind of cash." She sighed. "But why?" She tilted her head back and squeezed her eyes closed.

When Celeste and Patterson entered the room filled with locked boxes, Celeste's stomach plunged like an out-of-control elevator. She was about to discover a daughter she had never known.

The clerk told Detective Patterson, "Doctor Brookstone came here at least once a week. She kept a large box." She patted number 311 and inserted her key. She turned to Celeste and waited for her to put the second key into its space.

Celeste's hand moved as though attached to another person and brushed over box 311. She held it there for several seconds. How would she handle what was inside? Finally, she inserted her key. Once she opened the door, the clerk removed her key and left.

Celeste's throat seemed to close as though preventing a large foreign object from going down. In slow, agonized motion she pulled the metal box from its chamber and placed it on a table.

Patterson sat down. He waited without speaking. Celeste took the chair near him and lifted the top. The box brimmed with papers, mostly love letters from Chad.

Celeste started to speak, but the words stuck. She cleared her throat and announced in an almost inaudible tone, "He's a prisoner." The book Celeste took from Pilar's apartment flashed into her mind. Pilar was reading about herself. Celeste knew she had to read it, too.

"We suspected Pilar was involved with an inmate at Hawk Haven," the detective said, interrupting Celeste's reverie. "At least from the information Warden Whitefeather gave me. And when you mentioned Chad today, I was sure."

The hair on Celeste's arms prickled as though a thousand ants marched on their surface. She rubbed the imaginary bugs away. As she went through the box, each letter uncovered in great detail Pilar's deep involvement with Chad. "She was going to get him out of prison," Celeste stated without looking away from the stack of letters. "Is that possible?" She rubbed her arms harder.

"I doubt it. Chad Wilbanks is a serial killer serving life without parole."

A knife jabbed at Celeste's heart and bile advanced into her throat as it had so many times over those past days. She swallowed hard and asked, "Why, Pilar, why?"

Over that past year, Pilar had become distant about her friends, even Julie who had called Celeste many times to ask why Pilar had been unresponsive. Pilar seemed hesitant to share any information with either her own mother or her best friend. But how could she hide a romantic involvement with a murderer?

Patterson squeezed Celeste's shoulder. His hand was both powerful and comforting. "If there's one thing I've learned in this business," he explained, "people do odd things, often out of character."

Celeste pulled a small journal from the box. "It's her diary."

"We'll need to go through that. You can have it after, if you don't mind." The detective sounded more business-like than usual.

"Of course you can take it. I doubt her diary can be any more damning than those letters," Celeste answered as she lifted the last paper from the container. "It's her will," she whispered. When she finished reading it, she handed the will to Patterson. "Pilar left him everything."

How could she be so stupid, so näive? A brilliant doctor, no, a brilliant person. Since other documentation proved the will was filed with the county probate court, Celeste saw little recourse but to accept Pilar's decision. What did it matter? No money would bring her back. And if Pilar wanted Chad to have it, who was she to disagree?

Clipped to the will was a picture of Chad in his cell. "How can that be?" She passed it to Patterson.

"What, Mrs. Brookstone? How can what be?"

Celeste saw Marcus playing tennis at an age approximately that of Chad's in the photo. "Oh, I just can't understand how Pilar could have been involved with a murderer."

"It's always a mystery." He took the will from her. His hands were soft, clean.

"And that picture," Celeste added. "Are prisoners allowed to take pictures?"

"Yes. But normally in a designated, less secure area than a cell. I'll ask the warden to investigate how Wilbanks got the inmate photographer to do this."

A second picture was tucked behind that of Chad. "Who is this woman?" Celeste asked.

Patterson turned the picture over. Printed on the back was the name Maryann Wilbanks. "I assume she's Chad's mother, or some other relative," he answered.

Then they both examined the picture of Chad one more time as though it would bring forth an answer. Patterson finally packed it. "I'll need to take the contents for evidence." He lifted the safe deposit box. "Is that okay?"

"Certainly." Celeste was only half paying attention while he filled out a receipt for all the items he took from both the apartment and the bank. Celeste signed it and they each took a copy.

"What I need you to do for me," Celeste declared, "is to arrange a meeting with this Warden Whitefeather. I want to know more about what Pilar was doing up north."

"That can be arranged." Patterson shoved the contents of the safe deposit box into his overfilled attaché. He leaned one hand against the case to force it together and then snapped it closed. He lifted the attaché and looked at Celeste. "If you do find out anything at Hawk Haven that might help us, be sure to call me."

"You can count on that, Detective Patterson." She pushed away from the table and watched his precise movements as he replaced the deposit box. Once again, she thought, here was the kind of man she had hoped Pilar would marry. Wholesome looking. Caring, not self-centered. If only . . . Celeste stopped herself from dwelling on the past. "If onlies" would get her nowhere. She set her sights on how to avenge Pilar's senseless murder.

"I also need to meet face to face with Chad Wilbanks," Celeste said, sounding almost like a detective herself. "There's something about his part in all this that I need to figure out."

chapter eighteen

ENCOUNTERS

As CELESTE PLACED THE single red rose on Pilar's coffin, she imagined a little girl skipping across their front lawn, Bud jumping and trying to grab one of those iridescent, pink tennis balls from Pilar's hand.

That happy memory was erased when the casket was lowered into the dark cave. As Celeste watched it disappear, she was reminded of the words from the play, *I Never Sang for My Father,* "Death ends a life. But it doesn't end a relationship."

Marcus stood to Celeste's left. They didn't touch or speak to each other. Julie, the single comfort for Celeste on that grim day, was at Celeste's right. Though he said little, Detective Patterson lingered at the back of the group. Was it compassion, or investigative curiosity that brought him?

A quirky, anorexic-looking character hovered on the other side of Julie. She had introduced herself earlier as Lorrie and said, "I knew Pilar from work." Lorrie had placed her hand on the coffin. "I told her something bad would happen."

Celeste didn't have the where-with-all at that moment to press her for an explanation. But she was overwhelmed with an ominous vision, which was quickly suppressed when Emmett Carson suddenly appeared. He confessed to Celeste he had stalked Pilar. He claimed he had to blame someone for Jane running away with an escapee. Carson fell to his knees before Celeste. He sobbed, "I had no one else to accuse. She had to know about Jane and that convict and didn't do anything. But, I didn't think it would come to this." He pulled up a handful of loose dirt and threw it at the coffin. "Tommy and Jane took my kids away. I have no one now."

Other mourners gasped. Celeste leaned over to help Jane's husband up. "Perhaps none of us did what we should have done," she said. "Perhaps we all missed the clues." And there they stood, Celeste comforting the conspirator's husband rather than him consoling her.

WHEN THE LAST GLINT of brass on Pilar's casket passed from view, Celeste vowed, "I will find your murderer if it is the last thing I do." She threw Emma, Pilar's stuffed toy rabbit on top of the casket.

Everything smelled damp and woodsy from the humid summer air and newly disturbed earth. Celeste dropped to her knees. Marcus bent down. "Get up," he ordered. "You're making a fool of yourself."

Celeste stayed put and begged, "Forgive me, Pilar, for not helping you."

Marcus seized her arm. Celeste wrenched it free. She got up and faced him, her jaw jutted upward. "You will never change."

Celeste turned and walked to the mortuary's limousine without brushing the dirt from her knees. A gang of reporters followed close behind shouting questions, while cameras flashed. "Do you have any idea who may have killed your daughter?" one voice rang out.

"Was she having an affair?"

"Mrs. Brookstone, what are you going to do now?" another voice bellowed over the din from the crowd.

"Mrs. Brookstone."

"Mrs. Brookstone."

Their lack of any common decency was staggering. Celeste reached the limousine though she had no idea how she managed to get through the reporters. She told the driver to take her home.

"What about Doctor Brookstone?" the chauffeur asked as he opened the rear door.

"She's dead."

"Oh, I mean," the driver stumbled over his words, "uh, your husband."

A shameful smile formed across Celeste's face. "He's dead, too."

The confused driver got in and sped away.

After the chauffeur dropped her off, Celeste drove herself to the scene of Pilar's murder. She laid a bouquet of spring flowers on the roadside where the police found her body. "I will find the person who did this, Pilar, no matter how long it takes." Celeste knelt on the dusty tire tracks. "Why didn't you ask for my help?" she asked as though Pilar could hear. She placed her hand on an invisible image. The ground shuddered as though taking its last breath.

Too late to think about that. Celeste got in her car and pulled into the heavy freeway traffic. She was anxious to get back to the gathered mourners and get that part of her obligation over.

While she drove, Celeste went over her schedule: As soon as all the friends and family left the Gross Pointe house, she planned to drive to Marquette. She had no intention of spending another night in the cheerless mausoleum. Marcus could wither away by himself in his parents' legacy.

Julie held Celeste close in a sympathetic farewell. "I'll miss Pilar. Though she often seemed to be troubled, she was such a good friend," she asserted. "Take care of yourself, Mrs. Brookstone." Julie raced off in tears.

"Keep in touch," Celeste called out as Julie got into her car.

The hum of the mourners' sad discussions and offered condolences finally ended. Celeste thought Julie was the last to leave. But once she turned from the closed door she spotted Cleo, a nurse from Scott Women's Facility.

She cornered Celeste and disclosed that she and Pilar had become friends because they shared the same concerns about inmate welfare. "Neither one of us was popular." She wiped a tear away. "Our colleagues thought we coddled felons." Cleo's nose was red from crying.

"Pilar was always caring for the underdog." Celeste forced a feeble smile and recalled that other nurse, Jane, who was on the run. "Pilar believed she was lucky to be raised with privilege," Celeste went on. "Even as a child she wanted to give back to the community, to share her good fortune with those who had less."

"That characteristic probably got her killed," Cleo blurted without a thought as to how that would pierce Celeste's heart and feed her guilt.

Celeste placed a hand on the door jamb to steady herself. She didn't want to go any further in this conversation. She was sure Cleo meant well, but then . . .

The decision wasn't Celeste's to make. Cleo confided in her whether Celeste wished it or not. "The day before Pilar was murdered, she told me she feared for her life." She enunciated each word as though each one formed a separate sentence.

The nurse's words tore at Celeste's flesh. "Did she say why she was afraid?" Celeste asked. Despite that anguished question, Celeste really wanted to tell Cleo to get out. But she knew the more information she had about Pilar, the better chance she had at coming to terms with everything that had happened over the past year.

Cleo leaned closer so as not to attract the attention of the servants. "Pilar said she was in a dangerous and precarious position, but it wasn't her job she was worried about." This time she spoke in a low clip.

How could Pilar confide in this woman, but not in her? Celeste faulted herself for Pilar's perception of her lack of understanding.

Celeste's attempt to close the door wasn't a good enough hint for Cleo. "Pilar wasn't afraid of the women prisoners. She wasn't afraid of anything at that prison. She was really dedicated to her work. It was something or someone else." Cleo wept as though she deserved the sympathy and not Celeste. "I knew her well. I can't go back to that prison now. Not after this."

Cleo placed her hand over her lips and closed her eyes, then suddenly hugged Celeste and dashed away. For an instant Celeste allowed herself the consolation that perhaps Pilar hadn't told her everything because she didn't want her to worry.

As Celeste watched Cleo drive away, she realized the Lorrie person hadn't come to the house. Celeste needed an answer to Lorrie's queer comment that she knew something bad would happen to Pilar, but she didn't even know her last name or how to find her. Celeste would have to let that go for the time being. Maybe forever.

Glad Cleo left without making a scene, Celeste

retrieved her suitcase and raced to her car, thankful it was parked behind the house, away from the hungry reporters. Fortunately, Marcus got a long distance phone call and was sequestered in his office. In the past, such secrecy would have upset Celeste. Today, it made her getaway easier. No questions. No fuss. And she had to get away. She needed to get to the bottom of Pilar's mysterious life. It would be the only way she'd get through her grief.

THOUGH CELESTE CHOKED BACK tears every time she visualized Pilar's face, the ride along I-75 was emancipating. "Tomorrow, Pilar," she spoke to the road ahead, "I will meet Warden Whitefeather. I'm determined to get to the bottom of all this." Still, she was uncertain what she'd achieve in meetings with the warden and Pilar's lover. Closure?

When Celeste passed a billboard advertising a McDonald's restaurant, her tears flowed freely. "Thanks to you, Marcus, we spent what should have been one of Pilar's most joyous moments in that hamburger hell." If anyone had to die, why couldn't it have been Marcus? For a fleeting moment, she despised herself.

LAKES MICHIGAN AND HURON merged to form the straits that flowed like rapids under the Mackinac Bridge. The churning water rolled into an unlit shoreline and disappeared into an almost invisible horizon. Celeste was terrified to cross the bridge, so seeing the blankness more than six hundred feet below only made her five-mile trek over the water more frightening. Thankfully, there was no wind to either close the bridge or blow a small car over the railing, as had once happened. Though daunted at first, her self-assurance grew with each click of the tires hitting the metal grate.

She was exhausted when she finally made it to the Upper Peninsula side. It was as though she had been on the bridge for hours rather than the twenty minutes it took to cross. Her hands were so clammy they slipped from the steering wheel. Yet she was elated by her bravery. By the time she exited the mighty steel suspension, she wanted to give someone a high five. For twenty blessed minutes Celeste's mind was taken off Pilar.

After winding along the incredibly dark highway, Celeste parked at the Landmark Inn, her base in Marquette. It was midnight and she was both exhausted, yet awake with anxiety. Though her room was refreshing and charming, it was no suite at the Ritz Carlton. She specifically asked for a lake view. Pilar would have liked that. Since her move to Ann Arbor the lake was the one thing Pilar missed from Marquette that Celeste knew about, until she discovered Chad.

The only thing lacking in the room was a fireplace. As Celeste unpacked, she chuckled at the memory of Pilar saying, "All the apartments have fireplaces because it's so damn cold up here."

A rush of other remembrances followed. Their weekly telephone chats. Pilar's complaints about the bad and unpredictable UP weather. Hints about what it was like to work in a maximum security prison. Specific critical incidents such as prisoners' fights and drug abuse. Celeste shuddered at the thought that her beautiful daughter wanted to work in that hostile environment.

Celeste stared at Lake Superior as she was sure Pilar had done many times. Pilar would be amazed at the person her mother was becoming. First, a victim counselor. Then, a woman of emerging independence, no longer seeking permission from Marcus. And now, more confident enough to confront the truths of Pilar's life in Marquette. And most important, finding Pilar's killer.

Though it had been difficult to sleep the past horrific week, in those seven days that forever changed Celeste's life, she had to get rest if she was to think clearly when she met Chad Wilbanks and Warden Whitefeather. So she swallowed a sleeping pill and climbed into bed.

As she succumbed to the medication, Celeste mentally reviewed the letter Pilar sent to her the day she was murdered. It was delivered a few days after Celeste and Detective Patterson were at the bank. She hadn't decided whether to share it with him or not. It was so personal. In it Pilar disclosed how she felt about Chad and that she fully believed the police used him as a scapegoat. She also explained Susan Mitchell's murder as an accidental killing during a lovers' quarrel. Pilar had been totally taken in by that killer. The letter was her farewell to Celeste, because Pilar thought she and Chad would be living together in Africa. How had Pilar really believed that?

"Poor Pilar. I should have warned you." Celeste brushed her hand across the framed photograph she had brought with her. But would her daughter have listened?

WARDEN WHITEFEATHER GREETED CELESTE at the entrance to the prison. How long had he been waiting for her?

While the two introduced themselves, Celeste saluted herself for taking a sleeping pill. As she anticipated, the intimidating surroundings did lessen her confidence. Without a good night's sleep, she doubted she could face Chad Wilbanks.

Pilar had mentioned the prison looked like something out of a Gothic horror movie. That was an understatement. Celeste's attention was drawn to the marigolds around the flag pole and impatiens lining the shaded front walls. They seemed out of place, frivolous and silly under the gun towers.

Whitefeather released Celeste's hand and said, "I've been looking forward to meeting you. Your daughter was a special and unique person." He spoke with a brusque, yet quiet clip. Had that tone developed over his years in corrections?

Celeste was taken back by his un-Grosse Pointe-like frankness, but answered, "Thank you. I think so, too." Her hands were frigid though it was rather hot for the Upper Peninsula. Had the warden noticed?

"I'm sorry to stare at you. But, you and Pilar look so much alike," Whitefeather remarked without embarrassment.

"Looked so much alike." Celeste couldn't help correcting him. "Yes. I've often been told that."

Without apologizing for his remark, the warden led Celeste past the prying glare of his secretary and into his office. "Please." He pointed to a chair opposite his desk, which was practically obscured under mounds of files and stacks of paper. There were even files heaped on the floor. "Coffee?" He held up a full pot.

"No, thank you. I was hoping to meet with Chad Wilbanks this morning."

"You will." Whitefeather poured himself a cup. He sat in a chair near hers rather than behind his desk "He's being brought up to the visiting booth as we speak, " Whitefeather assured. "It takes time to get him there."

"Good." Celeste noted his serious eyes were embedded in hammock-like folds, perhaps from lack of sleep, almost hiding the lines which mapped his life.

"I just thought we could chat first. Get to know each other." He tasted the coffee and reached into a drawer. When he closed it, he chuckled. "I keep forgetting I quit smoking. Doctor's orders."

Celeste noted the absence of an ashtray. She also eyed the permanent stains on the warden's desk from rings made by coffee mugs. Those circles surrounded Whitefeather's work surface like a fence. Celeste took a moment to marvel at the soft yellow walls, a far cry from the institutional beige in the lobby. Did the warden or his secretary pick that color?

Pilar never talked much about Whitefeather except to say he was a chauvinist like all the other men she encountered. Her angry descriptions of the warden often ended in her affirming, "He reminds me of Father." So far, Celeste didn't see the likeness.

Celeste often speculated that Pilar had brought some of that on to herself. Perhaps she was so entrenched in being a feminist that she saw all men as sexist idiots. Except Chad, Celeste guessed.

"How much do you know about your daughter's work here?" the warden asked in a soft tone similar to that used by Detective Patterson. Was it part of their formal training, perhaps, to get what they wanted when interrogating someone?

"Not much. She told me about her general work in the infirmary. She hardly spoke about the prisoners or co-workers." Why hadn't she pressed Pilar more about her day-to-day world?

"Umm." Warden Whitefeather brushed his full head of unruly hair away from his weathered, but affable face. Celeste wondered whether he treated his wife like Marcus had treated her, as an occasional ornament. By the way his shirt looked, no one ironed in his family. What a stupid thing to think about at a time like this. It must be a diversion for her anxiety.

The warden's brow furrowed when he said, "Pilar also seemed to have a deep concern for social problems, especially the humane treatment of inmates." He stopped to answer his telephone. He hung up and announced, "It's time for you to meet Chad Wilbanks."

When Celeste stood her knees buckled slightly. Whitefeather caught her arm to steady her. "We'll talk more when you have completed your visit."

"Visit?" Celeste made no attempt to hide her sarcasm. "I intend to find out who this man is and how he was able to manipulate someone as intelligent as my daughter."

Whitefeather didn't respond.

Celeste started to walk away, but stopped and faced the warden. "Do you know who killed my daughter? Do you believe Chad Wilbanks orchestrated the whole thing?"

The warden lowered his head and examined the floor for a few seconds. He looked at her and said, "I can only speculate about who did what and that won't get you or the police any closer to the real culprit. I'd prefer to leave all that to the proper investigators."

Although not satisfied with his answer, Celeste understood his hesitancy to venture a conclusion that could be wrong, or even hurtful. She didn't prod him further, for the time being.

Whitefeather escorted Celeste past his secretary's

curious gaze once more and through the gates into the visiting area. Thankfully, Celeste wasn't subjected to a shake down like those Pilar described. It was bad enough to be exposed to the security officer's gape. Celeste noted his name, Leonard, on the tag fastened above his chest pocket.

Good thing she remembered what Pilar told her about visiting. Celeste wore a slack suit and locked her purse in the trunk   "Just bring a picture ID," she had instructed. "That's all you'll need if you visit me here."

Each time a gate clanged shut behind her, Celeste's heart raced a little faster. Did Pilar ever get used to that sound? If she were alone, Celeste would take deep meditative breaths.   But she refused to let the employees believe she was a wimp, which of course was exactly how she felt. So she held her head high and suffered the echoing clicks of her heels as she walked at the side of Warden Whitefeather. Her breathing and the clicking were all that was heard as the two traveled the empty corridor. Whitefeather, on the other hand, made no sound as though he wore only socks, or was a ghost.

"Here we are, Mrs. Brookstone." The warden opened the door to a booth. Once you're settled in here, that officer over there," he pointed to a door on the other side of the booth's window, "will bring Wilbanks in."

Celeste looked at the officer near the entrance and back at Whitefeather. She forced a smile.

"When you're done, just press this."   He placed a

finger on an object that looked like a button for a door bell. "And an officer will come for you. You can take as long as you like."

Did he really want to say, "as long as you can stand it"?

"We'll talk some more when you're done." White-feather's smile brightened his face and temporarily eased the tension. His grin lingered in Celeste's memory for a few moments after Whitefeather closed the booth door.

Celeste's heart pounded so hard she thought everyone heard it reverberate back and forth against the walls of the small enclosure. Surely one could suffocate from the heat if kept in that chamber too long. Though there was no air conditioning, her hands felt as if she had been in a blizzard without gloves.

The stainless steel table bolted beneath the viewing window was sticky. She tried to clean it with a hanky without success. She wouldn't lean on it, that was all. It probably had never been cleaned after any visit.

Celeste took a sniff. The mix of odors reminded her of moldy laundry, body odor, and grease. She placed a hand over her nose and mouth to stifle the smell and prevent herself from gagging.

The chamber's ceiling leaned on her while the floor pressed up. She became light-headed from the oppressive heat and stench. She was about to keel over when a sound of a gate opening startled her. Celeste lurched forward. She hit her head on the glass that separated her from the room on the other side. She quickly checked to see if anyone noticed her clumsiness. She pressed her forehead against the window and struggled to see to the end of the room from where the sound came.

Suddenly, with little warning, a young man in prison blues and leg shackles shuffled past the line of windows and stainless steel stools. His leg chains scraped against the floor like those worn by the ghost of Christmas Past.

Chad sat opposite Celeste. With his hands chained loosely together, he lifted the receiver from a telephone mounted to the wall and gestured to Celeste to do the same.

Celeste's thoughts spun in a dizzying motion, almost blurring her vision. The man facing her was alive and no longer in one of Pilar's photos. She pressed the receiver to her ear.

"Pilar looked exactly like you," Chad said as though he were Celeste's good friend.

Suddenly Celeste regretted being there with the man who took Pilar from her. She might be no match for a convict, yet Celeste was determined not to let it show. She stared at Chad Wilbanks and answered, "I'll take that as a compliment."

"Pilar told me a lot about you. She loved and respected you."

This murderer spoke to Celeste like he would to his next door neighbor. She wanted to slap him, no — beat him. How could he even dream they had anything in common?

Yet, they did. Pilar. Celeste took control of her anger and began her questioning, "Look, Mr. Wilbanks . . ."

"Chad," he interrupted, "call me Chad. After all, we were practically relatives."

His bright, childlike smile disgusted Celeste. His cockiness portrayed arrogance. "Look, Mr. Wilbanks," she repeated with more forcefulness, "I am not here to chitchat. I'm here to find out what part you played in my daughter's death." The man on the other side of the glass so reminded Celeste of Marcus. Both could be charming and nonchalant in a situation like this one. Even their physical resemblance seemed uncanny. She had often heard everyone has a double somewhere in the world. Although if the two were placed side by side, the likeness would probably be less visible.

Chad never flinched at her sudden accusation. He was more in control than Celeste thought. Perhaps the visit would prove futile. Yet, Celeste wasn't about to waste the trip and decided she didn't have the time to pussyfoot around. "I'm going to ask you straight out," she stated. "Did you have Pilar killed?"

Chad squeezed his eyes shut and remained like that for several seconds. When he opened them, he said with syrupy persuasion, "I thought we could be friends. I thought we could help each other grieve."

"Grieve," Celeste slammed her hand down.

Chad jumped at her sudden outburst.

"What do you know about grieving?" she yelled. "What

do you know about losing your only child?"

"I loved Pilar. I. . . ."

"You wanted her money."

Chad laid the receiver on the table. He glared at Celeste with more hate than she had ever seen in anyone. His eyes changed from a radiant mink brown to vacant black. She was sure he'd have killed her if he were a free man. After all, it had once been easy for him to commit murder.

Narrowing her own eyes to show as much determination and fearlessness as she was able, Celeste mouthed with exaggerated movement, "Pick up the receiver."

Chad's face immediately turned into the little boy's she saw earlier. He coiled the telephone chord in his hand. A tear fell from his right eye. He was a good actor, really good.

Chad lifted the receiver and said, "I would never have hurt Pilar. She was different." His voice was quiet, yet squeaky like a teenager going through puberty.

Chad's acting wouldn't persuade Celeste. "She had money, right?" she challenged.

"No. That wasn't it. She understood. She really loved me."

"You used that love. You used her trust. You had her killed, didn't you, Chad?" She leaned against the glass separating them to show she would not be intimidated by someone locked in a cage.

"No!" he shouted, and stood. The officer who brought Chad into the room scurried to his side. Through the receiver held in Chad's hand, Celeste heard the officer's muffled orders, "Calm down or I'll terminate the visit."

Chad nodded without looking away from Celeste. As he slowly sat, he said, "I thought maybe she really could get me out of this place, either by paying someone," he glanced over his shoulder, then back to Celeste and whispered, "or helping me escape. We had plans. And now I'm back to these." He jangled the chains secured around his waist.

It was worse than Celeste thought. "So, she paid someone to help you?" she asked. How could Pilar help this criminal escape? Either way, paying off a convict or being an accomplice in a prison break, Celeste believed that in the end Pilar would have been murdered.

"Yeah. The warden and cops know everything. Pilar told me not to keep her letters. But." Chad rested his forehead on the table and rolled it back and forth. Then he smashed his head against the table over and over again. With each impact he yelled, "Damn." Then he raised his head — nostrils flared, eyes on fire, and mouth grotesquely wide — and shouted, "She could have saved me."

Celeste was awed by his behavior but believed Chad had been rewarded for such outbursts in the past. She visualized him lying flat on the floor of a supermarket, pummeling the tile with his heels and screaming, "But I really need that Snickers bar." Like that incorrigible boy, Chad seemed to believe his unruly whining would convince Celeste that he was innocent. He did not.

Celeste pushed the button. The officer dragged Chad away. His face was smeared with blood. He twisted his head so that his wild, accusing eyes never left hers. Within seconds he disappeared behind a door and Celeste was escorted from the booth. Barely able to keep her legs from giving way for the second time that morning, the officer secured a hand under her arm. Celeste pulled away. "I'm fine." She left the area more determined than ever to find Pilar's killer.

WARDEN WHITEFEATHER WAITED IN the lobby as though he'd been warned of Celeste's abrupt departure. Once again his vigilance surprised her. He signaled the officer to withdraw and asked, "Are you okay, Mrs. Brookstone?"

"Yes." She gazed over her shoulder to the visiting area. "But, I wasn't as ready to meet Wilbanks as I thought."

"Would you like to come to my office for a few moments?" The warden took Celeste's arm and ushered her in that direction.

"No. No, I need time to myself to get a grip on what just happened." She gently drew away. Wilbanks had been too self-assured. And she was also taken back by how much he resembled Marcus. Maybe there was something to the theory that rejected daughters like Pilar searched for a father figure with similar characteristics to the natural parent.

Warden Whitefeather answered in a soothing tone, "I understand. Perhaps we could have dinner this evening and talk."

"Perhaps." Celeste offered her hand as a thank-you gesture. "Call the Landmark Inn later. I'll see if I'm up to it." Dinner with him could garner some answers to her many questions. Then she remembered that book about women in love with murderers she had brought along. There just might be an answer in it, too.

"You have to eat, alone or with someone." Whitefeather's endearing smile once again brightened the entire area. He wasn't at all like Marcus. In a similar situation, Marcus would have gone to the club without even asking Celeste.

chapter nineteen

SLEUTHS

OVER DINNER THAT EVENING Celeste and the warden shared their first names. Maxwell, or Max, somehow suited Whitefeather. Celeste discovered he was part Chippewa Indian and had lived in the Upper Peninsula most of his life. "Used to have a black ponytail in college." He chuckled as he fingered the now mostly gray hair.

Celeste pictured Max as a gentle warrior. His facial features were chiseled into a finely honed image reminding her of the sculpted figure of Crazy Horse in South Dakota. Like that stone rendering Max looked more proud than handsome.

"After getting a degree in criminal justice from Michigan State," Max explained, "and several assignments in other areas of the state I asked to be transferred back home." He tilted his head to the window. "Never wanted to live anywhere else, I guess, despite the harsh winters."

Celeste grinned. "There's something to be said for the serenity of the north."

"Mrs. Brookstone . . ."

"Call me Celeste, please. If we're going to be sleuths together, we should be on first name basis." She questioned her real motive for the intimacy, especially after the care she took in choosing her dinner outfit, a most flattering royal blue dress.

Max smiled, displaying a healthy set of teeth. "Good idea, Celeste," he answered. "Let me get started by telling you right off that I had Chad Wilbanks' cell searched when I got the news about Pilar's murder." He hesitated and studied her face as though looking for a sign that he might be treading too fast on painful territory.

"Go on," Celeste encouraged and dabbed the napkin at the corner of her mouth. "I'm here to find out everything I can, no matter how disturbing."

"Well," he sighed. "We know Chad was good friends with an escapee named Tommy Johnson." He stopped again. Celeste nodded to indicate he could keep going.

"We also suspected Chad was involved with your daughter. There were rumors. And she was so eager to help the inmates. I tried to warn her right from the beginning about getting in a relationship with a prisoner."

Celeste now understood Pilar's rants about how Warden Whitefeather thought she was vulnerable. He was correct and Pilar never liked it when her weaknesses showed. "What did you find in Chad's cell when you searched it?" Celeste wasn't confident she was prepared for his answer, but she had to know.

Max sipped his wine. "Unfortunately, nothing that ties him to Tommy since he escaped. But we found these." He picked up a large envelope from the floor and handed it to Celeste. "You may wish to look at the contents later. They're rather revealing, and provocative."

Celeste took his offering. The touch of their hands created an intense warmth where their skin met. For a second she mulled over the idea of revealing the note Patterson found by Pilar's telephone about meeting Tommy. She reconsidered. She'd better not say anything until there was no question about Max's motives.

"Or if you'd like, we can go over them together." Max sounded hopeful.

"I may need your support, or perhaps your explanation of what's in here." She lifted the packet. "I'll have coffee sent to my room."

"Good." That charming smile spread across his face.

Celeste studied Max's hardy, north country features. How could Pilar have missed that man's warmth? Perhaps Celeste was too gullible in her vulnerable state. Perhaps she saw more pleasing elements in him than she should because she wanted to. Was that what Pilar did with Chad?

"Something the matter?" Max asked. "You've gotten pensive on me."

"No. Just going over how much I didn't know about Pilar's personal affairs." A lump formed in Celeste's throat.

Max patted her hand. "None of us know all we should or want to know about our children. My sons all left the state and it's hard to keep track of them now."

Celeste recoiled. She had forgotten he could be married. As though he read her mind, Max explained, "My wife died five years ago in a car accident outside Muskeegan. That's when I decided it was time to come home."

Ashamed that her inner thoughts were so easily unmasked, heat flooded into her face. "I'm sorry, I didn't . . ."

Max shrugged and stood. He pulled her chair out. "Let's get this ugly deed over. Maybe together we can come up with a plan to get Pilar's killer."

THEY SPENT SEVERAL HOURS going over pictures and letters that Pilar had sent to Chad. Though she used an alias, Carol Jones, Pilar's familiar voice was so obvious in each typed line. The most damning evidence was Pilar's description of her days at Scott Facility and the new medical and education programs she was trying to introduce. Given those facts anyone could guess that Carol Jones was really Pilar. Max explained that Pilar had chosen a name from a visitors' list. When the investigators followed up on what they thought was a promising lead, they discovered Carol Jones was an inmate's now dead grandmother.

The unabashed intimacy Pilar showed frightened Celeste. She appeared indifferent to being discovered in an affair with a prisoner, a serial killer. It was an involvement that would have ended her medical career and could have put her behind bars. Celeste showed the pictures to Max. "How could she be this derelict?"

"People in love often do funny things." Max examined the titillating photos one more time. Then they both thumbed through the stack of material from Chad's cell in silence.

"We also pulled Chad's visiting card," Max said, "to check who had been to see him." He gave Celeste the card.

Several names, all women, were listed including Jane Carson, but she was denied entry. More heart-stopping was a visit from an attorney the day after Pilar's murder.

Max also showed Celeste a *Detroit Free Press* newspaper clipping dated July18 that recounted Pilar's slaying and the manhunt. "What does all this mean?" she asked when she realized all Chad's visitors were women, including the lawyer.

"We can't prove anything," Max answered, "but I'd say Chad knows more than he's letting on."

Celeste put the visiting card aside and reread the letter Pilar wrote to Chad on Mother's Day after their brunch together. "So that's where the $3,000 went."

"What?" Max peered over her shoulder. "What $3,000?"

Celeste told Max that she and Detective Patterson talked about the odd withdrawal from Pilar's bank account. "But he should have copies of all these by now, shouldn't he, Max?" Celeste shook the letters at him.

"Yes, I'm sure I told Patterson about the deposit. But I'll call him first thing tomorrow to be positive."

Surprised by his answer, Celeste asked, "You knew?"

"It's prison procedure. Any time a large sum of money is deposited into an inmate's account, I'm notified. Then we monitor the prisoner's mail and phone calls."

"Why? What could you find out?"

Max returned what he'd been reviewing to the pile and patted his hands along the edges so the stack was even. A fastidious gesture when compared to his rumpled outfit and the disarray of his office. "Usually such a large deposit means the prisoner is dealing in drugs or is involved in some other illegal activity," he answered and sat near Celeste. "Especially someone like Chad Wilbanks who has attempted to escape already."

Celeste fumbled through the pictures over and over. Many were of Pilar alone in her apartments. The skin on Celeste's face tightened when she found the one that showed Pilar lying naked on a bed. "What desperate need did Pilar have that she succumbed to this?" she asked Max without expecting an answer. "She was so beautiful. So intelligent. She could have had anybody." Then she sat still and stared at the evidence of her daughter's hidden life.

"Celeste? A dollar for your thoughts." Max offered.

She chuckled, "What happened to a penny?"

"Inflation, you know."

Celeste looked toward Lake Superior. "I was just

thinking about all the nice young men out there who could have been Pilar's partner." She faced Max. "Pilar's world was always so much bigger than mine. Yet I never thought it would lead her to this."

"Umm," Max acknowledged. "No matter how we try as parents, it's not always easy to guide our children in the direction we desire."

Returning to the stack of letters Celeste noted they were all typed except for the two dated the week before Pilar died. They were in pen. Seeing her handwriting, Celeste felt as though Pilar was still alive. She ran a finger over the words and shuddered at the eerie sensation.

The handwritten letters also mentioned Pilar's contacts with Tommy and the plan to get Chad out of prison by bribing a judge. Max was right; the letters revealed Pilar's connection to Tommy, but there was no indication that Chad had influenced her. Pilar's words showed a woman in despair dealing with a treacherous convict or convicts. In her letters, Pilar repeatedly displayed her despondency as she went on and on reassuring Chad he was the only man for her. That she'd do anything to be with him. She never mentioned that giving up her life was in the plot.

"What do you suppose Pilar meant by Plan B?" Celeste asked Max.

"I can only assume there was some sort of escape scheme if the attorney didn't pan out." He shook his head. "A key to the infirmary windows was found in Chad's cell.

But an escape was fantasy."

The cheerful handwritten letter dated Mother's Day made Celeste feel left out and empty. Celeste read about Chad and Pilar's plans to settle in Africa. How silly of Celeste to think she would go with Pilar. Her heart sank even further when she read the part about Pilar's visit with Maryann Wilbanks.

Celeste laid the pile down and gazed out the window at a passing freighter. "Do you know that Pilar kept the letters Chad wrote to her?" she watched the freighter's lights flicker in the waves.

"No," Max answered, "but I suspected they would turn up."

"I don't believe Chad had never encouraged Pilar to help him. He confessed to me that he and Pilar planned his escape. Yet he was careful not to say anything in his letters." She paused to take a breath. "Chad's fantasy about his release was fueled by Pilar, especially after he accused her of seeing other men. I wish he was right and she had found someone else."

Celeste surrendered to the tears she held back all evening. Max circled his arm around her shoulders. They stayed entwined while Celeste cried harder than she had since Pilar's funeral. Maybe harder than any time before in her life. Max wrapped his other arm around her. His firm caress felt so good. "Celeste?"

"Yes," she sniffled.

"What do you say we take a short break from all of this tomorrow?" Max released her and examined her face. "You deserve it."

"Perhaps." She sat on a chair next to the window. "Actually, it would be good for me to have a day of no worry. Pilar's death has completely enveloped me."

"As it would any good mother, I'd hope." Max's gentle compliment was endearing. She couldn't remember the last time a man of her own age had been that interested in her well being. Max was an intriguing person.

A carefree day alone with him was the perfect plan, although Celeste felt like a young girl sneaking out behind her parents' back to meet a boyfriend. How exciting that adventure would be. It just might be the spark needed to re-motivate the life changes she initiated before Pilar was murdered. She was curious to discover what about Max had so troubled Pilar. If she had been open to his kindness, perhaps she'd be alive today. Celeste did need that day off. Though she experienced a twinge of guilt – having pleasure when Pilar could not. Then Celeste recalled Pilar's often repeated phrase, "Get over it."

"I'll pick you up about 11:00, okay?" Max asked.

"Perfect." She walked with him to the hall.

Max took both her hands and quietly said, "Good night, Celeste."

"Good night." She watched him until the elevator doors closed.

Once ready for bed, Celeste retrieved the Isenberg book from her luggage. She propped the pillow against the headboard and reread the jacket: "They may be teachers, reporters, nurses, social workers or housewives. On the surface, these women seem like ordinary people. They aren't. They are the women who love and marry men who have killed — and their numbers are growing."

Celeste sighed in disbelief and opened to the first page.

LAKE SUPERIOR SHIMMERED IN the sun like a thousand rainbow-colored jewels. Max and Celeste drove along the shore to indulge in brunch at Thunder Bay Inn. "It's one of my favorite spots," Max told her earlier when he helped Celeste into his truck. "I like the nearby Big Bay Light House, too. It's a fun B&B. If you catch Chuck, the owner, at the right time, he'll give you a hilarious history of the old place."

When they parked outside the inn, Celeste remembered why the building was familiar. "Max, isn't this the place featured in *Anatomy of a Murder?*"

"It sure is." He reached for Celeste's arm to help her from the truck's high passenger seat. His eyes were wide awake, the puffiness she saw the day before had nearly disappeared.

"What fun!" she announced. Then she thought of the irony. To allay her sudden sadness, she asked, "I wonder if Pilar ever came out here?" She quickly added, "Sorry, no work and no grieving today. That was my promise."

"Good." Max beamed, his grin enhancing the creases around his eyes and mouth.

They sauntered toward the entrance as though they wanted to fill their lungs with the warm, entangled scent of woods and water, while listening to the silence of a fairy tale moment. Max moved his arm in a circle to show off the locale. "It's like having my soul massaged," he said in a subdued voice so as not to disturb the surroundings or stir up the deer that lingered in the brush on the other side of Lake Independence.

In response Celeste sniffed and admitted, "It's both refreshing and soothing." Sticking her nose up to the sky like a howling wolf, she took another exaggerated whiff. "And makes me hungry." She giggled. She had never shared such a moment with Marcus, not even in college.

AFTER ENJOYING A SLOW, scrumptious brunch, Max drove them out to the Big Bay Lighthouse. The historical building appeared to hang precariously from the perilous rock cliffs overlooking the unimpeded expanse of Lake Superior. "What a magnificent place," Celeste commented as she peered over the craggy outcropping. "It's the perfect spot to hide from the daily grind." She turned to Max. His lined face was highlighted by the sun.

"You're absolutely right, Celeste." Max's cheery response was almost swallowed by the wind as it mingled with the crashing waves below.

Watching Max's hair dance in the breeze, Celeste was convinced that she belonged here. Not necessarily this specific location but in that confident serenity, so far from Marcus' chastising. How had she become so comfortable with Max, a man she barely knew? It was like a scene from a soap opera — immediate attraction between two strangers threaded together by a horrible event. Max's unyielding attention to Celeste and Pilar's death re-enforced her belief that he also sensed they were meant to be together in some fashion or another.

"I'd like to move to this very spot." Celeste laughed.

"The B&B is up for sale," Max said. "Chuck says it's time for him to retire. Want to buy it?"

For a moment Celeste was tempted to say "yes". She looked at Max's hopeful expression and then at the red brick and white clapboard building. "Maybe, but to live in, not run as a B&B. I'm not much of a cook."

"You could learn."

Celeste thought about all the scone and muffin recipes she'd been trying lately. She needed more than those to appease the appetites of hungry guests.

They sat on the stone bench near the edge of the property and watched the sun lower in the west. It became a spectacular orange, red, and purple sunset. And just as Celeste had hoped, the green flash shone as the red ball made its final descent. When it ended, Max held her arm and ushered her away in silence. It had been a perfect day.

Even without that ideal outing, Celeste couldn't look forward to going back to Grosse Pointe Shores. But she must leave the pristine north country and face Marcus for one last time in his own environment.

Thinking about all those years she wasted with Marcus, Celeste realized that she wasn't much different than Pilar. Hadn't she let herself be swept away by Marcus' charm, good looks, and his place in society? At first he made Celeste feel beautiful, smart, and capable until she couldn't deliver a son. She also chose to stay in a relationship she knew was not good. A relationship that sometimes blinded her. A bond that smothered and almost killed her. When Celeste read the Isenburg book the night before, the study brought home the truth: Pilar and she were both taken in by charismatic murderers of one kind or another. People only saw what they wanted in others. What had Celeste seen in Max?

chapter twenty

EXIT

AS QUICKLY AS CELESTE put clothes into a packing box, Marcus took them out. He threw them onto the bed they had stopped sharing long ago. Celeste never liked that bed anyway, but that wouldn't be enough to get her through this awful scene.

"You can keep this up all day, Marcus, but I'm not changing my mind." Celeste stood before him with a blouse in her hand.

Marcus seized her wrist. The force propelled Celeste forward. She dropped the blouse. "You can't leave. Think of what people will say," Marcus whined. "There's never been a divorce in my family."

"To hell with people and what they think." She yanked her wrist free and rubbed the red finger marks away. "Their thoughts never got me anywhere. Their thoughts didn't save Pilar, and neither did you." Though her eyes burned, she refused to cry in front of Marcus anymore, or to look away in shame. "I've had enough. What is left of my life is all mine, no one else's."

"But Celeste," Marcus shook her shoulders, "Pilar's funeral was only a few months ago. Give it time."

She shrugged loose from Marcus' clutch. "I gave it thirty years. I have no more time." The hate in her tone sounded good to her.

Marcus' eyes almost formed perfect circles as his voice gained an octave. "I've been honest with you since Pilar's death . . ."

"Murder," she chided.

Marcus disregarded her correction. "You can't do this," he shouted. He whacked his fist against the dressing table. Perfume bottles and brush bounced across its surface. Chad's tantrum flashed before Celeste.

"Watch me." Celeste picked up her purse. "I'll have my attorney send someone here to pack my belongings." She gazed around the bedroom. It looked as though it had been burglarized.

Before Marcus answered or had a chance to stop Celeste, she rushed out the door and slammed it. She skipped down the stairs and out the front entrance. As she drove through the gate and onto Lake Shore Road for the last time, Celeste hummed Frank Sinatra's hit song, *I Did it My Way*. Speeding to her new condo, she heard Pilar's voice kidding her about singing that song just as Celeste did the last day they spent together.

Celeste also reviewed the scene that took place earlier

that morning. Before the packing began, Marcus tried one more time to gain Celeste's sympathy. Maybe he thought if he shared proof of his other family she wouldn't leave him. When he handed her a stack of pictures and official documents to peruse, she had no intention of giving him any satisfaction. She refused to look at them. Those papers and photos only reminded her of how many years she let him fool her. "Just like Chad fooled Pilar," she murmured.

Though Marcus hadn't realized, Celeste always knew he had another woman. But Celeste didn't want to acknowledge there could also be a son. She remained in denial until she saw them walking together near Tiger Stadium. Pilar had just turned sixteen.

Celeste confronted Marcus that very night about the boy. When he gave his rationale, she was painfully aware of the familiar spin. There were many times over prior years Marcus tried to tell her about his son. Yet, like Pilar with Chad, Celeste wouldn't accept the truth. Celeste so wanted to believe nothing was wrong and that they could be happy.

Marcus' awkward, self-centered attempts at confession always ended in his need for Celeste to forgive him. "I don't see them anymore, " he had said so many times, as if it made it better. Though Celeste heard the word "them" when Marcus used it, she continued to tell herself there was only a woman. Never would she let herself believe there could be a child, until that day she saw Marcus and him.

"What about the boy?" Celeste once shouted back after she finally faced the dreaded reality. "Who will take care of him?"

Celeste remembered as clearly as though it had happened earlier that day. Marcus lowered his head like a hurt child, obviously hoping to stir compassion in her. "I arranged a trust for him," he said. "His mother gets an allowance, too. Both will be cared for as long as my identity remains unknown."

"How thoughtful, Marcus," Celeste responded with deliberate sarcasm. Marcus never let her know his mistress' or illegitimate son's names. He always said them, and her, and him.

That was as far as they ever got. Celeste never saw the pictures or copies of any documents until that morning. And Marcus sounded just as he did those other times. "I don't see them anymore," he said. He never realized that wasn't the point.

CELESTE SWUNG HER CAR into her new stall and bounded for the elevator. The quick ride to the top of the building took Celeste to her sanctuary far from Marcus and his childish pleas. Once inside her condo, Celeste calmed as she gazed out the cathedral window at Lake St. Claire across to the Canadian shoreline. While she once again pondered the drama of that morning with Marcus, Celeste retrieved the packet he had given her. She withdrew a picture and what looked like a contract from the envelope. "Poor Pilar." Celeste fingered a photograph of a thirteen-year-old boy nestled between some woman and Marcus. "Just like the winners of the perfect American family," she sneered at the threesome.   Still, she was curious about the actual reason Marcus wanted her to have the pictures and a document that set the rules for child support and a form of alimony. Knowing him as she did, it had to be a self-serving motive. Celeste would probably never find out his reasons and didn't care. She tossed the contents into a dresser drawer.

Celeste headed for her new, tidy kitchen to make a cup of tea. As she passed each room, she decided that condo living would suit her just fine. She liked the openness of the great room. She had picked the condo for its oversized windows which allowed in an abundance of sunlight. She no longer needed privacy and certainly had no reason to have space, as Pilar often put it. And like those silly gloves Pilar chided her about, Celeste didn't need all the adornment, the stuff which was only a façade and cluttered her life. Still, her quarters weren't as sparse as Pilar's. Celeste indulged herself in a few niceties with the help of a decorator, particularly for her own bedroom — the master suite.

"Besides, I'm still looking at beautiful Lake St. Clair," she told Phoenix, a tabby kitten newly adopted from the Humane Society. She scratched him under the chin. In response, he pulled himself into an arch. Then he stretched full length across the top of the couch to lounge in the sun.

Celeste picked up the gold frame holding Pilar's graduation picture. She touched Pilar's face, glowing with eagerness and hope. "I wish you could see me now. You'd be proud." She set the picture down on the grand piano on which Pilar rehearsed for hours as a teenager. The piano and Pilar's bedroom set in the condo's guest room were the only pieces of furniture she moved from the Brookstone house. "I wish we could share every moment I have left." Celeste stroked the piano.

While touring with the real estate agent on the day Celeste first saw the condo's guest-bedroom, she decided right then to recreate Pilar's room as though she would be coming home any day. Her antique canopy bed snugged one wall of the quarters painted in a similar soft pink as Pilar had chosen when she was eight-years-old. To either side were the matching night stands, and at the foot was Pilar's toy chest still overflowing with stuffed animals, doll clothes, small battery operated cars, and a play doctor's kit. Even the mauve floral print spread and awning, Pilar's secret garden, were ready for a welcome home.

Celeste pulled a tissue from a box on the kitchen counter and blew her nose. She wiped her tear-dampened face. Would she ever get beyond the heartache?

She sat at the breakfast bar stirring her tea. She was stymied over what she should do next. Though there was a nationwide hunt for Tommy Johnson and Jane Carson, the police investigation seemed stalled. There had only been a few hints of Johnson's whereabouts: Jane's abandoned car found at the airport in Knoxville, Tennessee shortly after Pilar's murder; their visit to Tommy's father in Florida; and the description of an armed robber that sounded like Tommy. The couple also rented a motor home in Miami which was later found in Albuquerque, New Mexico. Then there was that young man who was killed in Colorado.

"Oh, my God. How many more victims will there be?" Celeste asked herself.

She picked up the telephone and called Max Whitefeather. Over the past weeks he had become a friend and confidante. They also discussed ideas and thoughts about how they could help in the search for Tommy Johnson and Jane Carson, as if what they determined made a difference to the police. No matter, Celeste felt better thinking she contributed, even if in a minor way. Better than sitting on her hands.

When Jane's car was found in the early days of Tommy Johnson's escape, and other information had been gathered from hotel clerks along the I-75 corridor to Florida, Celeste and Max were certain Jane was with Tommy. Max never said, but Celeste was positive he believed as she did, Jane had been a willing participant in the extortion plot from the beginning. Jane might even have encouraged Tommy to kill.

While Celeste waited to be connected to the warden's office, she reminisced about past conversations with Max.

He told her that shortly after the news of Pilar's murder was out, Jane's husband, with their nine-year-old son and seven-year-old daughter in tow, showed up in his office. Emmet Carson told Max he suspected Jane's affair with a prisoner for months, but knew little about Pilar. Max admitted he was suspicious by nature, so he passed that information to the police. "One never knows who could be the murderer until he or she is caught," Max explained. Right after that visit Jane kidnapped her children.

"HELLO, MAX," CELESTE ALMOST shouted into the telephone. She was glad he finally came on the line and stopped her thinking about the Carsons. "What's the chance we can get together soon?"

Celeste and Max planned to meet the following night in West Branch, a city on I-75 halfway between their two homes. While they had talked about their rendezvous, Celeste asked Max why he cared about finding Pilar's murderer. She had felt he seemed concerned beyond a warden's determination to right a wrong or to get the offender. He was even more determined than Marcus, but that wasn't saying much. Through their telephone conversation Celeste discovered Max thought of Pilar as the daughter he never had. "I wanted to protect her without suspicion being cast that I favored Pilar, or give people reason to think I was overly fond of her," he admitted. "I shouldn't have given a damn about appearances. I might have saved her."

CELESTE'S SPIRITS SOARED. HER body burned in anticipation. She scolded herself for acting like a foolish girl swooning over a recording star. After Celeste changed into pajamas and robe, she asked Phoenix. "Doesn't this call for a glass of wine?" Phoenix purred as Celeste scratched his ears.

Celeste plopped on the couch next to the cat and turned on the TV. As she sipped the wine, John Walsh, the host of "America's Most Wanted", talked about a dangerous criminal who had eluded the police for nearly two years.

"Maybe Max and I should contact the producers of this show," she speculated out loud, but looked at Phoenix as though he would answer. "They might have better luck than the police have had finding Tommy and Jane."

CELESTE AND MAX MET at the West Branch Country Club for cocktails and dinner. Though they each booked a room at Tri Terrace Motel, a Mom and Pop business sprawled lazily along route 76, they left in separate cars so as not to fuel curiosity.

Celeste was refreshed by the short drive east to the outskirts of town. The perfect late autumn sunset highlighted the remaining gold, orange, and red of the almost barren oak trees lining the streets of the snug community. But when the horizon ahead glowed in that pink moment, the time of day that always thrilled Pilar, Celeste's heart sank.

She ached for Pilar to be there with her.

Celeste spotted Max waiting at the club entrance. The fading sunlight seemed to hesitate for a moment at the top of his head to show off his newly styled hair. She smiled thinking about how Max must struggle to keep its wildness under control without using hair spray, which he had at one time acknowledged he despised.

As suddenly as Celeste's heart had plummeted earlier, it leapt at the sight of his comfortable looks. She parked and checked her face in the visor mirror before hopping out, surprised by the quick return of her uplifted spirit. "Get a grip," she said, and then clasped her hand over her mouth in shock because she sounded just like Pilar.

Max placed a hand on Celeste's elbow and guided her through the entrance. He apparently hadn't totally given up on old-fashioned gentlemanly ways. When he helped Celeste remove her cashmere coat, she congratulated herself for leaving her politically incorrect furs with Marcus. It was one more positive step she had taken. It was a decision similar to the one Pilar made when she got rid of the Mercedes.

Once seated in the lounge before a newly kindled fire, Celeste eased into the cushions of the over-stuffed chair. "Thank you for coming, Max. I had to get away from all that media junk." She handed him a stack of newspaper clippings. "Here's the latest. At least the reporters' phone calls ended once I moved and delisted my number. Leaving my condo is also easier without the throng of photographers chasing after me."

"It had to be a horror show," Max acknowledged. As he took the articles, he paused long enough for his touch to register. Celeste's palm heated as though it was seared with a branding iron. Similar moments at the Thunder Bay Inn and the light house came to mind.

"I've been following all these from Marquette. The news is as big there because Pilar worked at the prison." Max set the stack to the side. "But not this one." He removed the top article from the pile. The headline jumped from the page: **DID PRISON ROMANCE LEAD WOMAN DOCTOR TO HER DEATH?**

"How did this journalist get that information?" Max asked.

The waitress brought their martinis. She glanced at the headline and said, "Terrible what happened to that doctor. I hope the police have better luck in finding her killer than they did the guy who murdered Mr. Batchelor and his girl-friend up here years ago."

Celeste covered her mouth to keep a gasp from slip-ping out. Then she checked her hurt feelings. The waitress couldn't have known she was Pilar's mother. When the waitress left, Celeste answered Max. "The story only refers to sources."

Max threw the article back on top of the others and tasted his martini. "Who told this guy about Wilbanks? I haven't let any reporters near him."

"Chad can call the reporters collect, can't he?" Celeste was amazed at how much she had learned about prison life.

"Yes. But we've been monitoring his calls and he's not placed one to a reporter." Max tapped his fingers against the table. He pursed his lips and became reflective.

The liquid of Celeste's martini flowed like a hot line of lava through her body. She set the glass down and said, "A dollar for your thoughts." An old Glenn Miller tune, "String of Pearls", played in the background.

"Sorry. I was thinking about Chad's phone calls. He may not be contacting the media, but his mother might. Then, again, there could be a leak in the system."

Celeste placed a hand on his to stop the tapping and said, "And there has been news about the cross-country chase for Jane Carson and Tommy Johnson since his escape. I'd think it would be easy for a good reporter to dig up the real dirt."

Celeste removed her hand from his. Max placed the freed hand in his lap and studied her for a few moments. "So, Celeste, why are you so anxious to see me, other than I'm such a fascinating and handsome man?" he asked, as his cheery smile relaxed her.

"What better reason than that?" she teased. The martini loosened Celeste's inhibitions and she decided to tell her whole story to that kind man. "Well, Max, here it goes."

An hour later, Celeste finished her tale about Marcus' affair, his illegitimate son, how alienated from her father

Pilar always felt, and how guilty Celeste herself felt because she did very little to stop Pilar's murder. Max's face reflected sadness more than sympathy.

The waitress saved him from a comment for the moment when she led them from the lounge into the dining area. In the candle light, Max appeared younger and less downcast. Did Celeste want to see him that way because she feared he didn't want to remain a friend with a woman with such a mixed up past?

"Well? Do you have anything to say?" Celeste finally asked.

Max leaned back in his chair. "Your family saga sounds like something from that soap, "The Young and the Restless"."

"That stings." Celeste scrunched her face in pretend pain and then took a hefty drink of her second martini.

"I didn't mean anything harmful, Celeste. It's just a lot to handle all at once." He gulped his drink. "But it doesn't change anything between us."

Celeste pursed her lips to one side and examined his face. Max seemed receptive. "You know, I took a chance letting you in on this sordid mess."

Moving closer to Celeste, Max lifted her hand and kissed the fingers. She sizzled from her face to her toes. He lowered her hand but didn't release it. "I know you did. The truth only makes us closer. Thank you for telling me before the story comes out in the tabloids."

"What?" Her sudden movement caused a small portion of her drink to spill. "I don't plan to tell anyone else. And I'm sure Marcus won't ruin his reputation."

"No, I agree. But then, there's Maryann Wilbanks or Marcus' mistresses." He beckoned to the waitress.

"Why would they want to say anything?" Celeste had never considered there could be more than one mistress in Marcus' life. She chose not to ask why Max said that.

"Money," Max answered with certainty.

That comment upset Celeste, but then she knew Marcus. He'd buy off anyone to keep his reputation intact. Hopefully, he'd have that chance before a tabloid was willing to pay a mouthy person.

After they ordered dinner and wine, Max asked, "Why didn't you have more children?"

"We tried, but something went haywire. I suffered a lot of problems and finally had a hysterectomy."

"I'm so sorry, Celeste." Max reached across the table and stroked her cheek.

"Me, too. Maybe things would have been different for Pilar and me if Marcus and I also had a son. We'll never know." Certain Marcus would have been different to her with or without a son, Celeste hadn't ever dwelled on that issue until Pilar's death.

Once their dinner was served, they ate rather than talked. Each needed time to process the evening, particularly the baring of Celeste's soul, and Max' unexpected and bold tenderness. Celeste ordered a dessert, something she rarely did. Yet she didn't want the time with Max to end. While savoring a small bite of the lemon soufflé, she decided to pose the idea of putting Pilar's story on "America's Most Wanted". What did she have to lose after she pulled all the skeletons from her closet and displayed them to Max?

Celeste set down her fork and pushed the plate to Max. He took a few bites as though it was something they'd done for years as a couple.

"Max?"

He swallowed, then answered, "Yes."

"You know how concerned I am about nothing new happening in the pursuit of Jane and Tommy," she said.

"Yes, I do, and I'm concerned, too."

"Actually," she said in a singsong voice, "I can't sit still and not do everything possible."

Max pushed the empty plate away and drank his coffee. He set the cup down. He was quiet for what seemed minutes. "I have a feeling you have something up your sleeve. Something a little out of the ordinary."

Trying to offset the inevitable shock of her plan, Celeste smiled coquettishly. "I want to contact the TV show "America's Most Wanted". They always seem to have such good luck finding fugitives."

Max' mouth dropped open. He combed his fingers through his hair several times. His face crinkled into a hundred distressed lines which now, in the candle's glow, became grotesque gray creases. He moved his lips from side to side.

That reaction didn't appear positive. Losing her patience, Celeste asked, "Well, what do you think?"

"I don't know. Those programs are more sensational than helpful. Those TV people are in it to make a buck from advertisers." He wiped his lips with the napkin and placed it on the table. Max signaled to the waitress for their check.

Distressed by Max's sudden need to leave, Celeste apologized. "I'm sorry you find our evening's conversations difficult."

Max paid the bill and walked to her chair. He pulled the chair out. When Celeste stood Max held both her hands. "Nothing is difficult with you. I'm just not sure about going forward with something that will reveal your whole life to millions of voyeurs. Besides," he pointed out the window, "it's beginning to snow. We better get back to the motel before the roads get too slick."

Celeste was relieved Max was being more practical than scared off. Sometimes she did let her distrustful nature get in the way. But she had a lot of years to practice. She probably passed a little of her doubting disposition onto Pilar, except when it counted with Chad.

In the morning Celeste and Max parted on good terms. They made plans to get together in a few weeks. "Soon?" he asked, as though he suspected Celeste might renege.

"Of course. Need I remind you we are sleuths in partnership?"

Max kissed her on the cheek. "Soon, then," he whispered. "Remember, I'm just a phone call away if you need to talk."

Celeste wouldn't confide to Max, at least for the time, that she had made her mind up to contact the TV producers after she passed the idea by Detective Patterson. She would need help from the police if she was going to pull that off.

As Celeste watched Max's car enter the north bound entrance to I-75, she believed she was one of the luckiest people in the world to have found Max Whitefeather.

chapter twenty-one

THE CHASE

DETECTIVE PATTERSON VISITED CELESTE two weeks after her rendezvous with Max. She had telephoned him about tracking Tommy and Jane by giving Pilar's story to the TV show. He was as skeptical as Max. So when Patterson showed up at her door, Celeste was a little embarrassed about her pushy suggestion.

Once inside Patterson accepted a cup of coffee and sat at the breakfast bar as though he were a family member and not the police. "Nice stools," he commented as he twirled around.

"Thank you." Celeste marveled at Patterson's self confidence. " Pier One."

He stopped twirling. The smile left his face. He leaned over the countertop and confided, "Now that we have more to go on, I've convinced my boss to contact that show." Patterson drank some coffee as the low autumn sunlight sneaked through the windows and streaked across his face. Celeste noted he was dressed more casually today in a tweed sports coat and a sky-blue turtle neck that matched his eyes. The detective reminded her of a young Paul Newman, although his lankiness and laid-back style was more Clint Eastwood.

"What do you mean that you have more to go on?" Celeste set a plate of freshly baked raisin scones in front of Patterson. She enjoyed her newly emerging domestic trait. "No one has told me about any new findings," she said in a less than agreeable tone. "As the victim's mother, I should be the first to know everything."

Patterson put his cup down. "We just got the lead a couple of days ago and had to check it out." He examined the scones and chose a medium-sized one. "I'm sorry if you feel we haven't been honest with you." His composure eased Celeste as it always did.

"Never mind. Just tell me the news." Celeste smoothed her silk tunic over the matching slacks and sat on a stool next to him.

"It's not pleasant." He bit into the scone and wiped the crumbs from his lips before chewing.

If Celeste could have had more children, she would have wanted a son just like Patterson. And like a mother, she tisked at his delaying tactic, and then sighed in exasperation. "Are you married?" she asked.

Patterson crunched his forehead. "Yes. Why?"

"Do you have children?"

"Two daughters," he answered softly and less authoritatively.

"Then you understand how desperate a parent can get when she loses a child. So, let's not play this game. Tell me."

"RIGHT." PATTERSON LOWERED HIS head for a moment. He appeared reflective as though formulating the best way to report his news. "Do you remember when the Colorado police found a body of a hiker and suspected Johnson was the killer?" Detective Patterson paused before he explained further. "We know Johnson has spent a great deal of time in the wilderness practicing survival techniques."

"What does this have to do with the hiker?" Celeste's stomach turned over when she thought about another dead person.

"Sightings of a man and woman that resemble Jane and Tommy have been reported in that area of Colorado." Patterson stopped until he heard Celeste's loud, fretful gasp. He went on, but with caution. "One such report led police to search a hotel in Bluff, Utah. The hotel clerk found a backpack the police identified as belonging to the victim. The police also found Johnson's fingerprints on the contents. He seems to be getting careless."

"Is that it?" Celeste had hoped he would tell her they knew exactly where Johnson was.

"No." Detective Patterson finished the scone. He glanced at the plate still filled with treats, but drank the remainder of his coffee instead. "Johnson and Carson have been seen in the Southfield area."

"Oh, my God." Celeste drifted into the living room and collapsed into a chair. How would she handle the end of that horrid affair. "Who saw them? Have they been arrested?"

Patterson's sad face said everything. "No. They got away. For now."

Celeste bounded from the chair and walked toward him. "They got away?" she screamed as she picked up a dish rag and cleaned the countertop in a manic flurry. She brushed crumbs into her hand and tossed them into the sink. She returned to the counter and scrubbed the surface, over and over, as though there was a stain that wouldn't come out.

Patterson stopped her hand in mid-wipe. He held it until she looked at him. "One of the police officers," he began, "assigned to the murder investigation spotted them at a Southfield Mall. The officer was there for another reason."

Though his voice maintained that therapeutic quality Celeste so admired, she wanted rapid-fire answers, not consoling. "Detective Patterson, please explain all the wretched details. Don't be afraid of adding to my pain. I'm prepared for the worst." Or at least she hoped she was.

He walked to the coffee pot and poured himself another cup. He leaned against the counter and faced Celeste. His eyes turned deep blue. "When the officer saw Tommy and Jane, he decided not to draw his gun in the crowded complex. He called for backup while keeping the couple in sight." Patterson sipped his coffee.

Too anxious to wait for him, Celeste asked, "What

happened? Why weren't they arrested?"

"According to what the officer reported he couldn't catch up to them and they sped away in a small sports car." Patterson put his cup down and headed for the front door. He stopped part way. "In case you're wondering," he said, "the officer didn't get the license plate number, either."

Celeste was glued in place. Her limbs were so heavy they felt as though they had been cast in concrete. "How can those two be so close and get away?"

"It's a judgment call every police officer makes at least once in his career. He couldn't jeopardize the safety of all those shoppers."

"I know, I know, but . . . they were so close." Celeste brandished the dish rag like a flag. "Besides, why did they come back?"

"We won't know that until they're arrested. Some speculate they want to get caught. That Johnson is on a planned self-destruction course."

"You know." Celeste stacked dishes in the sink. "Except for those blurred pictures in the newspaper, I don't even know what Tommy Johnson and Jane Carson look like, let alone who they really are and how they think."

"How much would you like to know?" Patterson asked as he returned to his seat at the breakfast bar.

"Everything." Celeste swiped a wisp of errant hair.

"Carson is a small, attractive woman; some would call her pleasingly plump," Patterson began. "You already know she is, or rather was a nurse, so she's educated. Johnson, on the other hand, is an aberration like Wilbanks."

"What do you mean?" Celeste asked and sat next to the detective, her voice quivering with the memory of Wilbanks' cockiness the day she visited Hawk Haven.

"As hard as it is to believe, women adore both of them."

Celeste clearly saw Chad's visiting card listing all those women's names as though it were before her. If she thought hard enough, she probably could recall most of the names.

"There are differences, though. Wilbanks is handsome, educated, and clean cut." Patterson's eyes narrowed as though trying to picture the two scoundrels. "Johnson is a high school dropout, has a lengthy juvenile record, wears his shaggy hair long, and sports a Fu Manchu mustache and a heart-and-dagger tattoo."

Celeste crinkled her nose as though she smelled a container of spoiled milk. "Not exactly the most desirable bachelor." Celeste tried to imagine Tommy's visiting card.

Patterson snickered. "There's more. Do you want to hear it?"

Celeste nodded. "It may sound odd, but the more I know about Jane and Tommy the more real they are. Maybe then I'll be able to handle them with less emotion and more intelligence when you find them and bring them back."

"I understand," Patterson said in a healing, less police tone again. Celeste chuckled and he asked, "What?"

"Nothing important. You just sound like my therapist,

if I had one."

"I guess I'm glad you want to know all you can because it helps with grief. Besides, I did major in psychology in college."

Celeste lifted the plate of scones. "Have another?" He would make a perfect counselor if he could stay away from the more conventional police clip. Patterson raised his right hand like a traffic cop and patted his taut, well-exercised stomach with his other hand. "Thanks, but no."

Celeste put the plate down, "Please, go on then."

"Let's see. This isn't Johnson's first affair, escape, or murder. He absconded once when he was nineteen, just before he was to be sentenced on a burglary charge. He eventually was arrested for assault and sentenced to prison."

How much had Patterson memorized about these characters? He recited as though he were reading from a police report.

"Johnson served only three years and was paroled." Patterson stopped and checked Celeste's expression to ensure she was still listening. Celeste nodded encouragement.

"While on parole," he said, "Johnson skipped the state with another married woman, Agnes Trudeau, after killing his crime partner, Denny Richards. Richards once described Johnson as a gun freak. The two were high on LSD and fooling around with guns in a remote, wooded area in Lapeer County when Johnson killed Richards."

Though Celeste wanted more than anything to hear

what Patterson was saying, she couldn't stop her mind from wandering back to Pilar. How could she have been involved with such creatures? Of course Pilar was a warm person always ready to lend a hand to anyone. But them?

Patterson released enough air from his mouth that Celeste expected to see him deflate like an emptying balloon. He must have realized her mind had wandered. When she reconnected with him, Patterson resumed his story telling. While he talked, Celeste visualized a B-movie. She laid her head on her arm. Patterson's recounting of Johnson's gruesome past paraded before Celeste as though it were all happening to her.

A FEW MONTHS AFTER he murdered Denny Richards, Johnson told Agnes that he believed the coast was clear for them to go back to Detroit. He wasn't aware that both the FBI and Detroit Police were keeping surveillance, anticipating his return. Johnson dropped Agnes off at her trailer in Hazel Park and headed out on an expedition to scope the area for potential jobs; illegal, of course.

As a man often on the look-out for new women, he picked up Agnes' fifteen-year-old niece, Candy. She, like Tommy, had many brushes with the criminal justice system and was always braced for an adventure, as she put it, "to get me outta the house and away from this boring life."

Johnson was sure Candy was ready for the ultimate hustle. He was positive she'd do anything he wanted. She later admitted she'd have followed him anywhere.

Their brief relationship ended when the two were tooling the streets of Detroit and an FBI agent spotted the couple. The agent pursued them. But Johnson wasn't prepared to give himself up. He tried to run down the agent.

Backup had been called when the agent first saw Tommy and Candy. The attempted vehicle assault was witnessed by the Detroit Police who apprehended Johnson. When the two were searched Candy was carrying a .357 magnum. She was turned over to the juvenile authorities and Tommy was booked at the county jail.

Having no solid evidence to charge Johnson with Richard's murder, he only got twelve months for the escape. Carolyn Williams, Candy's mother and Agnes' sister, had enough of that culprit and his constant ability to get less punishment than he deserved. So she went to the police. Mrs. Williams reported, "It's terrible that my sister Agnes had to be stalked by that animal, Tommy, but he's gotten too close to my own front door this time."

After that she chronicled events that should only be read in a Steven King novel. "Tommy Johnson told me himself he killed that Richards guy," Mrs. Williams reported to the investigating detective. "He didn't want to be arrested and planned to flee the state. But the clincher was, he insisted Agnes go with him."

Since Agnes had broken up with him, Carolyn Williams reported, Tommy had to devise a means to persuade her to run off with him. It wasn't romantic. He dragged Agnes from Mrs. Williams' house where she had sought refuge and took Agnes back to her own trailer.

Patterson's narrative created confusing and outrageous images that swirled in Celeste's mind like leaves in a dark, disturbed pool. Hypnotized, Celeste lifted her head and actually believed she was with Tommy and Agnes. Like the voyeur Marcus had accused her of being, she saw every move they made. Every touch was realistic. Suddenly Celeste became an eyewitness.

TOMMY DRAGGED AGNES ACROSS the trailer pressing the gun barrel to her head with one hand while his other encircled her neck. She kicked and screamed, "Let go of me. Help," she yelled. "Someone help me." Her pleas went unanswered. No one in the park interfered in what appeared to be a normal domestic quarrel.

Tommy shoved her to the bathroom floor and kicked her in the stomach. She gasped for air like a fish thrown into a boat's lazarette. The pleasure of the cool linoleum against her cheek lasted only seconds. Tommy ripped her clothes away, leaving her naked on the floor. She reached for the toilet. Before she was able to lift herself, Tommy grabbed a fistful of hair. He pulled her to her feet. Blood gurgled from her mouth, down her chin and onto a bare breast.

"Just kill me and get it over," she begged. Every labored word was like a thorn piercing her throat.

"I just might do that," Tommy chuckled. "If you don't do what I want."

She wanted to sleep.

As Tommy manipulated her body like a rag, he stood her on a stool. Within minutes Tommy looped one end of a belt around her neck and the other around the fixed shower curtain bar. She needed to fight, but she was so weighted, she couldn't move.

Tommy rummaged through a vanity drawer and found nail clippers. His victim calmed a little, thinking he was going to trim his nails as he convinced her to . . . to what? Be his steady girl again?

He opened and positioned the clippers to prepare for the task. He turned to his victim, eyes round, dark, huge. He circled in front and said, "I'm ready. Are you?"

No time to answer. The room filled with an insane wail like an angry wild cat or coyotes on a chase. Blood dripped from her breast. The wailing came from her.

Tommy snipped pieces of skin off her body while he chanted, "She'll go with me." *Snip.* "She'll not go with me." *Snip.*

The victim squirmed with each slice and tried to free herself. Tommy laughed, head thrown back, showing yellow teeth and dark spaces edged in red gums. Then he stopped abruptly. "You better not move, darlin. You don't want to hang yourself, now do ya?"

Though at that moment she believed hanging would be

better than what he was doing, she begged for him to take her with him to Florida. It was the only way to stay alive.

"THREE MONTHS LATER AGNES was found with Tommy when he was arrested at his father's home in Fort Meyers." Patterson's hand lighting on Celeste's shoulder brought her back to the present and out of that nightmare.

Celeste looked out the window at the last of the day's sun rays bouncing across Lake St. Clair. "What?" she asked. "What did you say?"

"Mrs. Brookstone, have you been listening at all?" Patterson sounded a little irritated about having rambled on if she hadn't listened.

"Of course." Celeste placed a hand on her chest to suppress the remaining twinges. She searched for blood seeping through the blue silk. She turned to Patterson, elated that he and not Tommy was in the room. She seemed adrift as though she had just returned to earth after a near death experience. " Please go on. I'm listening," Celeste assured Patterson. She had listened all too well to that incredible saga. Yet she couldn't explain to him or herself what had happened. Patterson hesitated, rubbed his chin several times, and then resumed. "By the time Pilar met Tommy Johnson at Hawk Haven he was at the end of his sentences for escape and attempted murder."

"It's hard to believe he wasn't charged with Richards' murder," Celeste said. She tried a sip of coffee. It refused to stay down.

"The judge," Detective Patterson's hand dropped from her shoulder, "felt there wasn't enough evidence to charge him because Agnes claimed she couldn't recall what Johnson had told her about Denny Richards' death. So the judge agreed to accept Johnson's plea of attempted murder."

"After what Johnson did to her, she protected him?" Celeste spat out. "How could she?" Anger tensed every muscle. "Johnson would have still been in jail and not on the loose." Celeste had a hard time breathing, but added, "And Pilar would still be alive."

Patterson ushered Celeste to the couch. "Don't blame Agnes. She was scared. So were all his other so-called friends. One told Lapeer police that, and I quote, 'Tommy goes crazy when he gets mad and you don't know what he's going to do. I know I don't want him mad at me.' End of quote."

From what Pilar told Celeste about that nurse, she was a confident, not frightened woman. "What about Jane Carson? Was she scared, too?"

"She's somewhat of a mystery. Best we can tell, she likes excitement. She's like Candy."

"If you're trying to tell me she did all this because she was bored, it isn't helping." Celeste raised her hand to her mouth and then to her forehead. She massaged the hair line.

"No. But you did ask to know more about Jane Carson

and I'm doing my best." Patterson sat next to Celeste. "We also discovered Tommy wasn't her first prison affair. Mrs. Carson had already been reprimanded for over-familiarity with prisoners."

"God." Celeste pounded her fist into a sofa pillow. "How could they let her stay employed?"

Patterson shrugged. "She had a good attorney in the arbitration hearing, I guess." He paused. "Despite her flaws though," he stumbled over the words as he tried to find some redeeming quality in Carson, "she couldn't shake her maternal duties. She must've convinced Johnson to help kidnap her children."

Patterson stood and paced. He displayed a restless side to him Celeste hadn't seen before. He tugged at the blinds' cord, opening and closing them. Sunlight striped his face and caused flashes like a blinking neon sign. He turned to Celeste again. "Jane called her husband and said she was coming home if he would send her the money. Mr. Carson obliged and wired money to her in Florida. Instead of returning to him, she and Tommy used the funds to fly home and take the children."

Innocent children in the hands of that mother. Celeste curled into a fetal position on the couch and gave into another episode of grief. She clutched a throw pillow to her chest and rocked back and forth moaning a chant, "It can't be, it can't be."

Detective Patterson sat beside Celeste. "I'm telling you

everything I know because this information will be in the papers in due time." His voice was tranquilizing. He rested a hand on her arm. "I'd rather you hear all this from me than some obscure, prying reporter."

"I know," Celeste could hardly whisper the words. The room was so quiet she heard the engines of a passing freighter on the lake. She lifted to a sitting position. She and Detective Patterson remained seated side by side for a long time without speaking. What else could they say? Exhaustion crept into every muscle. Even Celeste's brain seemed too tired to go on.

Patterson finally said, "At any rate, because the FBI found Johnson's prints at that Bluff motel, the positive identification reports, and another victim, the hiker, Southfield Police are willing to work with the TV people." Patterson considered Celeste for several moments. "You'll be interviewed also. Do you still want to do this?"

"Of course." Celeste jumped up. She was woozy and steadied herself against the couch's arm before Patterson noticed. "It's more than Pilar now." She flailed her arms. "Who knows where those two evil beings will stop?"

chapter twenty-two

SHARING

SEVERAL DAYS LATER, DETECTIVE Patterson appeared at Celeste's condo. After she hung up his trench coat, she announced, "If you're going to be a regular visitor, I think I should know your first name." She had barely seen his full name on the ID he flashed at her the first day they met.

"Jim, well, James," he smiled, "after my dad." He proudly explained that he and his father both graduated from the University of Illinois. Jim even joined his father's fraternity.

Celeste pictured the two of them on the fifty-yard-line cheering their beloved Illini. "Coffee?" she asked, and lifted the pot from the counter

"Please," he said. "And if you have any of those scones, I'd take one of them, too." His grin indicated his anticipation of the tasty treat.

Celeste laughed heartily. It was a good feeling after so many weeks of grief. "The truth comes out. It's not my good looks, it's my cooking you're after."

"It's both," the beguiling Jim said. Celeste imagined

his father saying the same thing to his mother. A pang of jealousy struck her.

Celeste placed the plate of scones and coffee in front of Jim. She stood opposite him on the other side of the bar and sensed he came with news about Tommy and Jane. "What does bring you here, Detective Patterson?"

"Jim, call me Jim."

"Yes, of course."

Jim laid a large manila envelope on the counter. "I want you to see this before you watch "America's Most Wanted" or hear it in the news."

Cautiously, Celeste opened the envelope and extracted the contents. A similar scene with Max marched across her memory. Today's envelope though, held formal paperwork, a police log. Investigators made abbreviated written entries for each lead in their quest to find Pilar's killer or killers.

"Read it," Jim urged. "You may know most of this, but sometimes the day-to-day events in black and white strike harder at us than a verbal report. Those often sound like stories rather than the real thing. This," he pointed at the packet, "is the real thing."

When Celeste started her review of the material, Jim softly added, "If you have any questions as you go along, just ask." Then he bit into the fresh scone.

July 8   Tommy Johnson and his father Hal Johnson at Custom Sportsmen Supply, Palm Beach

Blvd., Fort Meyers, Florida purchased a S&W
9MM auto. Witness – Pam Walker.

July 13   Bulls-eye Sports, Jane Carson purchased one box S&W 9MM hollow point ammo.

July 17   Brookstone, Pilar — Dead on I-696
from two gun shot wounds to the head. Two 9MM
shell casings found in car. '03 Subaru

Celeste put the papers down and drank some cold
coffee. "I'm not sure I can read any more of this. It's so
emotionless. It's such a casual narrative about the purchase
of the gun that killed my daughter."

"It's a part of the police file. No sentiment should be
shown." Jim's voice was barely audible. "Even if we feel
it." He paused. "It will be worse hearing this on TV. But
it's going to get even harder at the trial. Hearing a detective,
even me, presenting a detached accounting of evidence can
be heart wrenching."

Celeste fingered the pages. "I know, but it's so tough."
She bit her lower lip to stop its tremor. "I just want all this
to go away."

Jim's face softened so that there was hardly a line visible.
"The more you hear or read these facts, the more prepared
you will be for the trial and TV. It's just like the day you
wanted to hear all about Tommy and Jane." He lifted one

eyebrow, indicating she had to do that.

Celeste was comforted for the moment that Jim, like Max, had become as obsessed by Pilar's murder as if she were a wife and daughter of their own. Marcus had hardly shown interest in the case. Celeste picked up the report and resumed reading.

> July 19   Patterson interviewed Chad Wilbanks
> in Hawk Haven. Wilbanks stated he had heard
> Brookstone lost a lot of money and wanted to know
> if it was true.

Reading those cold words made Celeste queasy. Wilbanks asked about nothing else, except how much of his inheritance would be gone. It confirmed that all he wanted from Pilar was money. Celeste paced the living room while she read the rest. She hoped movement would ease the hate boiling inside her.

> July 19   Patterson interviewed Keli Lawrence,
> Citizen's Bank – handled the $25,000 withdrawal
> for Brookstone on 7/17 all in $100 bills.

> July 19   Bulls-eye Sports and Shooters Supply
> – Hal Johnson purchased a .12 gage shotgun, .45
> cal. Cap & ball, accompanied by W/M and B/F.

Celeste stared at the report and asked, "Does Tommy Johnson have a mother?"

"That's an odd question," Jim answered, sounding surprised by the query.

"This report," she held the papers out toward him, "says nothing about his mother, only his father, who seems to be an accomplice. So, I'm curious."

Jim tilted his head to the side. He looked sympathetic when he said, "From what we can gather, Tommy's mother left him and his father when Tommy was around five-years-old. No one has heard from, or seen her since."

Celeste fought back tears. "I'll never understand a mother who could do that. But then, how do you explain a father like Hal Johnson who helps his son commit crimes, even murder?"

"It's hard to comprehend," Jim agreed. "Maybe he's scared, too."

Celeste shook her head as she continued. The papers she held felt heavier.

July 20   Patterson took call — Mr. and Mrs. Taylor, Detroit, were on I-696 where they observed a W/M next to a small car standing upright near to driver's window.

July 20   Palmer   interviewed   George Livingston, B/M, Detroit, who observed a late model Ford pulled off the road and behind a small car parked on the shoulder and occupied by W/F.

July 21   Patterson interviewed Willy Samuels that at approximately 11:1145 A.M. on 7/17 he observed a W/M standing beside a small foreign type car on I-696 east of Inkster – W/M was standing straight up.

July 21   Tommy Johnson rented #103 mobile home off I-23 outside Ann Arbor.   Donna McGregger, trailer #102, ID'd photo of Tommy Johnson.

July 22   Palmer interviewed Cleo Spangler, a Scott Prison nurse.   Cleo Spangler and Pilar Brookstone had a conversation at the Del-Rio Bar on July 16.   Victim told Spangler that there was strong possibility Chad Wilbanks would be out of prison in a few weeks.   She told Spangler about having met Tommy Johnson at Hawk Haven.

Cleo's face flashed across Celeste's mind.   Why hadn't she tried to stop Pilar?   What good was it for Cleo to tell Celeste about her concerns the day of Pilar's funeral or talk to the police after Pilar died?   She wiped the moisture from her eyes so she could see the paper and went on.

July 24   Palmer interviewed Carl Simmons
W/M/44 of Novi.   Saw a dark color Subaru
occupied by a W/F and a W/M being followed
by an attractive B/F in a late model Ford. Both
vehicles pulled onto the shoulder simultaneously.
Simmons can ID B/F.

"All these people saw the two cars and no one stopped.
Didn't any of them suspect something was wrong?"
Celeste quizzed.

"Like most drivers, they're more curious than concerned.
Their glance at the two cars led those we interviewed to
believe there was no trouble." Jim breathed deeply. "But
even if they did have some suspicion, most people wouldn't
get involved, only after the fact. Like now."

"Umm." Celeste silently cursed each one. The freeway witnesses still should have stopped. Was that an unfair
conclusion? She didn't care. Celeste quickly read the rest
of the report. Recorded in the last portion, Officer Leonard
whom she met at the prison, saw Jane driving in downtown
Marquette with Tommy a few days after he had escaped.
Just before that sighting the manager of the Super 8 confirmed Tommy Johnson was registered there on July 16.

Celeste wanted to know why they hadn't reported the
escapee. Tommy's picture was plastered on local TV and
in the newspapers. They were like the freeway observers.

They didn't want to get involved until they were forced.

The hotel employee also said Tommy was picked up the next day by an African-American woman and at least one child. For just a second Celeste's heart went out to those children. She lowered the report to her side. How could Jane Carson claim she loved her children and then place them in such danger? How could a mother be that negligent?

"Is something the matter?" Patterson's voice interrupted her reflection.

"No," she shook her head. "I only have a few more entries to read."

"Good." Patterson circled his foot around the bar stool's lower rung and finished the scone.

The last item Celeste read further implicated Tommy's father. It stated that on July 29 Paula Neil of Western Gun Traders sold two .357 Magnum revolvers to Hal Johnson accompanied by a white male and an African-American female. Was it the gun that killed the Colorado hiker?

Celeste finished the entire police log and returned the tear dampened pages to Patterson. Seeing the whole case in a written report made the offenders even more real and despicable. The matter-of-fact way in which the report was stated also made it clear that most likely Pilar was only one of Chad and Tommy's victims. How sad to think that there were probably more casualties in the world because of them.

Patterson lifted his brows after he replaced the packet into the envelope as if waiting for Celeste to make a comment. When none came, he said, "I repeat: Reading this is tough and brings up all the horrid facts, some you weren't aware of, but . . ."

"But I did need to see them. I know. Especially, like you said, since I'll have to confront these issues sooner or later in a less caring environment."

"Yes, well. . ." Patterson shifted from one foot to the other like a very shy boy. It was the first time Celeste found the detective without words.

"I need some time to put all this into perspective," Celeste announced. "It's hard to believe that people can be so calculating and cruel."

Patterson frowned and smiled at the same time. His mouth stretched to a grin but turned down at the corners. "Take care," he then said. "If you need anything, especially before your TV interview, you know where to get me."

"Yes, thank you. You have been very kind." Celeste let him out the door and thought about Hal Johnson, Tommy's father. What kind of man would aid Tommy as he did? Or as Jim suggested, was he too frightened of his own son to do anything else?

"Monster," Celeste declared to Phoenix. "Tommy's nothing but a monster."

But what was Jane's excuse? Love? Excitement? Or was she some kind of fiend, too?

chapter twenty-three

AMERICA'S MOST WANTED

MAX AND JIM STOOD in the doorway of Celeste's condo. Both displayed sheepish grins.

"What on earth brings the two of you here on this of all days?" Celeste asked, hoping for good news. Standing together, Celeste realized how different they appeared. Jim's tall, lean body towered over Max's stout one. As pressed and intact as Jim's clothing was, Max' outfit was unkempt. In fact, he looked more like Columbo. The two men standing before her were as disparate as the characters in *The Odd Couple*.

Max looked at Jim who stared back at him and nodded. Max faced Celeste and said, "We want to be with you when that producer from the TV show interrogates you."

Celeste chuckled. "You mean talks with me, don't you?"

Max laughed. A hint of red showed on his cheeks. "Yes, of course," he answered.

"Come on in and take a seat in the living room. The producer is due here any moment." As soon as Celeste said that, she had another question. "How did you know when the producer was going to arrive anyway?"

Jim shrugged, "I'm a cop."

Celeste motioned them to chairs. "Do you sense trouble with this group, Jim?"

"No," he answered and sat on the edge of one chair, elbows resting against his knees and hands clasped. "I," Jim raised his eyes at Max, "we, thought you might like a little support."

Max slid into a wing-back chair near the fire place, as comfortable as if he had reclined there all his life. "Their questions can be tough," he chimed in. "You'll be forced to remember some emotional moments. These producers leave nothing to the imagination. It can be rather difficult for you on your own."

Celeste handed each man a cup of coffee. She was now thankful Jim insisted she read that police log. She also was enchanted by Jim and Max's need to protect her.

"Though I believe there is little left that can bring me to my knees," Celeste said to both but focused on Patterson, "at least not the way the first news about Pilar did, Jim, I'm glad you're both here." She sat on the couch next to Phoenix and scratched his ears. He rubbed his whiskers against her fingers. "Besides, I can always use your support. It gives me the confidence that I've made the right decision to go forward with this TV show."

Before either responded, the door bell rang. "That must

be the interrogator now," Celeste teased.

Max's face reddened again as the two men tittered. Both followed Celeste to the door like bodyguards. Before she opened it, she turned to Max and Jim with hands on her hips. They retreated to their chairs and coffee. As she watched them go to their respective areas, she was curious how often they talked to each other. And when did they decide to be there together?

DOTTIE CLARK WASN'T THE kind of interviewer Celeste had expected to show up that morning. The beautiful African-American woman in a red suit bounded through the door trailed by a man with a camera. Her purposeful stride opened the slit on the right side of her straight skirt, exposing a long slender leg. "Hi," she said as she offered her hand and introduced herself as the segment's producer.

"Hi," Celeste answered, caught off guard by the perfumed breeze Ms. Clark created when she passed and marched straight toward Max and Jim.

"And you two are?" she asked with enviable assuredness.

Jim and Max stood and introduced themselves by name only. Celeste jumped in. "Max is the warden at Hawk Haven Prison where my daughter Pilar worked. And where she met Tommy Johnson and Chad Wilbanks." Celeste directed her attention to Jim. "Jim is a detective with the Southfield Police Department and the primary on Pilar's murder case."

"Umm," Ms. Clark answered, "I spoke to you a few days ago, didn't I, detective?"

"Yes, and we set up an appointment to meet later this week."

"Yes, yes, but I didn't expect the two of you today. Hopefully," she said to Celeste as though Jim and Max weren't in the room, "they won't get in the way."

"They're concerned friends, Ms. Clark," Celeste answered with some vinegar in her voice. "I convinced them to go along with this TV thing even though they prefer more conventional and less exploitive methods."

Max cleared his throat and Jim rocked from one foot to the other as all three of them watched Dottie Clark's caramel-colored complexion deepen. She appeared miffed that Celeste had more control than she at that moment.

"Shall we get this over, Ms. Clark?" Celeste again motioned for everyone to sit. "I have gathered several copies of pictures for you. They are of Pilar and Chad, and Pilar's apartments. I hope they may be useful."

Dottie Clark crossed her legs and took the photos. When the skirt fell to one side and revealed too much thigh, Max and Jim shifted. Celeste chuckled at their discomfort and Ms. Clark's unabashed attitude.

As Dottie Clark rifled through the pictures, Celeste told her, "At the bottom of the stack are a few letters between Pilar and Chad that made references to Tommy Johnson and Jane Carson." Celeste didn't see the need to supply her with all the letters. Just enough to give the producer ideas to help locate the villains and not disclose anything more that might further damage Pilar's reputation.

"Can you speak freely" Ms. Clark asked as she eyed Max and Jim.

"Certainly. They know more about Pilar and this case than anyone." It pained her to admit once again that she knew less about Pilar's life than a cop and Pilar's former boss.

"I'm curious, though," Celeste said. "What made you decide to do Pilar's story?"

"Easy," Clark said. "Her story is about a beautiful, young female doctor who falls for a convict who may have set her up to get killed for money. Great stuff."

Celeste now was uncertain about the interview she faced. Ms. Clark lacked subtlety and had no concern that her factual and uncharitable rendition of Pilar's death would wound Celeste. She suddenly felt used. Pilar's story would get Dottie Clark kudos and make the studio money. Would it also catch Tommy and Jane?

Celeste needed to put her hurt feelings aside. Nothing could be as important as getting Carson and Johnson put away forever. So she answered Ms. Clark's prying questions with calm dignity.

THREE HOURS AFTER THEIR initial introductions, Dottie Clark and her male partner, sped out the door as unruffled as they had arrived. Celeste, on the other hand, felt shredded into tiny pieces and in need of a long hot bubble bath, her cure for almost everything.

Max and Jim went to the door with Celeste. All three watched the human whirlwind speed away in a cloud of dust. "Well?" Celeste asked as she closed the door and faced the two men whose mouths were agape.

Jim spoke first. "She's a typical reporter type. She's young, attractive, tough, and caustic."

Something like Pilar, until she met Chad Wilbanks.

"She won't let anything stand in her way of a good story," Max added. "I've dealt with a lot like her through the years."

"Me too," Jim agreed. "I usually don't trust them and don't like them."

"What I'm really asking you two is whether you think there is any chance Tommy and Jane will be turned in by a viewer?"

"Oh. Hard to say," Jim said.

"Don't know," Max shrugged.

They remained huddled in the foyer for a few more moments until Celeste announced, "This conversation doesn't leave me with much enthusiasm about what I just did."

Max hugged her shoulders and quickly released his grip when his eyes settled on Jim. "It's the way the reporters and others in that business are trained to do their jobs," Max said. "They can't let their true emotions get in the way or make them biased."

"Like the police," Jim reminded Celeste.

"I suppose." Celeste held the door handle. "I'm glad now that you two were here. I needed to believe someone was on my side and sharing my pain." She smiled, lips quivering. "Thanks." She kissed both on the cheek. "Now, I need to relax by myself for a while so I can breathe freely again. After what I went through today, I know I have to deal with my anxiety about what's ahead for me."

"Sure," Jim said. "Take care of yourself." He left first as though he knew Max wanted a few moments alone with Celeste.

"May I call you later to see how you're doing?" Max asked. "I swear I won't bug you." He held up his right hand as if taking an oath.

"Oh, Max," Celeste clasped his arm, "you can never be anything but a pleasure to have around. Anyway, I should be ready for some wholesome and fun dinner conversation."

His eyes brightened as a huge smile invaded his face. "Great! I'll call later and we can figure out where we'll go for dinner."

"We'll eat here. I don't want to leave the comfort of my home right now. Don't bother to call. Just come around seven."

"Right. I'll bring the wine." He kissed her lightly on the forehead. "See you later then." He almost skipped to elevator.

Leaning against the closed door, Celeste doubted she could overcome her exhaustion even to take that bath.

Finally, she pushed away and headed for the tub. A short nap, too. Then she'd fix an easy but tasty dinner. Perhaps pasta in tomato basil sauce with shrimp, a salad, and a baguette.   Hopefully, later she could laugh a lot over silly things with that wonderful man.

chapter twenty-four

CAPTURED

NURSE AND PRISON ESCAPEE ARRESTED IN DEATH OF PRISON DOCTOR.

The *Detroit Free Press* headline punched Celeste between the eyes. Coming face to face with those two villains, Tommy Johnson and Jane Carson, could easily turn Celeste into a murderer like them. What mother wouldn't feel that way? Despite that vengeful bent, Celeste was anxious for the whole nightmare to be finally over. Then she could get on with her own life, such as it was without Pilar.

Celeste reread the paragraph that fascinated her the most:

The Sacramento Sheriff's Department said they arrested Mrs. Carson on a shoplifting charge. When officers checked her out through the Automated Fingerprint and FBI computerized reporting systems, they learned she was wanted with Tommy Johnson on federal warrants. Officers said they convinced Carson to tell them

where Johnson was. When authorities tried to
apprehend Johnson, he grabbed a revolver, but
Johnson was subdued before he could fire it.

Celeste cut out the article and glued it into an album along with all the others she had saved. It might seem a grisly keepsake, but Celeste had no intention of forgetting one moment of the whole morbid affair surrounding Pilar's murder. It was one way to preserve her whole memory of Pilar. As she pasted the latest information in place, she again went over what possible reason persuaded Jane Carson to turn on Tommy.

Celeste picked up the newspaper and stared at the hole where the article had been. Perhaps the police offered Jane leniency. More likely they told Jane she would be solely charged with Pilar's murder if she didn't reveal Tommy's location. Whatever it was, Jane Carson informed on her partner quickly.

Dan Oliver, the Oakland County prosecutor, called earlier that morning to let Celeste know that the extradition order was signed and the two fugitives would be back in Michigan within a week. Celeste envisioned Tommy and Jane, wearing orange jump suits, chained separately to an airplane seat along with several other offenders.

It was hard to believe it had been almost a year to the day of Pilar's murder.

The store clerk not only caught Jane Carson red handed,

he recognized her from "America's Most Wanted". Celeste was thrilled Jane was nabbed and that no more family skeletons would be hauled out of the closet and shown to millions of viewers in follow-up shows.

Jane foolishly told the police her name was Jane Johnson. That, along with her finger prints, the TV show, and picture nailed her. Was she too tired to come up with a more creative alias, or did she want the chase over? What kind of life could it have been if she had to resort to shoplifting? Had she given up to protect her children from Tommy? Had she known the game was over once their crimes aired on nationwide TV?

Maybe Jane was weary of looking over her shoulder and living a lie, especially running with the children she claimed she loved so much. Celeste imagined it took repetitive tutoring to train the children to accept their new identity. Once reunited with their father they would have to learn who they were all over again. Those poor confused children suffered the most.

Celeste regretted she would never know the answers to her questions or understand a woman like Jane.

It wasn't just Jane's negligence that got them caught. Tommy Johnson followed almost the identical escape route he took with Agnes Trudeau five years before through Florida, Texas, New Mexico, Colorado, Utah, and Arizona. What did you expect from a convict who escaped within six months of parole and one year of his final discharge?

"Tommy's not a rocket scientist, is he, Phoenix?" The cat stretched and ignored her as he settled into a methodic licking of his paw that he wiped across his whiskers. Or, could the escape have been all Jane's idea, because she couldn't visit Tommy?

On the other hand, knowing Johnson, the whole escape could just be another vile game for him. He left enough clues to keep the police trackers busy and yet stayed ahead of them. Celeste fantasized Tommy watching the evening news in a white T-shirt with sleeves rolled up to show off his tattoos like James Dean or Marlon Brando in their movie heyday. Tommy chugged beer and laughed at the police as they bungled their way along the same escape route.

Unlike his last run across country, Tommy had continued to California and not returned to Michigan since that officer spotted him at that Southfield Mall. But, Tommy kept one too many clues with him, like trophies. When he was arrested, Johnson was still in possession of the dead backpacker's hiking boots and hunting knife. The hiker's name had been etched in both.

Black newsprint ink filled the creases of Celeste's palms and fingers. She put the remainder of the paper on the table and massaged her sore hands. The wall clock struck 10:00. She'd been adrift in events of the past year for over an hour. From the way her hands ached, she must have tried to squeeze the life out of Tommy and Jane via the newspaper.

CELESTE AND MAX ENTERED the Oakland County Court House just before the start of Tommy Johnson's sentencing. It took five long months from the day she was told the extradition papers had been signed to that December morning. She was surprised and pleased when Max asked if he could come along. Celeste needed someone to lean on for Tommy Johnson's day in court. After he pled guilty and exonerated Jane, there was no trial. She didn't know if she could handle any more surprises like that on her own. Hopefully, with no testimony or courtroom drama there would be little reason for media to be around. Most of the sensational part of the story — the soap opera love affairs, Pilar's murder, the children, the will — had already been covered on TV, radio, and in print.

To Celeste's dismay, Dan Oliver told her shortly after Jane Carson returned to Michigan there was no solid evidence she had anything to do with Pilar's murder. But Tommy Johnson's attorney, Lincoln McPhearson, told the media otherwise. McPhearson stunned Celeste and other readers when he reported without any hesitancy, "Johnson confessed to the murder of Doctor Brookstone to protect his girlfriend, Jane Carson."

When pressed for details McPhearson stated, "There are many reasons why Johnson confessed to both the Colorado and Brookstone murders. Most of all, he wants to protect the girl."

That day, as when she first read the lawyer's statement, Celeste sneered at the attorney's sexist use of the label "girl", though she had no desire to defend the person to whom he attached the title. The bottom line was, Jane Carson got away with murder because Tommy Johnson struck a plea bargain with Oliver. He'd only plead guilty to first degree murder if the prosecutor agreed not to charge Jane as an accomplice. Oliver agreed.

Even more sad, there had never been any mention of the role Chad Wilbanks played in the whole thing except as Pilar's lover. Chad must have pledged a portion of his inheritance, Pilar's money, to Tommy and Jane to keep them quiet. But as with Jane, police couldn't find any firm corroboration of Chad's role in the scam and Pilar's murder.

THOUGH PART OF CELESTE welcomed the idea of no dramatic and lengthy trial, the curious mother in her wanted to know what made Tommy and Jane tick. Without prosecutors digging into their psyche, and the daily analysis of the trial and characters in the news, Celeste believed she would never find out who those two really were. She needed to know why they felt Pilar's life was expendable. She wanted someone to tell her Tommy and Jane did what they did for more than just the money.

WHEN CELESTE COMPLETED A quick search of the courtroom for vacant seats, she spotted Jim Patterson, stern-faced and in a three-piece navy suit. He looked more like the conservative Detective his profession dictated than the caring young friend he had become. When he saw Celeste, Jim smiled and signaled to her with a thumbs-up.

Celeste raised her hand to acknowledge his positive gesture and continued her perusal of the area. She recognized Maryann Wilbanks from Pilar's photograph. She sat in the third row next to Jane's husband. "Do you think they came together?" Celeste asked Max after she pointed them out.

"I'd be surprised," Max whispered, his breath teasing Celeste's ear. "Probably it's just a coincidence that they sat together."

"Umm," she answered. Maryann's posture was straight and proud, while Emmet Carson seemed folded like a used up rag doll. "What about Jane Carson?" Celeste asked. "She's not here."

"No. She's still in custody."

When Max leaned close to Celeste, he smelled clean, fresh, not heavily perfumed with the latest cologne. A man's man. Without detection Celeste sniffed his delightful scent and remembered how difficult it was to pick an outfit for that occasion, one that would appeal to Max and yet be appropriate for her position in the court's view.

"Oh, yes, I forgot." Max's words suspended her silly thoughts. "Jane's being charged with conspiracy to obtain money under false pretense." Max shared that decision as though the criminal justice system had triumphed.

"Whatever that means," Celeste countered. "She only suffers for a few years in prison, while Pilar becomes part of the dirt she's buried in." She was unable to hide her bitterness. Celeste was positive Jane was as much a part of Pilar's death as Tommy.

Max patted Celeste's knee as though they were an old married couple. The action seemed both familiar and comforting, and one she hoped would go on for a long time.

Celeste placed her hand on his and asked, "How can such a cold-blooded killer, an animal like Tommy Johnson who shows no remorse for any of his actions, take the entire blame for Pilar's murder? How can he protect Jane when he's always put himself first?"

Max opened his mouth to answer just as the court bailiff yelled, "Hear ye, hear ye. All rise. The Honorable Judge Joseph Lawry presiding." Everyone in the gallery stood as a shockingly young man in a black robe, swept through the chamber's door. He climbed the stairs, exposing a hint of cowboy boots under his robe, and sat at the high podium.

"Court is now in session," the bailiff concluded. When Judge Lawry was seated, everyone else sat as well. One person took her time lowering herself to the bench. It was Lorrie. She sat in front of Maryann Wilbanks.

The door to the left of the judge's bench opened. The heads of those in the audience turned as though a part of a synchronized routine. An armed deputy sheriff wearing a familiar brown uniform walked through the opening. Tommy Johnson, dressed in street clothes for court, and two more deputies were close behind. Johnson, legs tightly bound in chains, an unusual security measure granted to the sheriff, shuffled across the floor to a seat beside his attorney, Lincoln McPhearson. Several onlookers shifted on the wooden pew-like benches when Tommy Johnson nodded at Celeste. The heart-and-dagger tattoo boldly displayed on his right arm mocked the observers. His Charles Manson eyes were like the dark caves in ice flows. Even more menacing were Tommy's enormous eyebrows that fluttered like bat wings with each facial movement. Celeste refused to let them intimidate her. She never flinched or looked away from his scowl.

Johnson turned his attention to the judge.

Seated beside each other, McPhearson's preppie, just-graduated-from-Harvard-Law appearance, was a stark contrast to Johnson's unkept shagginess. As Celeste tried to imagine how a woman of any caliber could fall for Tommy, Max told her, "Agnes Trudeau, Johnson's former girlfriend and victim, is in the second row."

Celeste searched for who it might be. Her quest instead temporarily ended in brief delight at how few reporters were present. There were only the main local networks as noted by the logos displayed on their notepads and cameras. Still, there were enough to get the job done in time for the evening news.

While happy about the lack of reporters, Celeste shuddered when she discovered that the room was mostly filled with women of all ages. Who were they? Relatives? Girlfriends? The curious? Maryann Wilbanks was among them, but why? Though heavy makeup adorned her face, she still looked as young as she did in Pilar's photo. Marcus came to mind when she thought of Maryann and how much Chad's manipulative behavior reminded Celeste of him.

Marcus. He wasn't there. The last time they spoke he said, "There's no reason to be in court. I'm not a witness and I'm not a voyeur. Besides, the whole thing was over when Johnson took a plea." Though still not sure Tommy didn't have something up his sleeve, Celeste didn't argue with Marcus. Now, she was relieved Marcus wouldn't be a part of that morning's events.

Sensing that Celeste didn't know which woman was Agnes Trudeau, Max said, "She's the third one in. The slender brunette."

"Is she here to watch Tommy Johnson get his just desserts or to mourn for him?" Celeste asked.

"God forbid, I hope it's to see the man hang." Max spoke louder than expected, causing those seated near them to adjust their positions as they glanced at him with disapproval.

Johnson and McPhearson stood in response to Judge Lawry's request. "Do you understand, Mr. Johnson, the plea of guilty to murder in the first degree and its consequences?"

"Yeah, Your Honor, I do," Johnson said almost as a challenge.

"To be sure, Mr. Johnson, tell me in your own words before I pronounce the sentence."

Johnson surveyed the audience as though they adored him. Did he know more about that congregation than Celeste?

"I'm waiting, Mr. Johnson," the judge said.

"FIRST I'D LIKE THE court to know I want to be extradited to Colorado and executed for murdering that backpacker."

Whispers rumbled through the room. Judge Lawry pounded his gavel. "That has nothing to do with the sentencing today."

"I've got the right to state my piece, and I demand to be extradited," he screamed. Johnson's face crinkled into a thousand angry lines. He looked much older than thirty-two. Mr. McPhearson snatched Johnson's forearm to calm him. Johnson wrenched his arm away as two deputies moved closer to their table.

How could Tommy Johnson think he had rights? Maybe Michigan should send him to Colorado. No. No. What's one more death going to prove to anyone? Celeste would rather he'd waste away in a cell and be tortured by knowing what he was missing on the other side of the gun towers and razor ribbon.

"Your Honor," the prosecutor shouted as he rose.

"Yes, Mr. Oliver." The judge answered in a gravelly,

annoyed voice.

"We've been over the issue of extradition several times with the defendant. He knows our position."

"You're afraid I'll escape," Johnson screamed back as he moved toward Oliver. "I just don't want to rot in jail. I'd rather die." The deputies approached and posted themselves on either side of Johnson. The onlookers heaved and leaned like one huge wave away from the front of the room.

Judge Lawry banged his gavel again. "No more of these outbursts," he ordered. No one would challenge that voice. "There will be no extradition to Colorado, Mr. Johnson."

Mr. Oliver returned to his chair and tapped his pen against a legal sized folder on the table in front of him. Judge Lawry frowned at the sound. The prosecutor stopped and faced Johnson to hear the rest of his story.

"Now, get on with your version of the charges and plea, Mr. Johnson," the judge ordered. "You're trying my patience."

"Yes, your honor. After I jumped the fence . . . "

"Excuse me," the judge interrupted, "please be more specific."

"Okay. After I escaped, I stayed at the Super 8 out on the highway and called Mrs. Carson. She met me there that night and we left for Florida in her Ford the next morning. We went to my father's house in Fort Meyers. We stayed there for two days, then went to Miami where I bought the Smith and Wesson automatic I used to kill Doctor Brookstone."

Tears streamed down Celeste's face as Tommy Johnson

recited his tale. He might have simply been the court reporter reading it from Tommy's deposition. Celeste had
practically memorized it herself when she obtained a copy.
Hearing it in his own surprisingly articulate and distant
voice pierced her heart. She absorbed every painful word
like a sponge.

Johnson paused and stared at Celeste. Her breath
stopped as if he crushed her throat.

Celeste reached for her breast. The sound of Tommy's
nail clipper snapped over and over in her head. She placed
both hands over her ears until the snipping went away.

As though he waited for Celeste to pay attention,
Tommy didn't resume his scenario until she lowered her
hands and focused on him. "After we got the gun and
ammo," Johnson continued, "Mrs. Carson and I went back
to Michigan, kidnapped her kids, and went to Ann Arbor."

Celeste recalled the detectives' log and clearly pictured
Tommy and his father at the gun shop. A loud sobbing
drew her attention away from that imagined scene. Celeste
searched each row for the moaner. Emmet Carson laid his
head on his arm which rested on the bench in front of him.
His shoulders heaved in tormented grief.

Tommy increased his volume to be heard over Mr.
Carson. "We got a trailer there and I called Doctor
Brookstone. She agreed to meet me at a nearby restaurant
that night. Jane drove me to the restaurant. She waited in
the car while I met with the Doc. That's when we made

plans for the Doc to get me $25,000 to help get her boy-friend get out of jail. I convinced her that it would be set up by a lawyer. We made arrangements to meet at the bank when she got the money." Johnson smiled at the prosecutor. "The Doc had already tried to get a lawyer to help her, but she couldn't find one. I told her I knew a guy that could do it." He laughed, shaking his head as if he couldn't believe Pilar was so gullible. "But it was a scam." He shrugged.

Celeste's hands tightened around the wooden seat as though she was about to propel herself over the bench in front. Max's eyes were red, moist. Would she be able to listen to the rest of Johnson's impassive rendition of the events, especially if he was as explicit in person as he was at his deposition? Marcus was probably smart to stay away. Celeste and the others in the courtroom were the captive listeners Tommy had hoped for. Their presence seemed to improve his horrid performance.

Celeste wished she could see inside Maryann Willbanks' head. She wished she could see Jane's face, too. What went through their minds?

Max loosened Celeste's grip from the bench and held her hand as though he knew she would need his support for the next part of the story. The outline of her hand damp-ened the oak.

Tommy drank some water and cleared his throat like someone giving a commencement speech. He presented a step-by-step account that appeared rehearsed. "Mrs. Carson drove me to the bank parking lot the following morning where I met Doc Brookstone. After I made sure she had the money, I got in the Doc's car and told her to drive to an office in Southfield. Mrs. Carson and her kids followed us. When we got on I-696, Brookstone panicked at the site of a police car flashing its lights and pulled off the road. She refused to go any further or cooperate, so I shot her." He shrugged again. "Twice. In the head."

"You animal, you maniac!" someone shrieked.

Celeste collapsed onto Max, weeping. Max circled his arm around her shoulders and drew her to him. "Ssshh," he said as the judge slammed his gavel so hard a vibration traveled the floor and through Celeste's feet. Celeste watched Maryann hurdle over a bench toward Johnson. Two deputies subdued her. She was forced from the courtroom kicking and wailing, "Ya don't deserve to live, ya bastard." Her handbag crashed to the floor scattering its contents, including a bottle of pills. Another deputy sheriff gathered Maryann's belongings and followed her.

Tommy Johnson laughed, mouth wide open, so sure of himself.

The reporters penned notes at a furious pace as cameras taped the dramatic scene.

Maryann's tears painted her makeup into a grotesque mask. As Chad's mother was dragged from the area, guilt overwhelmed Celeste. She should have been the one to curse Johnson. Yet, Maryann's outburst seemed irrational. Was she more angry because her son would remain in prison, or because her wealthy daughter-in-law-to-be was dead? Had she thought there could be money in that scheme for her?

Judge Lawry rapped his gavel several times and ordered in a loud and distinct voice, "Any other outbursts and I will clear this courtroom." He scowled at Tommy. "Now get on with it, Mr. Johnson."

Tommy, still smiling, answered, "Yes, sir, Your Honor. I didn't mean to kill her, but the Doc lunged at me."

He didn't miss a beat. Nothing seemed to ruffle Tommy Johnson.

"I had wrapped her beautiful hair around my hand," Johnson said, and demonstrated by holding an arm in the air and motioning a hand around it, "when she tried to jump out of the car right after she pulled off the road." He glowered at Celeste. "My hold stopped her from getting too far, but it didn't stop the gun from going off. It was already cocked, ya see. When she made a sound after that, I shot her again. I couldn't do nothin' else then, could I?"

"Oh, my God," Celeste gasped. The judge glared, but didn't say anything.

Johnson snickered. His mouth twitched in nervous eagerness. He enjoyed that whole episode. Would he also drool with pleasure at creating misery for so many?

"I took the Doctor's hanky and wiped the door handle," Johnson continued as if his evil tale were an ordinary event. "Then I got out of the car and threw the keys onto the expressway."

The courtroom was silent except for the sounds of disturbed breathing. Johnson was still for several moments while he stared at the judge. After what seemed like hours, the judge finally asked, "Is that it?"

"No. I tucked the gun in my pants, walked back to Mrs. Carson and got in her car. I told her to get the hell outta there. We drove to Knoxville, ditched the car, and flew to Florida. We stayed on the run 'til Sacramento. The rest's history." He cocked his head to one side. "The only thing Mrs. Carson's guilty of is stickin' by an escapee. She had nothin' to do with the murders." Tommy plopped down. His face beamed like a triumphant athlete's.

"Is that all you have to say now before I sentence you, Mr. Johnson?" the judge asked.

Tommy stood back up. "No, Your Honor. I'd like to see Mrs. Carson one more time before I leave the courthouse. It'll probably be my last time."

Emmet Carson stood and yelled, "Please don't let him. She's my wife. Not his."

The judge motioned a deputy sheriff to remove Mr. Carson. He left without a problem, his shoulders slumped forward. He looked beaten and old.

Once the doors were closed behind Emmet Carson, Judge Lawry explained, "It is my understanding that your attorney and the prosecutor's office have arranged the meeting between you and Jane Carson right after your sentencing.

You will meet with her in the courthouse holding tank."

"Max, how can they let them do that?" Celeste tugged at his jacket sleeve. "They're not married. Johnson didn't let Pilar meet with me one last time, did he? Why should . . . ?"

Judge Lawry directed Johnson to remain standing. Before stating the sentence, the judge blasted Johnson. "Your behavior has not only been grievous, but despicable and defies any human explanation. You show no remorse. In fact, you seem to get great joy from murdering a defenseless human being."

Tommy Johnson's expression was as blank as a black hole.

Judge Lawry adjusted his glasses. "The court is satisfied that you have met the terms of the plea agreement. On the sole count of Murder in the First Degree I hereby sentence you, Thomas Allen Johnson, to life in prison without the possibility of parole."

Several women wept. Women who clearly understood what Tommy Johnson could do. Celeste sank against Max. Tommy didn't even flinch.

Johnson jutted his chin forward, a slight grin surfaced when he was led from the courtroom. When the door to the inner chamber hallway opened, Celeste glimpsed Jane Carson in an orange jump suit being escorted by a deputy sheriff. Tommy's face brightened.

Celeste smiled queerly. A vivid image appeared in her mind's eye. She witnessed Jane still wearing an orange jumpsuit standing by Tommy's grave.

Max nudged Celeste. "Are you okay?" he asked. "You seem to be elsewhere."

"I'm fine. Just fine," Celeste answered, feeling sure Tommy would soon be dead. Perhaps at the hands of another inmate.

When Tommy Johnson could no longer be seen, the spectators shambled from the courtroom. Several conversations buzzed like wasps zeroing in on their prey. Celeste and Max were among those to leave last, hoping they'd miss any further commotion and a confrontation with the press.

Maryann Wilbanks snatched Celeste's arm when she entered the hall outside the courtroom. She whispered, "I am so sorry."

Celeste barely caught a glimpse of Lorrie rushing by and out of sight. Why was she so elusive?

Jim Patterson smiled. Cameras flashed and blurred Celeste's vision. Reporters swarmed around her. Their words jumbled. Everything was black.

chapter twenty-five

FOREVER

CELESTE'S BODY CRUMPLED ON the marble floor outside the courtroom was flaunted across the TV on the six o'clock news. A curious crowd including Maryann surrounded her. Celeste was amazed when one brazen reporter stuck a microphone in her face and said, "Mrs. Brookstone . . ." The rest of his statement or question was muffled by the shouts from other journalists circling like vultures about to pounce on their helpless victim.

Max shoved the reporter aside and lifted her from the cold tile. With careful, strong warmth, he secured his arm around Celeste's waist. Taking note of Max's confident command, the voyeurs parted like the Red Sea.

Max walked Celeste to their car as reporters, photographers, and the curious followed behind like a carnival parade. Questions were hurled as the couple made their way through the throng:

"Mrs. Brookstone, how do you feel about Johnson's sentence?"

"What do you think about Jane Carson getting off?"

"Where's your husband? Why isn't he here?"

Fortunately, the sheriff's deputies kept the frenzied mass at a distance. The deputies, guns holstered, but armed with night sticks, formed a gauntlet that slithered like a snake from the pressure of those standing behind the uniformed line. The sight reminded Celeste of the riot scenes from foreign countries she had watched many times portrayed on CNN. She and Max threaded their way through the wave to safety.

CELESTE RAISED THE TV remote control and aimed it at the camera's closing sweep of the crowd which pictured the wide-open mouths of shouting onlookers. The camera man focused on his final view of Max helping Celeste into their waiting car.

"Not exactly the portrait I wish everyone to remember me by." Celeste turned off the news with a quick, angry motion.

Max handed Celeste a glass of wine. "Don't worry. In a few days some other lurid event will take over the headlines and satisfy the news room hunger."

Celeste curled her legs under her and nestled into the couch. "Half of me never wants Pilar's murder and all the characters that had a part in it forgotten, while the other half wants to get over it so I can move forward. Yet, it will never be over, will it? I mean, Pilar will always be here." Celeste placed her hand over her heart.

"It'll take a while," Max sat beside her and laid his

hand on her thigh. A wide-awake thrill sparked deep in her chest.

Celeste forced the welcomed sensation from her. She reluctantly left the coziness of the couch and peered out the window. She bit her lip hard enough to draw blood. She was determined not to be one of those grieving people who gave into sexual desires as a way to feel normal, as a way to feel anything other than numb. The inevitable response to Max's suggestive touch had to wait a little while longer.

To help ward off that delicious desire, Celeste slid the curtain aside and gazed at the waves lapping Lake St. Claire's shoreline, barely visible in the fading light. "Do you think Tommy Johnson will ever get out of prison?" she asked. A vivid image of his grave again flashed into her head.

"Not this time." Max poured another glass of wine and freshened Celeste's. "He'll die in his cell, and hopefully at Ionia Super Max, as a lonely, forgotten man."

"By the way the courtroom was filled with women, I doubt Tommy will be without female comfort," Celeste sighed. "There's no way Jane Carson can visit him, is there?"

"I should say not." Max handed her the wine. The liquid swirled like a small red pool. Celeste held the glass in both hands until the spinning stopped.

"In fact," Max affirmed, "I suspect Jane Carson will hunt for a new thrill once she's paroled, although I do believe her life is going to be rather empty from now on. Especially since she lost custody of her children."

"Good." Celeste lifted her glass in a toast and drank. "It would break my heart if either Tommy Johnson or Jane Carson had any pleasures in the rest of their lives. And those poor children need a chance to have something better than being on the lam."

"There's some other positive news," Max announced. His cheerful voice was just what Celeste needed right then.

"And what is that?"

"It looks like the corrections department can seize half of Chad's inheritance that Pilar left him." Max's chest actually puffed out, taking great pleasure in revealing that lovely treat.

"Well, well. At least Chad won't get it all and Tommy Johnson gets no more." Celeste lifted her glass again in recognition. "A small miracle, but gratifying. Yet, I feel as though my family had to pay dearly to keep the two scoundrels off the street."

They finished their drinks in an easy quiet. Celeste set her empty glass down with a tad of caution. "Though it's early," she faced Max, "I'm exhausted. I think I'll take a bath and go to bed. You're welcome to stay. I'll prepare the couch."

"Good idea. I'm too tired to drive, and we both could use a good night's sleep."

SLAYER SENTENCED TO LIFE WITHOUT PAROLE
Max showed Celeste the headline from the morning

Free Press that he retrieved from the box. "This should be the last of it." He eyed the coffee pot as it gurgled and spit out its last drip. The fresh brew filled the air with a sharp, inviting scent.

Charmed by his out-of-control morning hair and un-shaven sleepy face, Celeste wanted to brush her fingers through his locks. Later, that would happen. Later. Instead she sighed, "I sure hope so."

"You know, Celeste." Max's voice was like heated syrup. She wanted to swallow every sultry word. "That couch isn't all that comfortable." He chuckled. "You might think of using the second bedroom as a real guest room."

Their eyes locked as Celeste handed him a cup of coffee. "It'll take time." She smiled. "But I'll do that. Soon." In the future Max would discover they wouldn't need the second bedroom. But she also knew the shrine to Pilar would come down. Celeste held her cup in both hands, allowing the heat to warm them and watched the steam rise in tiny spirals.

"IT'S BEEN EXACTLY TWO years, Pilar," Celeste told the marble headstone. She caressed the grass covering her grave. "I've planted your favorite flowers: princess daisies, pink tulips and one red rose bush. I had a tough time con-vincing the groundskeeper to ignore the bush. It's against policy, you know."

Celeste was at ease talking to the grave. She sensed

Pilar heard every word. Celeste didn't care if others did, too. More than any concern about eavesdroppers, she wanted to believe Pilar understood that she had finally restructured her future. She was moving in a positive and agreeable direction. "I only wish you were here to take this trip with me, Pilar."

A car circling the area lured Celeste. She raised up from the ground and brushed the damp grass from her knees. With a hand she blocked the sun from her sight as she searched the driveway. "One more thing, Pilar," Celeste said as she followed the motor's hum which came closer. "My divorce from your father is final. It took such a long time, but I don't have to deal with him any more. In the end he proved more than generous."

The automobile flickered in and out of the sun like motion in a strobe light. "I'm sorry," she continued her monologue before the driver got too near, "I hadn't understood both our survivals depended on making that move." She bent and smoothed the grass over Pilar's grave one more time. "I'm also sorry my decision came too late for you." One tear slipped from her eye.

The car stopped on the curve by Pilar's grave site. Celeste laughed, wiped away the tear and waved. "Don't feel sorry for me, Pilar." Warmth enveloped Celeste, as if she were covered in a fleece throw. "I just might have another man in my life. I think you'd like him if you got to know him."

A tanned Max sauntered toward Celeste. He wore khaki slacks and blue oxford shirt which was actually pressed. "I thought I'd find you here." He kissed her cheek.

His fresh scent excited her, as always. They had been casually dating, which was the best way Celeste could describe their relationship. No sex. For the time, it was good conversation and a good ear when needed for each of them. Sex had been delayed more from her fear of inadequacy in that arena than her lack of craving.

Celeste beamed with genuine happiness, a long overdue sensation. "You're just in time to celebrate my divorce decree with Pilar and me. I brought her favorite merlot and two glasses."

Max wrinkled his forehead as though questioning her sanity. "No, Max," Celeste answered. "The second glass is for you." He was more handsome than when they first had met. Maybe familiarity brought that about. His hair was still unruly and graying more by the minute. He would never be Mr. America. Yet, he had the comfortable, wholesome, hardy good looks and steady disposition Celeste could easily get used to.

"How'd you know I'd be here?" Max asked as he spread-out the University of Wisconsin stadium blanket Celeste brought.

They sat. Celeste handed Max a corkscrew and the wine bottle. "I'm a clairvoyant."

BLOOD TiES

LORi G. ARMsTRONG

What do they mean?
How far would someone go to sever . . . or protect them?

Julie Collins is stuck in a dead-end secretarial job with the Bear Butte County Sheriff's office, and still grieving over the unsolved murder of her Lakota half-brother. Lack of public interest in finding his murderer, or the killer of several other transient Native American men, has left Julie with a bone-deep cynicism she counters with tequila, cigarettes, and dangerous men. The one bright spot in her mundane life is the time she spends working part-time as a PI with her childhood friend, Kevin Wells.

When the body of a sixteen-year old white girl is discovered in nearby Rapid Creek, Julie believes this victim will receive the attention others were denied. Then she learns Kevin has been hired, mysteriously, to find out where the murdered girl spent her last few days. Julie finds herself drawn into the case against her better judgment, and discovers not only the ugly reality of the young girl's tragic life and brutal death, but ties to her and Kevin's past that she is increasingly reluctant to revisit.

On the surface the situation is eerily familiar. But the parallels end when Julie realizes some family secrets are best kept buried deep. Especially those serious enough to kill for.

ISBN#1932815325
Gold
$6.99
Mystery
Available Now
www.loriarmstrong.com

SIREN'S CALL

MARY ANN MITCHELL

Sirena is a beautiful young woman. By night she strips at Silky Femmes, enticing large tips from conventioneers and salesmen passing through the small Florida city where she lives.

Sirena is also a loyal and compassionate friend to the denizens of Silky Femmes. There's Chrissie, who is a fellow dancer as well as the boss's abused and beleaguered girlfriend. And Ross, the bartender, who spends a lot of time worrying about the petite, delicate, and lovely Sirena. Maybe too much time.

There's also Detective Williams. He's looking for a missing man and his investigation takes him to Silky's. Like so many others, he finds Sirena irresistible. But again, like so many others, he's underestimated Sirena.

Because Sirena has a hobby. Not just any hobby. From the stage she searches out men with the solid bone structure she requires. The ones she picks get to go home with her where she will perform one last private strip for them. They can't believe their luck. They simply don't realize it's just run out.

ISBN #1932815163
Gold
$6.99
Fiction
Available Now
www.sff.net/people/maryann.mitchell

BREEDING
Liz
Wolfe
EVIL

Someone is breeding superhumans . . .

. . . beings who possess extreme psychic abilities. Now they have implanted the ultimate seed in the perfect womb. They are a heartbeat away from successfully breeding a species of meta-humans, who will be raised in laboratories and conditioned to obey the orders of their owners, governments and large multi-national corporations.

Then Shelby Parker, a former black ops agent for the government, is asked to locate a missing woman. Her quest takes her to The Center for Bio-Psychological Research. Masquerading as a computer programmer, she gets inside the Center's inner workings. What she discovers is almost too horrible to comprehend.

Dr. Mac McRae, working for The Center, administers a lie-detector test to the perspective employee for his very cautious employers. Although she passes, the handsome Australian suspects Shelby is not what she appears. But then, neither is he.

Caught up in a nightmare of unspeakable malevolence, the unlikely duo is forced to team up to save a young woman and her very special child. And destroy a program that could change the face of nations.

But first they must unmask the mole that has infiltrated Shelby's agency and stalks their every move. They must stay alive and keep one step ahead of the pernicious forces who are intent on . . .
BREEDING EVIL

ISBN #1932815058
Gold Imprint: Available now
$6.99
www.lizwolfe.net

SUMMER OF FIRE

LINDA JACOBS

It is 1988, and Yellowstone Park is on fire.

Among the thousands of summer warriors battling to save
America's crown jewel, is single mother Clare Chance.
Having just watched her best friend, a fellow Texas
firefighter, die in a roof collapse, she has fled to Montana
to try and put the memory behind her. She's not the only
one fighting personal demons as well as the fiery dragon
threatening to consume the park.

There's Chris Deering, a Vietnam veteran helicopter pilot,
seeking his next adrenaline high and a good time that
doesn't include his wife, and Ranger Steve Haywood, a man
scarred by the loss of his wife and baby in a plane crash.
They rally 'round Clare when tragedy strikes yet again, and
she loses a young soldier to a firestorm.

Three flawed, wounded people; one horrific blaze. Its
tentacles are encircling the park, coming ever closer,
threatening to cut them off. The landmark Old Faithful Inn
and Park Headquarters at Mammoth are under siege, and
now there's a helicopter down, missing, somewhere in the
path of the conflagration. And Clare's daughter is on it . . .

Gold Imprint
June 2005
$6.99

Grand Traverse

Michael Beres

The year is 2040. The world is in chaos. A valiant few have taken on the struggle to help the planet through its violent, lethal pilgrimage into the future. A valiant few, dogged by evil.

Paul Carter, his family forced from their home by a toxic chemical spill, becomes an environmental activist. After winning a class-action suit against the chemical company responsible, he establishes a rural commune-style community. When his wife contracts breast cancer, his hopes and dreams rest on the destiny of his daughter, Jamie.

Jamie Carter, whose life has been irrevocably affected by the toxic chemical spill, is obsessed with the environment. Friends, including a Chernobyl survivor, encourage her to enter political life. Her ideas gain worldwide attention, catapulting her into a limelight that proves to be a double-edged sword.

Heather West has the compulsion needed for success in a politically divided, media-driven society. After a lawsuit that destroys her family, she uses her good looks and sex appeal to enter the world of television. But it's more than fame she craves. It's revenge.

ISBN#1932815341
Platinum
Price TBD
Fiction
September 2005

The Keeners
Maura D. Shaw

The rough beauty of County Clare is seventeen-year-old Margaret Meehan's whole world, and it is nearly perfect. Her family is well and thriving, farming Ireland's staple crop. She expects to marry handsome Tom Riordan, raise their children, and live in a cottage across the lane from her best friend, Kitty Dooley. She has found her calling and is apprenticed to the old keener Nuala Lynch. Together they keen for the dead, wailing the grief and pain of the bereaved in hopes of healing their sorrow. Margaret's life is full of hope, full of purpose.

But the year is 1846. The potato blight has returned. Pitiful harvests rot overnight and the people are dying. Ireland is dying. And Margaret cannot keen for an entire country.

Out of devastation, Margaret Meehan's tale begins. Leaving her decimated family, the tragic Kitty, and the death of dreams behind, she flees with her husband, now a wanted man, to America. In Troy, New York, where pig iron, starched collars, and union banners herald the success of Irish immigrants, Margaret discovers something even more precious than a new life and modest prosperity. She finds the heart and soul of Ireland. And she finds it in the voice of . . .
The Keeners . . .

ISBN# 1932815155
Platinum
$25.95
Historical Fiction
March 2005
www.mauradshaw.com

For more information

about other great titles from

Medallion Press, visit

www.medallionpress.com